PENGUIN BOOKS
FRENCH LOVER

Taslima Nasrin was born in Mymensingh, Bangladesh in 1962. After completing a medical degree, she turned her hand to writing. She has published, in Bengali, several volumes of poetry, collections of non-fiction writing, and a handful of novels. The first part of her autobiography, *My Girlhood*, was published recently. The English translation of her controversial novel *Lajja* (*Shame*), published by Penguin is one of the biggest bestsellers in the history of Indian publishing.

Taslima Nasrin is the recipient of several prestigious awards from both India and abroad for her writings. Her books have been translated into several Indian as well as European languages. Exiled from her native Bangladesh, she lives in Europe.

★

Sreejata Guha has an MA in comparative literature from Jadavpur University, Kolkata. She has worked as a translator and editor with Seagull Books and Stree Publishers, Kolkata, and works currently with Jacaranda Press, Bangalore. She has previously translated *Picture Imperfect*, a collection of Byomkesh Bakshi stories, for Penguin.

FRENCH LOVER

a novel

Taslima Nasrin

Translated from the Bengali by Sreejata Guha

PENGUIN BOOKS

PENGUIN BOOKS

Published by the Penguin Group

Penguin Books India Pvt Ltd, 11 Community Centre, Panchsheel Park, New Delhi 110 017, India

Penguin Group (USA) Inc., 375 Hudson Street, New York, New York 10014, USA

Penguin Group (Canada), 10 Alcorn Avenue, Toronto, Ontario, Canada M4V 3B2 (a division of Pearson Penguin Canada Inc.)

Penguin Books Ltd, 80 Strand, London WC2R 0RL, England

Penguin, Ireland, 25 St Stephen's Green, Dublin 2, Ireland (a division of Penguin Books Ltd)

Penguin Group (Australia), 250 Camberwell Road, Camberwell, Victoria 3124, Australia (a division of Pearson Australia Group Pty Ltd)

Penguin Group (NZ), cnr Airborne and Rosedale Road, Albany, Auckland 1310, New Zealand (a division of Pearson New Zealand Ltd)

Penguin Group (South Africa) (Pty) Ltd, 24 Sturdee Avenue, Rosebank, Johannesburg 2196, South Africa

Penguin Books Ltd, Registered Offices: 80 Strand, London WC2R 0RL, England

First published in Bengali by Ananda Publishers Pvt. Ltd., 2001
First published in English by Penguin Books India 2002

Copyright © Taslima Nasrin 2001
This translation copyright © Penguin Books India 2002

10

Typeset in Bembo by Mantra Virtual Services, New Delhi
Printed at Saurabh Printers Pvt. Ltd., NOIDA

Contents

Dumdum to Charles de Gaulle

The girl, with chapped lips, draped in a red silk sari with gold on her ears, nose and hands, got off the aeroplane gazing at the white people, stumbling on the moving staircase; she walked in the direction of the moving crowd, amidst the chatter and the buzz. The crowd stopped at one point, forming an impromptu queue—a huge boa constrictor—a little like the one that forms in front of the ration-shop when they give rice at a throwaway price. The girl tried to pass by the tail and sidle towards the middle of the boa. But the others shouted, you there in the red sari, go to the tail. The girl wet her chapped lips and went towards the tail, right at the end, all the way to the back, the place for the destitute. The boa slithered ahead with great speed. Only the tail got stuck in the thorny bushes.

With a smudged bindi on her forehead and sindoor smeared in her hair, the girl came face to face with a Black and a White. She passed the Black and moved towards the White, ignoring the dark new moon for the bright, white moonshine. The Black called, girl, you there, this way. Red Sari, hard of hearing, just stood before the White, graciously smiling. She could pass for the goddess Durga, couldn't she? But the White didn't care about goddesses. Without raising his eyes, he pointed to the Black. Red Sari was not short sighted. Two steps to the left would bring her before the Black. She didn't feel like taking those steps.

Black was bucktoothed. The girl smarted.

'Passport,' the booming voice came from the cavernous depths of Bucktooth.

The girl held up the dark blue passport, just as she had seen the people from the head and the middle of the boa do. Bucktooth swooped down on it and swallowed the prey: an Indian mouse in a black eagle's talons. Bucktooth had got hold of a great treasure. The girl noticed that he seemed to drool as he eyed his prey.

'Ticket.'

No dangling prey this time, the girl placed the two-page ticket in his black paws—Dumdum–Charles de Gaulle–Dumdum—22nd February–21st March 1999.

The mouse went under the scanning machine once, twice, thrice.

Boom: What have you come here for?

Chapped lips moved: To be with my husband.

Boom: In which hotel will you stay?

Red Sari had come from her father's hotel to her husband's. Life would pass between one hotel and the other.

Boom: What's the address?

A tiny square of paper passed into his hands: 112, Rue du Foubaud Sandani, Paris 75010.

Boom: How much money do you have?

Two hundred dollars went into his paws.

Any more?

Her hand groped eagerly in the bag and from the bottom of it, along with some dry flowers, two buttons, the skin of a peanut and a half-eaten orange, she dug out twelve hundred and twenty-five rupees.

Bucktooth scratched his bushy eyebrows with two fingers and asked smoothly, 'What is that?'

The girl sighed and said, 'This is money.'

'Money?'

'Yes, money. The currency of India.' Her voice was stern.

Bucktooth had never seen money like that before. The White glanced at the money and crinkled his nose as if a handful of excreta was suddenly placed before him. There was a new boa forming behind the girl, growing longer by the minute, thrashing impatiently. If the red nuisance wasn't standing there, it would have cleared the fence long ago. The girl too felt she was a nuisance.

The White twitched his chin, wagged his white finger and said, 'You there, Red Sari, go and stand in that corner.'

The nuisance was flushed out, into the corner.

The new boa moved briskly, now the head and now the tail. Not a single passport went through the scanning machine. No one had to dig out money from their bags. No one was sent to a corner—the girl was the only one. She felt the corner was like a cage in the zoo. Everyone looked at her through the invisible cage as they walked past—they saw a strange animal with black eyes, dark hair and dark skin. The girl kept her eyes, the guilty ones, on the ground.

When Bucktooth leaned towards the White and laughed as he said goodbye to the last swish of the boa's tail, the girl stepped across the line, one step at a time and spoke apologetically to the White, 'Everyone has gone. May I go now?'

The White head began to sway. She couldn't understand what this meant: that she couldn't go or the White was suddenly in the throes of an irresistible melody and couldn't keep himself from swaying to it.

Black saw White swaying his head and came out of the glass cubicle.

Boom: Walk.

Black came to a stop before a room, this one encased in steel walls. Red Sari was right behind him. Inside the room there were two white men in blue uniforms sitting on two chairs. One was elderly and the other younger. Black handed the loot and treasures to the older man and walked out. The younger man was laughing, but as his eyes fell on the girl he gulped his laughter and hung an expression akin to being in the throes of labour-pain in its place.

The older one looked impotent and there were no signs of labour-pains on his face. It looked like steel and if you knocked on it, you would certainly break your bones if not lose your fingers.

In halting English, the older one asked, 'Do you know French?'

'No.'

'What do you know?'

'English.'

'That won't do.'

Surprise shook the girl like a pendulum as she stood leaning on the steel walls. She had no idea that there could be a place in this world where English wouldn't work. In Calcutta the knowledge of English separated the civilized from the barbarians. She had always assumed that civilized people, in any country, always spoke fluent English.

The older one barked, 'What is your own language?'

Her voice was feeble, 'Bangla.'

'Bangla won't do.' The girl was prepared for this statement. But then he took her by surprise and said, 'We'll have to arrange for an interpreter.'

The interpreter would shoot questions at the girl. If the answers were satisfactory the panel of judges would declare in favour of freedom or else . . . it was back to wherever you came from.

Two pairs of eyes, Steel-face's and Labour-pain's, travelled from the girl's head to her toes. Steel-face closed his eyes and indicated that she should sit on a chair in the corner. Silk sari, smudged bindi, chapped lips went and sat in the corner. There were three chairs there. On the one that was closest to the wall, a very dark man sat wearing a light green robe. He had a head full of matted hair. The girl left one chair empty between them and sat on the third one.

The man craned his giraffe-neck and asked in a rasping voice, 'I'm from Senegal, and you?'

The girl's eyes remained fixed on the steel walls. The crow wouldn't stop crowing, 'Where are you from?'

Her eyes still fixed on the wall, the cold reply bounced off it, 'I am not from Senegal.'

A tiny sparrow of pride quickly took its place on her left shoulder because she was not from Senegal. The girl held her left shoulder stiff. She sat still and looked from the corner of her eyes: at the ugly feet of the Crow, there was an equally ugly, purple sack. He opened the sack, brought out a dirty bottle, leaned his head back and tilted its contents into the open jaws of a hippo. Half a bottle of water went into it. Giraffe-neck looked at Girl again and asked, 'Want some water?'

'No.'

'Is your passport fake as well?'

'No.' Her voice was rude.

'Are you from China?'

'No.'

'Oh, I know—from Pakistan.'

The girl rose, her sparrow was still on her shoulder. She leaned on the wall and continued to stare at it. Another white man entered the room and the girl's beseeching eyes turned to him. He took the chair next to the Senegalese. The girl let the sparrow fly off and came to sit contentedly beside the white man, away from Giraffe-neck. The white man's greasy clothes were giving off the acrid smell of urine.

She was blissfully nonchalant about it as she asked, 'Where are you from?'

'Russia.'

'Why have they stopped you?'

The man grinned and flashed his yellow teeth, 'Moscow.'

'Oh, so you live in Moscow?'

The man nodded.

'D'you know, once my uncle had gone to Moscow. I believe it's a beautiful city. My brother will probably go there next year for a holiday.'

Yellow-teeth smiled.

The smell of urine assaulted the girl's nose again.

'I am from India. Have you ever been there?'

The man nodded.

The girl came closer to the nasty smell, 'Really! Which cities have you been to? Did you see Calcutta?'

The man answered, 'Paris.'

'Oh, you have been to Paris before? This is my first time.'

The girl didn't expect an answer, but it came anyway: Moscow.

Now the girl shut her mouth and her nose. She could guess what the answer to her third question would be.

Question: Do you know how long we'll have to wait here?

Answer: Vladimir Alexandrovich Stanislavsky.

Meanwhile Steel-face and Labour-pains were jabbering away heartily in French. She wasn't able to decipher a single syllable. After an hour and thirty-five minutes, the younger man in blue uniform turned his chair to face the three offenders. He pointed to her and spoke in crisp English, 'You will have to go back to your own country, do you understand?' His face was now cleared of labour-pains and the extra wrinkles on his forehead were gone too.

The girl stood up nervously, 'You said something about an interpreter—where is he?'

'Can't be found.'

As the girl was waiting to get back her passport, ticket and other treasures, the older man in blue uniform entered with another white man. This one was chewing gum and his eyes travelled over Nila, from head to toe.

'Name?'

'Whose?'

'Yours.'

'Nilanjana Mandal.'

'Reason for coming here?'

'To live my life.'

'With?'

'With my husband.'

'Husband's name?'

'Kishanlal.'

'Age?'

'I'm not sure. He must be ten years older than me.'

'How old are you?'

'Twenty-seven.'

'How long has he been here?'

Nilanjana scratched her neck and said, 'Probably about fifteen years.'

'You are not sure?'

'No.'

'Is he a French citizen?'

'So I've heard.'

'What does he do?'

'I've heard he has a business.'

'You've heard—you are not sure? Who has said that he is your husband?' A spark of disbelief lingered on the corner of his lips.

Nila looked around her and answered in nervous, humble tones, 'I say so. We were married a month ago.'

'But you don't have the same last names,' the disbelief flies off the lips and settles on his eyes.

Nila gulped, 'That's not the same because . . .'

'Because?'

'I have deliberately not taken his name.'

Nila's heart was beating fast. Her dear husband had never told her that if their last names were not the same it would be disastrous. He had said, 'Keep the name and address handy, and the marriage certificate with you. They won't be needed, but just in case. It's a legitimate passport, legitimate visa—there's nothing to fear.'

Although no one asked for it, Nila groped in her bag and pulled out the long sheet of paper. 'Here, this is our marriage certificate.'

'Whose marriage certificate?' Steel-face asked.

Nila handed the paper to Steel-face and said, 'Mine and Kishanlal's.'

He glanced at the paper, but didn't touch it. Instead the younger one snatched it away. The one with the chewing gum spoke rapidly with the younger one for some time and went out of the room, swaying his hips. Steel-face's eyes followed the swaying hips. She looked at the younger one expectantly—how much longer would she have to wait? The man's senseless expression gave her neither hope nor despair. Nila began to feel her life would be spent thus waiting in the room, surrounded forever by walls of steel. Impatient and restless, she paced the floor. She could do anything now to leave that corner, even if it meant going back to Calcutta.

She stepped up to the younger one hesitantly after a while and asked, 'Where shall I collect my suitcases? Have you decided which flight I'll take for my return?'

He didn't answer, as if she hadn't asked a question or as if, Nila wasn't someone who had the right to ask questions.

'My husband was supposed to receive me—he is waiting outside. Is it possible to have him brought here?'

The man now simply opened a small box carefully, picked up a pinch of tobacco, pulled his upper lip with his left hand and tucked it in; his nostrils and upper lip were puffed up. There was silence. Stanislavsky snored. The Senegalese squatted and reached for that dirty bottle again: the hippo's jaws opened and soon the water vanished down it.

Nila was consumed by thirst and hunger. The whirring sound in her ears was from the spinning of her head. She longed desperately for a shoulder to rest her head on. Stanislavsky's head kept drooping on to her shoulders like a tennis ball. The acrid smell was going through her nose to her head. She felt like picking up his head very gently and throwing it somewhere. It would merely hit the walls of steel. Nila now wondered, why did she marry Kishanlal, whom she didn't even know very well. But Calcutta had been tormenting her and if she hadn't left that city, she would have surely died. Yet she could have left it without getting married. She could have gone to Delhi, Mumbai or somewhere far away, where the sound or the smell of Sushanta's name wouldn't even touch her.

'Can someone give me a glass of water,' Nila asked herself. Then she answered her own question, 'No, we cannot give you a glass of water.'

Nila wasn't used to sitting or standing in one place for so long. She hadn't even waited so long for Sushanta, ever. Whenever they had to meet somewhere, Sushanta would be there first. Her head was spinning faster. It wasn't just the spinning—she felt as if a heavy burden, Sushanta himself—was suddenly placed on her head again.

When the head was about to snap from the spinning, suddenly the Senegalese was released. He picked up his purple sack, flashed a smile and a cough in her direction and was off. Nila had a vicious desire to grab the man by the robe, drag him back into that room and be off with the sparrow on her shoulder.

The black man has been set free—why am I being held back.

She asked from her corner, 'Excuse me, what exactly is the problem? Is my passport fake?'

The younger man did not answer.

'Is my visa fake?'

No answer.

'Is the currency fake?'

He screamed, 'Hey Red-sari, shut up!'

Red-sari shut her mouth.

The older man, who had all her treasures, came back into the room. The man who was chewing gum earlier (but not now) was also with him. The wrinkles on his forehead were gone as well. One by one, her valued treasures were thrown into Nila's hands and there was an additional piece of paper, sort of like a question paper. Now she had to go to the younger man.

He twitched his brows and said, 'Lucky you! If Monsieur Bess wasn't so kind, you would have had it.'

Like his nostrils his lips also puffed up. He gestured her to go the way she had come. It was that glass cubicle again and the same Bucktooth. She handed him the form duly filled up: it was a declaration that she was speaking the truth and at the end of a month she would leave the country; she wouldn't take recourse to any illegal measures in order to stay on in that country and if she did, the punishment would be severe.

Nila cleared the fence, desperately concealing her dark skin, red silk sari, the sindoor on her forehead and hair, gold ornaments, the blue passport and the loose currency. She had been given a reprieve, which could easily have been denied. Monsieur Bess may not have been so kind. She may have had to return to that same house in Calcutta, staring at the same sky and the same clouds—that house where she had said her last goodbyes. When Nila, the pauper, came out with her two suitcases, it was past noon and almost dusk.

Kishanlal, Sunil and Chaitali were waiting still there. When they spotted Nila, three half-dead souls pounced and fell almost on top of her. The short, stout Kishanlal wearing boots, suit, tie and a coat on top of it all, grabbed the luggage trolley and said, 'What's the matter— what took you so long? We have been waiting here since early morning.'

Sunil, tall, fair and lanky—the matchmaker—gave a broad smile and said, 'We had almost given up hope.'

Chaitali was trying to neat n the smudged bindi on Nila's forehead as she said, 'Must have been a terrible journey.'

The moment she left the airport, the sharp, wintry needles pierced her to the bone. Chaitali took the extra coat off her own shoulders and draped it around Nila. For someone who had just come in from the burning heat, the wintry needles seemed to weave a wrapper of elation around her body.

Sunil said, 'We'd have waited for two more minutes and then called Calcutta to check if they sent you back by the return flight.'

Nila said, 'It was all because I haven't taken my husband's last name. Otherwise I'd have come out long ago, just like everyone else.'

Sunil bent down and got into the car as he said, 'Oh no, even if you had the same names, everything would have been the same.'

Nila relaxed in the seat beside the driver and said, 'If I had more dollars it would have been okay.'

Sunil cleared his throat, coughed and then laughed, 'Not at all. They would have still caused you the same misery.'

A thousand questions arose in Nila's eyes, 'The passport and the visa—they are all genuine. Why then?'

Sunil laughed and so did Kishan. It was as if the question demanded that one answer—ha, ha.

Nila wasn't happy with that. 'What was the reason for that misbehaviour?'

'The reason is the colour of your skin—it's not white enough.'

Before Sunil finished speaking, Chaitali added, 'And your passport—it's not of a rich country.'

Nila didn't think she was all that dark and in comparison with the Senegalese, she could be called very fair indeed. She crinkled her fair nose and eyes, described that man's stretching and drinking and then said, 'He seemed to get away.' Nila's voice resounded with indignation, mainly at the Senegalese's getting away.

She examined her own face in the car window and said, 'I didn't expect to see dark-skinned people in Paris.'

Kishan, Sunil and Chaitali all hated the black people: they were the root cause of all misery. They just sat idle and took the government's dole and indulged in antisocial activities. Because of them, the almost-whites like them had to suffer.

Sunil was the first to speak, 'These blacks have made our lives hell.'

For a while they bashed these people verbally, in pure Bangla.

In a group of Bengalis, the non-Bengali Kishanlal stuck out.

He eyed her: red, juicy piece of meat. Whoever said that vegetarians didn't like meat! When she sensed his lusty eyes on her, Nila immediately tensed, just as she always did when the roadside romeos whistled at her. She covered her bare arms with her sari and then realized that this was, after all, her husband and there was no need to hide from him. She had slept with him for only two weeks after the marriage in her Calcutta home. After the sex, they both turned the other way and slept. Except for a few urgent matters discussed in broken English and Hindi, Nila hadn't even talked much with her husband. Before Nila said yes to the match, Molina had said, 'Should you marry a non-Bengali boy whom we don't even know very well? Why don't we wait and look for a good Bengali boy?'

'Forget it, Ma—we've seen enough Bengali boys, haven't we?' Nila had gulped the tears and spoken.

Just those two weeks—within that time Kishan arranged for the passport, visa, tickets and then came back to Paris via Delhi.

Nila was supposed to fly after finishing her university exams. Her father, Anirban, insisted on her wearing her wedding sari and jewellery on the flight—perhaps men knew best what would appeal to other men. Kishan was her closest friend, he was her husband and she'd have to spend her life making him happy. Yet, there weren't any sweet glances or words exchanged between them except for a few questions like why they were driving on the wrong side of the road and some answers in monosyllables. The outburst of conversation was all in Bangla and addressed to the rear seat of the car.

'Tell me, the people at the airport—don't they know English very well?'

Chaitali's smooth voice was heavy as she said, 'Of course they know English; but they won't speak it. You've just come here—wait a while and see how racist these people are.'

Sunil tapped Kishan's head and said, 'What's the matter—why are you so quiet?'

Kishan twirled his black moustache between his fingers and said, 'Oh, I'm letting the poor Bengalis have their say first.'

'Ha, ha.'

Once the car entered the city of Paris, Nila's hunger and thirst vanished. All the ill-will that she bore towards the blue-uniformed men, Chewing-gum, Bucktooth disappeared. As the car passed Hôtel de Ville, Palais Royale, the Louvre and ambled along the Seine over the Boulevard Saint Michelle and headed for the Pont-Neuf, Nila asked herself, 'Is this heaven?' Then she answered herself, 'Yes, it is.'

The Visiting Bride

Nila felt like a guest in Kishanlal's home. It was a huge flat with French windows, heavy curtains and a balcony with flowerpots. The carpet was sky blue; Nila sank into the soft cushions on the sofa. In front of her there were bottles of wine, a female statuette and instead of fans, chandeliers hung from the ceiling. The metal box pasted on the wall was spreading heat into the whole room. Chaitali rushed her into taking a look at the whole house—this was the living room and this was the bedroom; that room over there was of no use except to tuck in excess baggage or people. The kitchen was here and the bathroom and the shower were there. Chaitali told her that the place was all set, really. There were machines to dust, wash, dry and even to beat the eggs, whip it, boil it and then to cut into pieces! Nila had once dreamt of a simple household with Sushanta, first it would be a small home and then a better place—it would always be a struggle to make ends meet; they'd love each other in the dim light of the lamp in the room and laugh at the materialistic world outside. The day Sushanta's persistence yielded fruit and he got a job in the suburban school, they would light the room with a thousand lamps and have a festival of music all night long! Oh no, not a thousand lamps, they were going to have the festival by moonlight, outdoors.

Nila had her share of dreams about the hard life sustained only on love. Perhaps every Bengali was born with that desire. But at twenty-seven her life was topsy-turvy, the tree of her dreams lay uprooted, the thousand lamps were blown out, a ghostly pall had come down on the music festival and the moonlight was covered by a chunk of clouds—Nila was flown on this destructive wind into a shining household with everything she could need.

Nila asked, 'Are there no maids?'

Kishan and Sunil had already opened the bottles. Chaitali slipped into that group and said, 'Hello there, Kishan's wife is asking about maids!'

Sunil guffawed and a smile played about Kishan's moustached lips too.

They told her, in this foreign country there were no maids to do the household chores; there were no poor people here who would do those things. If she called in someone to clean the place, they'd charge her at least fifty francs for an hour's work.

Nila counted on her fingers and raised her brow, 'Three hundred rupees? In Calcutta the people who work in the house day and night don't get that kind of money.'

Both Sunil and Kishan reminded Nila that this was Paris, not Calcutta.

'So I'll have to do everything myself?' Nila sat on the edge of the sofa.

Kishan was pouring alcohol into Chaitali's glass and he said, 'Are you scared?'

Nila glanced around the room and said, 'No, not really. The house seems quite well organized.'

'There's nothing much to do, except to keep the house the way it is.' Kishan laughed.

Nila gobbled down two slices of bread and then two glasses of water to appease her hunger and rushed into the bathroom to have a hot shower. The sindoor on her forehead and the dark circles around her eyes were washed away. Clean and fresh with her hair wound in a towel, she stood by the window to take in the sky and the heaven beneath it. Kishan scolded her, 'What's this. You're a bride, you can't dress this way. Wear a sari and jewellery—people will come to see you later this evening.'

Nila took off her jeans and draped a silk sari on her body. She donned gold bangles on her wrists, heavy gold earrings on her ears and a gold necklace around her throat. She brushed some powder on her face, drew a line of kohl around her eyes, wore a sindoor bindi on her forehead and drew the sindoor in the parting of her hair, applied some dark lipstick and then looked at herself in the mirror. This sindoor was supposed to be for Sushanta. A bitter smile played on Nila's lips—where was Sushanta now! He must be enjoying life. For a whole year he went around with Nila, everyone thought they'd be married soon. But finally he ditched her because they weren't from the same caste. Sushanta was a high-caste Brahmin: he could make love to Nilanjana Mandal of the scheduled caste, but marriage—never! Perhaps it wasn't Sushanta who had the problems but his parents. But he seemed to give up his choice quite easily and settle for the girl his parents chose for him. After that Nila had felt she had to leave Calcutta, the sharp talons of memory were ripping her to shreds every day. She got married to Kishan instead and then wondered if she had done so in order to live or was this a different kind of death, or did she do it because one *had* to get married; otherwise people would frown upon her. Perhaps she did it to defend herself against nasty conjectures about why she didn't marry until so late and also to prove to everyone that she wasn't deaf or lame and could still get a good match.

In the evening seven guests came to the house. Of them, six were non-Bengali Indians and one was French: Odil. Tariq Ismail's wife was Gujarati, two others came with their wives: Babu Gogini and Rajesh Sharma. Sanal Edamaruku wasn't married. Nila accepted the gifts they had brought—the colourful bouquet from Minakshi, the sari from Sahana Gogini and the one, solitary red rose and two noisy kisses on either cheek from Odil. They all pulled up some chairs and sat down. Nila was the only newcomer in that house—she was the stranger.

Kishan was shaking the bottle of Moët and Chandon as he said, 'I have just this one wife, everyone—so I think today I can drown myself in champagne.' He pressed the cork of the bottle lightly with his thumb and the cork flew open with a deafening sound. Nila was drenched in champagne. Kishan poured out the remainder into glasses.

Babu Gogini raised his glass and said, 'Welcome to France.' The rest of the people immediately raised their glasses and clinked them with each other's and said the same thing, 'Welcome.' For a while

there were great exclamations over Nila, 'Oh, what lovely eyes—
they literally talk.' Sahana leaned to the left, looked at Nila and poked
Babu, 'Doesn't she look a little like the film actress Rekha?' Nila sat
stiffly before the razor sharp gazes of the Goginis. Babu leaned to the
right and whispered, 'No, not like Rekha; I'd say a little like
Meenakshi Seshadri.'

'No,' Sanal jumped up, leaped over three or four people, squatted
down in front of Nila and said, 'No, she doesn't look like Rekha or
Meenakshi. Our bhabhi looks like,' he put on as sombre an expression
as he could, 'exactly like Nilanjana Mandal.'

Everyone laughed.

Sanal was a physicist. He had been in the country for ten years
and wasn't married. He lived alone and had bought a house in Noisee.
He was around six feet tall with a toned body and long hair that
reached his shoulders. When Sanal shook his head and talked, his
hair swung back and forth. Nila looked at Sanal and then at Kishan.
She gave Sanal eighty-five on one hundred and Kishan fifteen. Nila
thought she could easily have married Sanal. But she didn't. Fate
ordained strange things for everyone. Did it really ordain anything at
all? If only Sunil had sent Sanal Edamaruku to Calcutta to get married,
Nila's life would have been different. But that's not what happened.

Nila whispered to Chaitali, 'That man, the French girl's husband,
what does he do?'

'He writes. He lived in London, but now he's married the French
girl and stays here. He's written quite a nice book! I don't remember
the name ...' Chaitali rubbed her middle finger against her thumb
and tried to recollect, 'It's name is . . . Sunil, what's Tariq's book
called?'

Sunil answered swiftly, '*Why I Am Not a Muslim.*'

'Yes, *Why I Am Not a Muslim.*'

Nila said, 'Like Bertrand Russell's *Why Am I Not a Christian*. Tell
me, has anyone ever written a book, *Why I Am Not a Hindu?*'

Chaitali shrugged and shook her head slowly—not to her
knowledge.

Sunil was engrossed in summarizing the qualities of the whisky.
He took a minute off it and said, 'Yes. It's by Mr Sunil Chakravarty.'

Ha, ha.

'Kishan, what is all this? Fetch the malt, quick.'

Kishan brought out a bottle of Glenfiddich in one hand and a bottle of Lafroige in the other as he swayed towards them.

The crowd went crazy.

'We'll wind up with Springbank.'

'Oaao ho,' Sanal whistled.

The conversation flowed between English, French and Hindi. Gradually the voices rose, one by one. Nila sat in a corner of the sofa, close to Chaitali—Nila, the bride, the doll, the visitor. Everyone went into the kitchen and poured themselves orange juice, water or whatever it was that they needed. Nila and Sahana were drinking orange juice. Some had their whisky with water and some had it on ice. Tariq drank his neat. At least twice he'd remarked, 'The taste of whisky is ruined if you mix it with water. This is the problem with Indians—they don't know how to drink and yet they have to'

Rajesh said, 'We don't really drink for the sake of drinking. We drink so that we can get drunk, however that may be.'

'I agree with you, my friend.' Babu Gogini guffawed.

Sahana nudged him and said, 'Why are you laughing like the devil? Are you drunk already?'

Sanal caught her out, 'Why did you say "like the devil"—have you ever seen the devil laugh?'

'I have, I have. I've seen La Jaconda laugh.'

The room was filled with laughter. Nila wondered whether Odil declared that smile, made famous by Da Vinci, as a devilish one simply to make people laugh or was that truly her belief. She couldn't find out because Sanal had already leaped up to her again.

He poured a little vodka into her glass, which had only orange juice, shook it and said, 'Now drink this screwdriver like a good girl, our new bride. By tomorrow it'll tighten all the screws that are loose in your head.'

There was another roll of laughter. When Kishan laughed, his shovel-teeth were exposed. Babu Gogini had a golden smile. Two teeth in the upper row were made of gold and they sparkled when he smiled. Tariq Ismail laughed with his lips closed and his whole body shook from head to toe. Chaitali covered her mouth with her left hand and Sanal laughed loudly, haha, hoho. Odil's laugh showed only her pink upper gums and neither teeth nor sound. Rajesh's moustache and beard covered his whole face and when he laughed, all of it just stretched a little and the teeth were hidden in the hair. Sunil sucked in his breath when he laughed—air only went in and never came out.

Amidst such gusts of laughter, Babu Gogini had the urge to ask everyone a question: why do Frenchmen have such large mouths and small hands?

No one knew the answer to that.

Babu Gogini said solemnly, 'Because French women have tiny breasts and huge nipples.'

No one except Odil and Sanal laughed at that one.

Minakshi turned away and Sahana got up to go inside.

One question led to another. Sanal asked, 'Do you know what gender is Law?'

Everyone was silent. Sanal said, 'Feminine gender.' He then sat there quietly until someone was curious enough to ask him for an explanation. Odil did that.

'Law is feminine because it has holes.'

Chaitali asked if anyone wanted more orange juice. There were desperate attempts to change the topic.

Kishan smiled and said to Nila, 'Today you're on leave, but from tomorrow you'll have to get down to housework, okay?'

Kishan's comment didn't embarrass Nila at all.

Chaitali butted in, 'The house isn't just hers. Both of you will have to get on with the housework.'

Kishan did a bottoms up and said, 'I am not good at all this.'

Nila asked, 'And I have to be?'

'You do. You're a woman.'

Everyone in the room laughed—that was that for the educated girl.

Kishan looked at Nila with half-closed eyes and said, 'Come closer. You're my wife and you're sitting so far away.'

Everyone almost pushed Nila towards Kishan.

Kishan knocked on his glass and drew all eyes upon Nila as he said, 'Ladies and gentlemen, my wife here is quite a beauty, isn't she?'

'Certainly, sure.' The voices were unanimous.

Kishan patted Nila on the back and said, 'After all, she is *my* bride.'

Tariq said, 'Kishan really needed a wife like this.'

'Why so?'

'So beautiful, so good—so totally Indian. Foreigners are no good! They are good for a little lovemaking, but not for marriage. For marriage it has to be an Indian.' Tariq spoke in pure Hindi.

Chaitali shouted, 'Will someone please translate what Tariq said for Odil's benefit?'

Odil was immersed in a whispered conversation with Babu and Sahana. He looked up and said, 'Has someone said anything odious about me?'

Sanal said, 'No, no, not odious at all. Whatever he said is true, but it is all made up.'

Tariq laughed and said, 'I have seen many women, but none so beautiful as my wife.'

Odil's pink-gummed smile was in place for a long time.

No one noticed, but the roomful of people broke up into smaller groups. Rajesh and Tariq were in one group.

'India's economy is going in for a massive change in the next ten years.'

'Nonsense! It's a poor country and it'll stay poor—the country is corrupt from top to bottom.'

'All of Silicon Valley is in the hands of the Indians and even Europe is trying to lure software professionals from India.'

'Only a handful of people have money in their hands—the rest are all dying of hunger.'

'I have never seen a man die of hunger in India. It is all Western propaganda.'

'Population is killing the country.'

'But why! Human resource is a great strength, if it is used properly. Once the factories of Europe almost closed down and they had to fall back on labourers from other countries.'

In another group Kishan and Babu Gogini were frothing at the mouth: 'Congress is gone. Not even in a hundred years will they be able to come back to power.'

'But the BJP also can't be relied upon. Vajpayee is our only hope.'

'The Left and Right wings are all the same. Do you know Jacques Chiraq has taken a huge bribe for his party?'

'It's not as if Jasper's party doesn't have thieves.'

'The rate at which Jose Bovain is gaining popularity, he's sure to win if he contests this election.'

'Nonsense—just rumours. If it suits your business then MacDonalds is no inconvenience. Let them give food so cheap—the very idea of competition will be a death-blow to them.'

In one corner it was Sanal and Sunil: arguing non-stop in French. The subject was cricket.

Minakshi and Odil sat on one side; they talked mainly about their children.

Sahana came and joined Nila and Chaitali.

The topic was the home—a new home; markets: where one would get river fish or which shop sold the five spices that were used in Bengali cuisine. Then it was a discussion of recipes.

In Kishan's group politics was nudged out and industry inched in.

Salmonella in chicken, mad cow disease!

All propaganda!

Fish and meat were being imported heavily and so mutton was very expensive.

'Damn, there's no sense in running a restaurant in this country! England is the best for that. All the immigrants are migrating to Italy in hordes—where is my workforce?' Kishan said. Then he looked at Nila, crinkled one eye and said, 'I guess I'll push my wife into the business—she'll cook and I'll serve. How good is your cooking?' Kishan nudged Nila's stomach with his elbow.

Nila edged out from her group and said, 'I don't know how to cook.'

Kishan laughed out loud, 'What's this—how can you be a woman and not know how to cook? Go and check out my restaurant—those boys who never even peeped into their kitchens at home are cooking away merrily. So you'll do just fine.'

Sunil put his cricket talk on hold and said, 'Hey, hey, don't bombard your new bride with talk of cooking just yet. Let a few days pass.'

Nila pressed Chaitali's hands and said, 'Enough of this meaningless jabber. Why don't you sing something?'

'Sing? No way. That's for the Bengali group. Non-Bengalis know nothing of singing! Philistines, all of them.' Chaitali spoke in Bangla.

At eight o'clock a man in a black suit and a necktie came with packets of food. It was from Kishan's restaurant: rotis and vegetable curry. Kishanlal was a vegetarian. Meat and fish weren't allowed in his house.

Mojammel, in the black suit and tie, kept the food on the table and came to see Kishan's wife. He wore a broad grin and his eyes were so dark that he looked like he was wearing kohl in them.

'Didi, I work in Kishanbabu's restaurant. I am from Bangladesh.'

'Bengali!' Nila's eyes brimmed with joy.

Chaitali laid the table. Some people sat on the sofa and some at the table.

As they ate, Sunil said, 'Nila, whenever you feel like having fish curry and rice, come to our place. Chaitali is a great cook.'

Nila said, 'I feel like going right now. I can have roti and vegetables one day, but not two.'

Mojammel smiled and said, 'Don't you worry, didi, just come to Taj Mahal. Our chef cooks fish and meat quite well.'

The banter continued until well after dinner. Kishan opened a fresh bottle. The Tariqs left early because they had left their schizophrenic son alone at home. Rajesh and his wife also left. Sunil and Chaitali had left their daughter, Tumpa, at a friend's place in Sandani and so they were not in a hurry. Once the bottle was empty, Sanal rose to go. As he put on his warm jacket which was hanging on the coat rack by the door, Sanal said loudly, 'Nila-bhabhi, it's customary to kiss you on both cheeks as I leave. But I won't. Today the honours belong to Kishan and I leave him to do it, right Kishan?'

Kishan was lounging on the sofa and his tummy bulged out of his shirt; more fat than stomach. He laughed crudely. His shovel-teeth bulged out and the fatty stomach bulged even more.

Once Sanal left, Sunil and Chaitali also made a move to go.

'What's this, all of you are leaving! The house will be so empty. Why don't you stay here tonight?' Nila held Chaitali's hand firmly in her fist.

Sunil drew his breath in and laughed, 'Crazy girl.'

Chaitali took her hand out of Nila's grip and put on her warm jacket.

The moment they left, a strange silence broke into the house. Nila felt lonely, though she knew that the man in the house was her closest one, her husband.

She went to bed in her full finery of sari and jewellery and lay in a foetal position. Kishan broke that posture, straightened her, undid the buttons of her blouse and unhooked her bra—Nila's breasts jumped out. Kishan mauled them the way he'd mash boiled potatoes with his hard fingers and soon rendered them lifeless. The room was silent except for Kishan's panting. Nila lay inert beneath Kishan's hairy body. She asked herself, 'Is this pleasure?'

The answer came from within, 'No.'

Life at Home

'Wake up, wake up, it's pretty late.'

Nila hadn't slept all night. Towards early morning her eyes drooped and she fell asleep. Now she woke up, startled: where was she; this wasn't her bed. Her glance fell on Kishan and as she registered his thick, black moustache, beady eyes, pockmarked face, she realized that this was her husband's house and she was here in Rue de Sandani on the sixth floor in Paris, lying on snow-white bedsheets. Kishan wrapped a towel around his waist, headed for the bathroom and said, 'Just look at all the dirty dishes of last night—they're still lying there.'

Nila had seen them last night. In Calcutta she would never have spared them a second glance. There were people to take them away, clean them, wipe them and put them away. Kishan reminded her that the luxuries of Calcutta were not available in Paris, where they even had to clean their bathrooms themselves. If it had been Calcutta, Nila would have stayed in bed a little longer. Once Chitra gave her the tea and the newspaper, she'd have drunk the former, read the latter and only then left her bed. There'd be another round of tea after that. But in this house there was no sign of Chitra. Nila must get up and deal with the dirty dishes of last night.

She draped a cotton sari around herself and went into the kitchen. A massive hunt didn't reveal where the tea was. So she stood at the bathroom door and asked, 'Where do you keep the tea?'

Kishan had come out of the shower and was halfway through his shaving. He looked away from the mirror in surprise and said, 'Who'll drink tea? I don't drink it.'

'What! You don't drink tea?' Nila's eyes were tinged with scepticism. She had never come across a person in India who didn't drink tea.

'No.' Kishan turned back to the mirror and continued with his shaving.

'I can't do without tea; I need at least two cups in the morning,' Nila stood at the door and rubbed her sleepy eyes.

'Are you addicted to tea?'

'Not really addicted—habit, you could say.'

'Now that's a problem.'

'Problem?'

'Two kinds of habits in the same house is definitely a problem.'

As she moved away from the bathroom, Nila heard Kishan say, 'I'm late.'

She set the table and placed the bread, butter, jam and orange juice upon it. For as long as she could remember, Nila had never seen Anirban reminding Molina that he was late. Molina left her bed at dawn and went into the kitchen. She made hot chapattis, or fried dalpuris or whatever Anirban liked to eat. Molina could never be faulted in the art of homemaking. Nila was Molina's daughter and people said she was as sweet, polite and gentle as her mother. So she should be flawless as well in serving her husband.

Nila quickly removed the dishes of the night before.

Kishan came out dressed in a suit, looked at the table and said, 'Well, you're quite a good wife.'

'Why are you calling me good? Just because I've laid the table and put food upon it?'

'That's not all,' Kishan crinkled his eyes and laughed.

Anirban had never smiled like that at Molina. Instead he usually complained about the vegetable not being cooked enough or the egg-yolk not being whole or one side of the bread getting charred. Nila thanked her stars that Kishan was not displeased—on the contrary he looked quite satisfied with so little.

'When will you be back?' Nila asked.

'Not sure.' Kishan didn't do a nine to five job that he could say, 'I'll leave the office at five and head for home; the traffic on the road should take me thirty-five minutes to reach here and finding a parking spot will take six minutes, two more minutes to come up, so I'll be back at five forty-three.' Kishan ran two restaurants. One was called

Taj Mahal at Montparnasse and the other was called Lal Killa in the fifteenth arrondissement. The latter wasn't doing too well. Kishan believed a change of name would help.

'Try to think of a new name for it,' he told her.

'What will I do all day?' Nila sat in front of Kishan, leaned on her elbows and asked.

'Sit and think of me.'

'And?'

'And what? Wouldn't that be enough for the day?'

'If it isn't?' Nila was remote.

'That's true.'

He said he'd take her out very soon, to buy warm clothes and shoes. But he didn't specify when that 'soon' was.

Nila's eyes shifted from Kishan to the window—to the paradise outside.

'What's that? Is that a palace?' She pointed to an impressive building with stone statuettes outside the window.

'That's the station—Gare du Nord.'

'Really? A railway station and so pretty?' Nila ran to the window. 'When will you show me around the city?' Her voice was childlike, excited.

'You did see some of the city yesterday. Why are you so restless? You've just arrived and you have the rest of your life to see the city.' Kishan left the house.

Nila knew she had the rest of her life to look around. But she felt a dance of impatience in all her nerves. She had felt the same way in that room with walls of steel. Waiting to be free, although she didn't know free of what or free to go where. In this room too, her heart beat like a caged bird. The walls of this room were no less disciplinary than those.

Nila sat at the window impassively and observed the flow of people and cars down below: the urbane, smooth, busy lives of people midst silent loneliness. At this time of the day Calcutta would be lit wide open by terrible sounds—a siren, a truck's tyre bursting, push-carts, hawkers, beggars, dogs bickering, women quibbling at the common tubewell, and so many other sounds that make life unbearable. Nila felt she had landed somewhere outside the planet where there was no dirt, no hassles, nothing that piqued the eye, nothing uncontrolled, uncouth or ugly.

This city never burst at its seams, never screamed. But in this city everyone had somewhere to go to, except she. No one waited for her, anywhere. Absent-minded, Nila began to sing, '*Break free these doors and take me away*!' As she sang, the sound of her own voice startled her. The Gare du Nord began to seem like the palace of the king of France; the prince stood at the window and looked out. He saw the princess, with long dark tresses, trapped in the house of a wicked giant. The prince charged up on horseback, to rescue the princess. He held a magic wand in his hand—a touch of that wand and the lock on the giant's doors would break free. He would take the princess and they'd both alight in front of the huge gates of the palace. Then they would walk inside, hand in hand. Nila looked at her own hands. She couldn't remember Kishan ever taking those hands in his. Perhaps their hands had brushed accidentally. But Nila couldn't remember him ever looking at them with even the mildest appreciation or desire. When he got down to pleasuring himself with her body in the dark, she never felt Kishan's body cry out for each and every part of her body; at the most, only one part of his body panted for one part of hers. Nila's delicate fingers, shapely nails, large dark eyes and masses of black tresses lay untouched in the dark, as untouched as a low-caste untouchable.

She moved away from the window and hunted for books in the house. She looked high and low and the only things in print that she could find were five mammoth telephone books, an English-French dictionary, three cookbooks in Hindi, seven *Le Monde* which were two years old, four *Herald Tribunes* and three porn magazines. She gave up and looked for music instead. That yielded some Hindi film songs, four English, some Bhangra and one Edith Piaf. There wasn't a single Rabindrasangeet or even any Hindustani classical. Nila put the Edith Piaf on and found that the French sparrow was chirping away in the same tune over and over again. An unknown chirping in an unknown land can make one feel even more alone. She switched it off and walked from one room to another, her footsteps her only companion. Eventually Nila, who didn't follow a single word of French, turned on the television and concentrated on the conversations and antics of the white people. It was broken by the sound of the phone, when it was nearly evening. It was Kishan, 'Hello there, wife, what have you cooked today?'

'Wife hasn't cooked anything.'

'What shall we eat then? Do you want to starve your husband to death?'

Nila couldn't decide what to say. She had no intention of becoming a widow so soon.

Kishan's voice was solemn, 'Something had slipped my mind totally, you know. I should have left a door-key with you, in case there was a fire or something . . .'

'Why should there be a fire?'

'Accidents—they happen, don't they? It's good to be prepared in such cases.'

'That's true.' Nila wondered how she would react if there was a fire, how she would put it out and for the life of her, she couldn't tell what was the connection between a fire and the door key. She asked, 'What happens if there's a fire?'

'Then, if you had the key, you'd have been able to leave.' Kishan answered as simply as if she had asked what should she do when she was thirsty.

'Oh.' Nila understood—if the house was on fire, she had the freedom to run outside and save her life. But if there was no fire, the question of saving her life didn't arise.

But if it did?

She went into the kitchen and as she washed the dishes and started cooking rice, daal and vegetables, the thought kept humming in her mind—what if the question arose?

Nila's rice was burnt, the vegetables were half cooked and the daal had too much salt in it.

Kishan returned home after dark and hurled his heavy body on to the sofa.

'Change into something more comfortable and wash up—you've had a tiring day at work,' said Nila. Immediately she realized her voice was dripping with sisterly concern.

Kishan laughed. 'Do you think this is your dirty Calcutta that I have to wash my face and hands the minute I come home from work?'

'At least take off those heavy shoes that you've been wearing all day.' Even as she said it, Nila remembered that this was the exact tone Molina used when she asked her son Nikhil to take his shoes off.

'Why don't you do it for me,' Kishan stretched out his legs.

Nila sat at his feet and untied the shoelaces with her slim fingers and took off his socks.

Now she felt like the housemaid, a little like Chitra who used to take everyone's shoes off, just as she was doing.

'There's a basket for unwashed clothes in the bathroom. Keep them there and do the washing tomorrow.'

Nila took the dirty socks into the bathroom and thought that at night she'd have to be the perfect whore and sell herself just as they sold their bodies for some money. Nila wondered if there was any difference between a prostitute's client and a husband. The only difference she could find was that the client can get away only after paying off the prostitute whereas the husband can get off the hook without ever paying his wife's dues. She felt the prostitute actually had more freedom than the wife in more ways than one.

A mother, a sister and a prostitute—were they the three roles which a woman had to play to the hilt or were they merely the three personas that a woman was born with.

Kishan asked, 'How do you like it here in Paris?'

Nila looked soulfully outside the window and said, 'This is my first time outside the country. Although there were no oceans to cross, I feel I've crossed the seven seas to get here. It's a whole new world, totally strange.'

Kishan nodded unhurriedly and spoke slowly, 'Let a few years pass and you'll see yourself finding India a strange place. That's life, Nila: a habit and nothing else. Once you get used to the life here, you won't be able to adjust in India although that's where you were born and raised.' Then he changed track and asked, 'So what did you do all day?'

'I felt very lonely the whole day. If I had their phone numbers I could have talked to them . . .'

'Who's "they"?'

'Those who were here last night . . .'

'Why would you call them for no reason? Last night was over once they left. It's more important that you call home.'

Kishan called Calcutta. It was nearly midnight there and everyone was getting ready to sleep. Kishan informed them all that Nila had reached safely, that she was fine and they had had a small reception the night before. After speaking to Anirban, she spoke to Nikhil and finally Molina's voice floated down the receiver, 'The house feels so empty without you. You've never been away, you see.' Molina was crying.

Nila chided her, 'Stop it. You're just being silly. Would you rather I rotted in that house in Ballygunge?'

Molina asked, 'Tell me how you are.'

Nila was ecstatic, 'I'm fine, really. Everything here is very beautiful. Last night we had a great time, many people were here. Everyone is very nice.'

At the other end Molina was still sobbing.

It got to Nila. This 'mother' business was very messy—they'd cry if the daughter didn't get married and cry if she did.

Kishan poured himself a glass of Scotch and relaxed on the couch. As he drank he told her that his restaurant, Lal Killa, was going bankrupt. The name would have to be changed very soon. Nila couldn't really understand how a change of name would rejuvenate the business. When she asked as much, Kishan laughed and said, 'You won't understand these things.'

Nila pleaded, 'If you explain, I'm sure I will.'

Kishan didn't think so. As far as he knew, women had no business sense.

Nila proposed the names 'Suruchi' 'Khabar-Dabar' or 'Tripti' for the restaurant. But Kishan blew them off into his alcoholic haze.

They won't do. So what would? Something like Gandhi. How was Gandhi related to food? Even if they were not related, the French could relate Gandhi to India. They knew Gandhi's name far better than they did the Lal Killa. And would the food in the restaurant change? Not at all—that'll stay the same, the same chef and the same waiters.

When the bottle was half empty Kishan sat down to have dinner. Nila served him the food and regretted that the cooking wasn't up to scratch. She sat in front of him with an apologetic face. As he ate, Kishan said, 'However, a wife's cooking is something else.'

Nila knew that all husbands liked their wife's cooking. Though Anirban would always criticize Molina's cooking, he would never eat the food if it was cooked by Chitra. Once Molina was down with fever and Chitra did the cooking. Nikhil and Nila both ate. But Anirban refused to eat. Molina got up and cooked, despite her fever, and only then did he eat. Not only did this satisfy Anirban; it gave great pleasure to Molina as well.

When he finished, Kishan said, 'One day I'll send Bachhu, the boy who cooks in the restaurant, to teach you some cooking.'

Nila laughed and said, 'Cooking is also a matter of habit.'

Just as cooking was a habit, so was sharing your husband's bed. After their marriage, when Kishan slept with Nila for the first time, she had felt stifled because she couldn't throw about her arms and legs and roll all over the bed. Gradually she got used to leaving more than half the bed for him, restraining her arms and legs and listening to the sounds of his snoring.

When Kishan lifted her sari and dipped his head into her breasts, Nila said with a childlike excitement, 'Tomorrow I want to walk on the streets for a bit.'

'Why?'

'Just.'

'No one walks around without a reason.'

'I won't go far, just close by.'

'Why do you want to walk in this dirty locality?'

'Dirty? But it's sparkling clean.'

'Alone? And if you get lost? Next Saturday I'll have some time and I'll take you to see the Eiffel Tower.'

Nila was lost in her dreams of the Eiffel Tower even as Kishan lost himself in Nila's depths.

After the six days' wait the promised Saturday arrived. Kishan bought some warm clothes and shoes for Nila, took her to see the Eiffel Tower and finally stopped in front of the Taj Mahal restaurant in Montparnasse. News travelled fast that the boss's wife was here.

Mojammel came forward with a wide grin, dressed in a black suit and a tie. He said, 'Hello didi, what would you like—tea, coffee or something cold?'

Nila wanted some tea. She felt it was years since she'd had any.

'What kind of tea, the Indian kind or black tea?'

Nila was surprised. 'What's the Indian kind of tea?'

'With milk, cardamom and cloves.'

Nila shuddered. She didn't even have milk in her tea, let alone cardamom and cloves.

The tea arrived and also a bunch of Bengali youth. Even Bachhu dropped his cooking and came forward. Some were from Jessore, some from Rangpur and some from Barishal. Nila was bursting with happiness as she said, 'My father came from Faridpur. At the time of the Partition he came over to Calcutta and never went back.'

The boys found a long-lost sister in Nila and talked to her of their faraway homes. Kishan observed all this from where he stood near the cash-box and shouted, 'Is that the Bengalis having their famous adda? There isn't a race lazier than this one, really! Eat, sleep and chatter. Come on, get back to work.'

Nila raised her voice, 'Let me finish the tea at least.' This was the effect of finding so many Bengalis. Her voice gained strength. Nila presumed even her soul was strengthened.

As she drank the tea, Nila came to know that Mojammel, who came to France three years ago because he couldn't find a job in Dhaka, had completed his master's degree in chemistry from the Dhaka University. He was still on a cut-throat passport.

'What is that?'

'This is when they remove the neck upwards from someone else's passport and stick your own photo in it.'

Nila shivered.

Mojammel said, 'I had no choice. There was no way I'd get a foreign visa . . . so you get to buy passports with visas. I sold the land and whatever else my father had and bought such a passport for five lakhs of rupees and then . . .'

Nila was curious.

'Then I came to France and started working.'

'What kind of work?'

'Selling roses on the streets.'

'Selling roses after studying chemistry? Couldn't you get a good job here?' Nila's voice shook with anxiety.

Mojammel laughed and said, 'Our education has no value here. I have even worked as a janitor for a while.'

Before he got the job at the restaurant, Mojammel used to work in a packing-box factory. There was less money in these jobs because they used illegal labour. The government of this country didn't allow you to apply for a proper job until your papers came through. So whatever you did, it had to be illicit and surreptitious, giving the police the slip. Nila was curious about these 'papers'. It wasn't just Mojammel, she'd heard it from an innocent-looking boy called Jewel as well. Nila could tell that the thing for which they all waited eagerly, for which they hoped and prayed and with which their lives could become brighter and more comfortable, was 'papers'.

What *were* these 'papers'?

'The permission to live in this country.'

Nila's curiosity mounted. Mojammel spoke candidly, 'They tried to evict me twice from this country. Finally I sued them, showing a valid cause for staying on and the case is still pending. As long as it's not decided, I can stay on.'

'What was your reason?'

'Didi, how do I say it . . . it's really a shame . . . I got a new passport with a Hindu name and said that Hindus are being persecuted in Bangladesh . . . it wasn't safe for me to go there.'

An utter and complete lie, Mojammel admitted it himself readily.

Nila, who could never tolerate lies, when she heard Mojammel's story, felt no anger.

Mojammel scratched his head and said, 'Didi, these are not things we can hide. Everyone knows how the poor young boys from our country come here, how they stay, what they do . . .'

'Isn't it possible without such lies?'

'No. If I say that I'm educated and I was jobless in Dhaka, that I want to work here, build myself a healthy, beautiful life, the kind of life that everyone dreams of, they'd just throw me out of the country. Political asylum they may just allow, but economic asylum—never!'

Nila had had a minor experience of how they threw people out of the country when she had arrived at the airport. So she didn't probe any further.

Jewel sat beside Mojammel and rattled out his story; that he used to sell fruits near the underground station; that the police got after him and he had to quit that.

'Why would the police be after you?'

'You're not allowed to sell fruits over there. They often take us to the police station and ask for the papers . . .'

'And none of you have them?'

'Yes, some do. There were some people who married French women in exchange for a lot of money. Such a marriage got them the papers and even a citizenship. And if you hang on for many, many years, eventually they do grant you permission, sort of like throwing a scrap to the dog.'

Mojammel and Jewel lived in the same apartment in Belle Ville along with five other Bengali boys—all in the same room.

'Seven of you?' Nila took the last sip from her cup.

'Cutting cost, didi—we really have no choice.'

Kishan finished tallying the accounts and said, 'Come on, come on, get going all of you.'

Nila said, 'But I wanted another cup of tea.'

'You just had tea.'

'But one cup is hardly enough. I've told you how I love this drink.' Nila raised her head and stated, not pleaded.

When Kishan shouted out, the boys straggled off, one by one, except for Mojammel.

Nila lowered her voice and asked, 'Why don't you go back?'

'Home? I've spent so many years in the hope of earning some good money. What will I do if I went back home now? At this age I won't get any jobs and what will I eat? How would I show my face there? I can't go back with nothing. Even with such menial jobs here, I'm able to send back some money home. At least I pay for my younger brother's studies.'

Jewel brought her another cup of black tea. Nila took a quick swig from it and asked, 'So what's the use of all your education?'

'No use, didi.'

'All those others, are they all like you—I mean, have they all come here the same way as you have?'

'All of them.'

Nila was concerned, 'Are they all educated?'

'Yes. Bachhu is a doctor.'

'Why doesn't he practise here?'

'Who'll give him a job? Even if you have studied medicine in your country, you have to appear for fresh exams here. If you are an illegal immigrant, you can't sit for those exams. Language is a problem. Even if we can speak it, we can't write.'

'Do the people at home know that you work in a restaurant?' Nila sighed and asked.

'I haven't told them . . . I'm ashamed . . .' Mojammel laughed and said, 'Do you know what I've told my family? I work as a DC— people think it's Deputy Commissioner. I know it as Dish Cleaner.' Nila laughed with him. Kishan walked into their midst uninvited and asked, 'What's so funny? Come on now, let's go.'

Mojammel moved away.

'I want to see the kitchen.'

Nila went into the kitchen and found Sohail from Barishal chopping onions there. Bachhu was pouring oil into the kadhai. Jewel was washing the dishes.

'So doctor, what's cooking?'

Bachhu laughed, 'Gravy.'

'Gravy for what?'

'Everything.'

'What do you mean everything? Fish or mutton, which one?'

'The same gravy for chicken, beef, lamb, fish and vegetables.'

'Oh dear me. Why would you have the same curry for everything?' Nila asked.

'That's the way it is, didi.'

'But then, this is not true Indian food.'

'Not exactly Indian. But it is Indian food tailored to the French taste.'

Bachhu told her that he had done the same work in Germany as well and there it was suited to the German palate.

Nila said, 'It's quite a sight: men chopping onions and cooking and cleaning. I have never seen this in all my life.'

Bachhu poured the bowl of onions into the oil and said, 'I had never poured myself a glass of water. Someone would pour it out and then I drank from the glass. I never knew what a kitchen looked like or what it was all about. I learnt it all when I came to Europe.'

The onions began to brown in the oil and Nila raised her voice above the sizzle as she said, 'In a way it's a good thing, don't you think? Now you know what women suffer in the kitchen.'

Bachhu sautéed the onions and looked away from the smoke, smiled sweetly and said, 'Didi, come here one day and teach us some dishes.'

'I am no better in the kitchen. I'd never gone in there either. I always thought it was the mothers who did it.'

It was the mother's job. Molina's job. That's what Nila had known. All her life she had seen Molina cooking and bringing the food to the table and then serving it to her husband and children. They talked as they ate. Molina stood by the table just in case someone needed something—more salt or gravy or water or something, anything. Nila tried to remember if she had ever actually seen Molina eating with someone. No, she hadn't.

Nila wanted to go out into the bright sunny day without any warm clothes. Kishan pulled her back into the heated room and explained to his novice of a bride that the sun had no warmth here. She understood the truth of it when she stood in the sun, wrapped up from head to toe and still felt the sharp wintry needles pierce her whole body. Nila looked for a post office to mail her letter to Molina. Her chin wobbled from the cold. In this city you never really had to look for anything. Everything was close at hand—you just had to open your eyes and look around. At the post office she saw the long queue and as she tried to avoid it and headed for the front, Kishan impatiently pulled her back by the hem of her coat and whispered, 'Whenever you see a queue in this country, respect it. This is the land of equality. The one who comes first is served first.'

But they didn't have to stand in the long queue. There were machines in the post office. When she placed the letter on a yellow machine, it told her what the postage on it would be. She put in the money and the stamps came out. She stuck the stamps on to the letter and dropped it into another machine. That was it! A matter of minutes. It was magic. There was such magic at every street corner in the city. You put in a card and the machine spewed out money, you put in coins and got hot tea, coffee or a cold drink from the bowels of the machine, or little toy cars, chocolates, biscuits. Nila wanted to see more of the city and more such magic.

Kishan wanted to buy a gift for Nila. They had a lifetime to explore the city.

'What is the gift?'

'I can't tell you that.'

Kishan got into the car with a spring in his step. The car drove by the Montparnasse, through Rue de Rennes keeping Saint-Germaine-des-Pres to the left and along Boulevard Saint Germaine—Nila watched in awestruck wonder as the sparkling cafés, restaurants and cinemas whizzed past. She wanted to get off the car and walk like so many others, stop at a café and drink some tea and watch the people, the beautiful people.

Kishan parked the car in Saint Michelle and went into Jibarre. It was a sea of books. Nila drowned in the sea without a trace. This was not an ocean she knew. She owned a little pond of the familiar waters, which she had left behind at home in Calcutta. She fingered the books by Balzac, Victor Hugo, Gustave Flaubert, Maupassant, Albert

Camus, Jean Paul Sartre, glanced through Baudelaire, Rimbaud, Paul Verlaine and Paul Eluard. She had read them in Bengali translations. When she picked up the books in the original French, she felt strange. In a trance, Nila handled the books one by one, smelt them, hugged them to her heart. Kishan was calling out to her, but she didn't hear him.

He had to almost drag her out of Jibarre. Nila's eyes were still glazed, in a trance and she felt euphoric. 'I must learn this language.'

Kishan walked towards the car rapidly as he said, 'Of course you must. You have to learn the language of the country where you live.'

Nila said, 'I want to learn it so that I can read their literature.'

'Oh, I have heard that you're a bookworm.' Kishan cackled and his lips twisted.

In Calcutta Nila had the notoriety of being a bookworm. Once she started reading, she forgot to eat or bathe and even forgot her own name—at least that's what her friends and family claimed.

Kishan rushed her, 'What's wrong? Walk faster.'

'Let's sit beside this fountain.'

'No, not today.'

'That's the Seine. Let's walk along it a little.'

'Another day.' Kishan brushed her off.

In the car Kishan handed her a gift-wrapped packet. 'Open it after we reach home.'

Nila kept it on her lap and grew restless again. 'Let's go to a movie.'

Kishan shrugged, 'You won't even understand, it's all in French.'

'Why, aren't there any English ones?'

'The French don't know English and they don't want to know it.'

'Don't they have plays here? Don't you ever go to watch any?'

'Where's the time!'

'There are so many museums in Paris—let's go to the Louvre.'

'We don't have the time today. We have to shop and then go back home.'

'Then let's go to a café and have a cup of tea.'

'But you just had tea at the Taj Mahal.'

Nila sighed. True, she had had tea and not one, but two cups.

Kishan blissfully ignored Nila's eager pleas. Apparently he had been taught from the age of six that it wasn't right to indulge such pointless pleas and whims of womenfolk. Kishan was laughing as he said that once his mother had craved for some ripe mangoes. His father went to pluck them from the tree, slipped and fell and broke his leg. That day his father had called his sons and warned them never to give in to these whims and fancies.

The car crossed the Seine swiftly and they were in the minipris at Chatal. Nila stared in amazement at the rows and rows of food: cooked rice, cooked fish and meat, vegetables in colourful packages. All you had to do was take them home and heat them and they were ready to eat.

Nila said, 'Don't they ever cook? Do they always eat from packets and bottles?'

Kishan replied, 'No one really wants to waste their time cooking.'

There were peas, okra, carrots, tomatoes soaking in brine in cans. They'd stay fresh even after nine years. There were powders for chicken and fish gravies, which would last several years. There was even mashed potato granules. Nila stood in stunned surprise.

When she came to the vegetables section she asked, 'Do they have the saag we eat at home here—I really love it.'

'None of the greens that you got at home.'

'Bottle gourd or pumpkin?'

'Are you crazy?'

'Why are the fruits and vegetables so large here?'

'They're all hybrid.'

Nila saw five strands of coriander leaves in a colourful packet and jumped up, 'Coriander, lovely. I love it.'

'I'll buy you lots and lots of it from the Chinese stores . . . these cost twelve francs for just five strands and there it's eleven for the whole packet.'

Nila put it back on the shelf.

'Tea?'

'All right, take some tea. But you know, it's a bad addiction.'

There were five hundred kinds of cottage cheese. Nila picked

up the most expensive one and brought it up to her nose to smell it—
she almost threw up. With the bile stuck in her throat, she managed
to get out of that section. In the meat section she breathed again.
There were pieces of meat in plastic packets: lamb, chicken, turkey,
duck, rabbit, beef, pork. The beef was the most expensive and chicken
the least. In Calcutta it was the other way around. Why was the meat
boneless? The bones were the tasty parts. People here had the meat
without the bones or the skin. Apparently that's what people did if
they had any sense. There was class division amongst the meat too—
the breast was better and cost more and the thighs were lower on the
scale.

There were many kinds of fish, scaled and deboned.

Nila pointed to the pink salmon and asked, 'How is this one
cooked?'

'It's eaten raw.'

'And prawns?'

'That too.'

Nila shuddered. But she still walked around the magnificent
displays in the shop. So many kinds of chocolates, wines—it was a
sight for sore eyes.

Nila grew more curious about the packed foods. She picked up
one bright looking packet and immediately Kishan said, 'What are
you doing? That's dog food.'

She reached for another tin and was in even more trouble. Kishan
snatched it from her hands, placed it back on the shelf and said in an
undertone, 'Why are you going for the cat food? Do we have cats at
home?'

Nila was dumbfounded—there was food for dogs and cats,
packaged just like human foods and kept along the same aisles! She
had been to the markets in Calcutta many times. Each time she would
have to duck under the stench of sweaty necks and armpits, scream at
the shopkeepers and bargain for the goods, aim a kick at the seedy
looking stray dog that stood in the dirty drain among buzzing flies,
drowning in cacophony and filth, before she could buy something.

Kishan put some greens, vegetables, flour, onions, garlic, ginger,
milk, eggs and two bottles of Johnnie Walker in his cart and hurried

her along. When they went to the counter, Kishan didn't do any bargaining. A machine read the prices off the goods and totalled it up. Kishan handed a blue card to the machine. It noted the number. The machine would get the money from Kishan's bank account.

Nila wanted to spend some more time in the supermarket. This was nothing like the market in Calcutta. But Kishan wanted to go home. At home she opened the packet and found a cookbook. It was a book on Indian cuisine by Madhur Jaffrey.

As usual, Kishan switched on the TV and opened his bottle of Scotch. Nila got the message: shopping done, cookery book bought, now it was up to her to get into the kitchen and start cooking the dinner. She tucked her sari into her waist and started doing just that. Kishan raised his voice and said, 'It's been a long time since I had malai kofta. Why don't you try that today?'

'What else?'

'Make some naan. And a vegetable dish would go well—make palak paneer.'

'But these are not Bengali food.' Nila stood at the kitchen door, onions stinging her eyes and the smell of garlic on her hands.

Kishan laughed, 'I am not a Bengali.'

'Oh, that's true.' Nila brushed the stray hairs away from her eyes and laughed.

Nila cooked all evening. She laid the table and called Kishan. As he ate, Kishan said, 'What did those boys at the restaurant want with you?'

Nila smiled, 'Just a fellow Bengali to talk to.'

'What was all that chatter with Mojammel?'

She put some malai kofta on to his plate and said, 'How he came to this country, what he does, etc.'

'What else?'

'Just that, and he said he can't get a good job without papers.'
'And?'

'And that he lives in Belle Ville.'

'And?'

'And that they stay seven together in one room.'

'And?'

'And that the people at home think he is a DC.'

'And?'

'And that he wouldn't get a job if he went back home, he's too old for that.'

'And?'

'And that Bachhu is a doctor.'

'And?'

'And he asked if I'd like more sugar in the tea. I said no. If I'd wanted it he'd have got me some. He also said that if you put salt in the tea instead of sugar, it tasted different. I said, yes it does. He asked if I'd like a pinch of salt. I said, no I don't like anything bitter. He asked if I wanted a slice of lemon. I said no, I didn't have my tea sour. I also said that too much lime in the tea could make it bitter.'

Kishan asked, 'Tell me, can you make daal makhani?'

'No.' Nila answered.

'But you know something, today's dinner is a definite improvement on the other day. The book will come in handy for you.'

Nila got up without finishing her dinner, 'You don't have meat at all. Will you never even try it?'

'You know very well that I don't have it and I'll never ever try it.'

'I am used to eating fish and meat. I cannot have vegetarian food always.'

'But you agreed to this match knowing full well that I am a vegetarian, didn't you?'

'Yes, I did. But I never said I will also give up eating meat.'

'Did you think you'll cook two kinds of food in the same house?'

'I didn't get the time to think so much.'

Nila picked up the dirty dishes and took them into the kitchen. Kishan burped loudly, stroked his immense tummy and said, 'If I get such great food everyday, my pot belly is here to stay.'

Nila raised her voice over the sound of running water in the kitchen and said, 'You do eat eggs; that's not vegetarian. So why won't you have fish and meat? Is it just habit or do you believe it is wrong to kill?'

Kishan didn't reply.

Nila said, 'Fine, I'll go to your restaurant sometimes and eat. Mojammel also suggested that.'

Kishan didn't reply to that as well.

At night, when Kishan began to take off her sari like every other night, Nila said irritably, 'I'm sleepy.'

'Go ahead and sleep. Let me do my work. You won't know a thing.'

Nila knew that this was Kishan's work and she had no role to play in it.

When Kishan was kneading her breasts in his palm she turned over and said, 'Please let me sleep.'

Kishan had no objection to Nila sleeping. But she shouldn't move her hands, legs, mouth and head so that he could get his work done easily. Nila wondered if Kishan really even needed a live female body to satisfy his hunger. She lay there still and motionless as Kishan's heavy body did its own work upon hers. He had been right about one thing: she didn't feel a thing.

Nila knew what would happen next. Kishan would get off her body and fall asleep, snoring. She would lie awake for many hours. In the morning Kishan would shake her awake, 'Wake up, wake up, it's getting late.' She wouldn't feel like getting up but she would. She'd make his breakfast, set the table and pour orange juice into his glass. She'd make tea for herself. When she drank the tea, Kishan would say tea makes your skin darker.

Nila would ask, 'When will you come back?'

'I don't know.'

Then Nila would stand by the window and watch the people in the street below.

On a Friday Kishan took Nila to Sunil's house for dinner. Sunil lived on Rue de Rivoli, which was named after the village in Italy where Napoleon defeated the Austrians in 1797. There was a station, a street and a bridge in this city, which were named after Austerlitz in Czechoslovakia because there too Napoleon had defeated the Russian and Austrian armies in 1805. There was also a street named Friedland because that was the Russian town where Napoleon had defeated the Russians in 1807. The war fields where Napoleon was victorious were the only ones that were honoured in Paris. Nila hadn't found anything named after Waterloo when she'd searched the map of Paris. The Hôtel de Ville was on the left and the Louvre on the right. Its roof was clearly visible from the window. Nila stood at the window and gazed at this vision of loveliness as she said, 'Kishan, can't you live in such a pretty place?'

There was a crude smile on his crude lips, 'If I got a big fat dowry from your father, I could have done that right now.'

Nila turned around, 'Why, has Sunil bought this house with money from his dowry?'

'Don't compare Sunil with me—he's a doctor and he mints money. I am just a hardworking businessman and my business is almost bankrupt.'

Nila didn't feel like a visitor in Sunil's house. It felt more like her own house or at least a close friend's. She noticed that she was more at home here than at Kishan's. There were pictures of Rabindranath Tagore, Netaji Subhash Chandra Bose and Vivekananda on the walls: the three famous Bengalis. Nila was a little sceptical about Vivekananda—he was in favour of child-marriage for girls and had opposed widow remarriage, hadn't he? When Nila asked, Sunil said he didn't know. Chaitali knew and she was busy cooking. She wouldn't be interested in discussing the moral fibre of Vivekananda. The bookshelves were full of Bengali books and a Bengali song was playing on tape. Nila bent down to look at the books as she hummed the song that played; the smell of hilsa fish cooked in mustard sauce wafted from the kitchen. She picked up three Bengali novels and a book on the French artistic sensibilities in the nineteenth century. As she glanced at Sunil for permission to borrow them, she found him already nodding and waving away the question of permission. And two cassettes of Rabindrasangeet by Kanika? That too.

Delighted, Nila crossed her legs and tapped her feet, a book by George Pereq in her hands. Her tapping feet went up on the sofa as she slowly reclined on the sofa and her legs stretched out to one corner of the seat. In her home in Calcutta Nila used to forget about the world thus, lost in her books, stretched out on the sofa, the bed, on the porch or the floor.

'What's the matter—did you come here to read?' Kishan's comment brought her upright. There were two men conversing in the drawing room and it didn't look proper for Nila to stretch out thus on the sofa, reading. She should go to the kitchen and try to help Chaitali.

But she didn't go to the kitchen and instead asked Sunil to form a sentence without an a or an i.

For a while Sunil stared at the ceiling and muttered but he couldn't do it.

George Pereq had written that massive book without a single 'i' in it. Amazing! Nila was still lost in her book. 'What a talent.'

Sunil showed some interest momentarily and then went back to discussing the restaurant business with Kishan. Nila put the book on top of the pile she was borrowing and slowly crept across the wooden floor towards Tumpa. 'Tumpa-rani, can I play with you?' The child was lost in her own world and didn't respond.

'Tumpa-rani, will you give me that talking doll?'

Tumpa didn't speak. Sunil said, 'She doesn't know Bengali.'

Nila was surprised—a Bengali child who didn't know Bengali but only French? She spoke French at home and in school. Although Sunil and Chaitali conversed in Bengali, they spoke French with the child.

'Why don't you teach her Bengali?'

'She won't be able to take the pressure of two languages.' Both Sunil and Chaitali were of the same opinion. What was the use of teaching her Bengali—she wouldn't need it.

Nila had seen this in Calcutta too: Bengali children were sent to English medium schools and spoke English at home, as if Bengali was a low-class language. The same logic applied there too: English helped in getting jobs, while knowing Bengali added no value. In spite of this factor, Nila had studied Bengali literature. Anirban had said this degree had no value. But she had argued that twenty-one crore people spoke this language and so it couldn't be that worthless.

It was the sixth most spoken language in the world and the written literature of this language alone went back to a thousand years. The deeper she had plunged into the language, she had surfaced with ever more valuable treasures, like coming upon a secret gold mine.

Chaitali laid the table with a variety of dishes and Nila's mouth watered as the smell wafted towards her. As she ate the daaler bara, shukto, posto, begun bhaja, kopi bhaja, chhoto machher chochhori, rui machher paturi, shorshey ilish, chingri malaikari, chicken curry and lamb curry, Nila felt she'd been on a starvation diet for many days. She ate to her heart's content and reclined on the sofa. Nila knew that if she asked, Chaitali would give her detailed directions of where she had found which fish and she also knew that it was of no use to her. None of these were allowed in Kishan's house.

After the meal, Chaitali sat down in front of Sunil with betel leaves in her hand, like the grandmothers at home. 'Are you inviting Paban Das Baul for Durga Puja this year?'

Nila put a betel leaf into her mouth and asked, 'You have Puja here in Paris?'

'Why not? And a big one at that.'

Sunil scratched his head. He was the president of the Puja Committee for that year and the pressures were just too much for him. He wanted to hand over some of the duties to Jayanta.

'Why Jayanta—he's from Bangladesh.'

'Still, he is a Hindu.'

'No, you'd better try Ashim Roy. Don't you remember, last year the Bangladeshis took money to decorate the dais and then just disappeared?' Chaitali complained.

Sunil remembered.

Nila sensed the mighty wall dividing the Bengalis. Those from Bangladesh were mostly illegal immigrants. All those unlawful, low-class people! The Bengalis from West Bengal were more Indian than they were Bengali. They'd embrace a Punjabi, Maharashtrian or Gujarati as their brothers and speak in broken French, Hindi or English. But they'd keep the Bengali in them suppressed like holding back nature's call. Bengali was for the bedroom—secret and surreptitious.

Amongst the three Bengalis Kishanlal stood out like a sore thumb. Nila prayed fervently that the sore thumb would go back home alone, drink alone and fall asleep alone and when he woke up alone in the morning he'd find that there was no one there to make his breakfast, to tie his shoelaces; at night too he'd come back home alone and find no one there to take his shoes off, to cook, lay the table and serve him dinner. Let him talk to himself and cry in solitude.

But of course Kishan wouldn't go home alone. Even if such a question had arisen, Sunil would never have allowed it. Nila looked at Sunil's longish, bespectacled face and remembered this was the man who had studied with Nikhil in Presidency College. He had been to their home in Ballygunge many a times and Molina had cooked and served her son's friend with great care. 'Aunty really knows how to cook!' this man had burped loudly and exclaimed many times. When Nila came home from school, swinging her braids, he had said, 'You crazy girl, what's the use of all this studying? Eventually you'll have to handle the kitchen in your husband's house.' Nila often stuck her tongue out at him and went into the other room. That same girl, who didn't have a care in the world, did successfully finish her college and university, without turning into an uneducated housewife. She didn't have to enter the kitchen. She had dreams of teaching in Lady Brabourne College or in Calcutta University. But finally, this man, Nikhil's friend Sunil, sent an ugly businessman to trample over her dreams, to bring her here and push her into the kitchen. She felt a little surprised to realize that her future had lain in this man's hands who had always believed that Nila would have to slog in the kitchen, however hard she studied. And that was so true. She could no longer stick her tongue out at him. Her tongue lay so heavy and stiff that even if she wanted to, she couldn't do it.

On their way back home, as she looked upon the dazzle of Paris by night, Nila went back to her childhood and smelt again that perfume called Evening in Paris. The streets bustled with people, women walked nonchalantly. There wasn't a trace of terror and their steps didn't falter.

Nila asked, 'Women are out in the streets even at this late hour—

aren't they scared?'

Kishan replied, 'Scared of what?'

That's true, Nila thought, scared of what? This wasn't Calcutta that five lusty men or a bunch of robbers would pounce upon a girl and snatch away her money, jewellery, honour or even life.

Nila pointed to a girl and asked, 'Take for example this girl, she's about sixteen or seventeen and she just came out of that house over there. Where do you think she's going at this hour of the night?'

Kishan answered, 'Perhaps to a bar, or a disco. She'll talk through the night, dance and have fun.'

Nila looked at Kishan with round eyes, 'And her parents wouldn't mind?'

'If on a Friday night girls of this age sit at home, if they don't have a boyfriend or sleep with a boy, it's then that parents would be worried. They'd wonder if something was wrong with her, physically or mentally. If the girl goes out, the parents sleep in peace and if she stays at home they'd have a sleepless night. Besides, most of them leave home at this age. They stay alone or with a boyfriend.'

'Without marrying them?' Nila asked again.

'Sure. These days no one marries and even if they do it's not until much later—after living together for five or even ten years or after children come along.'

'Education?' Nila's curiosity was aroused.

'In this country you don't need money to study, the government pays for it. The girls study and work part time—they get by.'

Nila said, 'It's a free life.'

'Yes. Over here they believe in enjoying life, in whatever way.' Kishan twisted his lips and crinkled his nose. 'Bullshit! Do you know when these girls lose their virginity? At age five or six when they play doctors and nurses. Even before they're twenty they must have bedded a hundred boys. There are no principles, really. If they love someone today, tomorrow they leave him—there are no enduring ties. They don't know how to settle down, when and with whom. They don't know it and they can't do it.'

Nila heard the splash-splash of water somewhere in her heart, 'Kishan, let's go to that bridge, let's walk on that Ponf a while. Why don't we bend down and take a look at the Seine, see how the waves are breaking and how the lights from the distant towers of the Notre-Dame are crowning the waves.'

Kishan didn't stop the car. He held the steering wheel. Nila realized that he who held the steering held all the power. But Kishan had to stop when thousands of roller skaters came charging from the Republic crossing, flying like thousands of butterflies. Nila looked with wonderstruck eyes at these young people flying on their wheeled shoes. She had never heard such a vibrant call of youthful life, such display of young energy.

'Why are they doing this?'

'Just for fun.'

'For what?'

'Fun, fun,' Kishan had to scream.

'*Just* for fun?'

'Just.'

Nila got out of the car and feasted her eyes on the speeding people. They left her behind and rushed ahead, in the flash of an eye, at the speed of light, with the energy of life, and immobile Nila, stationary Nila looked on, her eyes full of surprise and awe.

When Kishan called her, she had to get into the dark car again although she felt like walking or running on the streets; she wanted the speed of a cascade on her body and she wanted to exult in the feeling of youth all night long.

'So wonderful! There was no darkness; everything was light, bright and alive,' Nila said again and again.

Once they reached home, Kishan had to look for a parking spot from this end of the road to the other, from this alley to that and finally he found one after an hour.

Nila got down and said, 'Why are you keeping the car on the street and not in the garage?'

'Does anyone have a garage? Everyone parks on the street.'

Nila had never seen cars lying about on the streets of Calcutta. Anirban's ambassador had a dent on the bumper and the doors were rusty and yet it was kept in a garage which had huge padlocks on the door.

'All these cars parked on both sides of the road—will they stay here all night?'

Kishan nodded, yes they will, they always have.

'No one steals them?'

'Why would they?'

Nila thought, indeed why would they. This was not a land of thieves and robbers.

When life was so monotonous, the chances of an unfortunate event were less but it did happen in Nila's uneventful life. She slipped in the bathroom and hit her forehead on the corner of the bathtub. There was a steady stream of blood. Fortunately, she had the strength to call Kishan. He rushed home and quickly took Nila to the Lariboisière Hôpital, near the Gare du Nord. Nila was used to the hospitals in Calcutta with their swarming patients. Here, there were hardly five or six people in the waiting room dressed in immaculate clothes. They looked nothing like patients and more like guests at a banquet. Nila's sari was soaked in blood and a thin towel was wrapped around her wound—she was the living image of the outpatients room at Nilratan Hospital.

One by one they were summoned inside. When Nila was called in, the nurse said she'd have to take off her clothes, wear a front-open tunic and lie down on the examination table. Nila couldn't understand why she'd have to take off her clothes for a head X-ray. That was another hassle—she'd have to lie on the X-ray table, stark naked. Nila asked why would she have to be naked for an X-ray of her head. They said it had to be done—they'll take X-rays of her chest as well. But why would she have to be naked for that? They said she had to, for an X-ray of chest, stomach, legs or even toenails, she'd have to strip— that was the rule. Nila's father, Anirban, was a doctor and Nila had gone to the hospital many times. She had seen all the departments and once she even had to have an X-ray of her chest, but she didn't have to take her clothes off. This rule of stripping over here made her writhe in shame. It wasn't possible for her to strip and walk around before the nurse and the doctor with all her private parts showing. She was told that in that case they would not be able to treat her. The nurse and the doctor failed to understand why Nila was refusing treatment. Ashamed, she finally had to utter the word 'shame'. But they still couldn't understand the simple fact that she was feeling shy. When she repeated herself, the nurse and the doctor looked amazed.

'Shy of whom?'

'You. Him.'

'Why?'

Nila didn't answer that one. Instead she wore her clothes and walked out of the place and informed Kishan that she was unable to accept the obscene proposal of the hospital.

Kishan grinned with his buckteeth and pushed her towards the X-ray room; he advised her to strip.

'You wouldn't mind?' Nila asked.

Kishan was at his magnanimous best when he said it wasn't wrong to take her clothes off in front of the doctor.

Nila swallowed her shame and X-rayed her head. Her head received two stitches. She didn't have to strip for that.

There was a mark from a long-ago cut on Kishan's chin. Nila had never said that it detracted from his looks in any way. But Kishan often soulfully commented on the tiny mark on her forehead, which was usually covered by the fall of her hair, and said that her fiery beauty of old had gone.

Once the wound healed, it took her a while to take the medicines and recover fully. She spent the spare time after cooking and cleaning by reading books. The days were passing in their own fashion, lying on the ground, face down. One day, after his business picked up with the new name of Gandhi, Kishan wanted to take Nila to Gallerie Lafayette.

As they entered the place Nila was duly startled.

'We-ll, I thought it was a gallery and there'd be pictures in it.'

It was a store, a hundred under the same roof. Her eyes lifted to the colourful ceiling high up and she didn't want to look away from that amazing beauty. Kishan's nudge made her walk straight again. It was more like a golden palace. Nila had never seen such a beautiful store or even a palace for that matter.

Kishan went on and on, 'Buy this, buy that, buy some shoes, some clothes.' In spite of the mark on her forehead, Nila was still beautiful and her cooking was improving every day. Since Nila was his wife, his property, his wealth, since her life was in his hands and if she looked beautiful people would praise him, since Nila's recovery brought him the praises of how he'd looked after his wife, since everything of Nila's was actually his, Kishan's generosity knew no bounds.

In the shoe store the attendant asked for Nila's shoe size. But she didn't know it. How could she? In Calcutta she was used to picking up the shoes or sandals that fitted her. If a size eight fit her one month, the next month she'd find the size seven too large for her. Were her feet shrinking? Oh no, it was the shoe size that wasn't constant. The shoemakers just put whatever numbers that came to mind. When someone wanted to buy shoes, they'd just come to the shop, try out a few and take the one that fitted them—that was how it went.

Kishan picked up a pair of boots from the shelf and told her to try them on.

'But these are for men,' Nila pointed out.

'These are women's,' Kishan said and the attendant confirmed it.

Once the shoes were bought, Nila came to the clothes shop and there again she was in trouble. She reached for the trousers and Kishan said, 'Those are men's.'

'These shirts?' Those were also men's.

Nila was curious, 'What's the difference between men's and women's clothes?'

In Calcutta the differences between men's and women's clothes and shoes were many. Saris, salwars and slippers were for women and dhotis, shirts, T-shirts, trousers, ties, socks and shoes were for men. The difference was apparent. In this country men and women wore the same kind of clothes and it was hard to tell the difference. The buttons would be on different sides, the chest a bit narrower— one had to look very hard to be able to tell them apart. Kishan felt they were hugely different, at the waist, hips, length and breadth.

The gold jewellery shops were the least crowded and Nila was drawn to one.

'Why is the gold reddish in colour?'

'That's what 18K gold looks like.'

'Only 18K? But why? We wear 22K.'

'People here don't wear much gold and neither do they like it much. They prefer precious stones.'

These people were so rich and yet they didn't like gold. But in a poor country like India gold was an imperative. Gold spelt class and status. Without gold a wedding was incomplete. For Nila's wedding Anirban gave eighty grams of glittering gold. He probably thought that streams of joy flowed from the gold and held his daughter in its grip. Every Indian woman was attracted by gold, as was Nila. But she wasn't interested in buying the reddish 18K gold.

She wanted to buy perfume. In the perfume section she lost herself. There were so many perfumes in the world! This was the birthplace of all perfumes. Nila liked Givenchy's Organza and Kishan voted for Christian Dior's Poison. So which one should they buy? Easy—they'd buy Poison.

'Why is Poison so expensive here? It's much cheaper in Calcutta.'

'That's because those are fakes. Here they are real, okay?'

Nila floundered in the crowd of 'real'—everything was real, good and pretty.

Although they bought the perfume, Nila didn't want to budge from there. She was looking for a particular perfume—Evening in Paris. Although she hunted high and low, she couldn't find that tiny blue bottle of Evening in Paris. Instead, her eyes fell on a bottle of Chanel no. 5. She'd buy that, with her own money. Kishan was surprised. 'For whom?'

'For dada.'

Sunil had told her that a friend of his was going to Calcutta and she could send something if she wanted to.

Kishan said, 'For Nikhil? Why don't you pick something from the cheaper ones?'

Nila was adamant; she'd buy Chanel no. 5 because that's what he liked. Kishan took the bottle from her hands, returned it to the sales attendant and dragged her from the shop. In an undertone he said, 'You have no sense at all.'

Nila spoke calmly. 'Actually dada had given me two hundred dollars to buy just this perfume and send him.'

'Just this one and nothing else will do?'

'Yes, this and nothing else.'

Nila cashed her dollars and bought the Chanel no. 5. She found it gave her a strange kind of pleasure to buy something with her own money. It was much more than getting a bag full of gifts from Kishan.

When they returned, Kishan sat with his Scotch and Nila doused herself with the Poison as she hummed, 'I've drank of the dreaded cup, knowing all too well; I've waived away my life in the hope of living.'

'What's that song?' Kishan asked.

'Rabindrasangeet.'

'That Bengali chap who got the Nobel Prize?'

'Yes, it was written by that Bengali chap. That same guy wrote a beautiful song about this same poison and I'm singing it.'

'This same poison?'

'The very one.'

'Why don't you translate it for me?'

Nila laughed and said, 'There are some songs that are untranslatable.'

Kishan sighed and said, 'There are some people who are untranslatable.'

Nila stood by the kitchen and as her perfume wafted all over the room, she said, 'There are some people who can be translated very easily.'

When Kishan finished his dinner and went to bed, Nila sat down to write to Molina.

'You'd wondered how I'd run my home all alone over here. Just come here once and take a look. True, there are no maids. But there's no need either. The place is full of machines and the only work is in switching them on. Do you know Ma, I cook. But don't worry too much. It's no trouble at all. Today Kishan has bought me many things and made it very clear that *he* has bought them. That's life, isn't it? We are almost prisoners of these "things", aren't we? I've seen you too— if Baba bought you two saris you'd be over the moon. You would cook him something special, serve him and sit by him when he ate. Perhaps you did it for love and that can't be bought with things. Or can it? I don't know. Tonight I cooked daal makhani for Kishan. He really loves it.

'Paris is a stunningly beautiful city. Today, when we drove past the opera I thought it's a good thing I got married to Kishan or I would never have seen this city. And it'd be a shame to die without seeing this place.

'Ma, you have wasted your entire life trying to please other people. Now you should think of yourself, enjoy your own life. After grandfather died, the inheritance was split up and you got a fair amount of money from selling your share. Who are you saving it for? Spend it—on yourself. Life isn't forever. The people here have enough to eat and good clothes to wear. So they enjoy life to the hilt. They laugh heartily. And we are afraid to laugh because we are in fear. Why? Because some stupid man somewhere has said that if you laugh too much you'll pay for it with tears.'

She wrote this far, added a PS and wrote, 'I'm sending a Chanel no. 5 for dada. It's a very expensive perfume. This wasn't bought with Kishan's money. I paid for it myself with the money I'd saved by giving tuitions.'

'Can I please have some money? I'd like to go out alone since you don't have the time.'

'Alone? Are you crazy?'

'Why can't I go out alone? Am I a small child?'

Kishan caressed her cheeks and said, 'To me, of course, you are a small child.'

Nila laughed, 'But I'm not a small child to myself.'

'What are you then—a big child?' Kishan also laughed.

'I am twenty-seven and a mature adult.'

'And do you have to walk the streets if you are a mature adult?'

'It doesn't have to be walking around. I might go to Sunil's house, have tea in a café or visit a museum or a bookstore. Perhaps I'd want to see the opera from the inside. I read some books when I knew I'd be coming here. I want to see those places.' Nila looked out of the window listlessly as she spoke.

'You want to do all this alone?' Kishan's tiny, beady eyes grew as big as potatoes.

'Well, since you don't have the time . . . I thought I might even just walk around a bit, even if I don't go anywhere.' Her voice was dejected.

'Walk? But why?'

'No reason—just like that.'

'Does anyone ever walk for no reason? Look, just take a look,' Kishan dragged her to the window, 'Those people there—do you think they are walking there for no reason? They all have reasons, they are all busy. So am I. If I didn't keep busy, we wouldn't have food to eat or a roof over our heads. One day I'll show you how the refugees live on the streets, even on winter nights. Then you'll know that it doesn't make sense to waste time for no reason.'

Nila wound the corner of her sari around her finger and said, 'Actually, my time weighs heavily on me. I haven't been educated to just sit at home. If I found myself a job . . .'

'Job? Why on earth? Am I not earning enough?' Kishan asked in stunned surprise.

'Yes, you are.'

'This "not having the time"—it's for the sake of this household alone. If I didn't work, where would you live, what would you eat?' His voice rose higher as he spoke.

'Are you doing all this for me? You were working even before we got married. You haven't started working simply to be able to take care of me, have you?' Nila's voice was strangely calm.

Kishan sat down upon the sofa and said, 'Oh Nila, you have quite a way with words. Where did you learn to talk like that?'

'Nowhere. Everyone can talk like this.'

Kishan shook his head violently and said, 'No, no, no. Indian wives can't talk like this.'

In the same calm tone, Nila said, 'Which Indian wife doesn't speak like this—your grandmothers, right?'

'None of them,' Kishan screamed.

'You should have married a dumb girl who'd silently do the housework and never protest at anything, who doesn't have a soul to call her own and cannot read or write, who didn't have her wits about her and didn't dream a single dream.' Nila spoke slowly and succinctly.

Kishan's voice rose by another octave as he shouted, 'Why are you so proud of your education? It's not as if you're a doctor or an engineer. What can you do with your degree in Bengali literature? You can't earn a single franc. You'll have to depend on me all your life— you have no other choice. So quit that ego. If you had any sense you'd see how pointless it is.'

Kishan got up. Without any reason, he paced the floor. He walked with resounding steps. Then he drank water—one glass, another glass. Finally he spoke gravely, 'Listen, both Sunil and Chaitali work. They are never at home in the day. Why would you go to a café—make yourself a cup of tea at home and drink it. Why spend money outside? I don't go to museums, or movies, but if you are so keen on it, I'll take you when I have the time.'

He left. His steps sounded loudly on the stairs.

The bunch of keys was on the table. Nila took them in her hands many times—Kishan had advised her to use them only if the house was on fire.

'When will you have some free time?'

Nila was stroking Kishan's head as she asked him one Saturday morning.

Kishan edged closer towards Nila, threw his right arm over her and said, 'I have just this Saturday and Sunday to give you some time. All week long I work hard. There's just these two days for leisure. I want to enjoy my wife's touch all day long.' Kishan laughed, trying to hide his buckteeth. This smile was his best. He probably thought this was a lover's smile. This was how all lovers smiled at their women when they first fell in love.

'All day you'll just lie around and do nothing?' Nila asked. She was restless.

Kishan shook his head—nothing else.

'Once you'd told me the weekend was for cleaning the house, doing the laundry.'

'That's true.' Kishan was sleepy.

All day long Nila cleaned the house diligently, watered the plants and cooked. She wasn't used to doing all this, but she did. As she worked Nila wondered if she was doing all this because she loved Kishan or to please him, so that he would be able to love her. There had to be a reason to love someone. His reasons were perhaps her cooking and cleaning. She couldn't expect him to love her out of the blue, just because she was his wife. Nila could sing very well, she was well read. But these were no reasons for Kishan to love her because he didn't understand Bengali. If she abused him in this language, he'd not even know she was calling him names and just smile sweetly. If she spouted poetry in this language he'd sit with just as impassive a face. This language was as worthless in this house as broken shards of glass.

After lying around all day, Kishan came to the sofa for the second round of lolling about, and put on a Hindi film in the VCR. Nila had finished cleaning the carpet and she was wiping the glass in the window. She finished it, cooked and then showered. Not just qualities, beauty was needed as well and so she did her face, wore a nice sari and came and sat in front of him: Nila the wife, Nila the beauty, Nila the homemaker.

'How do I look?' She leaned closer to him and asked.

'Nice.'

'Let's invite them over once?'

'Whom?'

'Sunil and his family.'

'Where's the time?'

'Call them tonight.'

'You can't invite people like that. You need to tell them at least two weeks in advance. But why are you suddenly thinking of them?'

'It's been ages since I spoke in Bengali.'

'Hm, that's true. You should have married a Bengali.'

'It's a good thing I didn't marry one—they can't be trusted.'

Kishan smiled his lover's smile, 'Why don't you try and pick up Punjabi while you sit at home?'

'How?'

'Listen to Punjabi songs, watch movies, talk to me a little—it'll be easy.'

'Wouldn't it be better to learn French?'

'If you have the brains to do it, why not.'

Both Kishan and Nila knew that she couldn't learn French by sitting at home and going out with him every now and then. So she changed the subject and said, 'Well, the other day you turned down the invitation to Sanal's. So let's invite him over tonight.'

'Nah. That boy doesn't know his manners. Didn't you see how he was fooling around with you that night?'

'Fooling around?'

'What else? Even Rajesh commented later that he shouldn't have done all this. He always covets the other man's wife. Every time an Indian bride arrives, Sanal pounces on her. I don't understand why he doesn't get one for himself instead of eyeing other men's properties.'

Nila could clearly see that Kishan's eyes were bright with jealousy. The previous Sunday when Sanal had invited Nila and Kishan, he'd responded with 'Sure'. Later he said, 'Let's see,' and even later, 'Perhaps it won't be possible.' Eventually he'd said, 'Sorry mate, I have some urgent work and I have to go to Lyon.' But of course, he didn't go to Lyon.

'That night he shouldn't have poured you that drink. If anyone had to do it, it should've been me. I will see to my wife's needs.' Kishan's hackles rose as he spoke.

Nila said, 'What rubbish. He's a friend of yours. He was just joking with his sister-in-law.'

'You wouldn't understand. This isn't just joking. In these fifteen years I have heard some scary stories about Indian men: eloping with others' wives or having illicit relationships.' Kishan wrinkled his nose, forehead and lips with distaste. Nila moved away from the wrinkled Kishan and stood by the window, 'Then, let's have dinner at your restaurant.'

'You must be out of your mind. I spend the whole week in that place. I won't go there tonight. Of course, next week I'll take you there, to have some fish and meat.'

Nila turned around and walked towards him, one step at a time, 'Is that a promise?'

'Of course it's a promise.'

Kishan pulled Nila's right arm, placed it on his head and said, 'An Indian girl has something else in her touch—she tastes altogether different.'

Nila stroked Kishan's hair and bald pate with a tiny smile on her lips and asked, 'And how do foreign women taste?'

Kishan shrugged.

She leaned over his face and said, 'Did any of them run their fingers through your hair like this?'

Kishan shut his eyes. The big fat cat shut its eyes. Purrrrrr.

'Why don't you tell me, did someone do this?'

'They don't understand these things.'

'How do you know that?'

The eyes stayed shut. 'I know, I know—who doesn't!'

On Monday morning Kishan took Nila to the police station at Îl de la Cité and applied for her citizenship. When they came out after two hours, Nila wanted to go to the Notre-Dame, but Kishan didn't. Nila wanted to walk along the Seine, but Kishan didn't. Îl de la Cité is an old colony and a group of fishing folk called the Parisee lived there. The Romans came and conquered the place and built houses along the Seine. Some remnants of those buildings still stand on that bank of the river. Did you know that Paris was named after those original inhabitants? Earlier it was called Lutetia. Kishan didn't know this and neither did he want to know. He was in a hurry to go to the restaurant. He dropped her home and left. In his hurry he forgot his little address book. Nila picked up the tiny blue notebook and read all the entries from A to Z. Most of the names were unfamiliar. Nila's name wasn't there, but Nikhil's was and beside it their Ballygunge phone number. There were five numbers against Sunil's name, of his house, two of the clinic, one of his mobile and the last of his Calcutta home.

Nila lay down, picked up the phone and dialled one of his office numbers. A girl spoke rapidly in French. Nila asked if she knew English. The girl said no and slammed the phone down.

She tried the second number, got the same voice and the same treatment. Nila looked above Sunil's name and found Sanal's. He also had two numbers. She feared another slamming of the phone and didn't dial the office number.

Finally she called the Taj Mahal to tell Kishan that he had forgotten his notebook. He wasn't there. He hadn't reached yet. The restaurant had just opened. The tables were being laid and napkins were being arranged in glasses. Loban was being sprayed.

Nila asked, 'Don't you hate the smell?'

'People here like it. I hate it. Feels like someone has died,' Mojammel replied.

'What's the menu for lunch?'

Nothing new was ever cooked. There was always half-cooked food in the fridge. It was fried afresh and mixed in the same old gravy. But the tandoori chicken and naan needed special attention. That's what was most in demand.

'Oh.'

'You haven't visited us in a while.'

'I'll come one day, to eat. I've almost forgotten the taste of meat, just chewing greens and vegetables like a goat.'

Mojammel laughed. He said, 'But you know, they have a lot of vitamins.'

'That's true. The cup runneth over with vitamins.' Nila also laughed.

'Didi, are you studying or working?'

'Not studying. But working, yes—running a household. Without pay.'

Mojammel and Nila both laughed.

'Mojammel, you have worked in many places—could you look out for a job for me?' Nila's tone was serious.

'You'll work? Why don't you tell Kishanbabu? He knows many people. I do small jobs and I know nothing of the good jobs.'

Even before Mojammel finished, Nila said, 'I want a small job.

You've done your master's in chemistry and you wash dishes—I may as well sweep the floor after a master's in Bengali literature.' Nila's tone was as serious as before.

'Oh no, no, didi. I do this because I have no choice.'

'And do I have a lot of choice?' They both laughed.

'Kishanbabu earns a decent living.'

'So?'

'But that should be enough.'

'Mojammel, Kishan earns and that's his money, not mine.'

Mojammel was embarrassed. He spoke haltingly, 'If you speak to Kishanbabu, I'm sure . . .'

'He doesn't approve of his wife working outside.'

'But his first wife did.'

'First wife?'

Mojammel was silent. Then he asked, 'Didn't you know?'

'Well, no . . .'

Mojammel mumbled about some customers and hung up.

That evening Nila called Sunil at home and asked about Kishan's first marriage.

'But didn't you know?'

'No.'

'Well, he had a French wife—Immanuelle. Didn't Kishan tell you?'

'No.'

'Really! I thought you'd agreed to the marriage knowing all about it.'

Nila wondered if this fact about Kishan's past life affected her in any way. But strangely enough, she didn't feel anything. Nothing at all.

'What's wrong with you—sleeping at this time of the day?' Kishan woke her up in the evening and asked.

Nila stretched and said, 'Time is my biggest enemy and I'm trying to kill it—by sleeping.'

'I've invited two people for dinner. You have to cook up a few dishes. Why don't you get going.'

Nila laughed and said, 'See, you've just given me work. Who are these guests?'

'A Punjabi couple. You haven't met them.'

'All these Indian friends—don't you have any foreigners for friends?'

'I do, but they're for the workspace. The closer friends are all Indians.'

'Was Immanuelle also a friend in the workspace?'

'Who's Immanuelle?'

'Your wife.'

'Oh. Who told you?'

'Does that really matter?'

'Looks like you're upset.'

'Not at all—that won't do, right?'

'If I hadn't married Immanuelle, I wouldn't be a French citizen and neither would you.'

'But you never told me about Immanuelle.'

'If I did, would you have agreed to the marriage?'

'Perhaps not.'

'Yes you would.'

'How are you so sure?'

'Because Sushanta, the great love, had ditched you and if I didn't marry you, no one else would. News travels far and fast. You had slept with the guy, hadn't you?'

A deluge of cold water flooded her heart.

'Are you going to go on sleeping? There's cooking to be done.' Kishan raised his voice as he loosened his tie.

After Kishan left the next morning, Nila lazed around in bed. She was thinking of the big hubbub with his Punjabi friends the night before. She had heard them laughing and talking until midnight. Kishan told her that the cooking wasn't up to the mark, the naan was burnt and there was something missing in the daal makhani and although the Punjabi friend's wife said the cauliflower curry was good, Kishan felt it could have been better. Nila suddenly felt she was her mother,

Molina. Anirban used to invite friends suddenly, just like this, and ask Molina to cook dinner. She would slog in the kitchen and then Anirban would criticize it all, just like this. Molina tried very hard to please her husband, but she failed miserably each time.

Nila called Sanal. He didn't recognize her voice. There was no reason for him to.

'Nila, Nilanjana Mandal.'

'Oh, Mrs Kishanlal.'

Yes, Mrs Kishanlal.

'So, Mrs Lal, what's up?'

Nila could tell that he was expecting some significant news.

'I just called you . . . no reason . . . just got your number and I thought I'll ask you how you are doing.'

'I am fine. Doing very well indeed. And how are you?' Sanal's voice was merry as usual.

'Oh all right I suppose. Why don't you come over some day, it's been a while since we saw you.' Nila's voice was fervid.

'So where is the husband, is he with you?'

'Oh no, he is busy all the time.'

'Hm. In this country you have to be busy. So, bhabhiji, I also have a lot of work. I must rush.' Sanal's tone was impatient.

'Oh, fine. I'm sorry for calling you at a bad time.' Nila hung up. She was angry with herself. She didn't know why she made that call, to hear how busy Sanal was, so busy that even though Nila called him, not only was he unable to talk, he didn't even say when he'd be able to talk. He was so busy that even after Nila hinted that she wasn't fine, Sanal had no interest in knowing why or what was happening in her life. Why did she want to talk to Sanal? Was it just to talk to someone? If that was it, she could have talked to Molina or any of her friends in Calcutta. Although Calcutta was far away and Kishan had warned her that if she made international calls too often, the sharp razor of French telecom would slit their throats, she could have talked to Sunil and Chaitali here in Paris. She didn't because she wanted to talk to Sanal and no one else, the Sanal who was infamous for fooling around with other people's wives, pouncing on them and eloping with them—Nila *wanted* him to take her away from that house, somehow. She asked herself if that was indeed the reason. She didn't come up with the answer. These days she felt she didn't know many things. She had no idea why she was lying around all day or why she didn't even get up and have a cup of tea. She had no idea why she didn't get up to bathe, eat or even look out of the window, why she started reading the books she brought from Sunil's and then couldn't go on.

In the evening the phone rang. Nila turned her back on it and lay there. When she heard Sunil's voice on the answering machine she picked it up.

'What's wrong Nila, why didn't you pick up the phone?'

'I was sleeping.'

'Now? How are you doing?'

'Okay.'

'Is Kishan at home?'

'No.'

'But he's not in the restaurant either and he isn't answering the mobile. So I thought he must have come home.'

'No, he hasn't.'

'How do you spend your time—what have you seen in Paris?'

'The Eiffel Tower.'

'And?'

'And some shops.'

'You haven't been to the Louvre?'

'No.'

'Musée d'Orsay?'

'No.'

'You haven't seen Picasso or Rodin?'

'No.'

'I'd asked Kishan to let you come with us one day so that we could take you to the exhibitions—there's so much to see here. But he said he'll take you himself and anyway, the first few months after marriage everyone sticks to their wives.' Sunil laughed his familiar laugh. 'I've seen it with myself. After my marriage to Chaitali, I didn't even go to work for two months—we were stuck to one another with glue.'

Suddenly Nila asked, 'Sunilda, do you know of any jobs?'

'Jobs? Why? For whom?'

'For me.'

'You will work?'

'Yes.'

'Have you told Kishan? What does he say?'

'I haven't told him.'

'But that won't do!'

'Kishan, Kishan, Kishan—it's as if there's nothing else in my life!'

'It's not that. But you must learn the language first . . .'

'Where can I learn the language?'

'Why don't you go to the Alliance Française? Just tell Kishan—'

'Give me the address and tell me how to go there—I can find the place.'

'Kishan would mind . . .'

Nila sighed.

Sunil said, 'When Kishan comes home, just tell him to give me a call at home.'

'Anything important?'

'Yeah, it's about that Puja Committee. He had said he'd find some people who'll give donations.'

'Oh.'

Nila used the key, which Kishan had advised her to use only when the house was on fire—and walked aimlessly on the street. She had a map of the city and some money in her pocket. She went into that palace called Gare du Nord and saw people milling around, catching the train and getting off it, trains starting and stopping. Nila leaned against a pillar and watched them; she wanted to go somewhere far off. The blue-eyed, blond-eyed princes were dashing off on those trains; no one asked Nila to come with him. Suddenly she wondered if she was visible. She looked at herself, dressed in a pair of new black jeans, a white silk shirt and a pink cardigan, shining black shoes on her feet—Nila didn't think she was ugly. In fact if she walked like that in the streets of Calcutta many men would have turned to look at her.

She came out of the palace and walked aimlessly again. When she came to a bus-stop, she found buses arriving by the minute and she boarded one, without knowing where it went or what number it was. Kishan had once said that she could get lost in the city if she went out alone. She felt it could be a nice thing actually. She wanted to lose herself, to go to a place from where she wouldn't know her way back. She went as far as the bus would take her. Then she got into another bus. Her eyes held a mixture of sorrow and excitement. In Calcutta the buses were crammed full, it was sticky and hot and you got dust in your eyes and face. Here the buses were air-conditioned with lots of windows and no dust at all. You had to get in by the front door, hold up the ticket in front of the driver (the orange ticket for the whole month) and go in. If you didn't have the orange ticket, then you bought the green ticket from the driver for eight francs, put it into the small machine which would noisily stamp the date and time on it. Then you sat on the cushioned seats. There was no ruckus, no stories about politics or the fish market or household gossip. Everyone was calm, everyone wore a smile and no one poked their nose in other people's lives. A brown-skinned girl sat among a sea of white faces. No one came forward to ask her where she was from or where she lived. Nila gazed at the happy faces all around her. A couple got into the bus, with a child in a pram. The baby slept while the young couple kissed in front of the busload of people. An intimate kiss, it was a French kiss. Nila's ears burned but she noticed that no one else in the bus was even glancing at the kissing couple. In Calcutta they would have been promptly pushed out of the bus for indecent behaviour. Nila felt that this kiss, simply because they wanted it and didn't want to keep it for the bedroom or a secluded spot, was the most decent and beautiful thing in the world. In Calcutta she had never been able to hold Sushanta's hand for fear of people's gaze. That same fear had driven them four miles out of Calcutta to a secluded place behind a shanty to steal the odd kiss or two. Nila and Sushanta had feared people the most. They hadn't minded the odd fox or two behind the woods, but it was people they had been terrified of.

Nila saw the young man kissing the woman and stroking her back lovingly. The two bodies were entwined. Nila wanted to be kissed like that; she wanted such a handsome young man to love her, hug her and kiss her as deeply. When the bus reached the Seine, Nila got off. She walked along the river looking at the rows of green box-like bookstores on the pavement. There were tourists thronging the place, not to buy books but to take pictures. As she walked she came up to the Louvre. Like a crazed being she ran towards the museum. She felt like a tiny ant before the massive structure and surrendered the minuteness of her existence before this vastness with pleasure. She lost herself in the endless world of the Louvre. She no longer remembered that she was Nilanjana Mandal, daughter of Anirban Mandal of Calcutta; she didn't feel her existence anymore and the occasional hand that brushed her shoulder or neck went unheeded. She walked from Rassolio to Soulis, from Soulis to Denot like in a trance as if she wasn't walking but was being carried on wings from one section to another. It was way past noon and Nila felt no hunger or thirst—she was far removed from this world. Nila's evening passed in the throes of a beautiful trance. Even after she left the Louvre Nila wasn't herself. She sat like a statue beside the glass pyramid. Nila forgot that she had to go back home, forgot that she had just one identity—that she was Mrs Lal, Mrs Kishanlal.

She returned home to find that Kishan wasn't back yet. Nila had a good soak in the bathtub. She didn't feel like getting out and cooking. When Kishan came back, he found her immersed in the white froth. He stood at the bathroom door and said, 'What's wrong? Why are you having a bath at this time? Come on, get up.'

'Why?' Nila's voice was stone cold.

'What d'you mean why—I have come back!'

'So?'

'So you have to get up. The other day you wanted some pumpkin. Look, I've brought it today. Make something with this. I believe this makes a very good pickle—do you know how?'

She sank a little lower in the white froth and answered, 'No.'

'Then use your head and make something nice with this.'

'Why don't you do it—you are very bright.'

'I don't know how to cook!'

Nila knew very well that he knew how to cook. He used to cook for himself before she came to this house. Nila also knew that she'd have to get up although she didn't feel like it and she'd have to make the pickle, even if she didn't know how.

When Nila came out of the bathroom, Kishan was with Minakshi on the telephone, asking her how to make pumpkin pickle. It'll have to be washed and peeled, diced and punctured and then sugar syrup would have to be injected into those holes and the pieces simmered on low heat in the syrup with four cardamoms and some cloves etc. etc.

Etc. etc. etc.

That night Nila made the pumpkin pickle, gratified Kishan and then sat down to write to Molina: 'If I had money, Ma, I'd have lived happily. My own money, Ma. Without your own money you have to obey the person who has money for all your life. If you are a pauper, your wishes don't count. You can't live on someone else's money and also have your freedom. Don't tell anyone, but could you send me some money? The money I brought with me is almost over. It's good to have some pocket money of your own.'

In the morning Nila read the letter to Molina twice and then tore it up. Then she called Mojammel and said, 'Could you please find me a job—anything—one that doesn't need me to know the language?'

'Didi, I can do that, I will be in trouble for it.' Mojammel's voice was tense.

Nila was desperate, 'I know that. I won't tell anyone.'

'Didi, I will lose my job . . .'

Nila promised him that she wouldn't let Kishan find out that Mojammel had anything to do with her finding a job. She would take the entire blame upon herself.

That day too, Nila went out. She ambled along all day and returned in the evening.

Kishan came back his voice bursting with pent-up anger, 'Where were you? Why didn't you answer the phone?'

'When did you call?'

'In the afternoon and also in the evening.'

Just once Nila thought she'd say she was sleeping. Then she thought perhaps it'd be better to say she was in the shower. No, not shower, she was watching TV and didn't hear the phone. As Nila was searching for something to say, something that wouldn't make Kishan see red, she blurted out that she'd gone out. Kishan was livid. Gone out—where? Was the house on fire? No. Was there an earthquake? No. None of that happened. Nila had just gone out. She'd gone out because she wanted to. Nila knew that Kishan could have taken her out and yet she went alone because she wanted her own company.

Kishan loosened his tie and went towards the liquor cabinet without saying another word. He took the bottle from there and went to the sofa, without another word. He fetched the glass from the kitchen. He poured himself the drink and began to drink silently.

Nila heated the food and placed it on the table, silently. She kept a single plate on the table and didn't say a word.

The next night Kishan came back home to find Nila sitting on the sofa and watching TV with her feet up on the coffee table. It wasn't a film or a play but the news in French on TV. Nila sat there as he entered the room and she asked, 'Did you call home today?'

'Why?'

'I'm asking because I wasn't home.'

'Where did you go?' Kishan asked.

'Nowhere in particular. I took bus number 48 and went to Saint-Germaine-des-Pres and had a cup of tea at the Café de Fleur. Then I walked along Boulevard Saint Germaine. There were so many people. I went into a beautiful garden, the Luxembourg Gardens. Then I had lunch at a brassérie and then, then what did I do . . .'

Kishan gritted his teeth. He could see that she was exceeding her limits. She hadn't put her feet down when he came in; instead she was forthright enough to describe her terrible behaviour in the most calm, unperturbed and serene manner. Kishan held his hands tightly to his sides and balled them into fists or he would have dragged her by the hair and thrown her out of his house. 'Go and roam around to your heart's content.'

Nila reclined and said blandly, 'Now you see, I could find my way around quite easily. I did have to ask a few people on the street sometimes about the bus numbers and all. But you see, I am not a little girl after all.'

His teeth were on edge. 'I can quite see that you are not a little girl. Why are you sitting like a man with your feet up?'

Nila's laughter rippled around, 'Who says it's like a man? I have put my feet up in true female style.'

'Put them down.'

'Why? Are you not able to sit?' Nila's asked innocently.

'I am not able to look at you. I can't stand the sight of you sitting with your legs apart.' His teeth were still gritted.

'Then don't look—simple!'

Kishan's tone was simmering, 'Fine, I won't look. Go away.'

'Why don't you go away!' Nila brought her feet down, because at this point Kishan could utter a simple truth: this is my house and you will not tell me where to sit.

Kishan scowled, 'Give me my dinner.'

'Why? Won't you drink first?' Nila asked.

'You don't have to tell me whether I'll drink or not. If I feel like it, I'll drink.'

Again the same command barked out, serve me my dinner.

Nila was calm, 'I haven't cooked dinner.'

'Why?'

'I didn't have the time.'

'I thought time hangs on your hands and you don't know what to do!' Kishan's eyes grew smaller.

'That was when I used to sit around at home with nothing to do.' Nila was chewing her nails as she crossed her legs and said, 'Tomorrow you'll have to give me some money.'

'Why?'

'I want to buy some books.'

'What books?'

'Today, when I walked along the Seine I found an English bookstore. Actually there are quite a few in this city. A few books would help me pass my time.'

Kishan got up and took his tie off, 'Nila, I have to be very careful with my money.'

'Why don't I take up a job, instead of sitting around like this . . .' Nila looked at Kishan expectantly.

'You are really very impatient, Nila. You are very greedy. How long is it since you have come here? Two or three months and you are already restless.'

'I have never been so dependent before. In Calcutta even when I was a student I also gave tuitions. I earned my own pocket money.'

'I have never said I won't give your pocket, picket, rocket or any other money.'

Nila laughed, 'So give me—I haven't asked for picket or rocket.'

'I don't understand why you even need this pocket money. This house has everything you need and I have bought you the rest.' Kishan walked towards the bar.

'I need to have ice cream and there isn't any in the house.'

'Fine, I'll bring ten packets tomorrow and you can stuff yourself.'

Nila stopped chewing her nails, laughed loudly and said, 'I need to eat fish and meat.'

'Who says you need it? People live without it—don't I?' Kishan slammed the bottle of Scotch on the table.

'Yes, you're alive, but I don't just want to live. I need more.'

'What do you need?'

Nila looked him in the eye, spoke softly and calmly, 'You're talking of bread, but that isn't all. One needs the lily as well.'

'Fine, I'll buy you a hundred lilies tomorrow.'

'You will, Kishan, you want to buy me things. But I also want to buy myself something sometimes.'

Nila got a job, packing computers in boxes: fifteen hundred francs a week. It was a lot to her. In the morning, Nila woke up with Kishan and followed him out of the house. He went by car and she took the metro: the number two line from Gare du Nord up to Belle Ville and bus number eleven from Belle Ville to Metro Telegraph. The factory was right on Rue Pelleport. At first Nila didn't tell Kishan about her job; she didn't want him to raise hell in the house.

Kishan was from Chandigarh and Kurukshetra was in his blood. He had told Nila many times that he'd take her to Chandigarh for Janmashtami to see how grandly the Lord's birth was celebrated there. He wanted to show her Holi as well and if Nila wanted colours on herself, he could dip her in colours that'll take a lifetime to wash off. If Nila was amazed at the architecture in Paris, she'd be equally stunned by Chandigarh. It was built by the French architect, Le Corbusiere. He was no less that Monsieur Housmann! If Nila was excited by Jardin du Luxembourg and Jardin de Planot, she'd be thrilled by Pinjore Garden, Sukhna Lake and Shantikunj in Chandigarh. But Kishan's varied descriptions never elicited the slightest interest from Nila. The few of Kishan's relatives who had come to Calcutta for their marriage had not seemed like the kind of people whose company she'd appreciate for one moment in Chandigarh.

The news travelled and Kishan found out that Nila had started working in a box-packing factory. He called Sunil to their house the very day he found out about it.

Sunil came in, walked from room to room, sat in front of Kishan and said, 'Tell me, what's the matter—why the urgent summons?'

Nila was lying down, reading a book on how to teach herself French. A cassette was playing French pronunciations. When she saw Sunil, she kept the book away, switched off the cassette and came forward with a smile. 'Well, has our friend dropped in at last?'

Sunil's face was solemn. He was still unsure about the summons from Kishan.

'What is this girl you found for me, Sunil—she doesn't obey me.' Kishan lodged his complaint before he even greeted his friend. Nila pulled up a chair from the dining table and sat down.

The matchmaker was now the judge, 'What has she done?'

'Why don't you ask her?' Kishan pointed his chin in her direction. Before Sunil could ask her, Nila said, 'I'm not doing anything bad.'

'She has taken up a job without asking me first—just look at her nerve.'

'Is that so?' Sunil looked at Nila inquiringly.

Nila nodded in agreement.

'She gets a pittance there; wouldn't I give her that money if she wanted it? She doesn't have to leave her home and hearth and work with some worthless black people for that.' Kishan said all this in one breath and finally let out his breath, his fat stomach threatening to burst through the shirt buttons.

'And are you white?' Nila went into the kitchen to boil water for tea.

'My prestige and honour, all are gone.' Kishan heaved a huge sigh.

There was no alcohol in front of them, no TV, just a dry stillness as they sat there.

After a long time, Kishan asked miserably, 'Sunil, why don't you say something? This situation has to be resolved.'

Sunil looked at the blank wall absently and said, 'What can I do? You are the married couple and you have to resolve it.'

'Tell her to quit her job.' Kishan growled like a tiger, his fingers impatient in the fist.

Sunil turned away from the wall and glanced at Kishan, 'Why should I tell her? You do that.'

After a pause, Sunil spoke hesitantly, 'I feel, in this foreign land, it is good for both to work and supplement a single income. Chaitali and I both work and we live well. If you think that you have a lot of money and you can afford to keep your wife in high luxury, that's entirely up to you.'

Kishan got up, drank a glass of water and came back. 'Yes, I know it's good for both to earn and it improves the quality of life. But how can she know better than me about what kind of job to do, what will be decent work and also fetch some money?'

Sunil shook his head, that's true.

Nila had never seen Sunil look so grave before. He spoke in English, the language they were all using, and said to Nila, 'You should take Kishan's advice before you do something. After all, he is your husband and he wouldn't wish you any ill.'

They both waited for Nila's answer, expected her to say, all right, I was wrong and from tomorrow I won't go to that job anymore. From now on I'll do what my husband tells me; I'll work from the day he tells me to and do the job which he suggests because he knows better than me about which job is better and which one isn't. No one else cares more about me, etc. etc. etc.

Nila was silent.

Sunil broke the silence. 'It's possible for her to teach Bengali to the children here, start some classes at home.'

Kishan was sceptical, 'She might as well become a professor of Bengali in Sorbonne. It's not that easy. I had to wait for twelve years before I could open a restaurant.'

Nila spoke in Bengali, 'It *would* take an ass like you twelve years.'

Nila turned to Sunil and began to speak, totally ignoring the fact that Kishan, her husband, had called this urgent meeting in a bid to get back his honour, 'I am very impressed by the café culture of Paris. People sit around, drink coffee, read the newspaper, write, and literary groups also convene at the cafés—wonderful, isn't it? I believe Jean Paul Sartre and Simone de Beauvoir used to frequent the Café de Fleur? There's a bookstore opposite the Notre-Dame, called Shakespeare and Co. Do you know, Sunilda, that James Joyce's *Ulysses* was first published from there?'

'Who is James Joyce?' Kishan asked Sunil.

She answered, 'An Irish writer.'

Nila went on excitedly, 'Hemingway also came there and he used to borrow books because he didn't have the money to buy them.' The moment she said it Nila was afraid Kishan would ask who Hemingway was. Good thing he didn't because she had the answer ready, 'Hemingway is my cousin brother.'

That evening nothing happened. Sunil started about the Puja donations, leaving Nila's issue unresolved. Nila brought tea and biscuits on a tray. She asked Sunil about his friend who was supposed to go to Calcutta. He had gone and reached the Chanel to Nila's house and he was scheduled to return very soon. Nila wanted to know when he would go again and if he wasn't going this year, who else would go. This year Sunil himself was supposed to go, after the Puja. When would Nila go? Oh, Kishan knew that, of course.

That night Kishan woke up the sleeping Nila and his dark, hairy hands reached for the buttons on her dress. Nila shoved his hand away. Kishan gripped her hands in steely fists and said, 'I want a child, Nila.'

She said, 'Let me sleep.'

She had almost said, 'Why, didn't Immanuelle give you one?' But she didn't utter that name because she was afraid if she did, Kishan would bring up Sushanta and whether she had slept with him or not. Yes, she had. The guilt that Nila used to feel because she wasn't a virgin, had disappeared since she came to know about Immanuelle. Instead, she felt rather relieved. In a way, Immanuelle saved her.

At her work Nila found that most of the workers had black, brown or yellow skin. Only a handful were whites. On the very first day Monsieur Gigout described her job and what it entailed in great detail in French. Nila heard him out without following a single word. After Gigout left the room, out of the handful of whites one girl came forward and asked her if she understood anything.

Nila sat with a glum face; she hadn't understood a word.

Danielle explained it to her.

Since then it was Danielle who always translated Gigout's words from French to English for Nila. Danielle took her to the nearby café for a cup of tea and Nila talked to her about her arrival in Paris, about her life with Kishan.

One day, Catherine, another white girl, asked her in faltering English, 'You are from India, aren't you?'

Before Nila could say yes, Catherine explained that she'd love to go to India the moment she could save enough money. She did this job and saved the money to travel to faraway places. Last year she had gone to Malta and the year before that to Martinique. Catherine had studied Indology and her subject was the bauls of Bengal. Before she wrote her thesis she even went and stayed in a baul's house in some tiny village of Bengal for two months. She was yet to submit her thesis and she wanted to go again, to that village.

With the baul topic between them, Nila felt close to Catherine very quickly. That afternoon they had lunch together at the brassérie. Over lunch Catherine described how she had eaten with her fingers at the baul's house and walked for miles through mud and slush. She hadn't stayed in Calcutta and she hadn't wanted to. She'd preferred to see the lives of the bauls in villages. The one thing that she liked the most, and she even brought it with her, was . . .

Nila stopped chewing to hear her better.

'Bidi.'

For a long time Nila forgot to chew the food in her mouth.

After the meal Catherine carefully brought out a packet of bidis from her pockets, extracted one even more carefully and began to smoke it. In her entire life Nila had never smelt a bidi that close. She had seen labourers or beggars smoking it. She had never known that something could smell that disgusting.

That evening Nila went into a café with Danielle and Catherine. They asked for coffee and Nila tea. Nila said, 'Look there are empty seats there. Let's go and sit.' They said no, you were supposed to have your drink standing.

Nila didn't know that there were three kinds of prices in a café. For example tea: if you stood and drank it was seven francs, if you sat down it was eighteen francs and if you took it out in the terrace it was thirty francs. Danielle rolled her cigarettes and smoked, dropping the ash on the floor. Apparently this was also a rule; those who took their drink standing by the counter, would never get an ashtray.

Nila asked, 'Do you like Bengali food?'

'Sure,' Catherine replied.

Danielle had never had it. She jumped at the invitation. Nila invited them then and there, for dinner the following evening. They decided Nila would collect her week's pay the next day, go home and cook and they would join her there after work. Nila left her address and phone number.

The next day Nila did just that—she picked up fish and meat from Belle Ville and went home and spent the whole evening cooking. Danielle and Catherine arrived with two bottles of wine. Nila set the table with nine kinds of dishes. Both her friends exclaimed over it and then asked who else she had invited. Nila assured them it was just the two of them. They looked at one another in surprise.

'Nila, are you in your right mind?'

No, she wasn't. She was very sad.

'Why?'

She had wanted to cook two more dishes, but she didn't get the time.

Danielle uncorked the wine bottle and poured it into three glasses.

'Santè!'

'Bon apetit.'

Nila served them the food. But they didn't like her way of serving. Nila wanted to give the greens first and then the vegetables and then the fish fry followed by the fish curry and finally the meat, because that's the way to get the best taste. Danielle didn't agree with that. She took a bit of each of the dishes at one shot. Nila was uncomfortable because her plate looked like the discarded mess of marriage feast plates. She felt they'd never get the taste of the individual items. But Danielle and Catherine exclaimed over the food: it tasted great.

The fish curry made Danielle's eyes burn, it was too spicy. Catherine was used to some spice in the baul's house, so she was okay. As they ate, both said they'd never had so many dishes at the same time.

'But when we invite people in Calcutta, this is how we cook. It's nothing great.'

Nila served them more fish when they finished one, more rice and more meat. Even if they said no, and covered their plates with their hands, she forced them to take more because that's how it was done. Danielle laughed and said, 'Why are you behaving like a grandmother?'

Nila couldn't explain to them that guests were like gods to the Bengali. They'd always give them the bigger piece of fish, the best seat, the nicest bed. It was difficult for Bengalis to say 'I love you', but they'd show it by giving and feeding.

Danielle and Catherine drank wine as they ate. Nila sipped at it occasionally. The feast wasn't over. Her guests were resting in between the courses. Danielle had smoked twice in the gaps and Catherine smoked her bidis. At this time Kishan arrived, to spoil the fun.

Both Danielle and Catherine said bonjour. Kishan wished them and disappeared into the bedroom.

'Is this your husband?'

Nila nodded, this was her husband.

Ashen faced, Nila went into the bedroom and muttered, 'What will they think if you don't even talk to them?'

'Who are they?'

'They work with me. Please don't misbehave with them. Come on.'

'Why?'

'Can't you see, they are white and not black, brown or even yellow.'

'So?'

'So come and eat. I have cooked many things today.'

'What have you cooked?'

That's where Nila was in trouble.

'What have you cooked? Why do I smell meat?'

'They don't eat anything but fish and meat.'

'That's not my concern. You are not supposed to cook it in my house.' Nila stood with her head lowered in front of Kishan's indignant eyes.

'This is the last time. It won't happen again, I promise.' Nila pleaded. 'At least don't create a scene in front of the guests.'

'There's no need for you to cook anymore. Now go away, get out of my sight.'

Nila moved away.

All the time that Danielle and Catherine were in the house, Kishan lay in the bedroom with the door shut.

From Gare du Nord to Gare d'Austerlitz

'Why don't you leave that house?'
   'Where would I go?'
   'You can stay with me for now and then we'll think of something.'

Here are your keys and everything else. I have taken my things and nothing else. The house is just as it was. I am leaving because we don't get along, and you know that as well as I. Life isn't easy in this foreign country. I'm seeing a different you ever since I've started working. You are insulting me at every step. But have you ever thought that I can't possibly be enjoying that box-packing job and that I didn't take a degree to do this kind of thing? The reason why I took that job is that I hate begging from you. I know you don't consider it begging. You feel you're looking after your wife, doing your duty. But it comes with a price: I have to live according to your wishes because you are the master, you are the boss; without you my life is pointless and I am a mere servant who'll clean your house, cook, serve and provide sexual gratification at night. Is there any other role in which you see me? Oh yes, the other day you said you need a child. I have to give you an heir. I have to because you want it, as if it has nothing to do with me, and everything to do with you. We could have both wanted it together.

   The other night I invited two of my friends and realized that I don't have the right to do that. Probably I don't even have the right to *have* any friends. I have tolerated your nonsense about fish and meat; but you take that smell all day long in the restaurant, don't you? You just want to force me to give it up. This I, who has evolved over so many years, has to give up her habits, her language, her culture, her nature

and fit herself into your mould. You know that I haven't
done anything wrong. The main reason why you are angry
with me is that I haven't obeyed you. I cannot survive within
so many restraints and strictures.

If I leave the house, both of us will be glad. I'm setting
off for the unknown, for a friend's place to start with.

Don't try to find me.

Nila.

The next day, Nila kept the letter on the dining table, placed the
bunch of keys on top of it and left the house with Danielle. From the
Gare du Nord to the Gare d'Austerlitz. The dirty dishes of the night
before were still in the kitchen. 'Let them be,' Nila thought.

Danielle lived in one of the tenements in a five-storeyed building
just behind the Gare d'Austerlitz. Once these rows of tenements had
housed the servants of the rich people. The tiny rooms were hardly
eight square metres in size. There was no bathroom and just a toilet
at one end of the corridor. When the country freed itself from the
class war and got rid of masters and servants, the houses fell empty.
These days, they were rented by students or people with very small
incomes. Danielle paid eight hundred francs a month as rent. She had
stayed in that room for the last two years. She didn't have much
money. Sometimes she took up odd jobs here and there. She wrote
book reviews for a women's magazine. They were usually reviews of
books written by women. Danielle was Canadian and was fluent in
French, although her mother was Irish. In the nineteenth century,
during the famine, Danielle's grandparents had immigrated to North
America. Danielle's father was born in Canada and he had French and
native American blood in him. Perhaps her grandfather on her father's
side was a native American, although Danielle had never seen him
and her father never spoke much about him. Her father was so
embarrassed about it that if the subject ever came up, he either left
the house or he shouted down the person who dared to raise the
subject. Danielle's brother Phillippe had no signs of it, but she bore
the marks of that forefather in her nose, eyes and chin, although her
skin was white.

In her eight-square-metre room, Danielle had a bed, one table with a small computer on it, a tiny fridge in one corner and a cooking stove on top of it. Next to it was a basin and tap. There were bookshelves on the wall crammed with books, piled one on top of the other and there was one chair with armrests—just one.

'I have just one bed and there's no room for another one. I don't even have spare mattresses to make a bed on the floor.'

Nila said, 'I'm sure we can squeeze into it and manage, can't we?'

Nila had slept like that many times before. Whenever there was a village wedding, hundreds would go from the city. Big beds were made on the floor and people would just jostle on them and sleep. She was quite used to it. Besides, even in her home in Ballygunge whenever there was an aunt visiting, they'd be assigned her bed. She would snuggle up to the aunt and drift off to sleep, listening to her stories. She still remembered the spine-chilling ghost stories of Manju aunty!

That night Danielle wanted to treat Nila to dinner at a fancy restaurant.

'In that case, let me dress.'

Danielle went outside. Nila took her clothes off and got into a pair of blue jeans, a red shirt and a denim jacket. When she said she was done, Danielle came in and raised her eyebrows, 'I thought you were going to wear a dress.'

'That's what I'm wearing.' Nila laughed.

'But these are jeans, not a dress.'

Nila couldn't understand what Danielle was saying. Puzzled, she stood there and asked, 'Am I looking bad?'

'Not at all.'

Outside, Nila wanted to dance. She had never felt so happy, so free in Paris. She raised her hands in the air and said, 'So you wanted to keep an Indian servant. Now where is she, Kishanbabu? Why didn't I do this sooner?' She hugged Danielle and shouted, 'You have set me free!'

'You would have left that place sooner or later. No human being can live like that.'

Nila laughed and trembled with joy as she watched the lights of that beautiful city, shining down on the boys and girls who were out on the streets. She felt as if she was flying. She took Danielle's hand in hers and flew along the street.

'Nila, you look so beautiful. This is the real you. You were hidden behind the mask of Madame Kishanlal. But now, you are so alive! So beautiful! There's no sign of worry on your face. This is a different you!' Danielle looked at her with admiration. Her fist within Nila's hand trembled, sweated.

Inside the Café Jimmare, Danielle browsed through the menu and asked for a spaghetti Bolognese and red wine. Since Nila wasn't familiar with anything else in the menu apart from the sandwiches, she asked Danielle to choose something for her, even if it was the same dish.

Each time Nila tried to pick up the spaghetti with her fork, it slipped away. Finally she gave up. It was impossible for her to handle it with a fork and even if she did, it tasted too much of flour. Instead she looked around her and watched the people. At the next table a young boy sat, wearing earrings and the girl with him had six in each ear. She also had her brows, lips and her tongue pierced.

'Why has that girl pierced her eyebrows, lips and tongue?'

Danielle didn't find it unusual at all. 'Yes, she's done it because she wanted to.'

Nila thought of her own life: she never could do what she wanted to. If she ever tried to go out in trousers, Anirban would bear down upon her. She would always have to change into something more feminine.

They left the café and walked. Nila saw some young boys and girls with their hair dyed and raised high and stiff. Why had they done that? Danielle said it was because they wanted to. Nila wanted to know why they had such a need.

'They don't like many of the rules of society and so they do this—sort of like a protest.'

Nila also didn't like many of society's rules. But she would never dye her hair. She wasn't spunky enough to do that. She asked Danielle what these people were protesting against, in such a lovely, healthy society with such admirable rules. But Danielle's eyes were on the peaks of Pompidous and she wondered how Paris would look from up there. Nila wondered aloud if Pompidous was an oil factory and Danielle laughed so hard that she was embarrassed. They went into Café Bo-Bo. It was crowded and there was no place to sit. People stood and drank wine. Nila watched as a girl, tall as a beanpole and mounted on high heels, drank wine and swayed as she talked to two men. The girl was pretty with a red dress, red lipstick, matching shoes and hat. She puckered her lips like a bird's beak and kissed first one man and then the next. Nila whispered to Danielle, 'That girl has just kissed both the men. Who do you think is her lover?'

Danielle was indifferent, 'That's not a girl, it's a man.'

For a long time, Nila was struck dumb, 'Why has he dressed like a woman then?'

'Because that's his wish.'

Fine, Nila accepted that it was a man, but then why would he kiss other men? She shuddered when Danielle told her that they were homosexuals. This was the first time Nila saw a homosexual. She was dazzled by the extent of freedom in this society where they kissed whom they wanted and dressed as they pleased.

They got a seat and their wine was served. Nila sipped occasionally.

'Why aren't you drinking?'

'I am not used to drinking wine.'

'Not used to it? So what do people drink in your country?'

'Whisky.'

'That's before the meal. What about during the meal?'

'Water.'

'The other people in your country?'

'Everyone drinks water.'

'Everyone?'

'Yes, everyone.'

But Nila was realizing that it was customary for the French to drink wine at all times of the day. In Calcutta she had seen people buying liquor surreptitiously, wrapping the bottle in newspaper so that others couldn't tell. When Nikhil drank, he bolted his door from within. If someone came visiting then, he'd wash his mouth umpteen times before presenting himself to the guest. Molina always thought bad people drank alcohol. Nila thought so too. But when she saw Sushanta drink a few times she was disabused of that notion though she still believed if you drink, you should do it in secret. Now, in this amazing city of freedom, Nila realized she need never do anything in secret. In this city, she noticed, it was wrong not to drink; people thought you were uncultured and uncivilized.

Since the spaghetti had hardly gone into her, Nila wanted to eat something at Café Bo-Bo. She wouldn't have beef, and lamb had a funny smell; would grilled chicken do? That'd be fine. And what would she have to drink? Coca-Cola. Coca-Cola? The waiter at Bo-Bo laughed his head off. Who was this strange being who drank Coke with meat? Nila noticed Danielle was looking embarrassed.

This was shameful, not drinking wine—this won't do at all.

Nila decided she'd have to get used to drinking wine and save her face.

They left Bo-Bo and Danielle took Nila to yet another café and from there to an Irish pub. After that they went to a disco with strobe lights, loud music and swaying people. Danielle was exuberant and pulled her hand, 'Come on, let's dance.'

Nila shrank back; she didn't know how to dance.

She noticed this too was a cause for embarrassment. Only strange beings didn't know how to dance. But she realized that by dancing what was meant was just a rhythmic swaying to the music. There was no pattern—it was each to his own.

Danielle danced alone. Then she sulked and said, 'Do you hate me so much?'

'Why?'

'You didn't dance with me.'

Nila lowered her head in shame, 'I don't know how to dance.'

'What's there to know in it?'

Nila had assumed that dancing was something one had to learn. She had wanted to learn, but Anirban wouldn't let her. He bought her a harmonium and asked her to learn singing instead. He hired a good teacher for her and though she was no star, she could hold her own in a small gathering.

Out in the street, Danielle said, 'It was quite obvious that you were insulting me.'

Nila was startled, 'When? When did I insult you? What are you saying, Danielle?'

'I poured you a glass of wine and you didn't even thank me,' Danielle said.

What was she saying! Nila already thought of Danielle as a close friend. Did friends ever thank each other? That's not what Nila was taught. In Calcutta if Nila thanked a friend for pouring her a glass of wine, that friend would have felt insulted. There was a saying in Bengali: please don't trifle with me by thanking me.

'So if you don't thank your friends, whom do you thank?'

Sheepish, Nila said, 'An unfamiliar person or an acquaintance— if they give me something or do something for me.'

'But that waiter in Café Jimmare wasn't your friend and you didn't thank him either.'

'Why should I thank him?'

'You asked for water and he brought you some. You should have thanked him. You commanded him, not requested him, to bring you a glass of water. He is not your slave. He just works at that place.' Danielle spoke in one breath.

Nila was lost for words. She had asked for the water the same way she usually did in a restaurant: Could you bring me a glass of water? A command would be brusque and a request would be softer, with a smile—that was the only difference. Danielle's objection was that Nila hadn't uttered the word please. She should have said, 'Could you please bring me a glass of water?'

Nila's voice cracked as she spoke, 'Actually Danielle, I am not used to saying thanks and that's why I slipped. But I don't think any less of that man.'

'Not used to—well, why? It's because you don't think very highly of people.'

'Not really.'

'Yes, really.'

Nila mentally rebuked herself for this bad habit of not giving people their due credit. In this land of equality, everyone was the same. Some had better jobs and some didn't, but everyone had their human dignity. Nila thought to herself: that's how it should be. She had always thought she didn't believe in class distinction. Danielle had caught her out today. Nila bit her lip and her eyes smarted.

As a child had Nila often seen Nikhil reading the communist manifesto. What did it say? It spoke of the class war. When she was nineteen, Nila was inspired by her reading of Marx and Engels. She hung out with the communists in college and participated in meetings and processions. And today she was being told that she believed in hierarchy, that she considered the waiter in a restaurant to be a lesser human being? Shame!

Nila's voice was humble, 'Danielle, I know it was wrong. It won't happen again. Please forgive me?'

Danielle was relieved.

In her effort to make her friend happier, Nila continued, 'Do you know which party has ruled West Bengal for the last thirty years? The Communist Party.'

Danielle stopped walking and her mouth fell open.

'Thirty years?' She spewed out some white smoke and these two words alone.

'Yes.'

'Why?'

'What do you mean why? We like them, we vote for them.'

'You vote for the communists?'

'Sure.'

'Shame!'

Danielle shook her head all the way back home and exclaimed that Hitler had killed far less people than Stalin. She claimed Marx was wrong and so was Engels, Lenin was a fake, he was actually a terrorist.

The Invitation

Danielle and her Indian castaway of a friend were invited to dinner at Nicole Nemeret's house. Danielle had a rendezvous with a reporter of a new magazine at Café Cairo. Before going there she told Nila to be ready for the dinner party at seven.

When she returned, Nila was still lying and reading *A Moveable Feast*. Danielle was puzzled, 'What's up? Why aren't you dressed yet?'

Nila stretched lazily, 'So soon? What time is it?'

'Seven.'

'That's not too late.'

'I told you to be ready at seven.'

Nila sat up, 'I haven't even showered yet.'

'What?' Danielle was amazed.

'I haven't ironed my clothes.'

Danielle dropped down on the chair, 'We have to reach Nicole's place at seven thirty. I told you that.'

Nila couldn't understand what was the harm in reaching a half-hour or so later. In Calcutta they always attended invitations a few hours late. It was rude to reach at the invited time. For Danielle, of course, the opposite was true. Nila would have to use the common bath for her shower and by then Danielle would kill herself. Danielle was wearing a long black dress. Nila didn't bother with ironing and pulled on whatever came to hand. Nila knew that few people wore ironed clothes here. Most of the winter months the clothes were hidden under heavy coats or sweaters.

'Jeans? It's a dinner party.'

'Does it look bad?'

'Jeans are for the daytime, the workplace.'

They were so short of time that Danielle went along with her jeans. Nila quickly stuck a red bindi on her forehead, hoping that'd make up for her lack of formals.

It was two and a half minutes from Danielle's house to Gare d'Austerlitz; from there to the metro station near Nicole's house was twenty-two minutes and then it took five minutes to walk to Nicole's house. That left them with one and a half minutes. One minute would be needed if they came up against a red light while crossing the street and another half a minute to take the stairs if the lift was too crowded. They didn't face a red light and the lift wasn't crowded. Still, when they entered Nicole's house, it was seven thirty-seven.

Danielle apologized for the delay as soon as they entered. Nicole, with red hair and green eyes, dressed in a long black dress, taller and older than Nila, forgave Danielle.

There were three others invited: Maria Svenson, Michelle Kauz and Rita Cixous. Everyone was standing with champagne glasses in their hands. Only Maria had orange juice in hers. They all wore long black dresses. Nila assumed there was an intimate connection between a dinner party and long black dresses. The minute they entered, Nicole and her guests kissed Nila and Danielle on both cheeks.

Maria was from Sweden and she headed a feminist organization. She'd come to Paris to give a speech at a conference about women's participation in politics. Michelle wasn't from Paris. She lived in a place called Fizaq in the south of France and she was here to attend the same conference. Rita Cixous was Jewish, born in Algeria and she lived in Paris; she directed films, was a close friend of Nicole and was always present at any gathering in her house. Nicole taught at College de France. Danielle also had an identity: she was a writer. Nila's singularity? She was from India. What did she do? Nothing.

Nila thought, 'That's true; in Paris I am either Mrs Kishanlal or Nilanjana Mandal, labourer.'

Danielle took pity on her and gave her another identity as her friend. Nila was relieved. But just then two huge dogs pounced on her. Nila screamed and ran for life; the whole room burst into laughter. Danielle called out to one, picked it up and began to kiss it. Nicole picked up the other one and began to rock it as if she was soothing a baby.

Maria asked tentatively, 'Are you scared of dogs?'

No one in that house had ever seen anything as strange as someone screaming instead of hugging dogs. The way the five pairs of eyes were observing her, Nila felt they suspected her to be crazy.

Rita asked very mildly, 'Do you have any problems? Sometimes there are certain conditions in which if you see a dog . . .'

Danielle rescued her from the fate of being diagnosed as mentally ill, 'Perhaps she has never seen a dog before. They don't have dogs in her country.'

If Nila could have gone along with that, she would have been safe. But she said, 'We do have dogs.'

'You do?' Nicole was startled.

The five pairs of eyes held the same question, 'Why were you afraid?'

Nila didn't dare to answer. The eyes looked away, as did the dogs and the four black cats.

In the lengthy discussion that followed, Nila's participation wasn't solicited. The discussion over champagne was all about cats and dogs, which one Nicole found still asleep in the morning and which jumped up on her bed, which one looked at her and then moved away and which one didn't like the food that morning, who was sleeping on the sofa watching TV and forgot to eat and which one was sulking for the last two days, etc. etc. Nila noticed everyone joined in with great enthusiasm, exclaiming and stroking the pets as they nodded and talked. Nila was holding her breath because she couldn't stand the smell of cats. She found everyone standing and talking although all the seats were empty. Perhaps they wanted to show off their dresses or the accessories. Nila glanced down at her blue jeans, bright yellow, crumpled T-shirt and green jacket and realized that she looked quite hideous. In order to spare everyone the sight of her, she broke the circle and curled up on the sofa. Immediately she realized she had done something terribly wrong. You should keep standing in the circle until you were asked to take a seat. If you wear something crazy, don't know your manners or have any decorum, don't know how to stand upright and carry yourself, then let that be so. Nevertheless Nila now sat there and sweated heavily; she realized that everyone had hung their coats as they entered the room because it was warm inside, with the warmth of people, animals, culture and pride.

The fireplace in the corner was lit and a grand piano stood in another corner. These two were indispensable in a rich home. Carefully, without attracting their attention, she went and hung up her green jacket. But the bright colour gave off the sparks of uncultured taste, nonetheless.

'Flune loves spring,' Nicole came towards the sofa and asked them all to take a seat. 'Can you smell spring in the air?'

They all acquiesced: the smell of new leaves, new blooms; the windows were open and the smell tumbled in. Nila took a deep breath to get what they were talking about but all she got was the stench of animal coats.

Rita said, 'The winter was terrible.'

Maria and Danielle didn't agree that it was colder than Montreal or Upsala. Danielle had left Canada six years ago. She didn't want to ever go back to that cold country or even take its name because that brought on a snowy mountain of memories upon her, like an avalanche.

Now they looked at Nila, who sat in one corner of the sofa, picking her nails, 'What season is it now in India?'

It was Danielle who asked the question. Perhaps she wanted to show off that her friend wasn't all that dumb and she knew what season it was in India. She also wanted to rescue Nila from her solitude.

Actually Nila wasn't feeling lonely till now. In a rueful tone she said, 'Spring.'

'Spring?' Nicole's brows were tinged with disbelief.

'Is India to the north or the south of the equator?'

Rita said, 'North.'

Nicole said, 'Oh no, it's to the south.'

Danielle said, 'If it's spring there, it must be in the north.'

Nicole got up and returned with a huge book. Five heads were gathered over the world map: red (Nicole's), blonde (Maria's), black (Rita's), chestnut (Michelle's) and titian (Danielle's).

Nila looked at the five heads from afar.

Now Rita, the one who gave the right answer, leaned towards Nila and said, 'What was that director's name, the one who made *Salon de Musique* . . . Satyajit Ray. I have seen his films.' Rita's face wore a wide grin.

Nila smiled and asked, 'Which ones have you seen?'

'Almost all of them.'

Nila was eager, 'Have you seen *Pather Panchali*?'

'Yes, but I didn't like it that much.'

'No?' Nila was surprised. '*Charulata*?'

'Yes. But his best film is *Salon de Musique*.'

Since Nila liked *Pather Panchali* the best, she was a little taken aback to hear Rita's opinion; but then Rita was the only one in the room who had some thoughts about an Indian and a Bengali. So, even if she'd said she liked *Kapurush Mahapurush* the best, Nila wouldn't have shown any surprise. Actually Rita was the one who rescued Nila and truly set her free.

Nila asked, 'Have you seen the films of any other Indian director?'

'I've seen a few. But there're too many songs and dances in your films.'

'That's true, cheap fights and no taste.' There was no way Nila could disown those Hindi films.

Have you seen films by Ritwik Ghatak, Mrinal Sen, Aparna Sen, Budhhadev Dasgupta? No. Have you heard of them? No.

So far Rita hadn't made any full-length films. They were all short ones, two minutes, five minutes or fifteen minutes. She had made three films on the life of Kurdish women and another one on the prostitution of Russian women in Turkey. A full-length film? It was easy but getting a producer was tough.

Danielle said, 'If you set out to exhibit women in a film, producers would queue up at your doorstep.'

Nicole corrected her, 'Male producers.'

There were many kinds of liquor on the table and they were all helping themselves. Nicole was pouring out the drinks. Maria shook her head vehemently, she wouldn't drink because she would be driving. Why had she rented a car for just these two days in Paris? She was headed south, to Cannes, after her stay in Paris. Was she speaking there as well? No, she would sunbathe in the southern sun.

Michelle Kauz winked, 'She's Swedish and if they know nothing else they know how to obey rules. We, the French, can never touch the steering without a few pegs down our throat.'

Nila asked for a Porteau as the bottle looked prettier than other bottles and she had to drink something because otherwise they'd think her unsophisticated. When Nicole handed her the glass, she remembered to thank her, 'Merci beaucoup.' It had taken her a long time to learn to pronounce these words. She used to pronounce it phonetically and people would look at her strangely. Nila was convinced that this was one language that you couldn't learn from books.

The discussion veered from male producers to female producers to female directors—from there it shot back a hundred years: Susan B. Anthony, Elizabeth, Cady Stanton, the suffragettes. From there it was one jump to the labour movement and from there to birth control to the number of women in the parliament of egalite: not even ten per cent. Such a shame! Elizabeth Gigout deserved some credit— fifty per cent women should be nominated by a party! That was a lot.

Maria's nose was high in the air when she said, 'We have no such hassles. Women are more than forty per cent in the parliament.'

Nicole looked crestfallen, 'Whatever happens, it's all in Scandinavia.'

Maria's tone was angry, 'Rubbish. Take a look at the academic positions, they are all filled by men.'

They all listened to Maria intently, Maria of the snowy lands. It was originally the land of the Vikings who used to attack other villages, loot and kill. Now their scions were known to be the most civilized in the world. Equality and peace reigned supreme in the Viking lands.

Michelle said, 'Times have changed, you must admit. Just think of the condition of women once in Europe—the church used to burn them alive, didn't it?'

Nicole raised her hands and silenced everyone. Then she uttered each word slowly and clearly, 'Things have changed only on the surface; beneath it all, everything is the same as always: man still exploits woman and the frameworks of exploitation haven't changed at all.'

'What do you mean by always, Nicole. Once there was a matriarchal society. Man used brute strength to snatch power away from woman.'

Nicole was vehement, 'There was never any matriarchy anywhere in the world. What there was once, was matrilocal and matrilinear. Women inherited property and children took their mother's name. That doesn't make it matriarchy.'

Danielle had said that they'd decided to speak in English for Maria's and Nila's sake. But if Maria wasn't there, Nila knew they'd have spoken in French because it wasn't a discussion in which Nila could even participate. So she tried to show off her knowledge of French and compensate for the lack of her knowledge of feminism: 'Jay pore avoir du bhin rugee, sil bhous plait.'

No one understood what she said. Finally when she repeated her request in English, everyone was rolling with laughter. Danielle corrected her, 'Je peux avoir du vin rouge, s'il vous plait.' Nila kept her lips tightly shut as it seemed every time she opened them, she was in trouble. In the wave of laughter Nicole raised her head like a seal and began to discuss the menu for dinner. She wanted to cook some pork with garlic.

Mmmmm, everyone else said.

'Mashed potatoes, salad and cheese. There's also some tart,' Nicole said.

Mmmmmm.

'Finally, coffee.'

Mmmmmm.

Nicole went into the kitchen to take the pork out of the fridge. Danielle and Rita followed her. Nila was sure it would take ages for the meal to be ready. But hardly a few minutes had passed and the pork was on the table. Nila had no clue how the meat cooked in such a short time. Quickly Nicole pointed to each one her chair and ordered them to come to the table with their respective drinks. 'Help yourselves to everything.'

'How has this been cooked?'

'Fried in butter with a clove of garlic mashed into it.'

Garlic pork! Nila held the knife in the left hand and the fork in the right and tried to slice up the pork. The cutlery went flying out of her hands. She slid a glance around and realized she was holding them wrong. Quickly she changed them around and tried again. It was pointless. No one was looking at her, perhaps to spare her the embarrassment. But Nila felt, if they'd fussed over her instead and commented on her unwieldy use of the cutlery, she could also have laughed and said, 'Actually, we are used to eating with our fingers. The food tastes heavenly and brings you closer to it.' But the silence at the table only made her squirm some more and feel uncomfortable.

She tried to look sideways at Danielle and gauge how affected she was at this display of her friend's ineptitude. She was impassive. Nila now realized it was also impossible to chew the bland chunk of meat. She tried sprinkling it with salt and pepper, like everyone else. But the meat was still tasteless. Everyone else was exclaiming over it. Nila ate some mashed potato and half a lettuce leaf and got the smell of the meat out of her mouth. Then the cheese set her back to square one. Meanwhile, everyone had torn off pieces of the baguette and kept it beside their plates. With experienced and civilized fingers, they pierced the cheese with their fork, picked up a bite of the baguette on to it and expertly passed it into their mouth. The baguette was lolling on the dusty table. It was impossible for Nila to eat it.

Nila didn't want coffee; did they have tea? No. So she had to gulp down the water. She wasn't used to sitting around at the table after her meal was over. She was restless but she didn't dare go and sit on the sofa again. One had to sit around at the table after the meal. Nila noticed that they'd spent around five hours at the dining table alone. She noted that Bengalis and the French had five in common, the former spent five hours to cook and five minutes to eat and the French cooked in five minutes and ate over five hours.

Suddenly Nicole raised her glass in a toast to Nila. Why? There was going to be a documentary on India in a few minutes on TV. Everyone turned their chairs around. Nila was pushed to the front and all eyes, including the pets', was on the TV set.

The entire screen was filled by an empty steel plate with holes in it. The camera zoomed out, the plate grew smaller and the screen was filled with bare feet, walking. Now it zoomed out further, bare feet, bare bodies, an eight-year-old boy walked, with snot hanging from his nose. He shoved the empty plate at the people around him, begging. There were more beggars behind this one. The streets were crowded with a broken tram rattling away, the dilapidated buses and trucks were shoving their nose into the crowds, and amidst it all were scattered a few starving cows, some chewing cud by the roadside and some tied to bullock carts. The pavements were spilling over with beggars. The same boy with the broken plate returned home. A shack made of dry leaves was what passed for a home. It was by a pond and he had to walk across a rickety bridge to get to it. His siblings were leaning into the cooking pot.

Nila broke the silence in the room and said, 'They must be showing a very poor household indeed.'

'Shhhh.' She was asked to shut up.

The cooking pot filled the screen—it was empty. The mother was walking across the rickety bridge to fetch some water from the pond. She brought the water and lit the fire beside the rail tracks. Every time a train passed by, the fire went out. The mother shielded her eyes from the smoke as she cooked the rice. The camera caught the cooking pot again, with the children hanging around it and the mother pushing them away. The next scene showed the young beggar boy urinating under the open sky and below him was the pond.

As soon as the film ended, Rita spoke first. 'Wow, wonderful camera work.'

Nila leaned across the sofa, pulled out a magazine and pretended to read it intently. She knew she was hiding. Her ears were open and she heard Rita's excitement.

'Did you notice the background score when the camera zoomed in on the cooking pot? Isn't it that song by Edith Piaf?'

'Which one? *La vie, l'amour*?'

'No, *L'Oie Blessée*.'

Nila's eyes were still on the *Vogue*: a beautiful girl lay naked by the ocean, her eyes brimming with lust and at her feet was a bottle of perfume, Opium.

She looked up from the magazine when she heard the sounds of chairs being pushed back—time to leave. She was desperate to leave; so she jumped up and got into her green jacket. In case Danielle accused her of rudeness, she kept her head bent but managed to utter, 'A bientôt.' But that wasn't all. She had to kiss them all on their cheeks, except Maria because she gave Nila and Danielle a ride. They'd have to kiss her when she dropped them off.

Danielle also kissed the three of them and said, 'A bientôt.'

Rita said, 'It was my good fortune that I watched a documentary on India with an Indian beside me.'

Nila smiled because she was supposed to, or she'd be called rude and arrogant. In the car, Nila sat at the back and Danielle sat beside Maria in the front.

When they reached home, it was late. Danielle undressed and hit the bed.

Nila wasn't sleepy. Still she lay down, with all her clothes on.

Danielle said, 'Why are you sighing? What's wrong?'

'Nothing.'

'Why are you so quiet?'

'What should I say?'

Danielle touched Nila's shoulder, 'Is there nothing to say? What did you think of Nicole and her friends?'

'They're nice.'

'I can tell you're upset Nila. It's very obvious.'

'I'm just feeling very angry with myself.'

Danielle turned Nila to face her, 'Why?'

'I should never have gone to Nicole's.'

'Why not?'

In response to her question, Nila just lay deep in thought for a long time. When the question began to buzz in her ears insistently, she sighed and replied, 'Didn't you see what a fool I made of myself over there? I don't really fit in. Perhaps I was better suited to be Kishan's bride, the archetypal housewife who'll cook, clean and sometimes talk to an Indian or two. Actually I am not cut out for this society.'

Danielle sat up, 'What's wrong with you. I took you to a nice place to make you feel better and you are just complaining.'

Nila said in the same sad tone, 'Did you really like that documentary?'

'Sure. Didn't you?'

'No.'

'Do you know the significance of such an important channel showing a film on India?'

'Danielle,' Nila's voice broke, 'India doesn't just have all that poverty. There are many rich people, many middle-class families . . .'

Danielle laughed, 'But the TV channel wouldn't be interested in the rich people of India! If they want riches, they'll show Bill Gates. Besides, it's good for India if they focus on the poverty, she'll get more aid.'

Danielle tucked two pillows behind her back, reclined on them and rolled a cigarette and lit up. She took a long drag, exhaled, combed her fingers through Nila's hair and said, 'You can't deny the fact that India is a poor country. You can't deny that there are such families in India as the one they showed today. There are so many people all over the world living such subhuman lives, Nila. Something should be done for them, especially by the richer countries. It's true, there are the rich in India as well. But we already know how they live. Instead when they show us poverty, we sit up and think. Not everyone, but at least those who want to think, those who have a heart, they do think. You know Nila, this is almost like a whiplash for us.'

Suddenly Nila's cringing, shamed thoughts were free of the beggar's shanty. She took Danielle's hand in her own and said, 'You are so wonderful. The more I see you, the more I'm impressed.'

Danielle stroked Nila's fingers and it felt good.

'Why are you in bed with so many clothes; you can't sleep comfortably.'

Nila turned around, 'I'm not used to sleeping in the buff.'

She pulled the cover over herself and curled up. Danielle's fingers climbed her arms and reached her scalp via her neck. Nila always dozed off if someone stroked her head. Molina used to do it often and Nila would fall asleep. In this faraway land Danielle was like a mother to her. Nila's sleep went for a toss when Danielle's fingers danced on her breasts.

She pushed her hands away and laughed, 'Tickling me, are you?'

'No.' The tone was mirthless.

Nila turned and looked at Danielle. Her eyes held no teasing sparkle.

'D'you know, my mother used to stroke my hair like this and I love it when someone does that.'

'You like that? Here, let me. You have such lovely hair, such beautiful skin.'

'How can I have beautiful skin, it isn't white.'

'That's why it's beautiful.'

'You like brown skin?'

'Very much.'

Danielle kept running her fingers through Nila's hair. Nila turned and faced Danielle and curled into her like a child. She had slept like that many a night with Molina. Her past suddenly flooded through that tiny window and touched her.

Nila's voice was sad, 'But Danielle, I have nothing to offer.'

'Who said that? I like your artlessness the most.'

Danielle's fingers climbed over her temples, around her nose and descended on her lips.

'Your lips are beautiful. I want to kiss them.'

'Kiss? On the lips?'

'Why not?'

'No.'

'What does that mean—you don't want it?'

Nila shook her head—she didn't want it.

'Your feet are stone cold.' Danielle reached out and stroked her feet with her own.

Danielle's fingers didn't leave her body, her feet didn't let go of Nila's feet. Nila turned over and spoke sleepily, 'Let's go to sleep, it's quite late.'

'So what. Tomorrow is Sunday.'

There was no hurry to wake up the next day. So Danielle's fingers roamed Nila's body. They roamed all over and came to her thighs.

Date 4/2/05

M _____

Address _____

	Reg. No.	Clerk	Account Forward		
1				88	68
2				1	05
3				13	23
4					
5					
6					
7					
8					
9					
10					
11					
12					
13					
14		3990-46			
15					
35	Your Account Stated to Date – If Error is Found, Return at Once				

The more Nila pressed them together, the more the fingers prised them apart. Finally Nila jumped off the bed and sat on the chair, 'Danielle, what are you up to?'

'Why? Don't you want it too?' Danielle was surprised.

'Want what?'

'Sex.'

'What?'

'I thought you wanted it too.'

'How did you think that?'

Danielle said, 'You held my hand in the street.'

'So?'

'So I thought you liked me.'

Nila stared at her in open amazement, 'I liked you and so I held your hands in the streets. But sex . . . what's this? How can two women . . .?'

Danielle smiled, 'Who told you they can't?'

'I've never heard of it.'

Nila had not only never heard it, she couldn't even stretch her imagination as far as and come up with a mental image that vaguely resembled such a possibility. Danielle was also surprised, 'You didn't guess that I was homosexual?'

How could she? Homosexuals didn't look any different and Danielle looked like just another girl to Nila.

'No, I didn't.'

Nila was still confused. Before her eyes, the room began to spin, it flew in the air, the bed flew in the air. When she came back to it, Danielle's rapacious tongue licked her for the rest of the night. Nila lay there, speechless, breathless.

Paris in a Trance

Nila could hardly believe she was living this life. It was passing in a dream and when she woke up, she thought, she'd find herself back in Calcutta in her own room where the sparrows chirped at dawn and she'd talk to them silently. After she broke up with Sushanta, Nila used to spend sleepless nights and doze in the day. Sometimes she slept all through the day and woke up with strange dreams. Once she dreamed that she was running in a jungle and a lion was chasing her. She turned around and it wasn't a lion any more but a hundred snakes. Nila ran and fell into a vast ocean. She sank to the bottom and found the lion sitting there. It didn't do anything to her. Behind it there was a huge tree and on top of it a house. She entered the house and found Molina sleeping there. She opened the window in that room and looked out at the busy Chowringhee. When she came down to the street hurriedly she found the hundred snakes sitting there. In an instant the street was devoid of people. Just the snakes, and Nila. That day Nila woke up to find she was bathed in sweat and her heart was hammering away. Every time she thought of that dream, her heart pounded with fear.

On Sunday Nila woke and found she was naked. Danielle stood in front of the basin, brushing her teeth. She watched Danielle's body as she lay there and thought it was a living sculpture by Rodin. It was a body that could drive any man insane. But Danielle had never let a man touch her and never would. She claimed the male body was ugly and didn't excite her. The female body did. Nila's body did. Nila looked at Danielle's body and didn't feel that she wanted to love that body, kiss it. When Danielle finished brushing and kept the toothbrush aside, Nila noticed it was pink—the same as hers.

'Danielle, is your toothbrush also the same colour as mine?'

'I don't have a toothbrush.' Danielle's answer was simple.

'Then what do you use to brush your teeth?'

'I don't.'

'Whose is this then?'

'Yours.'

Nila sat up, 'You used my toothbrush?'

Danielle bent down and opened her mouth under the tap; the water streamed into it. She spat it out and said nonchalantly, 'Yes, yours.'

'You've brushed with someone else's toothbrush—on purpose? Or was it a mistake?'

'I knew it.' Danielle's tone was calm as if it was very natural. She seemed surprised that Nila was so agitated about it.

'Danielle, this is the first time I've seen someone use another person's toothbrush.'

Nila dived into her bedclothes.

Danielle put the water on the boil for her coffee. When she made her coffee and sat on the chair drinking it, wearing a T-shirt, Nila poked her head out and asked, 'Do you never brush your teeth?'

Danielle's tone was still unruffled, 'I do, sometimes, when I feel like it.'

'When was the last time?'

'I don't remember.'

Nila wanted to laugh. Then she wanted to cover herself and weep, weep for herself. But she did neither. Danielle went out and came back with the journal *Liberation* and four croissants. Nila was still in bed. When Danielle was drinking her coffee and having her croissant, Nila said, 'I want tea.'

'Have it.'

'Make some?'

'Make it yourself.'

Nila pouted indulgently, 'I don't feel like it.'

Danielle didn't have the capacity to pamper Nila. She had to get up, make her tea, drink it as she watched the tiny bit of sky that she could see from that window, and finally go downstairs and buy two toothbrushes: one for Danielle and one for herself. She threw the old one into the trash and brushed her teeth with the new one. When

Danielle suggested going to the market in Port de Sinequorte, she had to agree.

Danielle said, 'You'll like that place.'

'Why?'

'There are many black- and brown-skinned people there.'

Nila went to the market selling cheap, second-hand goods and found that she didn't like this multicoloured crowd at all. In fact, she felt uneasy. In front of her eyes, a little black boy picked up a watch, dropped it in his pocket and walked away. Another boy pretended to try on a pair of sunglasses and walked off with it without paying for it.

Danielle dug into a pile of old clothes and bought two dresses as Nila stared at this strange world. A few men in dark glasses stood under a bridge with black bags at their feet. There was some talk of the police coming and the men disappeared. Nila asked what was going on there.

'Illegal business.'

Nila couldn't fathom why people did illegal business in this wonderful city where everything was so good. Her curious eyes followed the crowd and settled on a dark man who was shaking a ball around in two small boxes. He shook them fast, dropped the ball into one and covered them. You'd have to guess which one had the ball. Gambling. You paid a hundred francs to guess. If you were right, he'd give you back two hundred. If you were wrong you got nothing. Even as she stood there she watched two men play. One got a hundred francs and one lost. When the ball was being dropped Nila saw clearly which box it went under and she screamed, 'I know, I know which one it is.' Danielle said, 'Don't Nila, you'll lose.'

'But why not. I know which one it is.'

Nila gave a hundred francs to the dark man, he lifted the box and the ball wasn't there. She tried again and lost again. Again and again. In two minutes Nila lost four hundred francs and came away. Danielle was leaning against a wall, smoking.

'You lost, right?'

Nila's eyes were pleading.

'I knew it.'

'How?'

'Because these are frauds. It's an illegal business, just to con people.'

Suddenly a few people broke away from that crowd and vanished. The group dispersed.

Danielle said, 'See how they run from the police.'

Nila wrinkled her nose, 'Where do these men come from?'

'Africa, Asia, South America.'

Nila said, 'I don't think any of these men are from India.'

'Most of them are from the Middle East.'

'Oh.'

Nila was relieved. Or at least she thought she was. Nila knew only too well that India didn't lack con men. On the streets, offices, courts of law and even in the parliament people were cheating others.

On Sunday Paris came alive with markets, selling food, clothes, furniture, everything. After losing four hundred francs, the two of them quit that area quickly.

Danielle wanted to go into an alley in Montparnasse where some people sold paintings every Sunday. The two sides of the street were lined with tents where artists, who couldn't sell their paintings otherwise, displayed their wares. As she looked at them, Nila flew back in time: once she had also painted for the love of it.

Danielle noted Nila's thoughtful eyes and said indulgently, 'Why don't you try it again.'

'It's no use.'

'Try it. You haven't come to Paris to make packing boxes. If this city of artists can't give you back what you lost, no place in the world can.'

'Danielle, I don't have the talent of an artist.'

'How are you so sure?'

'I am.'

'Nila, you never know who has it and who doesn't. Today Van Gogh's paintings sell for millions and when he lived, no one bought them. The man died in penury.'

As they walked towards Musée d'Orsay Danielle spoke of her own life. In Montreal she had begun to study law. She dropped it and chased horses. She used to ride and teach riding. But she soon tired of it too. So she just came away to Paris and at first took up a job in a Levis factory. But when Levis left the country, Danielle used to sit on the footpaths and watch the amazing beauty of this city and go round buying books from second-hand stores and read them lying in fields. As she read, she wanted to write. Gradually what she wrote began to be printed. Danielle had also written a book. It was about her father, Pierre Leroux. She'd mailed the manuscript to a few publishers. One of them had replied saying that with a few changes, it could be printed.

They spent the whole day at the Musée d'Orsay and on their way back Danielle loaned her money to buy an easel, paint and brushes. Suddenly Nila had wings and Paris was a dream.

Back home Nila was still in a trance and Danielle's hungry fingers and tongue roamed her body. The fingers knew every inch of the body, the lips and behind them another lip within which slept the magic bee: one touch and the bee spouted honey and swept away all, all. Nila wasn't a swimmer. She clung to Danielle, the expert swimmer, and crossed the ocean. Danielle swam ashore and whispered to Nila, 'Wake my magic bee.' Nila didn't. She feared that bee, she hated it.

Nila wanted to know when Danielle had realized that she desired women. Danielle said it was when she was still in school, twelve years old. She fell in love with a teacher and she'd stare at her face for hours.

'Then?'

Joselyn was married with three children. After school Danielle went to Joselyn's house every day. She'd scale the wall and peep inside and stare at Joselyn.

'Then?'

One day Joselyn spotted the two eager eyes at the window. That day there was no one else in the house. She called Danielle into the house. When Joselyn touched her and kissed her, she trembled. When Joselyn took her clothes off and undressed Danielle, she trembled.

'Then?'

Then Danielle didn't remember the details. But she remembered rolling on Joselyn's bed in the grip of a tremendous ecstasy.

The relationship ended after she left school. When she was fourteen, Danielle left home and started living in a commune. There were five women and two men living together. Of the five, Danielle had sexual relations with two of the women. During her stay there Danielle frequented gay bars and if she fancied someone, she went with them or brought them home to the commune. With the break of dawn the ties broke. If they ever met up in the day, sometimes they wouldn't even remember having spent the night in each other's arms.

'Then?'

Pierre Leroux died. Two months later Clara, Danielle's mother also died. The brother and sister divided their inheritance. With her share she bought a house in Montreal and lived alone. She wasn't in touch with any of her family, not even her brother Phillippe.

'Then?'

Then there were three or four relationships. They lived together and then broke up. When there was no one, there was always the gay bar. That was her life. As far as work went, she did odd jobs. But there was another excitement, that of revolution. She used to attend several meetings fighting for gay rights and screamed her lungs off at protests.

'Then?'

Then Nicole, who had come to the Concordia University to lecture on social history, made friends with Danielle and they slept together. When Nicole came back to Paris, Danielle missed her terribly. She realized it wasn't just a sexual relationship, it was love. That's what brought her to Paris. She lived with Nicole for four years. In those four years the love and the sex flew out the window. But the friendship stayed.

Danielle lit another cigarette and said, 'Has this ever happened to you: an event in your past is completely wiped out from your memory, say something that happened twenty years ago, and then suddenly one day it comes back to you?'

Nila shook her head, she'd never felt that.

'When I was six years old, my father raped me. Eight years ago, when I was sitting in Montreal, it came back to me one day suddenly as I was watching a snowstorm.'

Nila sat up, stunned. Her eyes were full of disbelief, 'Did it really happen or was it someone else's story that you suddenly imagined had happened in your life?' She shook Danielle's shoulders.

'It happened. I remember very clearly, Mother had gone out on an errand and I was alone at home playing with my dog. Father picked me up and put me down on the bed and raped me. He stuffed his shirt into my mouth to stop my screams.'

'Your own father?'

'My own father.'

In her trance, one day Nila began to paint in Paris—oil colours. A group of girls dancing in the field, sky dark with clouds. Danielle studied it from all angles and said, 'Too much of Matisse.'

'Not at all. Matisse did collages and this is a painting. Besides these girls are not even holding hands.'

'There's something sad about it.'

'It's a happy moment. They're happy as peacocks.'

Danielle frowned, 'Then why is it cloudy? Make it a bright sunny day. Cloudy days are sad.'

Nila gazed at the painting lovingly and rattled on, 'The girls are dancing just as peacocks dance when they spot storm clouds. Their bodies are burnt in the summer sun. The rains have gathered in the sky after a long time and the girls have run out of their homes joyfully into the light breeze outside. They'll dance in the rain, wet their bodies and cool themselves, cleanse themselves.'

Nila became erratic at work as her painting gained momentum.

Danielle had quit that job and taken up another one with the publisher who'd showed an interest in her manuscript. She read books and reviewed them.

Hardship made Nila open her suitcase one day, and hunt for her jewellery. But it wasn't there. She'd brought everything else from Kishanlal's house, but forgotten her jewellery. When Danielle heard it, she said, 'You can't afford to be so careless Nila. I've noticed, you spend rashly when you have money and when it runs out you depend on others.'

'Do you want to get rid of me? Why don't you?'

'I don't want to. But I think you should continue with your job for a while.'

'I don't like such menial jobs.'

'No one likes them. But one has to eat. If you don't like menial jobs, look for a better one—you have to search.'

So one morning Nila went in search of a good job. She would buy some dailies, and note down some phone numbers. When she went out, she bought the dailies, but couldn't go as far as look at the ads or note the phone numbers. She got lost in a huge procession. A joyful parade marched through Paris with red and blue balloons and Nila marched with them until Joan d'Arc. Nila had seen many parades in Calcutta, but nothing like this one. Overwhelmed and electrified, she bowed before Joan d'Arc and placed flowers at her feet, like everyone else.

When she came home and told Danielle about her expedition, the latter's eyebrows shot up, 'Terrible!'

'What's so terrible about it?'

'You're lucky to have come back alive.'

Nila was dumbfounded. Danielle continued, 'These are racist Lippens. They want to banish all non-whites from this country and Joan d'Arc is their idol. You went and rubbed shoulders with these extremists?'

Nila had walked alongside people at that march and no one had hurt her. She'd placed flowers at their idol's feet and no one had thrown dirty looks at her.

Nila justified their logic thus: if any country was thronged by foreigners and they threatened to take away the economic rights of the countrymen, then it was natural for the people to take up arms against these intruders. Imperialism was not the only big enemy of a nation. There was other kinds of coercion also.

Danielle said, 'I'm sure you can defend Hitler as well.'

Nila said her uncle Siddhartha could and many people in India believed it was difficult not to be impressed by the indomitable power of that man. Nila's father Anirban had a different logic. He believed the enemy of an enemy is your friend. Hitler had aided Subhash Bose in the freedom movement of India. Subhash Bose was a national celebrity who had laid down his life for the country. He didn't believe in compromises and he was against Gandhi's non-cooperation movement. He felt one had to fight fire with fire. Anirban found the West's adulation of Gandhi quite amusing. It wasn't his non-violence policy that drove the British from India. They'd become economically crippled after the Second World War and that's why they left.

Danielle bit her tongue in disapproval, 'The Bengalis are proud of the man who joined hands with Hitler?'

Nila laughed and said, 'Gunter Grass had a similar reaction when he saw the people of Calcutta honouring Subhash Bose's statue.'

One evening, feeling aimless and lost, Nila set off. She walked around randomly and rang the bell of Catherine's house. She thought she'd have a cup of tea with Catherine, chat with her about bauls and if she insisted, Nila would sing a few baul songs for her.

Catherine came out and looked startled to see Nila, 'Yes?'

Nila smiled sheepishly, 'I was feeling lonesome and thought I'd drop in on you.'

Catherine stood at the door looking thoroughly taken aback and said, 'But you weren't supposed to come?'

'No, I wasn't.'

'Do you have any urgent work with me?'

'No, not really.'

'So then?'

Nila looked down, embarrassed, 'Actually I wanted to look at the graves and . . .'

Catherine looked irritated, 'Oh. That's quite close by. You make a left from the door and then a right. The huge entrance will be right in front of you.' Nila moved away as fast as she could from Catherine with the irritated look and surprised eyes. She heard the door slam shut behind her. Nila had never experienced anything like this. In Calcutta she often dropped in on friends, not for any urgent work or with prior appointment, but just like that. Most of them dropped in on Nila the same way. She'd often had to deal with an unwelcome guest. But she'd invite them in, offer them tea and talk to them for a while. Nila had been taught that even a foe was never turned away from your door. Molina always used the proverb, offer your foe the best seat in the house.

Nila took long steps down the stairs. The sound of the door slamming shut followed her all the way to Gare d'Austerlitz.

The next day at work, Nila was surprised to see Catherine greet her with a grin and ask if she found the place.

Nila said, 'I did.'

'Which ones did you see—Jim Morrison's? Oscar Wilde, Balzac, Chopin, Edith Piaf? There's a very sad looking grave that's Paul Eluard's.'

Catherine didn't look as if she had any inkling that her behaviour had been unpleasant in any way. She didn't say a word about it, not even an apology that she was busy, or she was just going out. It was very natural: you weren't supposed to come to my house and you shouldn't have; wait till I invite you.

Nila was more embarrassed by Catherine's behaviour than she herself. So much so that Nila couldn't meet her eye.

'Is Baudelaire's grave also over there?' Nila's voice strove for normalcy.

Catherine's tone matched hers, 'You'd have to go to the Montparnasse cemetery for that.'

'Oh, thanks.' Nila didn't forget to thank her. She knew that the people in the factory talked about her, that she had no manners, she didn't say thank you and never looked at the person while they talked, her eyes wandered here and there and she didn't think much of anyone. So when she said 'thanks', Catherine's face lit up with a smile. Just such a smile had been there the day Catherine took Nila to the Bistro Romain. They sat face to face and ate entrecôtes and drank red wine. At the end of it the bill came to one hundred and ninety-two francs. Catherine kept ninety-five francs on the table and said, 'My share, for the food and coffee.'

'What do you mean, your share?'

'That's what I had. You'll have to give ninety-seven for the food and tea.'

Nila had pushed Catherine's money towards her, taken out a

two hundred franc note and handed it to the waiter.

Catherine's brows trembled with distrust, 'Why are you paying for me too?'

Her ashen face made Nila feel like a criminal, as if she'd committed a grave sin and she had an ulterior motive for it. She had to explain, 'In my country we don't pay like this. When we go out, one person pays, either I or you.'

When she saw Catherine's brows still creased in a frown, Nila touched her shoulder and said, 'Come on, let's go.'

Catherine's voice shook, 'But you paid for me; how do I pay you back?'

'You don't. Why do you always think of paying back?'

Catherine's brows cleared and the same brilliant smile lit her face, 'Thanks, thank you very much.'

Nila had thought Catherine's relief at not having to pay her back was behind the brilliance of the smile.

Just now the same bright smile was on her lips. Nila didn't know how to smile so brightly; if she smiled, her broken tooth showed. She broke it as a child when she slipped and fell in the bathroom.

La Familia

Sunil hadn't been able to get the address of Nila's factory from Kishan. He got hold of it from Mojammel and called twice; but he didn't find her. So finally he wrote, 'Your mother is seriously ill. Go back to Calcutta immediately.'

Nila laughed. She laughed because she simply couldn't believe that Molina was ill. If she was, it couldn't be anything more serious than a common cold. Sunil was advising her to go back home because of Nila's nerve, for having the nerve to leave Kishan, for putting Sunil in an awkward spot, for all the accusations that Kishan must be heaping on Sunil; because Nila must have become a juicy topic of discussion among the Indians in Paris: Kishan's wife has run away, ha ha ha. Also because Sunil probably felt Nila should go back to her father's house if she didn't feel like staying with her husband.

Nila shared the news with Danielle who said, 'It's a plot. You'll see, Kishan is involved in this too. Besides, if your mother is really ill, what will you do over there? Aren't there any doctors in your country?'

'Exactly!' Nila said.

'Exactly.'

The two of them finished a bottle of white wine. White because Danielle had just polished off a plate of escargot and mussels—it was her dinner. And white was the only wine to drink with it. Nila didn't like snails and shells. So she had rice. She was used to eating vegetables and going without meat these days.

Before they went to bed, Danielle gave her two pieces of good news. The first—Rita Cixous was making a film on foreign women living in Paris. She wanted to interview Nila and she'd give five hundred francs for it. The second—Danielle had asked three of her friends to look for a job for Nila. She hugged Danielle and waltzed around the room.

'There, you danced.'

Only if she'd had a few drinks and then only the random shaking around, not Bharatnatyam.

'Do you see how important it is to make contacts. See how handy that dinner party at Nicole's came in?'

Nila couldn't deny that.

She didn't sleep well that night. She got up many times to urinate. The urine was collected in a bucket and in the morning the full bucket had to be emptied in the common bathroom along the corridor. Nila always had to pinch her nose, hold her breath and perform this task. In the beginning Danielle used to do it. But eventually one day she got fed up and said to the pampered missy, 'You there, do you think I am your slave?'

No, that's not what Nila thought and to prove it to Danielle, she began to clean out the bucket five days a week.

At the first light of dawn Nila was ready.

Danielle asked her where she was off. Nila said she wanted to walk, have tea and croissants at a café and watch the city wake up.

Nila walked alone in the misty city streets. A few drunks lay around here and there, wrapped in blankets and empty bottles by their hand. Some people were out walking their dogs. Dog piss didn't bother anyone; it was dog shit that was a problem. There'd have been mountains of dog shit in the city if there hadn't been a green patrol to clear it up. The job of the green patrol was to go about on motorcycles, pick up the dog shit, dump it in boxes and carry it away.

A white beggar sat on the street even at that early hour, holding a placard that said We Are Hungry. Beside him sat a dog that was twice the man's size. If Danielle saw this sight, Nila knew she'd feel sorry for the dog and drop ten francs into the hat in front of the man. Not just Danielle, nearly everyone who gave money to this beggar would do so out of pity for the dog and not for the man. She'd seen many white girls in the metro station, with dogs. Danielle said they were from Kosovo and other poor countries in Europe.

So the people of the poor European countries came here to beg.

What was the use of communism's breakdown then?

Danielle said, 'Under communism they had no freedom.'

'Freedom to do what?'

'To go out of the country.'

Nila laughed, 'To go out and beg?'

Not just begging, many educated women of those countries lost their jobs when communism failed. They were rushing further west and taking up prostitution. Danielle didn't want to address these issues.

Nila walked all the way to the Louvre and behind it to Rue de Rivoli where Sunil lived.

He was surprised to see her, 'So early in the morning—where are you living, what do you do, you must keep us posted. Did you get my letter? Do you know how worried we all are!'

So many questions all at once. Nila didn't answer any of them. She just asked, 'What has happened to Ma?'

'I don't know that. Narayan, the man who went with the Chanel, has come back from Calcutta and said aunty is ill. Nikhil called twice and asked you to go to Calcutta, if possible immediately.'

After some social chit chat Nila came to the real point, her gold jewellery.

Sunil was out of touch with Kishan for a long time. The last time they spoke on the phone was when Sunil called to ask about Nila. Kishan said, 'Don't ask me. You must know her whereabouts better than me.'

Sunil was surprised, 'How would I know?'

Kishan replied, 'You've helped my wife run away; so you must know.'

Kishan believed Sunil had supported Nila in all this and she had taken his advice to leave the house.

'Don't mention that whore to me again.' Kishan had slammed the phone down.

Sunil hadn't called him after that and neither had Kishan. So it wasn't possible for Sunil to ask about her jewellery. But he could ask some of Kishan's friends about it. Sunil believed Kishan wouldn't give it back.

Nila wanted to blame Sunil for all this, for getting her married to Kishan. But then she thought, would it have been any different if in Kishan's place another Indian man had been her husband? Perhaps not. Even as she sat there, she noticed Chaitali made the breakfast and Sunil sat down to eat it. After Sunil left for the clinic, Chaitali would drop Tumpa at her school and then go to her own office She would pick Tumpa up on her way back from work. Chaitali would have to bathe and feed the child and put her to sleep. She would have to cook dinner and clean the house. Since she needed to give more time at home, Chaitali worked part-time.

In Nila's and Danielle's home there was no inequality. If Nila cooked, Danielle washed up. If Nila did the shopping, Danielle cooked. They paid the rent by turns. If Nila was short of money, Danielle paid and Nila repaid her later.

Nila finished her tea and rose to leave.

'Where will you go?'

'To work and from there, home.'

'And where is this home?'

'A friend's place.'

'How long will you stay with this friend?'

'As long as I wish.'

'This won't work, Nila. You have to take a decision.'

'What decision?'

'Either you go back to Kishan or return to Calcutta.'

Nila knew Sunil would say something like this. He continued without pausing for breath, 'You are doing just whatever you feel like. This doesn't work in life. There are bound to be some misunderstandings between husband and wife. Time heals everything. I feel Kishan is still waiting for you to come back. And if you try and it still doesn't work out, you should talk it out with Kishan and do something permanent. Then you can marry someone else and live your own life. What did Kishan do—did he beat you?'

'No.'

'Did he have an affair?'

'No.'

'Was it the Immanuelle issue?'

'No.'

'Then what?'

Nila gave a wan smile and set off into the misty morning.

She pondered over how to get her jewellery back from Kishan as she walked on the foggy streets. She didn't take the metro. Instead of going to work, she went into Café Rivoli and drank two cups of tea. Then she took the bus, like all those times earlier, and set off for nowhere in particular.

That day Nila saw something that she had never seen in a bus before. Two inspectors boarded the bus to check tickets. Nila sat right at the back of the bus. The white man came straight to her and asked for the ticket. She couldn't remember if she'd kept it in her trouser pockets or jacket pockets. She dug into all her pockets and many tickets came out. The inspector took each of them and discarded them as old ones. She would have to show him a valid one. Nila hunted in her pockets and purse and began to sweat as she realized a busload of people were staring at her. She was the only non-white in the whole bus, a strange being who didn't look anything like the other passengers. If she stood up, she was sure people would check for a tail. The inspector's lips were twisted in a 'See, I'm never wrong. I can make out from the colour who has bought a ticket and who hasn't' kind of smile.

The new ticket was tucked in behind some papers in her purse. She found it eventually. When she handed it to the inspector, he verified the time stamped on it and then let her off. She felt he was quite disappointed. He didn't ask the others in the bus for their tickets.

When the bus stopped in front of Hôtel de Ville, Nila got down. She adored this terrace; she could sit in front of it for hours and never tire of watching its architecture, its beauty. She called Danielle from there and told her that she hadn't gone to work that day because she didn't feel like it. She didn't know why she didn't feel like it. What was she doing? Nothing. Where was she? In front of Hôtel de Ville. Why was she there? She didn't know. When would she return? She didn't know.

Danielle said, 'Stay there. I'm coming.'

Nila hadn't wanted Danielle to come. She'd wanted to be alone. She wanted to make another call, but changed her mind. Nila didn't want to answer his questions about where she was, with whom and why she even left his home. She was afraid to hear him call her a whore.

Danielle came and took Nila into a café nearby, 'What's the matter?'

Nila laughed, 'Nothing.'

'You are upset Nila, tell me why?'

'Nothing has happened.'

'What did you do all day?'

'I'd gone to Sunil's house and asked about my jewellery. It doesn't look like I will get it back.'

'Is that why you look so heartbroken?'

Nila laughed, 'Is that how I look?'

No, Nila didn't look like that. In fact, her face didn't give anything away.

Danielle pleaded, 'Nila, I love you. Please share your feelings with me.'

Nila had heard the word 'love' from Danielle earlier, in their room. It had never made her uncomfortable. Now it did. She was afraid that if anyone heard Danielle they'd know that she was homosexual and her companion must, naturally, be one too. Nila still didn't understand how two women could be in love with one another and how there could be real sex between them, although on many nights she had lain beside Danielle and experienced an orgasm. But then, she could have given herself that pleasure quite easily and she didn't need Danielle for it. Nila had never played with herself and she didn't know it was possible. Danielle had told her that when she didn't have a lover, she brought herself to an orgasm. Nila was amazed. There were so many astonishing things in the world. Nila had been very shy about sexuality. In fact, all Indian women felt that was one topic which was taboo, secret and private. In her two years with Sushanta, they'd probably kissed about half a dozen times. And for those six kisses there was so much waiting, so many arrangements to be made. Over here, girls and boys kissed anywhere in public and this angered Nila as much as it delighted her. She was happy that they didn't hide their love and demonstrated it openly. She was angry thinking how much she had lost by growing up in such a restrictive society. For the longest time, Nila never could do as she pleased. Now, after leaving Kishan's home, she was doing as she pleased. Or at least, she guessed that's what living with Danielle and sleeping with her would be counted as, though Nila didn't think so because that sexual relationship was entirely for Danielle's benefit and not hers. Danielle had just assumed that Nila also loved her, although she noticed how on the streets or at a café Nila often gazed longingly at the handsome Frenchmen. Even now, as Danielle went on about her doctor's appointment with Nicole in an hour's time, Nila's eyes were elsewhere.

'What's wrong? Why aren't you listening to me?'

'I am listening.'

'No, you are not.'

'Yes, I am.'

'Then why are you looking somewhere else?'

'That's where you go wrong. When I listen intently, I don't look at the face. It spoils my concentration.'

'So where do you look?'

'At the walls, tables, chairs, things which don't distract.'

'Tell me what I said.'

'You said you have to take Nicole to the doctor.'

Was Nicole sick? No, no, it was for Pipi. Who was Pipi? Nicole's cat.

Danielle said, 'Pipi isn't peeing.'

So why does Nicole have to go to the doctor?

'Nicole is very sad and she has to see her psychiatrist.'

Nila was startled. She wanted to laugh out loud, but didn't. Ever since she'd learnt to kick, Nila had always aimed a kick at cats and dogs. It was a routine for cats to steal into the kitchen, go for the bowls of food and stick their tongue into it. So it became a habit to kick a cat whenever she saw one. If a mangy, stray dog wanted to steal into the house, they always had to kick it out. In this land of civilized cat and dog lovers, Nila rebuked her itching foot and tried to make it charitable.

Danielle's gaze followed Nila's and landed on a curly-haired youth. 'What are you staring at?'

Nila owned up she was taken by his looks.

'Yuk!' Danielle burst out, 'Do you want to go back to your old life? You've seen how life is with a man. Hasn't it taught you a lesson?'

'Not every man is Kishan.'

'If not Kishan, then Sushanta. All men are the same. They all exploit women.'

'Not all men are the same, Danielle. Some of them know how to love.'

'Love?' Danielle stirred some sugar into her espresso and said, 'It's a web. Men trap women in it. Women think they can't live without men. That's not true. Look at me. I don't need a man.'

Nila's tea grew cold as she looked into Danielle's eyes and listened.

Danielle could do without men, but Nila wanted to ask, if everyone became homosexual like her, how would the race continue? Nila sited the example of the animal world; almost all animals felt attracted to the opposite sex, mate with them and that's how the species continued. Otherwise all would be over, finito.

Danielle said, 'These are rules created by the men.'

Nila said, 'In that case I'll never be able to give birth to a child.'

Danielle was about to sip her coffee when she stopped and said, 'How many more children are needed in this world? There're enough. Besides, what's the point of bringing more children into this world of patriarchy and imbalance?'

'One day there will be no imbalance. We will all be equal.' Nila looked into the distance dreamily.

Danielle said, 'That's then . . . and for sex, the day women say they don't need men, will be the day men finally lose. Not before that.'

Nila sipped her cold tea. In this city people dawdled over one cup of tea or coffee in the cafés and spent a few hours chatting. Outside the cafés these same people rushed to and fro claiming to be very busy, frothing at the mouth. Nila often felt the people in Calcutta were far busier, in the truest sense, but they didn't talk about it so much. Here people had the whole weekend off, when they lazed around, read the newspaper and wiped the sweat off their brows. They knew nothing of hard work. If only they saw the rickshaw-pullers or the porters in Calcutta. The definition of hard work was different here.

For Nila hard work was when someone lifted heavy sacks of sand on their head from dawn till dusk, walked two miles and reached it to the construction site. One day Danielle had said, 'I've worked very hard.'

Nila asked, 'What kind of work?'

'I've read two books and written reviews for them.'

'Tell me about the hard work.'

'That's the hard work.'

Nila was surprised, '*That* is what you call hard work?'

'Yes.'

'But reading is the most pleasurable activity. What kind of books?'

'Fiction.'

'Wow, that's fun.'

'But I may not want to read that book for fun.'

'Hm. How many pages did you write?'

'Two.'

'If only I had such a job,' Nila said to herself.

She was drawn to Danielle and also repelled by her. Danielle's words had logic and also lacked it. Nila swayed between liking and dislike. Whatever Danielle said, Nila couldn't tear her eyes away from handsome men. She wanted a man to tell her he loved her. She wanted him to kiss her and make love to her ecstatically. But Nila's wishing didn't make it any more real. She noticed that no handsome man gave her a second glance. In Calcutta she turned heads. Here, even the idlers didn't bother to whistle when she passed by; it was as if she was nobody, a strange piece of flesh whom they'd all like to avoid. Back home she was beautiful. But that beauty was of no value here. Danielle valued it; Danielle's body may be as beautiful as a Rodin sculpture, but her face lacked grace and her voice was harsh

Nila could weave no dreams around Danielle. Did she know that? Nila believed she didn't.

Danielle finished her coffee and said, 'Penny for them, Nila.'

She didn't say what she was thinking about. But she asked Danielle if she could lend her some money.

'How much?'

'Say around five thousand francs?'

'Are you out of your mind? What will you do with that money?'

'I'll go to Calcutta.'

'Why?'

'Mother is ill.'

'Oh, that Sunil has stuffed your head with all this rubbish. Go on, go to Calcutta and see how they trap you there.' Danielle was really irritated.

'My mother is ill and I'll go to see her, that's all.'

'Will you go and treat her? Are there no doctors or hospitals in your country?'

'There are, but I still want to go and see her.'

'There's no point in going now. You should go when she's cremated.'

'It's not about cremation, it's about nursing her.'

'Aren't there any nurses to do that? You've mentioned there are many servants in your house.'

'They are all there. But I will go.'

'Go ahead. But I don't have the money.'

'Can you borrow it from someone?'

'No one will lend so much money.'

Nila sank her head into the lap of silence. Her tea was long finished.

'If you go now and come back, will you go again for her cremation?' Danielle tried to soften her coarse voice and asked.

Nila gritted her teeth, her jaws were set as she said, 'Don't keep on about cremation, Danielle. My mother isn't so ill that she will die.'

'Then why do you want to go?'

'Because she is my mother . . .'

Danielle made a face and broke in on her, 'My mother, my father, my brother, rubbish.'

Nila paid no heed to it and said, 'My heart tells me it's more serious than a common cold—it's something else.'

Danielle threw the change for her coffee on the table and pushed the chair back noisily. She held up her middle finger at Nila, slapped her left elbow with her right hand. Danielle was bursting with anger as she strode out of the café screaming, 'La familia, la familia!'

A Bientôt

Before she left for Calcutta, Nila went to two places: the first was Sandani and the second to a psychiatrist. Rita Cixous wanted to interview her in the gardens of Basilique de Sandani. Serge Santos's house was in that garden. Sandani was now a crowded suburb where very few white people lived. It was mostly inhabited by blacks and browns, the uneducated and the jobless, and the crime rate was high.

Nila looked at the brightly painted houses and wondered how they defined poverty. She saw the cars standing in front of the houses and asked, 'Who do these belong to?' They belonged to the 'poor' because they couldn't afford to buy new models of expensive cars. Nila's eyes had seen the slums of Calcutta and for those eyes, no other kind of poverty would ever match up. She had seen millions of refugees, homeless, hungry, half-clad, suffering with no treatment in sight. But that man who just came out of that house after a full meal, who got into his car and shook his head in time to the music as he drove off—he was no poor man.

Rita pressed a button, unlocked the gate and drove into the huge garden. It was more like a field. Gravestones were strewn around. Ann l'Or sat on one of them, drinking coffee. Rafael and Benjamin, Ann's sons, were playing around.

There was a round of kisses. Danielle exclaimed over the house at the foot of the Basilique. It was wonderful to get a house like that. Well, they wouldn't have got it if Serge wasn't the bishop at the Basilique.

Two other men had come with Rita; one held a camera and the other a microphone. Nila was scared; she had never faced a camera before. She didn't know what Rita would ask her. Her palms were sweating, and drops stood out on her nose.

Rita said, 'Would you like to powder your nose?'

Nila wiped it with the back of her hand and said, 'No, it's okay. I haven't brought any powder with me anyway.'

Rita blushed with embarrassment.

Danielle brought her mouth close to Nila's ear and muttered, 'Powdering your nose doesn't mean that literally. It means going to the toilet, peeing or shitting.'

'Why couldn't she ask me that then?'

'No, that's shameful.'

'Shameful?'

Nila could never understand what construed as shame in this society. It wasn't even summer yet and the girls walked around half-dressed. Clothes were a problem.

Before she came in front of the camera, the cameraman said, 'It'd be good if she powdered her face.' This time it was real powder. Ann l'Or took her in to dab powder on her face. Nila saw the perfectly arranged home and said, 'Have you been married for long?'

'Oh but we are not married.'

'So what is Serge to you?'

'He's my lover.'

'You live together?'

'Sure. We have been together for the last six years.'

Nila looked into the mirror and brushed powder on her face. Today she had worn a sari on Rita's request; dressed in a sari and a bindi, she looked the complete Bengali girl. In her mind Nila swiftly went to Calcutta and came back.

Two chairs were placed in the field. Rita checked if Nila's face and the Basilique in the background, the famous landmark of France where all monarchs were buried, were seen clearly through the lens. Now, they sat face to face and the questions began. 'Tell me, Nila, that symbol you have tattooed on your forehead is a mark to indicate that you are married, right?'

'No.'

Rita was flustered, but she sported a pitying smile as she waited for Nila's explanation of why not.

'This is not a mark of marriage. Most women wear bindis even before marriage, because it looks good.'

'Isn't it a permanent mark on your forehead?'

Nila laughed and took the felt bindi off. 'See, it comes off. Here now, gone next.'

Cut.

Rita didn't like the bindi magic. She'd have been happier if a permanent, red marriage mark was tattooed onto Nila's forehead. She glanced at the written sheet of questions on her lap and asked Nila the next one, 'You are from India and you have come from so far away to Paris, to live with your husband, haven't you?'

'Yes.'

'I've heard that you have left your husband. Will you tell us why?'

'Because I don't get along with him.'

'But why not?'

'We are two different kinds of people.'

'But your husband is also Indian. Why do you call him different.'

'We don't think the same way.'

'I've heard that your husband tortured you. Tell us what he did to you.'

'He's not really done anything that'll qualify as torture.'

'Your husband beat you—what did he use, whip, sticks or his belt . . .?'

'My husband has never laid a finger on me.'

Cut.

Rita raised her hand and stopped the camera. She came up to Nila, knelt down in front of her and said, 'Perhaps you didn't understand my question, Nila.'

Nila was in an awkward position. Rita noticed her discomfort and shouted for some water. Ann l'Or ran and got a glass of water. Nila wasn't thirsty, but she had to drink it and she kept half of it at hand for later.

The camera was aimed at Nila. Rita started again. 'You must be in touch with other Indian women like you here who have also left their husbands. What kinds of torture did their husbands inflict on them?'

Nila replied innocently, 'I don't know anyone like that.'

Cut.

This time Rita went up to Danielle. She sat on a gravestone and conferred with Danielle for a long time; then she came back with a smile plastered on her face and said, 'You're looking very pretty in a sari. I have seen you in Western clothes more often, but I think the sari suits you best.'

Rita's next question, 'I've heard of the custom of sati in your land. So when your husband dies, you'll have to jump into his pyre, right?'

'That is an ancient custom and it was banned in the last century.'

'It's customary to pierce the girls' clitoris in India. So what percentage of girls have this done to them?'

'That is not an Indian custom.'

'Tell us more about your married life—you had to do all the housework, right?'

'Yes.'

'What did you do?'

'Cook, clean, do the laundry and the dishes.'

'Which of the chores at home did your husband do?'

'Nothing much.'

'Did your husband ever cook?'

'No.'

'Clean the house?'

'No.'

'What did he do when he came back from work?'

'Watch TV, drink . . .'

Rita nodded, 'And? What else did he do?'

'What else? He ate and slept.'

'Both of you contributed to the household income, right?'

'No. I didn't. My husband paid the bills.'

'But your husband didn't want you to work.'

'No.'

'So your husband kept you locked in, didn't he?'

'He didn't want me to go out. But he didn't really lock me in. I had a set of keys as well.'

'Your husband has retained all your gold jewellery, right?'

'No, he hasn't. I forgot all of it and left it behind.'

'Didn't your husband pressurize you to maintain purdah and cover your head?'

'No. That happens in orthodox Muslim families, not in Hindu households.'

'Your husband didn't let you eat fish and meat. He forced you to eat according to his wishes, didn't he?'

'That's true. He was vegetarian and he wanted his house free of meat.'

'But if you disobeyed him what did he do—beat you up?'

'No, he's never beaten me.'

'Did he abuse you?'

'No.'

Then what did he do?'

'He'd be upset.'

Cut.

When they left Sandani, Danielle said, 'You seem to have a lot of sympathy for Kishan.'

Nila said, 'What should I have said? What would have proved that I don't have any sympathy for him?'

Danielle shrugged, 'Forget it.'

'What is this documentary on?'

'About women and how they are exploited.'

Nila had more questions. 'Which women? Any woman, even French women?'

'I've already told you that, it's foreign women.'

'Foreign? German, Swiss, Belgian?'

'They don't come to live in France. It's about those who come here to stay.'

'So it's women from Rwanda, Mali, Somalia, India, Pakistan, Iran and Afghanistan, right?'

Danielle was silent for a long time. The metro was unbearably crowded and as they jostled around, Danielle said, 'You don't know about the custom of clipping the clitoris? It happens everywhere, even in France this atrocity is being perpetrated in the name of culture. You seem to support it.'

Nila spoke vigorously, 'Why should I support it? But I spoke the truth—it doesn't exist in India.'

'Maybe it doesn't, but other things do. You could have spoken about those. This was the best platform to let the world know how women are deprived and discriminated against in the Third World. Normally you speak of so many issues.'

Nila said, 'I answered the questions that she asked.'

'To tell you the truth, Rita isn't very happy with your interview.'

Nila wanted to ask when and if at all she'd get the five hundred francs. But she held her tongue. Sometimes that was the best thing to do.

'Why are you so quiet?' Danielle's vexed brown eyes were on Nila's.

'What should I say, you haven't asked anything.'

'Your interview is over, now come back to earth, be normal.'

Nila laughed, just for the heck of it. She decided if Danielle asked her why she laughed, she'd say for no reason. And if she said only mad women laugh for no reason, Nila would say she was crazy.

From the Basilique Sandani they reached the Concorde. From there they'd have to take line number one and go to Charles de Gaulle Etoille. But the metro wasn't running in that direction. It wasn't running from either Concorde or Etoille. Danielle and Nila came up to the surface. They would have to catch a bus. They waited at the Concorde bus-stop. Buses were coming, but they wouldn't stop because there was no room in them. Some people at the bus-stop said it was because the metro had stopped. Danielle was trying to thumb down a taxi, but none of them stopped. Nila felt as though she was back in India. In a way she was relieved to see buses or trains running late. Here, where even the taxis were punctual, Nila felt stifled with the perfection. This chaos made her breathe freely again.

Very soon the police arrived and surrounded the Concorde metro station. Danielle asked one of them, 'What is the matter?'

'Nothing much. Two suicides.'

'Reason?'

'Same as usual. Spring.'

Nila's jaw dropped. Danielle shoved a pile of facts into that open mouth.

Spring was the season of suicides. Two youths had jumped on to the tracks. They wanted to die and so they did. It happened every spring. People killed themselves under the rail tracks.

Nila wanted to know, 'Why do people feel like killing themselves at springtime?'

As far as she knew, the people of the West were happy when spring came.

Danielle said, 'Those who are lonely, who don't have a partner, they kill themselves at this time. In the spring your loneliness taunts you because it tells you that summer is here; summer, which is the time of joy, of loving and enjoying life. All summer long lovers walk hand in hand, have fun and those who are alone feel even lonelier when they see so many happy couples. The distress drives them to suicide in spring, even before summer arrives.'

Nila didn't understand.

'Of course you wouldn't understand. What would you know of someone else's misery?'

Danielle's gibe didn't affect Nila. She grew pensive as they walked towards Equadore. She thought of those two youths lying on the rail tracks, their brains all over the place and their bones crushed to powder.

They killed themselves just because they didn't have a lover, because they wouldn't be able to enjoy the next months! Nila wondered if she'd do the same for the lack of a partner. She wouldn't. Love was not the only joy in life. There was so much more: listening to the sound of falling leaves, floating with a transient cloud, reading an entire book of verses in one long evening, so many ways of fulfilling life.

'Nila, learn to understand people, to appreciate their concerns.'

The throng of patients at the clinic in Equadore made Nila quite nervous. She wanted to know what ailed all these people. Some were reading journals, some talking to their neighbour in low whispers, and some others were dozing. Nicole had come here to rid herself of the agony of her cat not peeing. Danielle came because she wanted to get over her misery at Nila's impending departure to Calcutta. Nila assumed that the man who dozed was probably there because he hadn't slept well a few nights and the one who spoke in whispers was probably there because he normally spoke too loudly. The sixteen-year-old girl who sat gazing out the window, Nila was sure, had come because she was having trouble with her lover. The people of the First World couldn't have their minds in a less-than-perfect condition. It had to be a hundred per cent fit. The body may well be a little weak, but the mind had to be in the pink of health.

Danielle took about two hours at the clinic. She tottered out like a drunken Catholic would from a confession box. She walked towards the door and didn't glance at Nila, who had to wade through the crowd and get her attention. Danielle tore herself from Nila's arms, which held her, and said, 'Leave me alone.'

Nila didn't leave her alone. She wasn't used to leaving someone alone if they were upset. If she was ever upset, Molina would stroke her back, wipe her tears and all that love took care of the sorrow. Nila had never needed to see a shrink.

Nila held Danielle's chin, turned her to face her and said, 'Why did you have to go to a doctor? If I am the reason, talk to me, tell me what's on your mind. You love me, don't you? So talk to me!'

Danielle screamed, 'I've told you, just leave me alone.'

'You're upset and if you're alone, it'll get worse. It wasn't so bad before you went in to see the doctor.' Nila hugged Danielle again. Danielle tore out of her arms and went and sat on a bench. Nila sat down beside her and placed a hand on her shoulder very gently and said, 'It's such a lovely city, so pretty; everyone has food to eat, a roof over their head and clothes to wear and security. Why then do they run to psychiatrists?'

Danielle's eyes brimmed with tears. When Nila tried to wipe them, she snatched her head and her tears away.

'You wouldn't understand, Nila. Food and clothes are not everything. You want to judge the world with your Third World vision. There's such a thing as the heart and about that you know nothing.'

Nila said, 'The Third World also has a heart, Danielle, and it isn't made of stone. I know you are suffering. I also suffer often but I never have to see a doctor. Why are you so afraid of suffering? I have never heard of our people going to a doctor to cure themselves of sorrow.'

Nila didn't speak for a long time and Danielle tried to hide her tears.

'Let's walk on the Champs-Elysées; you'll feel better.'

Danielle didn't want to go anywhere. She wanted to go home. Alone.

Nila pulled her hand, 'Let's go to the cinema.'

'No.'

'Let's go to a café.'

'No.'

'Walk along the Seine?'

'No.'

'Theatre?'

'No.'

'I'll treat you to dinner.'

'No.'

'Oh, go to hell. You and your melancholia!'

Calcutta as Usual

Calcutta was just the way Nila had left it. Yet, she felt it looked a little dingier, there was more filth on the footpaths, the air was a little more polluted, there was more traffic on the roads, the incessant honking seemed a little louder. The houses looked more worn out with paint peeling off, the shops smaller, more cramped, damp and the people darker, there was less grass in the fields. As Nila was driven home from Dumdum, she said as much to Nikhil, 'Calcutta has changed a lot.'

Nikhil tried to find the signs Nila talked about and the driver, Ramkiran, wiped his neck with a dirty handkerchief and said, 'Didi, *you* have changed. Calcutta is exactly the way you left it.'

Nila entered her home in Ballygunge and felt that too had shrunk in size. Once, Nila had gone to see her old school building after she was grown up. But she could hardly recognize it. She was looking for the huge field where she had run around once, the immense pond that she remembered, had looked like a small tarn.

On her way home, Nila hadn't asked Nikhil or Ramkiran what was the matter with Molina. When she came in, Chitra ran to tell Molina, 'Didi has come, didi.' That's how it had always been, if Nila ever came home a little late, Chitra ran to give the news of her arrival to Molina thus. Today Nila felt as though she had come home a little late: there was traffic on the way; she'd gone to see Aparna Sen's new film.

She did what she always did when she returned home, called out for her mother. If she didn't find her in the bedroom, she'd look in the kitchen and then try the puja room. If Molina wasn't there, Nila would try the small patch of vegetable garden in their backyard and then she'd know that Ma was up on the terrace, drying out the clothes.

Today Nila called out to her and entered the bedroom. Molina lay there under the fan at full speed, sweating. She was sleeping.

'Ma is sleeping at this time of the day? Wake up, I've come.'

Nila has come. Molina, wake up. Give her some cool water, sit her down beside you and listen to her stories—she has lots to tell you. If her voice chokes as she talks, draw her head upon your lap and stroke her lovingly and say, 'Don't ever leave me, darling.'

Nila sat at the head of the bed and found Molina's long dark tresses had flown out the window and a skeleton swayed under that whirring fan.

'Didi, would you like some tea?'

Didi didn't answer.

Chitra burst into tears. Nila didn't ask why she was crying. She got up and went into her own bedroom upstairs. Chitra followed her, wiping her tears on her sari, 'Didi, don't go to sleep. Have a bath and eat something first.'

'Chitra, just go away. Leave me alone.'

Chitra continued to stand at the door and said, 'God knows what has happened to aunty! She was fine one day and bedridden the next. Now she can't even stand up. She just takes those sleeping pills and sleeps all the time. It's a good thing or else she'd be screaming in pain. You won't be able to stand that, didi.'

'Why are you talking so much? I haven't asked you anything!' Nila yelled at her.

Chitra moved closer to Nila, step by little step. 'Aunty was constantly asking for you, didi. Before she fell asleep she was giving us nonstop directions to cook three kinds of fish and get some sweets because you are coming today.'

Nila buried her face in the pillow. 'You go away from here, just go for a while.' She felt Chitra was hurling not words but balls of fire at her.

Chitra sobbed again, 'So many people came to see her, but no one could cure her. So many doctors. They gave so many medicines. But she isn't getting better. Every day she's getting worse. Until a few days back she could eat a bite of rice if it was overcooked and soft. Now even that she can't have.'

Soon she was joined by Manjusha. 'You have come home at last,

Nila.' She burst into copious tears.

She wept noisily and said, 'Why didn't you come sooner? She said she'd cook so many things when you came home, because you didn't get them abroad. But now I don't think you'll ever taste her cooking again . . .'

Nila raised her face from the pillow and shouted, 'What's wrong with all of you? Why are you all crying so much? Go away.'

Manjusha sat there and went on speaking. 'The doctors have stopped treating her; they say it's no use. Now they just give painkillers but even those have stopped working. I believe the cancer has spread from the intestines to the liver and yesterday he said it has affected the bones as well, and the brain too I believe. Last night didi howled in pain all night long and we could only watch.'

Now Nila got up from the bed and ran to the bathroom.

From outside, Manjusha said, 'Have your bath and come for lunch, Nila.'

Nila wanted silence. She didn't want anyone to describe Molina's condition or wishes in great detail. Nila knew about Molina's wishes from her childhood—none of them had ever been fulfilled. Molina had wanted a little love from Anirban; she didn't get it. It's not that Anirban Mandal didn't love anyone, he did. But not Molina. He loved Swati Sen. Once Molina had seen a Kanjivaram sari and exclaimed, 'What a lovely sari. I wish I could wear one.'

Anirban didn't buy it for her. But he bought it for Swati, who wore it and went to Simla with him. Molina had always wanted to go to Darjeeling. But Anirban never had the time to take her there. Swati was fairer than Molina. That was the one quality for which Anirban loved her. For as long as she could remember, Nila had never seen Anirban and Molina share a bed. Molina always made her husband's bed with great care. He came back from his hours of fun with Swati, critiqued every item that was put on the table, crashed on his neatly made bed and snored the night away. That was Molina's life. She had spent her years in this household by keeping her wishes collared and chained.

In the evening the house overflowed with relatives who'd come to see Molina. The road in front of the house brimmed over with cars. Molina's sister, her husband, their son, daughter-in-law and their children, Molina's aunt, Molina's cousin, her son Poltu, Anirban's elder brother, sister, cousin brother, his daughter Mithu and two women from the neighbourhood. The pile of shoes at the entrance grew as they all went into Molina's room. Some brought her apples, pomegranates, grapes, oranges, some brought Horlicks and some others came with a fish soup or homemade yogurt or even just flowers. Manjusha showed them to Molina and kept them aside. She knew that the smell of flowers was intolerable for Molina and she'd throw up if she had the juice of apples or oranges. Molina looked at her relatives with empty eyes and closed them again, as if she didn't even have the strength to open them now, after so many years of relentless service. They all looked at Molina and sympathized, some wiped their tears, some fanned her and some even stroked her emaciated body.

From the crowd the words floated around, 'She was up and about even a few days ago.' 'Dear me, how sick she looks.' 'Her stomach looks more puffed up today.' 'The eyes are more yellow.'

Nila waded through the crowd and came out of the room. Some of the throng followed her. Manjusha rebuked Nila, 'Go and wear the red and white bangles and sindoor. What will all these people say!'

'Have they come here to see my bangles and sindoor?'

'No they haven't. But they all have eyes. You'll see, there'll be talk of this.'

'I don't care.'

Nila had quit wearing all that long ago and she had no intention of starting again. She stood at the window, and looked out at the back wall of her neighbour's house and the pile of filth at the foot of it. Two stray dogs were picking at the pile. Nila's stupor broke when Molina's elder brother's voice, speaking in English, reached her, 'Why didn't he come, Nila?'

'Who?'

'Kishanlal. I thought he was in Calcutta and we'll have quite a chat. He is quite a gentleman.'

That's true. But he wasn't here. Nila came alone.

'I have never been to Paris. But I know it's a wonderful city. I'd love to go there. Can I stay in Kishanlal's house? I am sure he has a beautiful, big house.'

Nila said, 'Why are you using so many English words? We are Bengalis and you can speak in Bengali.'

He always spoke in a mixture of Bengali and English and Nila had never objected to it before. In fact, she had also responded in the same way. He laughed out loudly. His ego wasn't bruised. Instead, Nila felt, he was rather pleased. He was quite proud that his tongue rolled out more English words than Bengali.

Anirban's elder sister drew Nila back from the window. 'What's the matter, why are you so quiet? Talk to us. The less you talk, the worse you feel. What can we do? It's not in our hands to cure Molina. It's God's wish . . .'

Molina's brother-in-law reclined on the sofa, lit a cigarette and asked, 'So how is life in Paris? Is your husband a rich man? I heard he earns good money!'

Molina's cousin sister held up Nila's wrists and said, 'Look at this—bare hands. Why have you taken off all your jewellery and why aren't you wearing the red and white bangles and sindoor? You're looking like a widow!'

Another cousin asked, 'When are you planning to have children? Whatever you're planning, do it quickly.'

Now one of Nila's cousins spoke, as she shoved the milk bottle in her baby's mouth, 'Your child will be a French citizen by birth, right?'

Molina's aunt called out to Poltu and pushed him in front of Nila. 'You said you wanted to ask your didi about Paris, so ask!' Poltu was fifteen years old. He sidled behind his grandmother. 'Just try to take this Poltu abroad, Nila. The boy doesn't want to study here at all.'

Anirban's cousin brother, Sadhan Das took Nila aside, heaved a sigh and said, 'Nila, will you try to do something for Mithu? If you can arrange a match for her . . .'

Nila guessed that her relatives thought her to be very rich now.

They didn't know that she had borrowed her air fare from Sunil and come home. They didn't know that it wasn't possible for Nila to solve anyone's problems. They didn't know that Nila had no interest in who wasn't getting married and who wasn't studying. She wanted all the people to leave and for her to get some time to sit beside Molina, to gaze at her closed eyes until she opened them; when she did, Nila would show her the shoes she had brought for her, the watch and the face cream to stop ageing.

Chitra and Manjusha were busy looking after the guests. Tea and biscuits were doing the rounds.

Nila searched for the rare solitude.

Mithu stood in a corner of the room wearing a white cotton sari. She came up to Nila with hesitant steps, looked around her cautiously and said in an undertone, 'I want to talk to you.'

'Tell me.'

'Not here. Let's go to your room.'

Nila took Mithu to her own room upstairs. Mithu shut the door and sat down on the bed. She took Nila's hands in hers and said, 'Please do something for me, Nila.'

'What can I do?'

'Find me a man, anyone. You know I am four years older than you. Baba was a clerk and that job has gone. Now he is a watchman in that same office. Dada is jobless. Whoever comes to see me for a match, rejects me because of my dark skin. Baba doesn't have the money to offer me a fat dowry. Nila, you are married and you wouldn't know what a crime it is in this society to stay unmarried. I have passed my BA long ago and I am sitting at home. I am nothing but a burden to my parents. I am an eyesore. A man abroad . . . I am not particular about religion, anything will do, if only he agrees to marry me. There's no one in this country who'll marry me.'

Mithu's large eyes were brimming with tears. Her long black tresses covered her back. Fear was stamped on her heart-shaped face. Nila took in the graceful beauty of Mithu's tall, sparse frame.

'I ask dada why he isn't getting married. He sighs and says how can I until I marry you off? He isn't getting any younger. He can't marry because of me. I am scared, Nila. I can hardly show my face in society.'

Nila drew her hand back from Mithu's grip and said, 'You've done your BA. Why don't you look for a job? What's wrong in not getting married? It's not everything.'

'I don't want marriage for my sake, Nila. I can scarcely look at my parents these days—dark and hopeless. I see my skin colour on everyone's face. This is such a big crime of mine. Nila, if someone marries me and then treats me like a servant, I don't mind—at least please marry me. If you find someone, old, mad . . .'

Nila didn't give her any hopes. Mithu went away with the fear still on her face.

Anirban came home after dusk and called Nila to his room. He was just as he had always been. As usual, he came home and washed up, changed into comfortable clothes and sat on the sofa. He glanced through the day's news. When Nila came and sat in front of him, Anirban was still reading.

'What's wrong between you and Kishan?'

'Nothing.'

Anirban took off his glasses, wiped them in a corner of his kurta, placed them back on his nose and said, 'Can't you see that life is very short? You are seeing your mother's condition. If you don't recognize the value of life, go about doing whatever you fancy and ruin your future entirely, one fine day you'll find life is over. There's no time for anything else, to change or build something afresh.'

This man had always talked of the future to Nikhil and Nila, in just this way. Nila tried to remember if she had ever seen Anirban cry.

Anirban spoke again in sombre tones. 'I spoke to Kishan the other day. He said, if you behave yourself, keep your husband happy like most women do, do as he says, then he's prepared to forgive you and take you back. Otherwise he has no problems in ending the relationship legally. Nila, you have gone and upset this straightforward man. I could hardly sleep, I was so worried.'

Nila stared at Anirban's moving lips carelessly and said, 'Baba, have you ever cried?'

'What kind of a question is that?'

'Because I want to know. I want to know if ever, in your entire life, you have cried. Try and remember, have you ever wept for anyone? If not for someone, then at least for yourself, have you ever felt tears in your eyes? Eyes, I'm talking about those eyes behind the glasses, which you just polished and wore again, those eyes. Have they ever shed a single tear? Have you ever felt your heart ache, and suddenly reach up to find your cheeks wet? It happens, you know, your hand gets wet, or your pillow—has it ever happened to you?'

'Have you gone mad?' Anirban scolded her.

Nila's voice was strangely tranquil, 'Yes, I have.'

Anirban took his glasses off again. This time it wasn't to wipe them but to throw a keen glance at Nila. But she continued, 'There's a word—regret. Have you ever heard it? Have you ever felt it? No, you haven't. There was never any need. You married Ma because you needed money. That was taken care of by her dowry. You used it to study medicine. Ma was like a servant in this house, right? No one said anything because that's how women often are in their husbands' house. You've enjoyed lording it over her. And you had Swati Sen to give you other pleasures. People didn't care about that either because men are supposed to have a liaison or two, there's nothing wrong in it. In fact, everyone thought you are noble because you didn't throw your dark-skinned, plain-looking wife out. You had to prove that you are not sterile and so there were two children. It was a matter of pride that your children studied and did well; you won there too. You didn't have to shell out anything for your daughter's dowry and you were saved. In fact you had the added advantage of being able to say your daughter lives abroad. Naturally no one wants to know how she is because living there is always good enough. If the daughter served her husband the way her mother served hers, the circle would be complete. If the daughter took a divorce and came back to her parents' home, it'll be one hell of a mess. Your son has a good job and also dabbles in politics; perhaps one day he'll be a minister. The cup runneth over. A successful life! Whatever else you may do, regret certainly wouldn't be one of them, right?'

She didn't give Anirban the chance to speak and walked away to

Molina's room. Molina lay there with her eyes closed. Nila picked up her fingers to stroke them and suddenly, like a sunflower bud blooming slowly, Molina opened her eyes.

'Ma, do you want something?'

'Don't say anything to your father. In times of trouble, he will look after you.' Molina's voice was tired, broken.

'Ma, I'll take you to Paris, treat you there, you will get well. Have I told you there's so much to see in Paris? I'll show you everything.'

Suddenly Molina's eyes grew bright. 'I'll get well?'

'Definitely you will get well. There are such great doctors there. I'll build us a beautiful house by the sea. There'll be mountains behind it. You love the ocean, don't you?'

Molina nodded like a child.

'There's so much to see in this country too. I'll take you to Darjeeling, Simla, Kashmir.'

Molina's voice was the same, weary. 'No, not Kashmir.'

'Okay, not Kashmir, it's unsafe. Do you want to go to Jaipur, Ma? Goa? We'll swim there . . .'

The smile faded from Molina's eyes. She closed her eyes so hard that her face wrinkled up and looked like a balled up piece of paper.

Nila hugged her close.

Suddenly Molina screamed, 'Manjusha!'

'Manjusha isn't here, Ma, she's gone. Tell me what you want.'

Chitra came running. She said, 'Didi, give that red medicine to aunty.'

Painkiller. Nila dissolved three instead of two and gave it to Molina.

But the pain wouldn't go.

Nila woke Nikhil. 'Dada, how can you sleep like this? Ma is screaming in pain. Wake up. Call the doctor who is treating Ma.'

Anirban was snoring away. Nila woke him too and asked him to call the doctor. Anirban shouted, 'What doctor, at this hour of the night!'

The groans rebounded in the sleeping household. Molina

moaned all night long, she could not scream any more. Nila sat by her, helpless. She tried to will her own body to take all the pain from her mother into her own, all her sorrow unto her own heart.

A-la-s Familia

In the morning, Anirban peeped into Molina's room before leaving for work. Nikhil did the same. They didn't feel a jot of remorse in disappearing for the day after finishing their breakfast and the quick peek. Nila barred their way and said, 'How can you all blithely leave for the day, when Ma is so ill?'

'But we have work to do.'

'Work? You'll work all your life and get fat salaries for it. Take a day off!'

'What's the point? Will Ma become all right?'

'No, but at least be at her side; she can look at you.'

'She, and look at me? She's sleeping all the time.'

Anirban rushed Nikhil, 'Don't waste your time, you are getting late. Don't pay any heed to this impractical girl. Just because one person's life is at a standstill doesn't mean everyone has to stop theirs!'

'Go! Go and earn money. In fact, I guess you are not even needed here. Just send the doctor and if you can't, give me his address; I'll see to it that he gets here.' Nila spoke wearily.

In the morning the sunflower bloomed again.

'Do you want to stroll by the Ganga today?'

Molina's face had a childlike smile—she would go. It was ages since she'd stepped out of the house. She wanted details of what Nila was being fed. Her voice was weak, but she spoke; her eyes drooped but she tried to keep them open. She was being strong. Nila said she was eating very well, Chitra was cooking excellent fish curries . . .

'Did she put coriander in the curry?'

'Yes Ma, she did.'

She herself could eat nothing except for a cup of milk and even that she threw up. Nila looked at Molina and thought, once she used to eat the leftovers after feeding her husband and children. She had done what most women did. That's how she fell ill. She'd never looked after herself, paid any heed to her own pleasure or health. Nila, just like everyone else in the house, had also never spared a glance at what Molina ate, whether she was sick or not. Now Nila wanted to look after her, feed her with her own hands. She wanted Molina to get well. But Molina was beyond her love and tenderness, her respect and adulation. Nila had kept it all back until it was too late. She desperately wanted to turn the clock back, to correct her mistakes. But time swept on as usual, carrying with it all mistakes, all wrongs.

Dr Prashanta came in the afternoon. Nila's newly acquired habit made her reach her hand out for a handshake. But she saw the doctor's discomfiture and drew it back and pretended she was indicating which room was the patient's. Nila was thankful that she had remembered and not proceeded to kiss his cheeks! Otherwise it would have been all over the town that Nila was not only depraved, she was also crazy.

The doctor checked Molina's blood pressure, her pulse and told them to continue with the medicine he had prescribed.

'That won't do, doctor. Give her something stronger—morphine.'

The gray-haired doctor with the grimy glasses perched on his nose, shook his head from side to side. 'Morphine isn't for now. Later.'

'How much later?'

He didn't say how much later, just later.

The doctor eventually revealed the reason for his reluctance to give morphine; he didn't think it was good and it could be addictive.

Nila's surprise knew no bounds; it trickled down her body and drenched her nerve endings. She shook with rage. How could he bother about morphine addiction for a person who was breathing her last?

Nila said, 'Let her get addicted! My mother never had any

addictions. I want her to have a morphine addiction. Please prescribe it.'

'There's something called medical ethics! I can't overstep them.' The doctor pushed his grimy glasses back on his nose and said.

'Ethics be damned! Please prescribe it—I will give her the injection,' Nila shouted at the doctor.

The doctor was wallowing in his ethics and wouldn't prescribe morphine. Suddenly Nila felt the Western debate over euthanasia was worth looking into. Earlier, she'd thought it was cruel. But today she felt just as someone had the right to live, they should have the right to die. This was also a human right. What was the point of living if all you could look forward to was misery?

Before he left, the doctor said, 'Why are you getting so excited! The illness isn't sudden; it was festering for a long time. It was just a boil in her intestine at first and that was haemorrhaging. It could have been operated quite easily. But because it was allowed to grow, it turned into cancer. This is the problem with patients' families. They don't begin treatment on time and when it is too late they throw their weight around.'

In the evening the car dropped Nikhil home and went to the hospital to pick up Anirban. He came home and Nila said, 'Tell Ramkiran to wait; I'll go out.'

'Where?'

Nila didn't answer. She told Nikhil to carry Molina into the car. Anirban stopped Nikhil. 'Have you also gone mad, like her?'

Nikhil agreed with him, this was truly crazy. To go to the riverside with a person who couldn't walk or stand, who had no strength in her arms and legs!

'Are you going to kill her even before she dies.'

Nikhil pulled her into the balcony and shouted at her. 'What is wrong with you? Why are you acting like this? You can see Ma's condition. Dragging her around at this time just doesn't make sense.'

Nila stood there silently.

Nikhil sighed, 'God knows what happened to Ma suddenly.'

Molina was screaming in pain. She could hear those pitiful cries from the balcony. But she couldn't bring herself to face that ghastly pain, to look on that face crumpled in agony. She gripped the grills on the balcony tightly—she wouldn't go anywhere; she'd stand there and spare herself the sight of all this pain. But she went and as she looked back, she saw Anirban sitting on the sofa in his comfortable clothes, the newspaper on his lap, his eyes fixed on the TV, watching the nubile heroine's undulating hips.

Nila switched off the TV, sat down in front of Anirban and said, 'Yesterday I spoke to you of regrets. Well, do you regret anything?'

Anirban took off his glasses. It was the keen eyes again, 'Why should I?'

'You should because you never paid attention to Ma's health. For ten years Ma was bleeding from time to time and you said it was piles, didn't you? Now you know it wasn't that. When she had stomach aches, you said it's nothing, she was just acting up. Actually she wanted to just take the day off, isn't that what you said? You said she was complaining unnecessarily to get your attention. Now you know the truth. Don't you have regrets? When you sit here alone, don't you ever feel sorry, feel that you could have prevented this disease if you had treated her instead of ignoring it. You were a professor of gastroenterology, and still are. Don't you feel sorry that although you are a doctor and Ma relied on you, she's dying without treatment because you never spared her a second glance? You do regret, right?'

'But she is being treated. We tried chemotherapy too.' Anirban's voice rose.

'Rubbish! Chemotherapy is no treatment. You have caused this cancer and now you try chemotherapy to fool people and make them believe she is being treated! When she needed it, there was no treatment. You know that too. Do you have any regrets?' Nila's voice held fury, her eyes rained hatred.

'I sent an oncologist today as well.'

'That's mere pretence, to show people that you're getting her treated by great doctors.'

Anirban looked at Nikhil for support, 'What is this girl blabbering! He is the finest oncologist in the city . . .'

'Fuck your oncologist.'

'What?'

'Fuck yourself.'

Nila wept. She brought the house down.

Nila fell asleep weeping. She woke up to Molina's screams and Anirban's snores. While one howled with unbearable pain, in another room the other slept peacefully. They had lived under the same roof for forty long years. Stillness, there was a stifling stillness within. Nila was scared; scared to touch Molina. Under the whirring fan, Molina's feet were cold as ice even though it was summer. Oh, why wasn't Molina born as a foreign dog?

In the morning the sunflower bloomed. 'Chitra, make some tea for Nila.'

Chitra slept on the floor of the room, on a mat. She rolled it up and went to get the tea. Molina said to Nila, 'Shut the door and come near me.'

Nila shut the door.

'Take the keys from under my pillow and open my almirah.' Molina's voice was as faint as someone speaking from the moon. Nila opened the almirah.

'There are some papers in the right hand drawer. Bring them here.'

Nila brought the papers.

Molina said, 'Keep these with you. They are yours.'

Nila opened them and found a cheque for twenty lakhs made out to her.

She was startled to see such a huge amount on the cheque. 'Mother, why are you giving me so much money?' Nila saw the tears rolling from Molina's eyes and wetting the pillow. She wiped them and said, 'I will get you treated with this money, Ma, you will get well. You'll walk and sing like before.'

The voice from the moon came again, 'Stay in the country. Don't go abroad.'

There was chaos in the house. Nikhil told her there was a call from Paris, from a girl called Danielle. She was arriving tonight in Calcutta.

Anirban had gone to the market to buy good fish and meat for their foreign guest. Two of his friends were coming to lunch too and at night there'd be some relatives for dinner. The pressure would be too much on Chitra. So they sent word and fetched Chitra's mother and aunt. Nila observed the festivities in the house from a distance. She watched Nikhil running around. 'What will your foreign guest like to drink? Is it okay if we don't serve French wine? I can arrange for Indian wine.'

Nila's voice shook, 'Dada, please sit beside Ma, talk to her a little.'

Nikhil said, 'The doctors have said she'll live for another two months.'

'I am scared, dada.'

Nikhil went to the airport in the evening and brought Danielle home. There were lots of relatives gathered in the house. They had all come to see Molina. After the dinner party, Anirban went and felt Molina's pulse. After that, he started whispering with Molina's brother and brother-in-law about the crematorium, arrangements, money, etc.

The words fell on Nila's ears like burning logs of fire and she burned alone.

Danielle touched Nila's burning shoulders and whispered in her ears, 'I've come to you from so far away, and you don't seem to be happy to see me.'

Nila didn't answer.

Sleeping arrangements for Danielle were made on Nila's bed. It was as natural for Nila's woman-friend to sleep on her bed as it was for the sun to rise in the east and for Molina to suffer pain. Chitra made the bed with two extra pillows. Before they went up, Anirban and Nikhil talked to Danielle for a long time about the French Revolution and French perfumes.

Nila sat by Molina's bed, alone. After midnight Danielle came into the room as silently as a cat and said, 'Come, let's go to bed.'

'You go and sleep. I'll sit here.'

'You are very tired, Nila. You need some rest. If you make yourself sick like this, you'll never be able to help her. Your family will be fussing over you. Get some sleep tonight and come back here in the morning,' Danielle whispered.

Nila realized the house was filling up with whispers.

Danielle dragged Nila's tired body upstairs.

All night long, Danielle's thirsty tongue played on Nila's motionless body. Suddenly Nila's deadwood body was flooded with life. Like a skilled painter Danielle painted her dreams on Nila's body.

When Nila was drowning in orgasmic tremors, when the first rays of the sun were kissing her long black tresses, Nila heard Chitra's scream and turned into stone.

Danielle left. She had never seen a Hindu death ceremony before. This was a new experience for her.

Nila didn't leave the bed. Nikhil came and called her. Chitra came and said, 'Didi, aunty was restless and called out "Nila, Nila". That's what woke me up. Then I called her again and again. But she didn't answer. She didn't open her eyes.'

After Chitra left, Nila got out of the bed, naked. She locked and bolted the door. All day long there were sounds—some knocked, some pushed, some requested her to come and see her mother's face one last time, some commanded. Manjusha, Molina's brothers and sisters and for some reason, even Anirban came to call her. But Nila didn't open the door for any of them. She stared at the golden sun outside the window. The sounds of the streets, of the death rituals, didn't reach her at all.

At night Chitra's tenuous weeping tore through the stifling stillness of the house. But there was no sigh ripping Nila apart and no tears burned her eyes.

Nila had wanted to sprinkle rose water on Molina's sorrows as if they'd doze off to the sweet smell, somewhere on the streets of Calcutta. If she had gently lifted the sorrows and left them on the terrace at night, perhaps they'd have forgotten to be sad and played with the moonbeams. These sorrows had never left Molina's side, not even when she went for a bath. It was as if they were bosom buddies and without them Molina would be helpless, vulnerable. The people in the house were relieved to surrender Molina into the hands of the sorrows; they'd call them in, offer them a seat and some tea. Nila had wanted to take them away secretly, and set them afloat in the Ganga one day. They'd float like hyacinths, like bits of straw, like dead snakes and go far, far away. Not one of Nila's wishes had come true. Today the sorrows went all the way to the burning ghat with Molina.

Thus We Float Away

Danielle went back to Paris, after wilting under the dust, pollution, traffic jams and violent honking, and eating snacks off the roadside and falling ill, chatting with Monique Claude Mathew in her Park Street flat on two days and watching Nikhil perform his mother's last rites. Danielle had tried to knock on the boulder. 'Regrets? You may not have returned from Paris and Molina would have had to go without seeing you. Why are you feeling guilty? It doesn't help anyone. Never think that way. Do you want to be a stagnant pond?'

But the boulder didn't budge or speak. Nila threw away Danielle's words on the rubbish heap nearby and said, 'You have troubled me enough. Now go away.'

This one phrase should have been enough for Danielle to go back to Paris without a backward glance. But she stopped at the door, left a piece of paper with Monique Mathew's address on the table and said she was Nicole's friend, a very nice person. If Nila ever needed to, she could look her up.

The nights sank in deeper silences. No one moaned in the house, Chitra didn't weep any more. She had cleared out Molina's bed. The pillows and linen from Molina's room had been cleaned. Anirban wanted to see patients in that room. He'd set it up with chairs, tables and an examination table. The sun vanished from the window. Nila stared at the darkness, her eyes focused on the moonless sky. On one such night Nikhil came and sat beside her, stroked her back comfortingly and said, 'You are not the only one. We are all feeling sad. But we can't bring back Ma. Life has to go on. That's how it is. Reality can be very harsh, but we have to accept it.'

Nila began to speak in a trance. 'We had a mother; she used to feed us, put us to bed, never let us get dirty, never let us feel any hurt.

People called her dark and plain, we did too. We called her silly and naïve. She felt sad but it didn't matter to us. Nothing about her mattered to us. We thought she was mother, not another human being. Mother means the one who doesn't have a life of her own, who shouldn't have one. If she screams in agony, we said, that's nothing, just your imagination. When she dies, we just cremate her and think we have done our duty. That she no longer exists, doesn't matter to us.'

'Don't talk rubbish. Come and have dinner.'

Both Anirban and Nikhil took three days off. Those three days there would be just rice and boiled vegetables cooked in the house. After that they would call the priest and Nila would have to perform her mother's last rites. Nikhil's duty extended for a whole month. He had wrapped a piece of unstitched cloth around his waist, another on his body and carried a cloth to sit on. He would eat only boiled vegetables and rice and yogurt with flat rice. For a month Nikhil would carry his sorrow thus. For Nila, the sorrow wasn't for a month but for three days. She was married and had gone into another family. Now she didn't have so many duties towards her mother. Anirban also maintained the rules faithfully. He was already drawing up the guest list for Molina's death ceremony at the end of the month. After that both Anirban and Nikhil would get busy; they would leave the memories behind and move forward. Neither of them saw the point in looking back and wallowing in misery. It was Nila alone who stood between life and death, asking questions.

Nila entered Molina's room sometimes and called out, 'Ma' absently. Then she realized, the room was empty and a lonely lamp burnt in the middle of it. She felt like resting with her head on Molina's breast, as she had after Sushanta left. Chitra came and lifted her up from there.

'Chitra, what did Ma want to say?'

'How can I say that, didi?'

'Did she want some water? Or the painkillers?'

'I don't know, didi.'

'Did she want to hug me close? Was she scared?'

'I don't know how people feel at the time of dying, what they want to say! Only those who have died know that, didi.'

Molina's absence was tearing Nila apart. Everything felt like dust and ashes. Nila wanted to be gone, like Molina.

There were many ways of going and visiting Monique Mathew wasn't one of them. But Nila went to her house anyway.

Monique was the same age as Molina, but she was healthy and alive. Her finger- and toe-nails were painted neatly, she wore mascara in her eyes and make-up on her face, lipstick on her lips and her brown hair was dyed blonde; she wore a filmy dress that showed off her breasts. Monique quickly made them some tea and talked as they drank it, 'Do you know the meaning of life? Douglas Adams said life begins at forty-two; I think he was wrong: life begins at forty-seven.' Monique shook her breasts and laughed. Nila wasn't amused.

Monique was a lively and vigorous person. She had married a Bengali man much younger than her. Now they were divorced and she was moving to Delhi. She used to teach French in the Alliance Française. Now she had got a job at the French embassy and she would have to leave Calcutta. But she simply couldn't bring herself to leave her house in Calcutta.

'Nila, there is no city like Calcutta! If you want a city to live in, it is Calcutta.'

Nila sighed.

Monique asked her, 'So, are you going back to Paris?'

'No.'

Two German Shepherds walked around the room arrogantly—Lullu and Bhullu. Bengali names for foreign dogs! They were named by Monique's ex-husband. Monique cuddled them a little and then sent them out to the garden to play.

'They are my life. I have lived with many men and I find it infinitely more satisfying to stay with pets. Trust is a big thing. Men break your trust, but dogs don't. Do you have any pets?'

'No.'

Nila sat there with her sad face and aloof eyes. She wore a white cotton sari, her hair was dishevelled, her skin chapped and the paint on her nails was chipped.

Monique stared at her long and hard and then said, 'You make me feel as if you are eternal, you will never die!'

Nila showed no interest in hearing an explanation of this 'feeling'. But Monique continued, 'You have become so depressed because you saw someone die in front of your eyes, that you've forgotten man is one species among many others. In this universe, man lives on a planet in one solar system among many in one galaxy among many others. You are like a dot, even smaller. Can you feel your existence anywhere in this vast system? Or your mother's? That mud-eating tortoise lives longer than man. That is nature and we cannot conquer it. We come and we go; thus we float away. Man's life is over in a blink of an eye. Just think, for billions of years so many things live and die on this planet. Once the dinosaurs ruled, and now they are no more. One day man will no longer exist; man's history will vanish in the deep dark hole of the past. We are nothing, nobody on the face of this vastness . . .' Monique's green eyes were lost. But they brightened up instantly, 'Do you believe in rebirth?'

Nila shook her head, she didn't believe.

'Those who believe in it have one comfort, if they couldn't do something in this birth, they can do it in the next. But if you believe in just one life, then don't waste time. Each one has his own life and time flies swiftly. You must take all you get. You must be selfish, Nila, there is no other way. Seize it, have your fill.'

Monique spoke nineteen to the dozen. Nila knew it was easy to say many wonderful things, sitting with your feet up on the sofa in an air-conditioned room, watching the trusted dogs play in the soft sunlight out in the garden.

Suddenly Nila spoke out of context. 'Monique, is your mother still alive?'

'Yes. She is ninety-one and she lives in a village in Toulouse.'

'Who lives with her?'

'She lives alone.'

'Alone?'

'Yes.'

'Why don't you go and live with her?'

'I don't have the time. Mother also doesn't want her children bothering her. Each to his own, Nila. No one wants to give up their independence. We go to visit Mother once a year for Christmas. But even that isn't possible every year.'

'Your mother can do everything on her own? Cook?'

'She can, still. When she can't do it anymore, she'll go into the government home for the aged. There will be people there to look after her.'

When Nila came home after spending half the day at Monique's, Nikhil informed her that Mithu had hung herself with her sari and committed suicide the night before.

Au Revoir

Mithu was lying on the floor. She was dressed in a red sari, floral garlands around her neck and sandal decorations on her forehead. She had perhaps never dressed up so much when she lived.

People who came to see her said, 'Oh, what a perfect face, what a sharp nose! Such long black hair! The mole on her chin made her face even more appealing. Her nature—what can I say; she was the best: always looked down when she walked, never looked an elder in the eye when she spoke, never misbehaved. These days, educated girls don't respect tradition. But Mithu did. She did the housework alone, she was a gem of a girl.'

Nila saw Mithu's mother wailing. She wailed, but there was a tinge of relief in it.

Mithu's father, Sadhanbabu, was wiping his tears with his shirt. The worry lines on his forehead were gone. Now there was no need to worry about Mithu. Now it was just the burning ghats, the pyre and ashes. Mithu would be wiped off the face of this earth. No one would be hassled about the black ashes of her dark body. Mithu herself escaped from the humiliation of being dark. But her suicide brought even greater relief for her parents, her brother, who could now marry a suitable girl for a huge dowry.

Mithu's death left Nila speechless.

Anirban shook Nila and brought her to her senses as he asked her when she was going back to Paris.

'I am not going to Paris. I'll stay here.'

'Here where?'

'Here, in Calcutta.'

'Where in Calcutta?'

'In this house.'

'After marriage your husband's house is your home. There lie all your rights. Girls come to their father's house for a short while, not to stay.'

Nila looked around at her room. It had her bed, her books, clothes, old letters, her favourite tanpura, harmonium, everything. It was a broader horizon than her life out of a suitcase, in Paris.

Why would Nila have to go to Paris? Because the neighbours and relatives were already whispering that she had left her husband.

'Yes, I have. What is it to them?'

Anirban shouted, 'It is nothing to them. It is all to me. I will not be able to show my face to anyone. You want to disgrace the whole family?'

'If I don't get along with my husband, how is that a disgrace?'

'It is.' Anirban insisted. 'If you want to stay in this society, you have to do what everyone approves of. Either you go back to Paris, or kill yourself like Mithu and let us off. This is my last word.' After Anirban left with his last words, Nila soaked in the bathtub for a long while. No, she didn't have a single tear in her eyes.

Late in the night, when the whole house slept, Nila went into Molina's room and lay on the floor with one arm extended like she often slept hugging Molina close to her. She whispered, 'Ma, why aren't you here?' Nila's shadow was the giant that charged at her as she lay with her back to the lamp. Nila decided she would leave Calcutta.

'Go after your mother's shradhh.' Anirban and everyone else said. Nila had no interest in Molina's shradhh. She saw no point in feeding people and calling the priest.

'Your mother's spirit will suffer. Don't behave like this.'

Nila laughed, 'Ma is used to suffering and her spirit will also be able to take it, this is nothing.'

She packed her suitcase. But going away was not so easy. There were many hassles like buying the ticket, cashing the cheque, transferring the money, etc. Her return ticket had lapsed and so it would have to be a new ticket. Since she didn't want to stay until the shradhh, Anirban gave Nikhil some money to go and buy a cheap air ticket from Calcutta to Paris.

'Nila barred his way, 'Give him back that money. I will buy the ticket.'

'Where will you get the money?'

Gradually the facts emerged: when Molina got her inheritance, she sold everything and kept the money in the bank. Those papers weren't in her drawer, they were in Nila's hands.

'How much?'

'Twenty lakhs.'

Anirban sat down heavily, holding his head.

'What will you do with all that money? Kishanlal will pay for all your needs. Leave that money behind, we have a lot of expenses coming up. The house is old and it needs work.'

'But this house isn't mine and I am not of this house. This is your house; so you take care of it. Don't eye my money.'

'Do you know that as per the law, this money will be divided into three parts and you will only get one part of it? When have you ever heard of a girl taking her inheritance? They usually give their share to their brother.'

'If Ma had wanted it to be divided, she wouldn't have written that cheque in my name.'

'Writing isn't everything. There's such a thing as inheritance.'

Anirban invited all his relatives to explain this fact to his daughter. Molina's sisters, brothers, brother-in-law and even Manjusha came and tried: 'There is such a thing as inheritance. Although girls go away to their husbands, they don't forget their father and brothers. They'll die for them They never covet their father's property; if they do, people don't approve of them. Girls should be unselfish, unstinting, unspoiled, uncontroversial, unalloyed, undefiled, unassuming . . .

'Molina must have lost her mind; she didn't know what she was doing. One shouldn't take it seriously, even if it was really her signature [or perhaps Nila had forged it]. Even if it was a real signature, there was no point in taking so much money out of the country. It wasn't as if Kishanlal didn't make good money. With two restaurants, he lived comfortably. And if she insisted, she could keep that money in a bank here, for a rainy day perhaps. Or she could buy a house with it and the rent could be deposited into her account. People went abroad to earn money and send home. No one took money from India to a foreign country. Was Nila out of her mind?'

'Yes, I am,' Nila said.

Who could handle a lunatic!

Nila believed Anirban advised Nikhil not to sue her because it would look bad. Sometimes the censure of society made the wrong hold itself back. But the bankers made her life hell. The shrewd businessman talked himself silly. 'So much money going out of the country, it's not a joke. Why? Where? How did you come to have so much money? Tax papers? Get the permission from the Reserve Bank, etc. etc.'

After endless harassment, Nila was able to draw about fifty thousand rupees and the rest was supposed to be transferred to her account in Paris, for which she submitted the necessary papers, although the banker couldn't tell her when the money would reach her there. Nila surrendered herself to the uncertain and bought her ticket.

There wasn't a daily flight from Calcutta to Paris or Nila would have boarded it that same day. She would have to wait for two weeks. For her it was like two years. She wanted to escape from this dirty society. Now she didn't feel Calcutta was her own. She began to feel as if she had never known it, never played in the dust and grime of the city and never whispered to the breeze on the Ganga. For Nila, Calcutta was now a burning ghat. It used to be her mother's cotton sari where she wiped her sweat and tears and stood waiting at the door. It used to be Molina's large, black eyes, which flew into the sun, into the night and wherever Nila dived, they searched for Nila. It was as if someone had wrapped up the fun of curling up in Molina's rug in the winters, eating savoury snacks on fields of shefali, into a parcel of darkness and hurled it far, dug a hole in the silence and dropped Calcutta into its depths and run away. Now there was no one called Calcutta, nothing called Calcutta.

One summer afternoon, in the burning heat, Nila sought refuge in Monique's shade and grace.

'Talk to me about France, Monique, not Calcutta.'

Monique, drowned in red wine, talked of France. In the lazy afternoon Lullu and Bhullu were in the balcony, Monique's driver Suranjit lay under the tree to spare himself the fiery sparks, the cook Bindiya was humming as she braided her hair, the gardener Haridas lay beside the dogs like some elderly cousin telling them stories and in the cool room Monique's green eyes brightened as she told her stories. Her forefathers lived in the Chateau Montaigne in southern France. Monique was full of her aristocratic breeding. The next moment she could see the Chateau fall apart in her mind's eye and her eyes dulled, as if she was seeing the Bastille being stormed and heard the cry of the revolution for herself.

Then it was just that—egalite. She uttered the word twice.

'I am going to Delhi tomorrow for three days. But I am very worried about Lullu-Bhullu's feeding; who'll feed them?' Monique's mossy eyes held concern. 'Will you do this for me, Nila? I'll leave the keys with you and show you where the food is, some in the fridge and some outside and two bottles of mineral water. The water has to be changed thrice and they feed twice a day.'

'Sure, I can do it, but . . .'

'But what?'

'Won't this Bindiya, Suranjit or Haridas be here?'

'Yes, they'll be here.'

Monique lit a cigarette and smoked some rings into Sunil Das' Horses on the wall and said, 'They'll stay, but . . .'

'But what?'

'But my Lullu and Bhullu don't eat rubbish or leftovers like the dogs here. They have packed food brought from Paris.'

'So?'

'So I suspect they may not feed the dogs.' Monique's voice was low.

'Why wouldn't they?' Nila was curious.

'Because they'll eat the food themselves.'

'They'll eat it up? How strange! Have they done that before?'

'No.'

'So then?'

'They may.'

Nila returned home feeling positively ill.

Nikhil scattered some cooked rice in the courtyard and called to the crows to come and feed. Only when they did that, would he be able to eat. It wasn't easy doing your mother's last rites!

Nila stood behind him and said, 'Do you really believe that Ma has become a crow?'

Nikhil looked away from the sky and said, 'Are you mad? I'm doing it because it's a custom.'

'You call yourself a communist, but you go to the temple in Tarapith and feed the crows before you eat—it doesn't add up,' Nila said as she squashed a rotten tomato from the garden underfoot.

Nikhil gave a tired smile. Nila dragged him inside and took the cloth from his neck. 'Look at this, you have bathed in this and now you're wearing it till it dries? Leave this and wear a shirt. This is no way to rid yourself of your debt to your mother—rubbish! Go and have a bath and get dressed. Let's go to a restaurant and have lunch.'

'Leave it. Just a few more days to go.' Nikhil was weary. He wouldn't go anywhere and he wanted to eat the boiled fare.

'Then eat before the crows at least.' Nila shoved the food into his mouth.

After lunch, Nikhil left the suffocating heat indoors and sat on the grass with his legs outstretched. There was a light breeze. Nila came and sat beside him.

'Dada, tell me the truth: do you really believe in all these rituals and rules of Hinduism?'

'Does one ever believe in them?'

'Then why do you do it?'

'There's an element of fun in it.'

'Fun? I see no fun in a bunch of illogical rules and pointless emotions.'

'Suppose Pujas were suddenly cancelled, would you be happy? Won't you miss it? How would you have the festivities and the fun?'

'Dada, do you remember, when we played hide and seek here,

you often hid behind that stone bench? And I always found you first.'

'Your hiding place was different—the topmost branch of the mango tree.'

'Do you remember about Prafulla's guava tree? You went and stole all the ripe fruit and Prafulla came to complain to Baba.'

Nikhil laughed loudly.

'How did you like Baba's hiding?'

'And at night, full moon nights, when there weren't so many houses all around, Ma used to sit here and sing the songs of Rajanikanta. What a lovely voice she had . . .'

For a long time neither of them spoke.

Nila gazed at the spreading pink tinge of the sunset indifferently and broke the silence, 'Dada, Ma will come back one day. She'll wash her feet at the tap and say she'd gone off to Darjeeling suddenly and ask if we are all fine. At night she'll tell us stories of Darjeeling and feed us, she'll wear a red-bordered sari smelling of moth balls, sit on this field and sing to us like the old days . . .'

Suddenly Nila stood up and said, 'Today I saw an eighty-five-year-old man walking on the streets. He doesn't have to be alive! I hate to see anyone live these days. If all the trees in world die today, and all the mountains are razed to the ground and the rivers and seas dry up, all animals and men would die in that wasteland. And if only this earth fell off the orbit, went too close to the sky and burnt to ashes!'

Nila realized she was shaking. She felt weak. She lay down beside Nikhil on the grass and spoke softly, 'Do you know something, Dada? I feel alone, very lonely.'

'Are you really going back to Paris?'

'Do I have a choice, dada?'

'When will you return?'

'Where?'

'Where? To Calcutta, of course.'

Nila didn't reply.

'You are angry with Baba, right? But once you leave, he will worry about you as usual, how you are, whether you are happy or not.'

'Happy.' The word escaped on a sigh.

'Baba didn't know that Kishanlal had married once before. I came to know just the other day when Sunil told me. I haven't told anyone.'

'Don't tell anyone. What's the point? Baba will only get anxious about dishonour to the family.'

'Sunil said that's why you left Kishan. Apparently that marriage was an arranged one, to get him the citizenship. Don't take that to heart.'

'I am not.'

'This time, send me a good bottle of Chanel. The first one you sent was fake.'

'How did you come to that conclusion?'

'It doesn't smell right. The ones I buy here in Calcutta have a strong smell.'

'The one I sent was the real thing.'

'I have thrown it away.'

'You've thrown the real thing and kept the fake? All that money wasted!'

Nila enjoyed lying on the grass. The breeze blew her hair off her face. The birds were flocking to their nests. The two cats who were sitting on the neighbour's fence were also heading for home.

Nikhil also said, 'Let me go and chat on the Internet.'

Nila lay there on the grass. One by one the stars blinked in the sky and Nila looked for the brightest. When Nila was a child, Molina told her that people became stars after they died.

On the day Nila left, Manjusha came to pack her suitcase and kept on saying, 'Try to adjust with Kishanlal. No one forced you into this marriage. You opted for it.'

Anirban called Paris and told Kishanlal when Nila would reach there. He did his duty as the father.

Before she entered the airport, Nikhil took a bottle from his pocket and handed it to Nila, 'Keep this.'

'What is it?'

'Ma's ashes.'

'Ma is not ashes to me.' Nila gave it back to him.

Nila entered the aircraft, leaned back in her seat and bid Calcutta au revoir.

Then she asked herself, 'Nila, do you know where you are going, to whom?'

She answered herself, 'No.'

'Do you know what you want to do with this life of yours?'

'No.'

Benoir Dupont

From Dumdum to Charles de Gaulle.

In that journey, Benoir Dupont happened.

Nila had a window seat and Benoir sat next to her. Benoir was a blonde, blue-eyed, pink-lipped, Frenchman, six feet three inches tall in blue jeans and white T-shirt, black boots and with a Macintosh laptop.

His eyes were restless, alighting on Nila, on her aloof eyes, long black hair, the mole on her cheek, the tiny mark on her forehead. She stared into the strange darkness outside and looked for one lone star in it.

The puffy white clouds were flying somewhere, home perhaps. Everyone went home, except Nila. When they were served dinner she said she didn't want any.

'What are you searching in the dark?' Benoir finally asked her.

'Are you speaking to me?'

'Yes.'

Nila smiled wanly. 'I am searching in the dark for darkness.'

'Can you see anything in the dark?'

'Yes, you can see the dark.'

'Strange.'

'The dark is also beautiful. It's different.'

Benoir sipped his champagne slowly. 'I have never seen it.'

He finished his champagne and ate his dinner. Then he said, 'There's perhaps no one else on this flight who isn't eating or drinking, but just looking into the darkness.'

Nila didn't turn.

'Are you going to Paris as a tourist?'

Nila didn't turn.

'Sorry. I guess I am disturbing you.'

Nila turned, 'Did you say something to me?'

'Are you going to Paris as a tourist?'

'No.'

'Then?'

'To live.'

'What do you do there—study?'

'No.'

'Work?'

'No.'

Benoir's blue eyes held curiosity. 'Will you live alone there or do you have a family?'

Nila didn't answer.

'Do you have relatives there?'

Nila shook her head.

'Who is there?'

'No one.'

'So you live there alone?'

Benoir asked for a bottle of red wine after his dinner and said, 'I am Benoir Dupont.'

Nila nodded.

'You are?'

'Nila.'

'Nila, the Indian beauty.'

It was obvious to Nila that Benoir Dupont wanted to talk to her. It was normal. On a long flight it was tiresome to sit stiffly in one place and people usually asked their neighbours where they lived, if they were married or not, how many children they had, what they liked to eat, what was their taste in music or books, what their hobbies were, etc. Benoir Dupont also wanted to ease his boredom and was keen to uncover the mystery of this mysterious woman. On her first trip to Paris, Nila had posed similar questions to the Dutch lady next to her, more to discover about a white person than for anything else. Gabriella was forty-three and for the last five years she had been buying fabric from India and taking it back to sell in her country. She also bought paste, jewellery, incense, etc. She had given Nila detailed descriptions of how much profit she made after spending on her travel and capital expenditure, how much rent she paid and what the cost of food was. She even went personal and told her that she was single and lived alone, though not quite. She had affairs and sometimes lived with them for a year or two. Her last lover was Abu Nasser from Egypt. After a couple of months she'd said to Nasser, enough was enough and he should get lost. He didn't see her point and finally she had to set the police after him. Then she had gotten even more intimate and said, 'Nasser was done in two minutes flat.'

'Have you ever been to Amsterdam?' No; what were the attractions there? Prostitutes. Did one go to see prostitutes? Sure. Along the streets the whores stood naked behind glass windows and thousands of people thronged to see them. Nila felt sick. What else was there? Freedom. What kind of freedom? Freedom to fly. Marijuana lent you a pair of wings and you could fly all over the city. When the flight landed, Gabriella said bye and went away, without a backward glance. She hadn't asked for Nila's address. It was a similar experience on her way from Paris to Calcutta. She knew that all this talk was merely so that the twelve-hour journey felt a little more interesting. So she didn't pay much heed to Benoir's unbridled excitement.

This was his first trip to India. He went to Delhi and from there to Agra. Then he went to Chandannagar and Calcutta. Now he was headed back home to Paris without any major mishaps or illness. Of course, before he left, his doctor in Paris had inoculated him against malaria and every other disease there was in the world. It was the same when Benoir had gone to Africa.

'But I don't need immunization when I go somewhere. Why do you?'

'We do.'

'What do you mean "we"?'

'Europeans—whites.'

'Oh.'

'Tell me something, why are Indian women so beautiful?'

Nila was startled by the question.

'But I am not beautiful.'

Benoir smiled. 'I didn't know Indian women were such lovely liars too.'

'Why would I be beautiful, I am not white.'

'Are white women beautiful? They are anaemic. See how uncouthly they walk, how harshly they speak. Breasts thrust out, necks craned, they look like camels. One can sleep with them but not make love to them.' Benoir leaned towards Nila and spoke.

'So you have not fallen in love with a white woman so far?'

'I did fall in love with an Ethiopian; beautiful as fire. But she . . . is gone with the wind. I have decided, if I fall in love, it'll be with an Indian woman.' Benoir winked.

'Where will you find one? You don't live in India.'

'So? There's no dearth of Indian women in Paris.'

'They are all married.'

'Are you also married?'

'Yes, I am.'

Benoir's forehead creased in a frown. 'But you said you have no one there.'

'I don't live with my husband.'

'Quite complicated.'

Then Benoir told her about his marriage. He was married to a white woman and he had a daughter named Jacqueline.

'How old are you, Nila, not over twenty surely?'

'Twenty-seven.'

'Really? You don't look a day over nineteen.'

'How old are you?'

'Twenty-five.'

'Really?' Nila was surprised.

'Why? Do I look older? How old?'

Nila had thought he wasn't any younger than forty-two. But she lowered it by a notch and said, 'Thirty or thereabouts.'

Benoir laughed loudly, 'You make me feel ancient.'

How could she think otherwise when he had seven wrinkles on his forehead and four around each eye?

The lights in the aircraft were dimmed for the passengers to push back their seats and go to sleep. If they didn't feel sleepy, they could watch TV and if they didn't like that, there was always the music. Benoir didn't want to do any of these things. He finished one bottle of red wine after another and talked to her: he had married Pascale four years ago. Initially the marriage was good. But now the excitement had dulled. He hadn't really wanted so routine a life. He had wanted something else, something different.

'Like what?'

'I don't know for sure. But something different.'

Some passengers were reading with the reading light on and some were sleeping. Benoir spoke in whispers so that he didn't disturb anyone. And in order to whisper, he had to lean towards Nila. She also had to lean towards him.

'Where do you live in Paris?'

'At first I lived near the Gare du Nord, then in the fifth arrondissement, near Gare d'Austerlitz, at a friend's place.'

'Is that where you will go now?'

'I don't know.'

'Are you a lesbian?'

Nila looked out of the window; dawn was breaking.

'Or are you bisexual?'

Even Benoir could sense that Nila was like a reckless refugee. The hesitation showed in Nila's voice.

'Didn't you ever fall in love with anyone in Paris?'

Nila shook her head.

'No French lover?'

'No.'

'Do you always talk so little?'

'This is not little.'

'I know I am a little garrulous. But I've heard that Indians also talk a lot. I find you more European than Indian.'

'Europeans talk less?'

'They weigh their words. They don't talk to just anyone or for no reason.'

'And you?'

'Perhaps I'm not weighing my words, but it certainly isn't for no reason.'

'What is the reason?'

'You are still a mystery to me. The reason is to go deeper into the mystery.'

Nila looked into Benoir's blue eyes. He was far better looking than any of the handsome men she had ever fantasized about. His blonde hair lay carelessly on his forehead; Nila wanted to push them back. She wanted to touch his smooth skin under that pretext. Nila looked out the window instead. There was a strange light in the sky; she had never seen anything like that before.

'Amazing!' Nila murmured. 'How can colours be so beautiful?'

She wanted to touch those colours of the horizon, grab it by the fistful and spread it on herself. Benoir also leaned forward, to the window, to Nila.

Nila didn't realize that Benoir had taken her hand in his and was stroking her fingers.

He stared at the wonder in Nila's eyes and said, 'Wonderful.'

'Isn't it?'

'It is.'

'I have never seen such beautiful light before.'

'Neither have I. Where did you get such a light, Nila?'

Nila turned, startled. She realized Benoir's gaze rested on her and not on the sky.

'Haven't you seen the light in the sky?'

'I have; I've seen the light in your eyes.'

Nila knew in a short while Benoir's eagerness would dull. When they reached Paris, Benoir would say 'bye' and walk away. The dreamy eyes would be gone. He would merge into the faceless crowd and Nila would stand there, neither here nor there.

But she was surprised when, after reaching Paris, Benoir said, 'I'm sure you're not in a hurry. You will go near Gare d'Austerlitz, right? I'm sure your friend wouldn't mind if you stop by at my place for a cup of coffee?'

'She doesn't even know I am here.' Nila laughed.

'So there's no one waiting for you in Paris? How fortunate. Come on, let's go.'

Benoir had parked his car in the airport car park—a red Peugeot.

They headed for Rue de Rennes. Nila gazed out into the calm, pretty morning in Paris; she breathed in her fill of the clean air. She didn't have to stop and ponder if it was spring or summer, she smelt spring in the air. The grass was a banana-leaf green and Paris was decked in fresh green, with flowers on trees, on the grass, on the window sills. Nila looked at Paris in bloom with new eyes.

Benoir parked his car and took his own suitcase. Nila's luggage stayed in the boot of the car.

His home was beautifully decorated. Nila asked, 'Your wife isn't home?'

'She lives in Strassburg. She works in the mayor's office and comes home on holidays.' Benoir's voice was toneless as he delivered this information. Nila sat on the sofa and glanced around the room. The sunlight petered in through the heavy curtains. There was a futon beside the sofa and next to it was the tape deck and some books on a shelf, some CDs and some video tapes. There was a kitchen facing the room. Benoir poured water into the coffee machine and asked, 'Sugar?'

'I don't have coffee.'

'Then what do you have?'

'Tea.'

'I don't have any tea.'

Nila rose to leave. She guessed she should have told him earlier that she didn't drink coffee since that's what he'd invited her for. Since she hadn't told him and since it wasn't possible to arrange for tea now, she assumed it was only decent for her to leave now. Benoir came and stood in front of her. He held her gaze. She dropped hers.

'Just because there is nothing to drink, do you have to leave?' Benoir asked.

Nila didn't answer. She stared at her nails.

Benoir took her hands and began to move closer to Nila, as close as her hammering heart. Nila jerked away and Benoir grabbed the Indian beauty, brought her close and began to kiss her.

'What are you doing!' Nila pulled away.

Benoir spoke in an intimate voice, 'Drink me up, Nila, drink me.'

It didn't seem real to Nila. She felt she was still sitting on the plane, looking at the strange light in the sky and having weird dreams.

No one had ever kissed Nila like that. She didn't know a kiss could be so deep. Her whole body felt weightless and Benoir picked up that weightless body, laid her gently on a bed as soft as clouds and began to undress her slowly. 'You are so beautiful, Nila, oh Nila, the Lord has made you with great care.' He kissed her all over, on her forehead, ears, eyes, nose, lips, tongue, cheeks, chin, neck, shoulders, back, breast, arms, hands, fingers, belly, thighs, the joint between them, knees, toenails and soles. Nila's whole body was wet with kisses. She closed her eyes. She had never got such pleasure in all her twenty-seven years. She never knew she would ever feel such pleasure. She had never even imagined that in this cruel, grotesque world, love could be so intimate, sex could be so perfect.

In Nila's life, unknown to herself, Benoir Dupont had happened.

Benoir's Wild Elixir

Nila's day passed in a daze. In the evening Benoir dropped her off at Danielle's place and reminded her, 'Tomorrow evening, seven o'clock at the Closerie des Lilas, okay?'

'Okay.'

Danille was stunned when she opened the door and found Nila standing there. 'You? When did you reach Paris?'

'Today.'

Nila entered the room and found it the same except there was a different girl in it.

'That's Natalie, my lover.'

Natalie was lying on the bed wearing a flimsy dress. She sat up. Nila and Natalie did what everyone did upon being introduced, they shook hands and Danielle and Nila kissed each other on the cheeks.

Natalie was from Provence and she was new to Paris and yes, she would be staying here. She smiled sweetly. Her brown hair was shorn short and she had brown eyes. Natalie knew all about Nila. Danielle had told her.

Danielle said, 'I thought you were not coming back to Paris.'

Nila pulled up a chair. 'I didn't think so either. But I had to.'

'Where have you put up?'

Nila couldn't answer that one immediately. She thought she was putting up at Danielle's. But the question sat on her heavy tongue and wouldn't let it move.

Danielle took a long drag at her cigarette and said, 'Let me tell you right now that Natalie and I stay in this room. You'll have to go somewhere else.' She handed the cigarette to Natalie. 'So, do you know where you'll go?'

Nila had no idea where she'd go if she didn't get to stay at Danielle's. She fingered the piece of paper with Benoir's address in her pocket as if she was touching his body. Benoir's ecstatic cries still lingered in her ears, her body was still wet from his elixir and she was still in a daze.

Natalie handed the cigarette back to Danielle.

'Would you like some—marijuana?'

Nila had never had marijuana before; one drag and her head was spinning.

Natalie's clothes and shoes were strewn around the room. There were more books now and two, instead of one, computers on the table.

'My paintings? And the easel?' Nila asked.

Danielle puffed on the grass and smiled, 'There was no room. I had to throw them away.'

Nila thought Danielle was joking.

'Tell me the truth, where are they? I want to start painting again.'

Danielle repeated, 'They're trashed.'

Danielle had trashed them because she found them irritating, so she was sure to find a discussion about them equally trying.

Nila changed the topic. 'I met your Monique in Calcutta.'

Danielle was very excited, 'Really? Isn't she a wonderful person?'

Monique was crazy about Calcutta. Her knowledge of the city could put an expert to shame. She knew more than Jean Racine about Calcutta. It was so dusty, so crowded and so filthy and yet she loved Calcutta and stayed on there. She helped the poor generously. She had a big heart. No one else loved the Bengalis more than she did.

Nila halted Danielle's flow and said, 'I don't think so.'

'You don't think what?'

'I don't think that Monique has a big heart or that she truly respects the people of Calcutta.' Nila's words were enough to ignite Danielle who brought the roof down. 'You are a strange creature, Nila. You just cannot appreciate anyone. How can you not praise someone like Monique? I have done so much for you, I've gone all the way to Calcutta to hold your hand, to give you support and what have you done in return? You've behaved horribly with me, ignored me and humiliated me. I was the one who gave you shelter when you had nowhere to go. But you lied to me the very first day—you said you couldn't dance when you can. I got you invited to Nicole's and you deliberately wore jeans instead of a dress. Nicole was so courteous and you didn't even thank her before you left. Has Catherine helped you any less? But you landed up at her place out of the blue. No one does that in this country and if it had been someone else, she'd have called the police. But she's the one who introduced you in the factory, showed you where the post office or the restaurant was. Yet, you never spoke a civil word to her, never smiled at her. You feel others will slave for you, that it's their duty and you will lap it all up like a queen. I have seen what a bourgeois family you come from. That's where you got spoilt. You get whatever you want and you have never had to work hard for anything. Nila, change your attitude or you will suffer. No one is sitting around waiting to be your slave. Even the rich in Europe don't live in the style in which you grew up, in a poor country like India. And you have come back here to the life of a labourer? To live in poverty? You even have hobbies! You wanted those paintings and easel—I have trashed them. You know nothing of art. They were worthless and so I have trashed them. Now, it's getting late. We have a dinner to attend. We can't give you any more time. You have pestered me enough, no more.'

Nila quickly walked out with her heavy suitcases. She brought them down the stairs one by one. There was no Ramkiran here to help her and neither was her car waiting at the door. Here she didn't even have a destination. Once downstairs, Nila wanted to ring Benoir from the phone booth nearby.

What would she say! Let me stay in your house! But why should she feel shame? Hadn't all her shame flowed away in Benoir's wild lovemaking that day?

Nila hesitated for a moment and then dialled Benoir's number. He picked it up.

'What are you doing?'

'Thinking of you.'

'Really?'

'Really, truly, absolutely.'

'I am thinking of you too.'

'Your friend must be happy to have you?'

Nila stopped short. The words that her friend wasn't happy to have her back rolled around on Nila's tongue. If they rolled off it, Benoir would know that she was unwanted in this city. Nila was afraid Benoir would also not want her any more. She knew everyone kicked the dog that was kicked by one. She swallowed the words lolling about on her tongue and said, 'Yes.'

'Have you told her about me?'

'Yes.'

'What did she say?'

'She said, why don't you go and stay with him.' Nila waited, waited for Benoir to say why don't you? My heart and soul yearns for you, oh lover mine, come, come to me.

Benoir laughed and said, 'Tomorrow, Closerie des Lilas, one hundred and seventy one, Boulevard Montparnasse. Don't forget.'

Nila remembered. Her memory hadn't lapsed yet but at the moment she needed four walls and a roof over her head more than a meal at a restaurant. She asked, ' We'll go there and eat. Then what?'

'Then we'll come to my place for coffee.'

'Then?'

'Guess!'

'I can't guess. And you know I don't drink coffee.'

'Then you drink me.'

'I am not that thirsty.'

'You are.'

'How do you know?'

'I know.'

'Quite the expert, are you?'

'At least a little. Couldn't you tell?'

Benoir laughed. Nila was silent. She heard him say, 'Tell your friend you'll get back late tomorrow night. Don't worry, I'll take you home.'

If she had any money, she'd have gone to a hotel. She would have been spared the embarrassment of appealing to people and bothering them. But at this moment she could only think of Kishan and Sunil who could help her. When Anirban had spoken to Kishan, he hadn't said he was done with Nila for good. She took a cab and gave him the address of Rue de Foubaud. But then she changed her mind and asked him to take her to Rue de Rivoli.

Chaitali was at home. She was stunned to see Nila. 'Where were you?'

Nila realized no one was expecting her. Danielle had asked her in the same tone of voice. Everyone thought the girl from Calcutta would stay there. Even Chaitali had done the simple math and realized that Paris wasn't for Nila and she wasn't for Paris. She stepped around Chaitali and entered the house, unwelcome and uninvited.

Chaitali of the startled eyes wanted to know, 'What is the matter?'

'Nothing. I have come from Calcutta. I'm looking for a place to stay.'

'Just now Kishan had called. He said he went to the airport in the morning. That's what was decided.'

'Not with me.'

'He said you held a Frenchman's hands and walked out without even looking at him.'

Nila's head was spinning. She asked for some water.

'What is wrong with you?'

'Nothing!'

'There must be something.'

Nila reclined on the sofa. The suitcases stood at the door. Chaitali didn't ask her to take them inside or whether she had had a tiring journey or a bath or food. But this same Chaitali had cared for her like a sister when she had first arrived in Paris.

Chaitali sat with a doleful expression for a while and then called Sunil.

'What did Sunilda say?'

'Listen Nila, Sunil's relationship with Kishan is ruined because of you. Now if Kishan finds out that you are staying with us, he'll make life hell for Sunil. It doesn't look good.'

Nila said, 'I haven't come from Calcutta to go and stay with Kishan.'

'Then?'

'No, I haven't come to stay here either. I'll rent a house very soon. But I'd like to stay here until my money arrives from Calcutta. Please don't ask me to go somewhere else.'

Chaitali got up to make another call to Sunil. But the dejection on her face was enough to make Nila pick up her suitcases and walk out. Chaitali didn't call her back or ask her to stay. As she reached the street, Sunil's car screeched to a halt next to her.

'Where are you going, Nila?'

She didn't know where she was going. Sunil suggested that if she wanted to go to Kishan's, he could drop her off there. But Nila wasn't going there. Then was she going to her friend's house? Sunil could reach her there too. No, that wasn't where she was going either. So where was she going? She wasn't going to anyone's house. Any street, any pavement was her address now. At least no one could throw her off the street. Nila stood stiffly and Sunil dragged her inside. Then, after calming her down, Sunil asked her why she didn't want to go back to Kishan.

Nila was cool, 'I don't feel like going to Kishan.'

Chaitali's voice was hard. 'Women have to do many things they don't feel like doing, Nila.'

Sunil felt Nila should go back to Calcutta.

But Nila didn't want to do either. She wouldn't go back to that filthy society in Calcutta. If she returned to her father's house it would dishonour the family name and if she stayed anywhere else in that city, people would call her names. She could always take a job and live alone. But that would be a horrible life, she knew. A woman who had deserted her husband was a fallen woman, she was a slut and lusty men would pounce on her in no time at all.

They raised the question of marrying again.

Who would marry a woman who was once married? If someone did, he would be either seventy years old, or a lout or a lunatic . . .

Chaitali asked the relevant question. 'Whose hand were you holding at the airport? Who is he?'

Nila's throat was parched. This time she poured herself some water instead of asking for it. She gulped it down and said, 'A friend.'

'A Frenchman—did he come with you from Calcutta or did he go to pick you up?'

'I met him on the flight.'

'And you became friends so soon?'

Sunil laughed a mirthless laugh.

'It is not so easy to be friends, Nila. Even after knowing each other for twelve years, there can be no real friendship.'

'But sometimes you strike up a rapport in an instant, don't you?'

Sunil laughed. It was not in agreement. 'Let that be. You'll understand in time that life is not an easy game, whether in Paris or in Calcutta.' He stopped, stretched out his legs, spread out his arms on the back of the sofa and said, 'In Kishanlal's state of mind, he can divorce you at any time. Then you'll have to go back to Calcutta.'

Chaitali rose to go and put Tumpa to bed. As she walked to the bedroom she said, 'But why? All her troubles would be over if her French friend marries her.'

Nila now moved closer to Sunil and explained that she needed to borrow some money. She'd return it all, including the previous debt, when she got her money from Calcutta. Around five thousand francs would be enough. She could wait a couple of days for it. Sunil couldn't understand why she needed so much money; she would stay in his house, there was no rent or food to buy. It was true. But she needed the money. She had some plans. She had also not come to Paris to live hand to mouth. If Sunil had any doubts he could call Nikhil and find out whether she really had twenty lakhs of rupees or not.

A bed was made for Nila in Chaitali's puja room. She had to sleep amidst Lakshmi, Saraswati, Durga. She tossed and turned all night long. The night would end and then the morning, afternoon and finally the evening would limp around; then she could dive into that sea of pleasure again. Nila stared at the hands of the clock. Time had never moved so slowly for her.

She lay in the bathtub all afternoon, washed herself scrupulously and then tried on every nice dress that she owned. Finally she settled for the best one, made up her face, wore some lipstick, turned the bottle of Poison upside down on her whole body and was ready—it was just five-thirty. She sat still. If she lazed around the dress would get crumpled, her hair would be messed; if she ate or drank, her make-up would go. So she didn't do a thing except to hear the hammering of her own heart and watch the movement of the clock's hands.

When the Indian beauty came down to the Closerie des Lilas, the Frenchman stared at her wide eyed and almost flew to greet her, gather her in his arms and sink his tongue deep into her mouth. Their tongues spoke to one another. They drank each other's essence like nectar. The beauty trembled at this taste of a kiss that made her weak at the knees.

Benoir said, 'You drive me crazy, Nila.'

Her carefully reddened lips were back to their dark brown shade. Nila went to powder her nose and reapply her lipstick. She came back with red lips, reassured.

Nila sat in front of Benoir and asked, 'How could you do this in front of so many people?'

'What did I do?'

Nila bit her lips. Her lips smiled and the eyes held shame. 'Don't you know what you did?'

Benoir leaned forward, saw himself in Nila's eyes and said, 'Was it a crime?'

'You kissed me.'

Benoir laughed, 'You didn't resist.'

Nila pulled the menu towards herself and hid her face. He pulled it aside and looked into her eyes, 'Did you?'

She laughed and lowered her eyes, her chin with the mole on it.

'I have taken my kiss, how does it matter to anyone else?'

Nila had seen men and women kissing on the streets, in parks, in the metro all the time and gradually it had become something like the maple leaves or apples hanging from trees. But if it came on her, it was something else. Of course it was different, if the man happened to be blonde and handsome and the kiss a French kiss.

'What will you have? Foie gras?'

'What is that?'

'Duck's liver. Ducks are fed very well and then their liver is taken out to make this delicacy.'

Nila's appetite died when she heard this description.

'Then how about a salad—mozzarella and tomatoes?'

'Cottage cheese? I don't like it.'

'So what will you have?'

'Is there any fish? I come from a coastal land.'

'There're some sea fish.'

'No, those aren't good. How about river fish?'

Benoir glanced at the menu and shook his head, no.

'Do you want an entrecôte? But you can't have this either.'

'Why not? I have had it once.'

'But isn't the cow sacred to you?'

Nila hid a smile and said, 'I'll go for the entrecôte.'

'You are not religious?'

'My religion is private.'

Benoir wiggled his brows and said, 'So your private religion allows you to eat beef?'

Nila was grave as she said, 'It's not forbidden to eat beef in the Hindu religion. In the Vedic age we all ate beef. Then the Brahmins introduced certain restrictions to differentiate themselves and they gave up beef. Slowly, the castes below them also followed suit. That's how it became a status symbol not to eat beef and it became a custom.'

Benoir said, 'But here it is a status symbol to *eat* beef.'

Nila's voice held false disbelief, 'There's a class system here too? So the French Revolution couldn't get rid of it? It couldn't merge the poor with the rich?'

Benoir wasn't interested in the revolution. He was interested in Bordeaux. He asked for a whole bottle.

As they ate, Nila told him that she wasn't staying with her girlfriend, but at Rue de Rivoli.

'Quite a posh area. Is it a French household?'

'No.' Nila waited for Benoir to ask her whose house it was. But she realized he had no curiosity about it. So she herself said, 'It's an Indian's house.' Benoir's eyes were suddenly round with surprise.

'Why is it so strange for an Indian to live in a posh area?'

'No, that's not what I meant.'

He didn't specify what he meant. Instead he raised his glass of Bordeaux and said 'Santè.'

Nila also said, 'Santè.'

The names of the famous writers and artists who had once dined at the Closerie des Lilas were written on the tablecloth under their plates: Baudelaire, Ezra Pound, Scott Fitzgerald, Ernest Hemingway, George Orwell, Samuel Beckett. Nila glanced through the list and she was overwhelmed. 'Is this the place that was frequented by Lenin and Trotsky?'

Benoir looked around him and said, 'I don't think so.'

Nila pondered for a while and said, 'I think this is the place where Hemingway sat on the terrace and finished his *The Sun also Rises* in six weeks. He lived close by. Picasso also came here with his poet friend, Epolleniere.

'Picasso!' Benoir's eyes lit up.

'Yes, Picasso. But I don't understand about Hemingway—he lived like a pauper in a dank room with no hot water. He had no money to buy firewood and heat the room. The house had no toilets. He used a bucket. But he always went to the cafés and restaurants and drank café au lait at the Café aux Amateurs in Place Saint Michel. He even bet on horses. How did he do all this? A little strange, isn't it?'

Nila looked at Benoir. He was staring at her as he chewed on his rum steak. Nila's eyes saw the tinkling of glasses, the drunken screams and fresh words, prose, poetry. At the turn of the century, when America introduced prohibition, many writers came to Paris, drank themselves silly and hollered all night long at these restaurants, spouted words which had genius in them. The scene was fixed in Nila's mind and her eyes were unfocused. She came back to herself with the sound of Benoir gulping down his Bordeaux. 'Look at Hemingway's situation. He always ran short of money when he went to buy food. Of course, books too. He always borrowed books from the bookstores. He even described the marvellous experience of seeing Cezanne's paintings on an empty stomach. Once I went into a Dali museum on an empty stomach. My head was spinning. If there had been a tree in sight I would have hung from its branches like Dali's clocks. I had to come out and eat at one of those touristy places in Montmartre first. Then I went in again. I guess it'll be the same if I tried it with Cezanne.'

The wine was over. Benoir refilled both the glasses. Nila finished half the glass in one gulp and continued, 'But Benoir, Hemingway said something really valuable: staying in Paris was never in vain. Whatever you gave to Paris, the city paid you back in full. Of course, those were the old days. Paris was like that in those days and Hemingway and others may have been poor, but they were happy. Now it's different. If you don't have loads of money, you'd be on the streets.' Did Nila's eyes feel wet? Of course they did. No, actually she must have sprinkled too much pepper on her entrecôte. Benoir eyes or ears weren't burning, he wasn't blushing, though the tip of his nose was a little reddish from drinking too much Bordeaux.

Benoir asked her, 'Why did you leave your girlfriend's place, Nila?'

Nila didn't answer. She felt it was a good thing, in a way. Thanks to Danielle's relationship with Natalie, Nila was free of that voracious tongue every night. It hung in front of her eyes. She pushed it aside and said, 'Can you have sex with someone without loving her?'

Benoir said, 'That depends.'

'On?'

'On the circumstances and . . .'

'And what?'

'Emotions, etc. etc.' Nila heard his unclear mutter, lifted her face and said, 'I can't.'

The soft breeze of love made Nila prattle. 'I don't know when love suddenly engulfed me like this. When I'm walking, talking to someone, sitting alone, sleeping or waking, I can sense very clearly that I love someone.'

'You didn't eat your entrecôte.'

'I tried, but for one thing, I'm not used to such bland food, for another I am not used to eating beef.'

'And you are not used to eating gods! Ha, ha, ha.'

Nila smiled.

'There're no gods in ice creams. I'm sure you can have that?'

As she ate her ice cream, Nila told him her plans, of renting a house and getting a job. She had always wanted to be independent.

'Where will you rent?'

'I haven't decided yet. But I believe it's not easy—some rich person has to be a guarantor?'

Benoir said, 'Rent a place close to mine. That'll be great.'

Benoir reached for her hands and began to stroke her delicate fingers. 'How well these men can make love,' Nila thought.

The waiter placed the bill in front of Benoir. Nila snatched it away. He protested violently. 'What are you doing? I'll pay. I have invited you.'

'So what?'

She kept eight hundred and fifty francs on the table and said, 'Just because I am from a poor country doesn't make me a pauper.'

Benoir didn't stop her and said, 'All right, the next one is on me.'

Nila was sure the waiter had placed the bill before Benoir because he felt she wasn't capable of paying: black and a woman at that. She felt a sense of pride when she paid.

But the pride came with a price. With that in place, Nila could very easily place her lips on Benoir's pink ones.

They left the restaurant and went to Benoir's apartment in Rue de Rennes for coffee as usual. There was the same 'no coffee for me, tea please' scene.

'And if I don't have tea, can I give you something else? Will it quench your thirst for tea? Just try it.' Benoir played some music, filled the glass with red wine, sipped it and slowly came towards Nila, one step at a time. *'When you want it, when you need it, you will always have the best of me, I can't help it, believe me . . .'*

He laid her on the bed and tore her clothes off. Then a long kiss on the lips, sucking the red from it as if the honey was only in that red. Without taking his lips from hers, he took off all his clothes as well. Nila closed her eyes shyly and pulled a cover on herself. Benoir pulled it aside. Now Nila had her arms akimbo on her breasts. Benoir pulled them away, gazed at her in wonder and his voice shook, 'Nila, you are beautiful.'

Nila turned on her side, trying to hide as she said, 'What is so beautiful about me?'

'Your colour.' Benoir's voice was thick with emotion.

Nila said, 'Colour? But it isn't white.'

'That's what makes it so beautiful.'

Suddenly Mithu's face came to her mind. Poor Mithu, if only you could see how I am being loved for my dark skin. Poor Mithu, perhaps someone may have come along in your life too, if only you'd waited. Poor Mithu, you went away without seeing this amazingly beautiful side of life, poor Mithu . . .

'Your colour is beautiful, your skin so smooth; your hair is so black, so deep, dark black. Your breasts—I have never seen such breasts, like a pair of melons. You'll drive me crazy.' He poured drops of wine on her breasts and began to lick it up. 'The wine tastes better.'

'Really?'

'Really.'

Then he poured the rest of the wine on Nila's stomach, thighs and drank it. Nila sank her fingers into his golden hair, on his shaven cheeks, reddish nose tip, lips, chin and all over his face. Benoir sang with Bryan Adams, '*I may not always know what's right, but I know I want you here tonight, gonna make this moment last for all your life, oh yeah this is love, and it really means so much, I can tell from every touch . . .*'

At first a feather touch on her breasts. Then the beak-like nose kissed them and Benoir's tongue licked them. The nipples woke up slowly and he watched without blinking. Lips came down on the aroused nipples, kissed them lightly and when they were fully aroused, a reckless Benoir grazed them with his tongue as if they held some immortal fluid and said they were his cherries. Nila felt he was no Benoir; this was her Apollo loving his Aphrodite deeply, intimately.

Benoir moved lower as he kissed Nila's breasts and stomach. Her thighs were tightly pressed. He prised them apart with his hands and said, 'Let me taste you Nila, let me taste you.'

'No.'

'Why?'

'It's disgusting.'

'How lovely is your soft, downy fur. I know there's nectar beneath. Please let me drink it.' Slowly he prised apart her thighs. Nila covered her eyes in shame. Benoir soaked the lips with his tongue and went deeper in search of more overflowing rivers. In the dim candlelight he looked like a deep sea diver. He began to suck her dry like a blind maniac as if he had come upon a fountain of life and if he didn't drink it all, he would die.

Benoir whispered, 'Nila, open your eyes, look at me. Touch me. Kiss me.'

Nila opened her eyes and was shocked: a huge penis throbbed in front of her, like the flames of a bonfire. She shut her eyes in fear and shame. She had only ever been touched by two male organs in her whole life. Sushanta's she hadn't even looked at for shame and Kishan's, when her glance fell on it once by chance, was the size of a little finger or the tail of a rat. If his penis was an anthill, Benoir's was the Himalaya in comparison. Finally Nila touched the Himalaya. Her fingers curled around it, her hand trembled. Benoir brought the blazing flame, the huge giant near her lips for her to kiss it.

'Why do you lie so passively? Yesterday was the same. Open your eyes, watch, feel and have fun. Touch it, suck it, take it between your breasts, wake me, play with me.'

Nila was used to lying flat and passive. She thought that was the rule of the game, the woman would lie with her eyes shut and the man would climb on her body and take his pleasure. If the woman got anything out of it, well and good. If not, too bad!

Benoir didn't heave his body on to hers. He levered himself up on two hands and stayed suspended. His massive giant went on wetting its toes at the edge of her ocean. Nila was restless. She was consumed by a thirst. When she overflowed, the giant ran away to the shore. Her ocean wanted him and he wouldn't come near. What kind of a game was this? Nila opened her eyes and found Benoir laughing. She clung to him and drew him towards her.

Benoir whispered, 'Tell me what you want.' The faint light lit up his beautiful face. Nila had never seen so much beauty so close at hand. She trembled with love.

'Say what you want.'

Nila blushed in shame, she couldn't say it. Her head tilted to the right and so did Benoir's; hers tilted to the left and his followed suit.

'You can't wait, right?'

She couldn't but she had no way of telling him—she had never learnt to say it, wasn't used to saying it. Modesty covered her in a cloak.

Benoir smiled sweetly, mischievously, as he watched Nila bursting, parched. Suddenly, without warning, the Himalaya penetrated her shores and entered her deep waters. Nila shrieked and her body arched like a bow.

Benoir, or Apollo, wreaked havoc as he said, you are a virgin, untouched, except by me, me and only me!

He lifted her legs on his chest and raised a storm, kissed her feet and charged with a destructive madness. The storm whipped up, faster and faster, the storm gods laughed within and without. Nila's body was wracked with pleasure, the sharp, shooting pleasure of lightning flashes.

Suddenly Benoir lifted Nila from her supine position and sat her on his lap, laid down his tired arms and lay back.

'Have you ever ridden on horseback?'

No, Nila hadn't. She sat there, still and unmoving. Benoir lifted her with his hands and brought her down again, taught her how to ride, asked her to gallop fast, whispered into her ears to ride like an expert. He drew her to him, held her breasts with both his hands and got drunk on his cherries.

The two bodies entwined, enmeshed, rolled from one side of the bed to the other and fell on the floor.

'Can you dance?' Benoir whispered again.

Nila couldn't dance, she had never learnt.

'Dance, wildly, turn your back on me and dance.' Benoir turned her around and made her dance. She had never danced like that before. He stroked her back and taught her how to dance. Then he bent her forward and lay her face down and covered her lovely body with his beautiful one. The storm crashed on the backyard and it was havoc all over again. Nila shrieked as lightning flashed. The storm didn't abate one bit and just heaved Nila's pelvis up. Her hips were in his hands. He knelt down and raised waves in her ocean once again. Nila was panting. Benoir picked her up from the floor and put her down on the bed. He brought a glass of water, drank half of it and gave her the rest. As she drank the water, from the corner of her eye she saw that the red giant's tongue was hanging out and it was still quivering. Benoir picked her up, sat on the sofa and made Nila sit on him He kissed her all over, aroused her again and said, 'Why do you keep such lovely hips passive? Shake it, shake it, shake my universe.'

She didn't know how to shake it. Benoir had to do it for her. When the storm grew intense Benoir stood up holding Nila in place. He lifted her and pushed her against the wall, storming her insides again and again. The room swayed as Nila climaxed, Benoir swayed. As they swayed, he put her down on the bed, on her side, as if she was a little child. He held her from behind, her breasts, his cherries. Then the storm whipped up all over again, that destructive crazy storm which entered Nila's tranquil temple turbulently and ripped her apart, sweat mixed with lightning, the shock waves transmitted from Nila to Benoir and back to Nila. Benoir drowned her, soaked her entire world.

Sweat dripped off Benoir's chest, back and hair. He hugged Nila's throbbing body close to him and lay there.

The candle had gone out and Bryan Adams had stopped singing. The hands of the clock had moved past three hours, past midnight. Nila was half asleep, taking in the scent of Benoir's chest. She felt he was that prince of her dreams, who would come and carry her away on horseback. This was that palace and he was her prince. There was a strange calm in her body, joy in her heart. Nila believed no one could be happier than this. She had never felt love so strong. Her voice shook as she said, 'Benoir, I love you very much.'

Benoir opened his eyes, kissed her lips lightly and said, 'I like you, I like you a lot.'

Nila asked, 'Don't you love me?'

'Not yet.'

She sat up in bewilderment. 'What did you say? You *don't* love me?'

'No.' Benoir was calm.

'If you don't love me, how could do all this like the devoted lover? How does your body get aroused at the sight of someone you don't love?'

Benoir said, 'I like you. Why wouldn't it arouse me?'

'I hate myself. Yuck!'

Benoir sat up. 'What are you saying?'

'You thought she's from a poor country, she can hardly feed or clothe herself. I can easily talk her into bed!'

Benoir's forehead and eyes crinkled up. Nila dressed as quickly as she could.

'Are you a fool? How can you love someone so soon? Maybe I will, one day,' Benoir said.

'Maybe you won't.'

'Are you leaving?'

'Yes.'

'It's late, Nila. Stay here.'

'Stay here? Aren't you scared? Pascale, whom you love, may come over suddenly.'

Benoir, naked with a limp and sated penis, sat there stunned as Nila walked out.

Nila was stalked by the humiliation, it walked in front of her, it flanked her as she walked. It held her against the wall and wreaked havoc within and without. Nila now knew that what Benoir had done had nothing to do with love; he had enjoyed her body, just as a lusty rapist would enjoy a stupid silly girl. Shame, Nila, shame! Why don't you die? Hang yourself, like Mithu.

This wasn't Calcutta; it was Paris. It stayed awake all night. Lift your hand and a taxi was there; reach out and a lover was there.

Morounis Vernesse

When Nila came back home Sunil woke up from sleep and opened the door for her. He asked, 'Where were you?'

'At a friend's place.'

'One Mr Benoir called twice. He has asked you to call him when you return.' Sunil went towards his bedroom.

Nila also walked towards hers. Just when she had switched off the lights and was about to go to bed, the phone rang. Tumpa cried, 'Ma, Ma.' Sunil called out, 'Nila, it's a call for you.'

It was Benoir.

'Why have you called at this hour? People are sleeping.'

'I need to talk to you.'

'Now, at this hour?'

'Yes.'

'No. I am sleepy and I'm going to sleep.'

'Will you meet me tomorrow?'

'No.' Nila hung up. As she walked away, it rang again. She took it off the hook and went to bed.

Nila went out early in the morning. She knew that if she stayed at home she'd have to face a hundred questions, who was this Benoir and why was he calling late in the night and disturbing everyone, why didn't Nila finish her business with him outside, etc. etc. Once outside, Nila walked around aimlessly; there were people everywhere. Women walked around showing off their waxed, hairless legs, wearing backless dresses. They walked and their breasts, their hips swayed. All winter they had chewed on salads and maintained themselves, got rid of any flab and now they were showing off. It was summer, the time of joy. Nila was sweating in the sweltering heat and she searched for shade as others walked in the sun. Everyone was sweating, but they wanted the sun; their white skin would get sunburnt and yet they wanted the sun. People left their homes in summer when the sun poured out shafts of hot rays. The cinemas and theatres were empty. Four walls and a roof were for the winter, not summer. No one sat indoor in the cafés and restaurants—always on the terrace, basking in the sun, drinking, eating. In the scorching heat of the afternoon Nila saw a hundred men and women lying half naked in the Jardin des Tuileries. While Nila could hardly bear the heat, the people of this wintry land were lapping it up as if it was the tastiest dish in the world. In the milling crowds, Nila was the only one who walked alone. Everyone had a partner, everyone was busy kissing. It was the same in the Jardin du Luxembourg.

Nila walked around for a while after leaving the Luxembourg gardens, bought some books at William and Smith and went into Passage Bradis for some Indian food. Books were the only recourse for those who didn't have a lover. They used books to hide their loneliness in gardens, cafés, trains. At the Passage Bradis she saw, for the first time that day, a girl alone. The girl was very dark, but her nose wasn't snub and her hair wasn't curly, she couldn't be from Africa. She was the only other diner at the place. Nila took the table next to the girl and thought, 'She is bound to be an Indian.' But when the girl spoke in perfect French instead of any Indian language, and asked the waiter for water, food (less spicy), Nila looked up from her book and tried to gauge the girl in a new light. Their eyes met several times. So Nila felt a sense of obligation to exchange a few sentences. She asked, 'What is your mother-tongue?'

The girl replied, 'French.'

Nila was prepared for Tamil or Malayalam. 'Aren't you Indian?'

'No.'

'Then where are you from?'

'France.'

Nila was curious, 'Where were you born?'

'In India.'

Nila laughed. Foreigners dubbed themselves French the minute they got their citizenship and they forgot all about their country. Nila kept aside the Umberto Eco she was reading and asked, 'Where in India?'

'Perhaps Calcutta.'

'Calcutta?' Nila's eyes lit up and she spoke in Bengali. 'Since when are you here?'

The girl smiled and said, 'I don't know the Indian languages.'

Nila asked, again in Bengali, 'You are from Calcutta and you don't know Bengali?'

The girl stared at her blankly. Her food, non-spicy, arrived and she began to eat. Nila wasn't sure if she should go on talking to the girl or mind her own business. Of course, she didn't have a business of her own; bohemians seldom did. Nila looked at the girl's attractive face and large eyes and decided that she wasn't avoiding contact with Nila. She volunteered, 'I am from Calcutta.'

The girl extended her hand, 'I am Morounis Vernesse.'

Nila's lunch also arrived: rice and chicken curry. She started eating. But she realized her curiosity hadn't abated. She was curious that although she was from Calcutta, why didn't Morounis feel any interest in talking to her.

After the meal Morounis lit a cigarette. She wore a black T-shirt, shorts, white keds and carried a backpack. She stared distantly at the Passage.

Nila asked, 'I suppose you came here long ago?'

Morounis said, 'Yes.'

'I hope you don't mind my asking you so many questions?'

Morounis smiled, 'No, not all.' It was a sweet smile. Over coffee, Morounis spoke, 'Actually my English is not very good. So I am a little shy.'

'Who said it's not good? You are doing fine.'

Nila was eager to dispel Morounis's hesitation. 'I have heard much worse English than yours. Your grammar is fine and these days no one speaks proper English.'

Nila asked, 'Have you studied here?'

'Yes.'

'When did you come to Paris?'

'Twenty-seven years ago.'

Then Morounis Vernesse spoke in her broken English: she had been in Mother Teresa's Home in Calcutta when a French couple adopted her. Since then, from the age of two months, she had been in Paris. She was a Parisienne from head to toe. The people of the Home had picked her up from the rubbish heap when she was a month old. Her name, Morounis, was given by them.

Nila heard her story with wonder.

'Then?'

'Then nothing.'

'You don't know who your parents were?'

'No.'

Morounis asked for another cup of coffee.

'Have you never been to Calcutta since then?'

'No.'

'Don't you want to?'

Calcutta was just like any other city to her. She didn't have any special feelings for it to want to go there.

'Morounis, do you ever feel sad that you couldn't live in your own city, your own country?'

'No, why should I? Instead, I feel it's all for the best or else I would have died in that rubbish heap.'

She spoke the truth. But somewhere in Nila's heart the feather of a sorrow flew in and lodged itself.

Morounis didn't know who had dumped her there, nor could she ever know. She couldn't even have known where she was born. When she grew up, her adoptive parents told her all this. In the documents from the Home there was only her name; beside the birth date and birthplace there were question marks and beside the parents' names also there was a big question mark.

Nila said, 'Suppose it was your mother who dumped you there, do you have any idea why she would have done it?'

Morounis shook her head, she had no idea at all.

Nila said, 'It was because you are dark. No one marries women who are dark. Or perhaps your mother was unmarried and it is a great sin to be an unwed mother. Or perhaps because you are a girl. No one wants girl children; they need a dowry and maybe your parents were poor and already had a few girls.'

Morounis laughed.

'Doesn't it make you feel angry?'

Morounis laughed again and said, 'No.'

Her contentment surprised Nila.

'Do you enjoy Indian food?'

'Yes, very much.'

'If I had a home here in Paris I would have cooked Bengali food for you. You don't get the real Indian food in Indian restaurants. I have many photos of Calcutta, I'll show you. If you want to pick up some Bengali words, I'll teach you.'

Nila's enthusiasm amused Morounis. Nila didn't feel she had any desire to learn Bengali or see photos of Calcutta.

Morounis was a vibrant, lively girl and there wasn't a trace of sorrow about her. Even after Nila told her the possible reasons for her mother dumping her in the dustbin, she wasn't affected at all.

'Do you know any Indians in this city?'

'No.'

'Have you never wanted to meet them?'

Morounis shrugged. She had never asked herself that question. Nila realized that to Morounis meeting an Indian and meeting a Portuguese would be the same experience. Nila thought that if someone, her parents, hadn't thrown Morounis into the rubbish heap so cruelly one night, she would have grown up in Calcutta, spoken Bengali and worn a sari. She was dark and no one would have married her. Like Mithu, she would have had to hang herself.

After the third round of tea and coffee, a Frenchman, the same age as Morounis, came into the café, kissed her, held her around the waist and walked away. Before they left Morounis gave Nila her phone number and took Nila's temporary number. Nila saw that she was not only alive, she was happy. Nila assumed the Frenchman would kiss her all day long; like all other French people Morounis would also lie around in the sun and darken her already dark skin; she hadn't learnt to use sunshades, to wear lotions and creams and sit around all day long to make herself fairer. The Frenchman must have told her a million times, 'What a beautiful colour you have, Morounis.'

Nila came home. Of the twelve messages on the machine, eleven were from Benoir. 'Nila, please call me. I am thinking of you. Please come home, I am waiting for you.'

Chaitali and Sunil were not back from work yet. Nila erased Benoir's messages from the answering machine. In the evening when they returned, neither of them asked about Benoir or questions about his relationship with Nila. Tumpa was playing in the room and Sunil and Chaitali began to discuss whether they should go to India for the Pujas or not. Chaitali felt they should go, since there was a lot of politics in the Puja Committee in Paris already. Sunil said since they'd gone home last year, this year they should go somewhere else, in Europe perhaps. Where? Sunil had an uncle who lived in London, they could visit him. The Puja in London was no less than that in Calcutta.

'Nila, what do you feel?' Sunil asked.

Nila shrugged and said, 'It is entirely up to you two. But if I was given a choice between London and Calcutta, I'd have chosen the first.'

Chaitali said, 'All our people are in Calcutta and we get a chance to see them just once a year. We shouldn't waste the opportunity. If you want to go to London, we can take the Eurostar and be there on any Friday, spend the weekend there and come back by Monday.'

'Fine, then go shopping and fill your suitcases. The relatives are endless. You know Nila, everyone wants something. It's not that they need it. But they like to have some foreign odds and ends in the house. And we have so many relatives and friends. It's not possible to take something for everyone. Tumpa's clothes take up half the space. We have to see some disappointed faces, but that doesn't stop us from going to Calcutta.'

Two hours passed and they still hadn't decided about the holiday.

That night, before she went to bed, Nila got an unexpected call from Morounis. 'If you want to go anywhere in Paris or around here, I have the next two days off and I can take you.' Nila was delighted. She wanted to go to Giverny to see Claude Monet's garden. Morounis told her when and where to meet her. Nila thought about Morounis until late into the night. She need not have called Nila. This was what happened in Calcutta, but Nila had never heard of something like this in Paris. If Morounis didn't have anything of Calcutta, then why this generosity towards Nila? She believed that although Morounis had denied it, she had felt some sort of kinship with Nila. She also believed that Morounis sometimes thought of the mother who gave birth to her, what she looked like, what she was called. Had that woman ever forgiven herself for her cruelty? Did she ever wake up at night, having a nightmare? People could be so violently cruel and so pliably soft at the same time. Nila could never make sense of them.

The next day Morounis took Nila to Giverny in her Mercedes. When she was driving on the highway at a hundred and eighty kilometres per hour, her mobile rang many times. She held her phone in the right hand and the steering in her left. As Nila stood in front of the tiny pond in Claude Monet's garden and watched the lotus leaves floating on the restless water, she meditated on Morounis. Now Morounis was the pampered daughter of rich parents. She had studied philosophy in Sorbonne and perhaps one day she'd be a great philosopher. If she had lived in Calcutta, perhaps she wouldn't have known her alphabet, or got two square meals and she could have died from starvation and a hard life or ended up in a brothel. There too, she'd have had less customers because she was dark.

After a few hours in Giverny Morounis took Nila to Rouen, to that famous church which Monet painted in different lights. She showed Nila the place where Joan d'Arc was burnt at the stakes, behind another church. She showed her the churches, but also said she didn't believe in religion. Nila thought, if she had grown up in Calcutta she would have been religious, worshipped Shiva and bathed in the dirty Ganga.

When she learnt that Nila was interested in art and literature, Morounis took her to Ouver sur Oassee the next day. Twenty kilometres from Paris, it was a tiny town called Ouver on the river Oassee. Famous painters like Daubigny, Camille, Pissaro had lived here once. Paul Cezanne had also lived here and Van Gogh had come at the invitation of an art expert, Dr Gosset. They walked through the cornfields, entered the cemetery and Nila perched on the edge of Van Gogh's grave, covered in vines and creepers. Morounis sat on a corner of Theo's, Van Gogh's brother's grave.

Nila asked, 'Does anyone ever have all their wishes granted and all their dreams coming true in one lifetime?'

Morounis felt one didn't; it would take the fun out of living.

Nila said, 'Life is too short. Human beings should live to be at least two hundred.' Morounis didn't agree with her.

Suddenly Nila thought of something weird. 'Tell me, Morounis, if you find two people drowning in a river, me and a French girl, and you can save only one of us, whom would you save?

Morounis said, 'You.'

'Why?'

'Because I know you.'

'Suppose you know the French girl too, you are acquainted.'

Morounis laughed, 'Then it'll be difficult to decide.'

'Suppose you know her better, you are friends.'

'Then I'll save her,' Morounis replied.

'Suppose you don't know either and have never seen us before?'

'Then I'll save the younger one.'

'They are the same age.'

Morounis laughed and didn't answer. Nila noticed she didn't say she'd save the Indian girl.

The hot breeze from the cornfield swept Morounis's thick black hair back. Nila looked at her, reclined on the leaves and creepers and began to sing a Rabindrasangeet, *'Oh frenetic wind, blow softly, softly, softly.'*

Morounis listened to the song with rapt attention.

Nila asked her if she had heard of Rabindranath Thakur. No, she hadn't.

'Who is he?'

Suddenly Nila got up and said, 'Let's go, I'll show you something.'

They left Ouver and came back to Paris. Nila told her to drive towards Detally. There she stopped her in a small street and gripped Morounis's hand in excitement. 'See, this road is called Rue Tagore, the man whose song I sang.' There was a garden named after the Spanish artist Miro at one end of the street and on the other end was a road named after the Russian painter Marc Chagall.

Morounis asked, 'Was Tagore an artist like Miro and Chagall?'

Nila said, 'His name isn't Tagore, the correct pronunciation is Thakur, Rabindranath Thakur. Since the British couldn't pronounce it, they made it Tagore.'

Morounis took her hand from Nila's grip and walked in Miro's garden and Nila spoke as she walked beside her, 'Rabindranath also sketched, but his songs, poetry and prose were of greater renown. To the Bengali, he is almost like a god. Even today Rabindrasangeet is played in almost every Bengali home. It is eternal. No musician can ever do what he has done. His songs will be everlasting.'

Morounis said, 'Have you seen Miro's work?'

She told Nila about how taken she was with Miro's work when she saw it in Barcelona. She insisted that if Nila ever went there, she must see his work.

Nila said, 'I'll give you a volume of Rabindranath's poetry in French. Read it. I'm sure you'll like it.'

Morounis walked towards the car and said that she was busy writing a paper on Nietzsche at the time and wouldn't have time to read anything by Rabindranath. When she had the time, she'd let Nila know.

Suddenly, Nila felt an aching emptiness within herself, for no reason.

Je t'aime, Je t'aime, Je t'aime

Nila checked with her bank. The money hadn't arrived.

She called the bank in Calcutta. They said it had been sent.

Nila's days passed in the throes of an unbearable restlessness.

Every day she erased Benoir's ardent pleas from the answering machine.

She rushed Sunil many times to look for a house for her to rent. He wasn't making the effort. One morning when Nila again petitioned him to look for a house, Chaitali was right there and she said, 'How can he find the time?'

Sunil said he would, next week.

Chaitali said, 'It's not easy to rent. Who will stand guarantee?'

Sunil would have to do that as well!

Chaitali burst out, 'If he does it, there's no telling what may come of it. It's better for a Frenchman to do it. You *have* a French friend, don't you?'

Nila said, 'No, I don't have anyone.'

Chaitali's tone was the same as before, 'Why should Sunil take such a big risk?'

'Where's the question of risk? I won't default on the rent. Let Sunilda verify about my money before he does it.'

Sunil winked at Nila and she winked back—deal!

That afternoon Nila was restive in the heat. There were no fans here and outside the sun was blazing hot. She stood at the window and watched the people for a while.

She stayed at home all day and finished a book by Sukumari Bhattacharya. Then she made herself a cup of tea and began to read Joy Goswami's poetry, aloud. She always read poetry out to herself.

As Nila sat with the tea in front of her, Joy's poetry and immense pleasure in her heart, Sunil walked into the house and made straight for her room, the room of Durga, Lakshmi and Saraswati.

Nila said, 'What's up? Home so early?'

Sunil reclined on the bed, pulled up a pillow and said, 'Don't ask! I just didn't feel like it—work, work and nothing else!'

Sunil took the book from her hands, held it up and said, 'You're reading poetry. I haven't done that for ages! Gone are those days . . .'

Nila hummed a song. Sunil started. He sat up. 'Well, well, I had no idea you sing so well.'

Nila crinkled her brows. 'Not really. Once upon a time, maybe. Now I can barely hum.'

Sunil leaned back, pushed the book towards Nila and said, 'Read something to me. I've heard Joy Goswami writes really well.'

Nila turned the pages, looking for something good. Her left hand lay on her lap and Sunil picked it up. He looked at the lines on it and said, 'Let's see how many times you'll marry.'

'Marriage? Again? Once was bad enough.'

Nila lightly took her hand away and began to read. As she read, Sunil looked at her in wonder. He was half-reclined and so was she. Sunil sulked, 'You're having tea all alone? Can I have some too?' As though he was the guest here and not Nila. She made him a cup and poured herself another one. This time she took the chair instead of the bed, outside Sunil's reach and said, 'Tell me when will you find me a house?'

'What's the rush?'

'No rush! But how long can I impose on you like this?'

'Why, are you not comfortable?'

'I am very comfortable. But I am causing you a lot of discomfort, occupying a room like this.'

'Why are you making us sound so distant and formal?'

Nila knew Sunil was the only person she had in this city. If she thought he wasn't close to her, she wouldn't have been able to stay in their house.

She said, 'If only I could get a job, I'd breathe easier.'

'It'll work out, don't worry. I have told Narayan; he is a useful chap. He's looking out for jobs. But you'd have stood a better chance if you knew the language.'

'I don't need better; just about any job will do.'

Nila sipped at her hot tea and scalded her lips. 'Oh Ma.' The tea spilled on her lap and on the book. She put down the cup and looked at Sunil. His eyes were laughing.

'Did you scald your tongue?'

Nila looked away from his eyes and at the floor. It was like a chessboard, white and black, black and white. On this side there was no queen or bishop, just an unarmed pawn. From that side the knight moved two and a half steps, 'Let me see how much you've burnt it, show me your tongue . . .'

The next moment Sunil's long, red tongue advanced on Nila's scalded one. She pulled her tongue back in, leaned her chair back and removed herself from his reach.

'What are you doing!' Nila pushed him away and stood up.

Sunil pulled her down on the bed in one swift movement. The tea cup and Joy's book dropped heavily. Sunil jammed her body down with his own; with one hand he untied her salwar and pulled it down. He unzipped his pants and pulled them down too and pushed himself into her. Speechless, powerless, Nila lay there watching this ugly scene. There were no sounds in the house except Sunil moaning, 'Oh Nila, oh Nila.'

In a few moments Sunil was limp. Nila didn't even touch him to push him away. She stared at the blank wall fixedly.

Sunil quickly dressed and then noticed the tears rolling down and wetting her pillow.

'Are you crying?' Sunil wiped her tears and said, 'Why are you crying?'

She stared at the wall and spoke hoarsely, 'I am not crying. I don't cry. My mother left me all alone and I didn't cry. I don't break down under any kind of pressure. Life is so ugly. I . . . feel my brother, Nikhil, has just raped me.'

'I am not your brother, I am his friend.'

'We are taught to think of our brother's friends as brothers.'

'But sometimes one also gets married to them, isn't it?'

'True. But I haven't married you. I left Kishan because we were not compatible. I never felt close to him. In this city you were the only one who I thought was near to me. Perhaps it's better for me to go back to him rather than take this kind of humiliation. Even if he ravishes me, at least he is my husband, not brother.'

Sunil's voice was heavy. 'I thought you wanted it too. When you read Joy's poetry, you were giving me looks, weren't you?'

As soon as Sunil left, Nila went into the bathroom. She showered for a long time, finished a whole bar of soap—this wasn't a body, it was a rubbish dump. Nila spat on herself. She rubbed the soap into every nook and cranny and removed every bit of the greed, lust, hatred, mucus, spit, sperm, blood that was there on her body. She repeatedly told herself that nothing had happened, she was just using up the soap for no reason, it was a figment of her dirty mind. Sunil didn't come home early, didn't lie on her bed, didn't touch her, even if someone did it was a different man or perhaps Nila was asleep and she dreamt the whole thing. Or maybe a neighbour, a criminal forced his way into the house, found Nila alone and raped her, or perhaps she wasn't raped, she had wanted to be ravished. Sunil would come back in the evening, like every other day, sit down to chat with Chaitali and Nila, eat fish and rice and Nila would feel he was her nearest kin in the whole world.

At five-thirty she met Benoir in the Select at Montparnasse. He ordered tea for Nila and coffee for himself. They sat on the terrace, facing the street.

Nila wore a black T-shirt and white trousers. She hadn't done her hair, made her face up and her lips were dark brown. She wasn't going anywhere to 'powder her nose' and cover the true colour of her lips. She looked out at the street distantly and sipped her tea.

'What did you do all day today?'

'I read.'

'Didn't you go out?'

'No.'

'Why didn't you answer the phone? I called you all day.'

'It was off the hook.'

'So that you don't have to talk to me, right? What made you think of me suddenly?'

'I don't know.'

'Nila, look at me.'

She looked into his deep blue eyes.

'Can you see something in these eyes?'

'No.'

'Are you blind?'

'No.'

Benoir picked up her hands in his own warm ones and kissed them.

'Promise me something?'

'What?'

'Why are you looking at the street? Look at me.'

Nila looked into his eyes again.

'Are you upset?'

'No.'

'Tell me.'

'It's nothing.'

'The other night you left like that and I couldn't sleep at all.'

Nila was indifferent. She looked away from his eyes and back at the street. It was overflowing with people.

Benoir held her hands and walked along the pavement. Nila wanted Benoir to hold her hands forever, never leave them. Benoir lived on the fourth floor of a five-storeyed building at the crossing of Rue de Rennes and Rue Saint Placide. When they walked in, Benoir didn't kiss her. He offered her a seat and went into the kitchen. Nila was sure he'd bring a bottle of red wine, pour it on her naked body and drink it up. All said and done, it was better than being raped by Sunil.

Nila was stunned when Benoir came back with two cups of tea.

'I thought you didn't have any tea.'

'I've bought some Earl Grey, just for you. Will it do?' Benoir's voice was calm and beautiful.

Nila laughed, 'It will.'

He moved and sat at her feet, rested his head on her lap. She didn't know what to do with the head on her lap.

She didn't do a thing; just drank her tea. She sipped the hot tea and scalded her tongue again. 'Oh, Ma' slipped out and her heart trembled; any moment now Benoir would ask to see her scalded tongue and come at her with his tongue hanging out.

He looked up, 'What's the matter?'

'Nothing.'

He didn't ask if she'd burnt her tongue. He just looked unblinking at Nila drinking her tea and said, 'Je t'aime.'

The tea cup shook. She gripped it with both hands and asked, 'What did you say?'

'Je t'aime. I love you.'

Benoir's voice was unusually calm. The earlier restlessness was gone. There was no inebriated craziness to lose himself in her when she was so close at hand. He seemed to have changed in the last few days, grown much quieter, calmer. Nila rose to put the shaking tea-cup down on the table and also to hide her shock. She went to the window, watched people for a while and came back again. She sat far from Benoir, picked up her tea and started drinking it again, as if the words 'Je t'aime' hadn't been uttered.

Nila was afraid that if Benoir knew of what Sunil had done to her today, he wouldn't say 'Je t'aime' any more. She shut her eyes, gritted her teeth, balled her fist and took in her own loneliness, helplessness and all her secret pain. Benoir's love was her pride. She would not tell him about any of her humiliations. Nila had lost everything, and in that losing she had lost the pain of losing. Nila desperately wanted to live. In this grotesque world Nila would walk hand in hand with beauty and head for her dreams.

She took one step at a time and knelt down behind Benoir. Nila placed one hand on his shoulder and on that Benoir placed his own very lightly. Just two hands touching, and the happiness dripped down Benoir's hand, flowed through Nila's and filled her whole body.

'Do you really love me?'

Benoir turned around. His eyes were dreamy, very blue.

He drew Nila to himself and kissed her deeply and said, 'Je

t'aime, je t'aime.'

By now Nila knew that the French didn't utter the word 'love' very easily. They did it only when they loved truly. It wasn't like back home, where a Bengali youth had to just catch a glimpse of a girl standing on a distant terrace, to fall in love with her, write a hundred poems without knowing or understanding her but prepared to give his life for her. These people loved truly and this true love made her life worth living; it gave meaning to her life.

Nila rose from Benoir's lap and lay on the bed. Love had lent her wings and she wanted to fly out of the window, tell every soul on the streets that she wasn't alone any more, she wasn't being used, someone really loved her, truly loved her. Benoir lay down beside her and said, 'You wanted to learn French. Do you know the best way to learn it?'

'What?'

'You learn it from your lover, through pillow talk, lying on your back.' He pulled her close, smelt her hair and asked, 'Do you love me?'

'I do.'

'Then say, "Je t'aime".'

'Je t'aime.'

'Embrasse-moi.'

'Embrasse-moi.'

'Ça, la vie et belle.'

'La vie et belle.'

'Ça, c'est la vie.'

'C'est la vie.'

Benoir kissed her again.

He took off her slippers and kissed the soles of her feet, every toe on her feet. Nila thought of Sushanta. He had said he loved her, but never had he made love to her like this. Benoir had an artist within. Was he different from all the men in the world or did all Frenchmen love their women thus? Nila didn't know but she was drowning in love.

Nila said, 'I am older than you. In our country older women are called didi, like a sister.'

'If you want I can call you didi.'

'Please don't do that or I'll never be able to kiss you again.'

Benoir kissed her lips. He looked up and said, 'Didi.'

He did that again and again.

'So you are older; how does that matter?'

'In our society, love or marriage has to be between an older man and a younger woman.'

'This isn't your society, it's ours. It's lucky that it is, or I wouldn't have got you.' Benoir laughed.

'Don't you feel like saying je t'aime to any of these young, nubile beauties roaming the city?'

He shrugged, 'No.'

'You said you like brown skin. But they are also getting the colour from tanning, aren't they?'

Benoir laughed long and said, 'They'll lose that colour soon; it's fake.'

He kissed her again, 'It's a good thing that you are older. I can learn a lot from you.'

'You know much more than me.'

'What do I know much more than you?'

Nila tweaked his nose and said, 'You know what I'm talking about.'

'No, I don't. Tell me.'

'I won't.'

'No?'

'No.'

'Why?'

'It's my wish.'

'I also have a wish.'

'What is it?'

'It's not to be told!'

'Then what is it for?'

'It's to be felt.'

Nila closed her eyes. She waited for his touch, for the destructive storm. But for a long time she didn't feel his touch. She opened her eyes and found him on the floor, laughing, out of Nila's reach.

'Can you feel it?'

Nila came down from the bed, lay down with her head on his chest and said, 'Playing the fool, are you?'

Benoir hugged her close with one arm. Brown fingers roamed a white chest and from there, Nila's fingers climbed to his neck, chin, and lips.

Benoir held her tightly with both hands and said, 'Je t'aime, je t'aime, je t'aime.'

Why couldn't time stand still right there? She held her breath. Nila needed just a drop to quench her thirst and Benoir poured out the whole ocean for her. It was more than she deserved. She was Nila, the hunted, friendless, helpless animal whose backbone was broken, who was crumpled, crinkled and drowning.

She closed her eyes. Benoir kissed her closed eyelids. Nila perceived his love with all her body and soul. The deeper within her he penetrated, the more she realized this wasn't mere sex, it was genuine love. It soothed the body, relaxed it and cooled it. It cheered the soul, broadened and brightened the spirit.

The two of them went out at night. Though the sky was still bright with daylight. This was nature's reparation, for snatching the light away in winters. They sat huddled together on the grass at Champs-Elysées. Benoir picked up a tiny white flower called Marguerite and began to tear each petal one by one, saying, 'Je t'aime un peu, beaucoup, passionment, à la folie, pas du tout.' In this game of tearing petals, Benoir's last one was à la folie and Nila's was pas du tout. He said, 'See, I love you like crazy and you don't love me at all.'

Nila laughed, 'Is that what you feel?'

He kissed her and said, 'No. I know you love me very much.'

'And do you really love me à la folie?'

'Yes.'

As they dined at a café, Nila watched people, bright and lively. The Champs-Elysées was awake all night and was always crowded. There were sixty- and seventy-year-old women dining in the café. Nila said, 'Even the old people aren't sleepy.'

Benoir whispered in her ear, 'Those rich old fogies are sitting there to catch gigolos.'

'What's a gigolo?' Nila murmured.

'Young men will come and according to their taste, these women will pick them up.'

'What?'

'Just watch.'

Nila turned around frequently and it really happened. The elderly women held the young men's hands and walked away happily, like mother and son.

'What will happen now?'

'The woman will take the boy home, have fun, buy him gifts and dinner. They'll dance together, make love and when the boy asks for money, she'll give it.'

They walked from one end of the Champs-Elysées to the other, from the Arc de Triomph to the Concorde, holding each other tight. Sometimes they stopped for ice cream or coffee, sat on the terrace of a café and then walked on. Little bits of conversation floated between them: favourite colours, Nila's was blue and Benoir's light green. Nila liked to eat fish curry and rice, Benoir like canarre and potato. Favourite city? Nila liked Paris and Benoir Rome. Had she ever been there? No. Nila liked cloudy skies and Benoir liked it sunny. Nila loved the rain while Benoir didn't. Sad memories of childhood? Nila was thrashed badly by Anirban when she did poorly in her exams. For Benoir it was when Madame Dupont said to him too much chocolate was bad for the teeth. Happy memories? When Nila did well in an exam she got a red frock and when Benoir went skiing with his friends to Austria.

When Nila was exhausted and her eyes were drooping, Benoir said, 'Shall we go home?'

'Yes.' She said to herself, 'I'll go home and sleep, holding you tight, sleep in peace, without fear.'

Nila thought Benoir was crossing the Seine from Place de la Concorde, and heading for Rue de Rennes along Boulevard Saint Germaine. But after driving quite a distance, she realized they weren't near the Seine, but on their way to Rue de Rivoli from the Concorde.

Nila asked, 'Where are you going?'

'Reaching you home.'

'Oh.'

'They love you a lot, don't they?'

Nila wanted to say, 'They don't love me at all. Please take me to your home and save me from more humiliation, save me.' But something gripped her vocal chords and she couldn't speak.

'Of course they love you, or why would they have you with them for so long?' Quite logical.

'Won't they wake up when you ring the bell?'

'No, I have a key.'

'Okay, my kitten, go inside and sleep well.' He dropped her off, kissed her several times, reminded her when and where they were meeting next and drove away.

She punched in 30A59 on the big door and it opened from within. She climbed up to the second floor and then didn't feel like sleeping on that bed. So she curled up on the stairs and spent the rest of the night thinking, wondering why Benoir didn't ask her to stay with him. It wasn't like his wife Pascale's presence haunted the place. Nila was numb with fatigue, both mental and physical. Towards dawn she heard some footsteps and sat up in terror, perhaps it was someone coming to rape her. She cowered in fear. Some French people coming home after partying all night long. No one gave her a second glance or asked her who she was, why she was lying there. This was another reason why she felt at ease in Paris. No one poked their nose in your business; it was against their nature to impede the others' wish. If Nila wanted to sleep there, she had the right to, as long as it didn't disturb anyone else.

Nila walked alone on the streets at dawn, as the cool breeze fanned her face. It was perhaps the best time to view any city in the world. She drank tea in a café and whiled away the hours until ten o'clock. Nila's day had no beginning and no end, she had no office and nowhere to go. After ten, when she was sure the house was empty, she slipped in and packed her suitcase. She thumbed the phone book and looked for a hotel. Each one she tried, was either full or too expensive. Finally, after much hunting, she found a room in a studio hotel in Rue de la Corvosion and it cost three hundred francs. Nila booked it deciding to rely on her credit card and called a taxi. It was to come in three minutes. Joy Goswami's book was lying on the floor. She picked it and her suitcase up, walked to the door when the phone rang. She thought it could be Benoir and snatched it up. It was Danielle.

After the usual small talk, Danielle said, 'There's a letter for you; it looks important—from the bank.'

Nila was very excited, 'I need the letter.'

'I'd called your husband's place, no one answered. Then I called here at Rivoli thinking I'll leave a message at your friend's. If you say, I can forward it to your friend's place.'

'No, no, I have no friend. I thought this man was my brother's friend, but actually he is an enemy. I am leaving this house today.'

Danielle's voice was cool, 'In that case I am forwarding it to the bank.'

'Could you open it and read it for me?' Nila's voice shook with eager anticipation.

Danielle opened it. The money from India had arrived and now there was two hundred and ninety thousand, seven hundred and eighty francs in her account.

Nila had known this money would come, but once it was here, she felt surprised, like it was a lottery prize-money.

Her voice was warm, excited, 'Danielle, you have saved me.'

Danielle was detached, 'You weren't dying that I'd save you. You are doing well, much better than a lot of people.'

Then Danielle spoke about herself a bit; she was having tax problems. Nowadays half the income went in taxes and life was becoming increasingly difficult for the average people in this country. The government was busy giving aid to the poorer countries.

Nila left the key on the table, just as she had in Kishan's house. In the same manner she stepped out towards a new life. She knew it was an uncertain life, but she hadn't hesitated earlier and she didn't start now.

I stamp your name
on the sky, on the wind, in the water and
on grass—Liberté

Nila had a good night's sleep in the studio room and woke up ravenous. She had money in the bank, so she set off for a meal at a good restaurant. She had never come to this area before. As she walked around, she quite liked the area—cafés, restaurants, cinemas, metro, bus stop, grocery, boulangerie, everything was close at hand. It was a Thursday and market day in Corvosion. From beds and furniture to cheese and wines, everything was on sale. A girl was hawking rotisserie chicken and rabbits. Nila bought a rabbit. She waded through the festive market and bought two bottles of wine, some oranges, camembert cheese and that day's particulier with ads for houses for rent.

She came back to the hotel and called Benoir. He said he had called Sunil's place many times. No one knew where she was. He didn't like her disappearing like this without telling anyone.

'Where are you, mystery woman?'

'Didn't you say you like rabbit?'

'I do. Have you turned into one? If so, let me grab the salt and pepper and come to you.'

'Please do.'

She gave the hotel's address to Benoir. Before he arrived, Nila studied the papers for the houses which had a rent of five to seven thousand francs and called the landlords. Most of them were already rented out. For the ones that were left, she fixed appointments to meet them.

Benoir came into the hotel room and dropped into a chair. He simply couldn't fathom why Nila had come to a hotel.

'Was there a problem in that house?'

'No.'

Benoir drank some water and tried to guess her reason for staying in the hotel, 'It's better to have your own space, right?'

Nila said, 'Yes, like you have.'

The rabbit, wine and cheese lay on the table. He was thirsty and it wasn't for wine. It was for her kisses. He was hungry too, but he didn't want that dead rabbit that lay on the table. He took a long time over lunch.

In the evening they showered together and went out to see a house in Emile Zola Avenue. The rent was eight thousand. Nila liked it.

She asked Benoir, 'Should I take it?'

He shrugged, 'If you like it.'

He was right. She should take it because she liked it; he didn't have an opinion on it.

But Nila's wish wasn't everything. The landlord turned her down because Nila didn't have a job. But she had money in the bank. The landlord didn't care about that.

Rejected.

She saw and liked another house and asked when she could take it. The landlord asked her who would be the guarantor for her. Nila looked at Benoir appealingly. But she saw his indifferent face and shook her head, there was no one.

Rejected.

Benoir got into the car, shook his head and said, 'Without a guarantor you won't get a house in Paris.'

'Even if I am a millionaire?'

'Not even if you are a millionaire.'

'So what should I do?'

Nila hoped he would say he would do it. But he didn't.

'You have Indian friends—why don't you ask them?'

'No, I don't feel like asking them.'

'Ask your friend in Rivoli.'

'He is not my friend.'

'But you stayed with them for so long!'

It was on the tip of Nila's tongue to say, 'Why don't you stand guarantee Benoir; you have a well-paid job in Alcatel.'

But she didn't say it because she felt Benoir must have thought there was no telling what this girl would do next and she could easily default on her rent. She wanted to dispel any such notions he may have had and said, 'My mother has left me a lot of money. I can live comfortably in Paris without a job for three years at least.'

She heaved a sigh and said, 'My mother hadn't wanted me to live abroad. If I was in Calcutta, renting a house would be no problem at all. Over there, no one asks for guarantees. If the tenant has money, no landlord refuses him.'

Benoir told her that it was a very old system in Paris and even explained to her why and how it came about. He chanted a hundred rules of giving and taking a house on rent. He also said that he'd bought the flat in Rue de Rennes; if he hadn't, it would have been equally difficult for him to rent a place. Nila relieved him by not probing any further. He also didn't ask anything about how she'd find a place.

He stopped the car on the way to Pigalle, walked on the dazzling street and said again and again, 'Je t'aime.'

There were bright lights on both sides of the street. The sex-toy stores were selling plastic penises and vaginas by the dozen. There were sex acts on display, not on film, not by puppets but by live human beings.

Nila knew she would never have walked on this street alone. She would have been too shy and afraid. She could dare to walk comfortably here because Benoir was with her.

She said, 'Let's go to the Moulin Rouge.'

'Oh no. I don't have the money to spend.'

'I do. Come on. Let's go and see what kind of dance Toulouse Lautrec watched.'

'You won't get that these days.'

Nila knew that, but she went in. She knew it was nothing but a tourist trap. Nila wanted to show off her carte bleue to Benoir and pay the huge bill. She wanted him to see that she was no pauper and it was true that she had a lot of money, given by her mother. Let him know that she never lied.

When they came out of the Moulin Rouge, Benoir said, 'I have seen many women, but none as lively as you. You know how to enjoy life. No one is more spontaneous. You are exceptional. French women are very calculating.'

'And French men are not?'

Benoir was so lost in his praises of Nila, that he didn't hear her question.

That night Benoir stayed over in Nila's room. It was a night of love. In the morning Benoir left for work and Nila went out. She went into the bright and inviting brokerage offices and asked if she could rent a place. Of course she could, any time, but who would be the guarantor? She checked out two houses in Place d'Italie and Rue de Vouyeer, and lay on her bed feeling utterly helpless. She had shown them her bank documents and it was useless. Benoir could see her helplessness, but didn't offer to help her.

Nila called Danielle in the hope that her anger had abated, since she had called and informed Nila about the letter from the bank and not thrown it away like her easel and paintings.

Danielle said she was going to Sweden the following week with Nicole and Michelle. Rita also wanted to go but she had to go to Israel for the making of a film. Maria Svenson had invited them to her new house of redwood, by the ocean. She had built it with her own hands.

'With her own hands?'

'Yes. In those countries most people build their houses themselves.'

Maria would take them further north where the Lapps lived; they would see the midnight sun. Not once did Danielle ask if Nila wanted to join them. It was obvious that Maria had invited everyone from that night at Nicole's, except Nila.

Out of politeness, Danielle asked her about herself.

She lived in the hotel where Van Gogh had got a room for three and a half francs, a century lay between them and the price had increased hundred times.

'But you are rich, why are you worried! I have never earned or even seen so much money in my entire life.'

Nila said, 'Whatever you saw in Calcutta was my father's and brother's. My mother has left me some money and it is all I have for my entire life. I heard money could buy almost anything. But here, in Paris, one can't rent a house with it.'

Nila made a fervent plea to her to do something.

'What's the rent?'

'Say around six thousand.'

'Then you have to go to someone who earns four times that much. I don't. I'm of no use to you.'

'Any of your friends, Nicole, Rita, Michelle?'

'I doubt they will. Why don't you ask your Bengali friend? He earns well and I'm sure he'll agree.'

Nila didn't feel like talking to Sunil. She just lay there. Benoir came after work, to spend another night at the hotel. His touch woke her dreams, of a home, a family. The more he said Je t'aime, the more she wanted firm ground under her feet. She was afraid to live a loveless life like Molina.

When Benoir lay in her arms, like a child, Nila surrendered to wakefulness and gazed at his intense beauty. It wasn't like she didn't feel like pushing him off the bed at times, or even throwing him out of her room. But then her future loomed before her, hopeless, a victim of Sunil's desire everyday, living like a helpless woman. Although Benoir loved her, he didn't trust her yet. A vague sense of reproach kept her silent.

The next day she called Sunil and visited him at the clinic.

'Why did you leave like that? Even Chaitali said it wasn't the right thing to do,' Sunil said innocently, as if he had never stepped out of line with her or done anything objectionable.

Nila was exasperated and angry, 'Didn't you tell Chaitali the reason I left?'

'What reason?'

Nila balled her fists. She had never wanted to see this man or hear his voice or his strange laugh, but she had no choice, she needed a house for herself. She was surprised at her own tone of voice when Nila commanded, not requested, Sunil to be a guarantor for her house.

'Have you decided to live in Paris? Why don't you get your papers in order first? What'll happen if Kishan divorces you? Oh, of course, you have a French lover. So, are you marrying him?'

Nila shut him up, in the same commanding tone.

Eventually she was able to rent a place. It was in Rue de Vouyeer, seventy square metres, four rooms and the rent was seven thousand. She paid two months' advance rent and seven thousand to the broker, showed them Sunil's documents and guarantee and then got the key to the house. She entered the house on the fourth floor and took a few deep breaths of freedom. Sunil had said, 'What will you do with such a big house. You could have gone for a studio.' She could have; she could also have stayed in one of the tenements where the refugees lived without electricity and hot water, which were declared unlivable by the government and so the tenants occupied them and lived there for years without paying any rent. She could have rented a cheap place in Belle Ville where Mojammel and most black and brown people lived. Nila could have done many things, but she didn't. She had no regrets. She began to plan how she'd set up the house and how Benoir would be stunned when he entered the decorated apartment, how he'd kiss her and say, 'You amaze me every time I see you. You are wonderful.'

Nila opened all the windows and sat on the floor with her legs stretched out and leaned against the wall. The wind blew into the room; a lone bird came and sat on the balcony railing, shat on it and flew away. She had paid off her debt to Sunil and, Nila felt, he had paid his too. That's how he had looked, with that smile which people have when all their debts are paid off.

Nila threw up whatever she'd eaten at Chez Lullu.

A New Life

Life held little meaning for Nila now, yet she bought expensive things to decorate her home. Molina had never been able to decorate their home according to her wishes. It was always Anirban who decided where the sofa or the beds would be and even what was to be cooked that day in the kitchen. Molina was there only to execute his wishes. Anirban made it amply clear that the house was not Molina's and he was the lord and master. That's how it was until Nila left the country and Molina this world.

In the evening the people from the stores came and arranged the furniture, just the way Nila wanted it. It took her two more days to get the house looking the way she wanted, with flower pots in the balcony, orchids on the dining table, lilies on the coffee table, and a computer in the study in case Benoir wanted to use it. On that table she placed ten red roses.

Nila walked around in her home and felt delighted. A bedroom, a living room, a study and a guest room—now what, Nila, she asked herself, you've got everything! Then she answered her own question, but I feel so lonely!

She showered and stood on the balcony watching the people pass by and wondered whom, among them, she wanted, who would be nice to have here right now. If only there was a knock on the door and she found Molina standing outside! She had dropped by to see how Nila was doing in Paris. Nila would hug her, say, 'I love you, Ma. Don't ever leave me.' It was something she had never said before. She'd make Molina lie on the bed, lie down beside her and tell her all about the cruel world, everything. She would never be able to say it to anyone else. Bottling it all up, sometimes her heart felt like a dead weight.

She forgot her eager anticipation for Benoir in her conversation with her mother. When the day ended and the night bore darkness on its scavenging wings, she called Benoir and told him of her new abode.

'Why didn't you tell me what you were up to? Do I mean so little to you?'

Nila didn't answer.

When he walked in, Benoir was dumbstruck. 'Whose house is this?'

'What do you think?'

'I don't know. You tell me.'

Nila laughed, 'It's mine.'

Benoir sat on the sofa and frowned as he looked around. 'Yours?'

'Yes, mine.'

'How did you find a house? I thought you were looking for a place to rent and I was helping you do that?'

'You were helping me?'

'Wasn't I? I took you to see the houses in Emile Zola and Voissiray.'

'Oh.'

'Who else will live here?'

'Just me.'

'And?'

'And you?'

'How can I stay here?'

Nila said, 'If you don't want to, don't stay. I'll live here alone.'

'Such a big house just for you?'

'I'm used to a big place in Calcutta. I guess some habits die hard.'

'But you don't have a job. How will you pay the rent?'

'I've told you once, I can do without a job. Don't be afraid.'

'Hm.' Benoir sat there with a glum face.

Nila smiled at him and said, 'Aren't you happy?'

'What's there to be happy about?'

'Nothing? You saw me drifting around for so long, like a refugee, begging shelter here and there. My friend, Danielle, threw me out of her home. I wasn't happy in Sunil's house either, he has humiliated me in the worst possible way. I never had a truly dependable place to go to. I had no choice but to go to a hotel. Now I have a home of my own and you know how good that feels, to have your own home. Don't you know how peaceful it is? However much we love one another, I can only go to your home and stay in it, if you ask me to. If you wake me up at three in the night and tell me to leave, I'll have to, right?'

Benoir raised his voice and said, 'Have you gone mad? Why would I ask you to leave?'

'You haven't but you may one day. So can I, can't I?'

'Are you telling me to leave?'

She sat on the arms of the sofa, hugged him and said, 'Not at all. I want you at all times, in the day and at night, when I wake and when I sleep.'

Benoir looked around him and said, 'Have you won a lottery or something?'

The curtains were light green, just as the sofa and the bed linen.

'Are you also fond of light green?'

Nila laughed and said, 'Oh no, I like blue.'

'Then why is everything light green here?'

'That's because you like it.'

Benoir bit his lip and smiled sweetly. Nila placed her forefinger on his lips and said, 'When I love, this is how I love—one hundred per cent.'

'Do you know magic? How could you do all this in such a short while?'

Nila snapped her fingers.

Benoir heaved a sigh. 'Of course, if you have the money it can even be done in two minutes.'

Benoir walked into the bedroom, stood with his hands on Nila's waist, looked around at the light green bed, the two bedside tables, the lamps on them, the wall-to-wall wooden cupboard and clicked his tongue. 'You'd have got these much cheaper at Ikea. If you had waited, I could have taken you there.' He knocked on all the wooden furniture and said, 'This is not good wood; you've been cheated. Where did you buy these?'

'Habitat.'

'That's a useless store, rubbish. You should have asked me before buying all this. Ouf, you can be so stupid at times.'

Nila pulled his hand and brought him before the cupboard. 'Open this, and see.' Benoir opened it and said, 'Where did you buy it and for how much? I'm sure you'd have got it cheaper in other stores.'

'Just take a look inside.'

Benoir found men's clothes, shoes, shaving things, eau de toilette. 'Whose?'

'Guess!'

'Kishan's?'

'Question doesn't arise.'

'Then?'

'Take a guess?'

'Sunil's?'

'Why would Sunil's things be here?'

'Then?'

'Guess!'

'I can't.'

Nila laughed, traced her fingers on his chest and said, 'Yours.'

Taken aback, Benoir shouted, 'Have you gone mad, Nila?'

'Why?'

He sat down on the bed, the light green bed, and said, 'I have all these things already.'

Nila said, 'So what? But I have some doubts about the shoes; just see if they fit.' She took out the black Italian leather boots and kept them in front of him.

'Shoes? What size?'

'I don't know the size but I looked and thought they'd fit you.'

Benoir turned the shoe over, saw the number on the back and kept it aside; no, they weren't his size.

'Why have you bought all this for me?' Benoir asked, with fifteen furrows on his forehead.

Nila sat beside him, looked into eyes and said, 'I love you, that's why.'

One more surprise was yet to come. Nila took Benoir into the last room, with rows of books on the bookshelf and the computer on the desk.

Benoir raised his brows and said, 'You are going to use the computer?'

'No, I don't use machines. This is for you.'

'For me? But I have a computer.' Benoir tried to laugh.

'I know.'

He sat on the revolving chair. Nila plucked two wilted petals off the roses and said, 'If you feel like using a computer when you are in this house . . .'

'How many gigabytes is this?'

'I don't know that.'

'Do you know the RAM?'

'No.'

Benoir clicked his tongue again. Nila stood behind his chair and sank her fingers into his hair and kissed the thick blonde hair, 'Don't you like it?'

Benoir switched the computer on and said, 'Do you know more about computers than I do?'

Nila smiled sweetly. 'I didn't say I know more. I've bought it for you to use.'

He clicked his tongue again. 'I don't use these kinds of computers. You've just wasted your money.'

'Don't worry about the money; tell me what you like and I'll exchange it.'

'And they'll do it without a fuss?' He had the furrows on his face again.

'Okay, so you don't like the computer; what about the roses?'

Nila buried her nose in them. Benoir said, 'They look good.' But he made no attempt to smell them. Nila could tell that flowers were mostly a pleasure to the Western eye and not a delightful scent.

Benoir stood by the bookshelf and asked, 'Have you bought these books in Paris?'

'Some, yes. The rest I brought from Calcutta.'

'All of them are classics.'

'Not all, some. I have always wanted to have a home of my own which will have a library.'

He pointed to *Ulysses*. 'Have you read that?'

Nila shrugged. 'I never could go beyond twenty pages and I don't think I ever will read more than that.'

Benoir walked towards the kitchen. 'I need some coffee; do you have it?'

Nila followed him as she said, 'Of course.'

She leaned against the kitchen door and said, 'But I don't know how to make coffee.'

Benoir started making it for himself. Nila stood beside him and said, 'As you know, I am hooked on tea.'

Nila learnt how to make coffee in the machine; Benoir directed her. He took the cup of coffee and sat at the dining table. Nila made herself some tea and sat in front of him; her eyes smiled, her lips smiled. Benoir stirred some sugar into his coffee and asked, 'Have you read anything by Tom Clancy?'

'No.'

'Stephen King?'

'No.'

'Ed McBain? Tory Brookes?'

'No.'

'Then . . .' Benoir paused.

Nila said, 'Actually I haven't read too much of contemporary Western literature. I've read more of Bengali.'

'Elmore Leonard?'

'No.'

'George Simenot?'

'No.'

'David Eddings?'

'No.'

Benoir sipped his coffee.

'Have you read Terri Pratchett?'

'No.' Nila looked stricken.

'What? You haven't read such a famous writer?'

'No.'

'You haven't even heard of her?'

'No.'

'You said you love reading, and yet . . . don't worry, I'll lend you some of her books.' He poured himself more coffee.

'What kind of novels does she write?' Nila sat with the tea in front of her.

'Oh, I can't describe. If you start the book, you won't be able to put it down.'

Nila held his hand and said, 'Don't you want to see what else is there for you?'

Benoir's voice was cool, 'What?'

She brought a bottle of Moët and Chandon champagne and placed it in his hands. 'Just what is needed in a new house, the bubbly, right?'

'I have to drive. It won't be right to drink.'

Nila was startled. She had never seen him being so cautious.

'But you do drive after a few drinks.'

'Perhaps I did, but it's not right.'

'How can you think of right and wrong in this new house, today? Oh please, just pour the champagne, it'll be fine.' Nila brought two champagne glasses.

Benoir heaved a sigh, 'Well, if you insist, I guess I'll have to.'

He uncorked the bottle with a morose expression. The froth leapt out noisily. Nila's joyful shout drowned out that sound.

They went to the balcony, champagne glasses in hand.

'It's nice out here, isn't it?'

Before he could answer her, one way or another, the phone in Benoir's pocket rang. He went into the room as he talked into it. Nila stood outside, eyes closed against the pleasant breeze. He came back and said, 'Pascale is coming back to Paris tomorrow.'

The champagne glass shook in her hands. Nila drained it swiftly, 'It's a good champagne, isn't it?'

'Nila, Pascale is coming back to Paris tomorrow.'

'I heard.'

'So say something?'

'What can I say?'

'Do you know that I have told Pascale all about you and me?'

'No, you didn't tell me.'

'Well, I am telling you now. She knows about us.'

'So what do you want me to do?'

'Do you know that Pascale and I have a daughter called Jacqueline?'

'I know.'

'Can you imagine how difficult it is for Pascale to accept our relationship?'

Nila went inside to pour herself more champagne. When she tried to pour him some too, he moved his glass and banged it down on a corner of the table. He took her by the shoulders and shook her, 'Why don't you say something? Have you lost your tongue? Until now you had a lot to say, you showed me the house and all the expensive things you've bought. So talk now!'

Nila drank the champagne in long gulps as if it was water. She looked into Benoir's eyes, those blue eyes, the ones she loved.

She said, 'I know it's not possible for Pascale to accept this. You go and apologize to her and don't come back to me ever. I won't call you either.'

Benoir smashed his glass on the floor and shouted, 'Is that what you want?'

Nila trembled at the noise. He pulled her up from the chair and said, 'Look into my eyes.'

Nila stared at the shards of broken glass at her feet.

'What are you looking at—have I ruined your expensive set of glasses?'

She looked up and into his eyes, they were trembling with concern.

'Do you want to end our relationship? Is that your wish?'

Tear stood still in the corners of Nila's eyes. Benoir held up her chin and stared at those tears until they rolled down her cheeks. She sobbed, 'No, that's not what I want.'

Benoir hugged her close and kissed her like a madman. Nila went weak at the knees. He picked up her weightless body, laid her on the bed, rubbed his lips on her breasts and said, 'Je t'aime, je t'aime.'

Nila heaved a sigh of relief. Did Anirban ever love Molina like this? Anirban had never hugged Molina to his chest as Benoir was doing to her and never said he loved her. If only Molina could be a bird on the window sill and see how someone was loving her daughter.

'Hey, what are you thinking?' Benoir held her chin and turned her face towards him.

She sighed, 'Nothing.'

'It must be something. Tell me.'

'Benoir, do you really love me?'

'Why are you asking me this? Can't you tell?'

'Sometimes . . .'

'Sometimes what?'

'Sometimes I find it very strange that you love me. Who am I? I am nothing, nobody. I have no friends, no relatives. My life is a crumpled mess.'

'You have me! I will give you everything, everything.'

Benoir gave Nila everything, much more than her body needed. Not once, but many times, all night long.

When the dawn kissed her brow, she said, 'Don't you want to sleep? It's been seven times already.'

Benoir levered his head on his left hand, lay on his right side and played with his favourite cherries as he said, 'Nila, you have robbed me of my sleep. You are such a basket of surprises, the deeper I go, the more I want to know. Each time is like the first time. The more I quench my thirst, the thirstier I get. I love it when you writhe in pleasure. When you clench my shoulders in magnificent joy, I feel I am truly a man.'

In the morning Benoir's gentle touch woke Nila, 'Good morning, madame.' He held a tray in his hands, with croissants and tea in it. His face was tranquil.

Nila felt she was drinking nectar rather than tea.

Benoir said, 'I am sorry, Nila, yesterday I wasn't myself.'

He had made his own coffee. Anirban or Kishanlal had never made coffee or tea for themselves. Neither had she ever heard them apologize for their mistakes. Nila gazed at Benoir with wonder in her eyes, she gazed at herself and at her good fortune.

'I looked at you, sleeping, for a long time. You slept like a child. I crept away so that you didn't wake up, cleared the champagne glass, swept the place clean, had a shower and went to the boulangerie. I bought the croissants, made the tea and woke you up.'

Benoir counted as he kissed her a hundred times, picked one of the two keys to the house and left for work. Every two hours he called from work and told her that he loved her. He also told her that he'd have to go to the station after work to pick up Pascale and then go home. He would also have to stay at home that night, for Jacqueline and not for Pascale.

Nila spent her day reading, watching TV, lying down, listening to music. She went into the kitchen, but didn't feel like cooking; she picked up the phone, but didn't dial. She stood before the mirror, stripped and stared at herself, made faces and laughed.

At night she lay in her bed, stared at the black sky and thought of Benoir kissing Pascale, just as he kissed Nila. Pascale came into the bedroom after putting Jacqueline to bed and Benoir hugged her and said je t'aime, je t'aime, je t'aime passionment. Then he stripped her just as he took off Nila's clothes. If Nila's nipples were cherries then Pascale's were lingonberries. He was stroking her white skin and saying, 'What a lovely colour, how smooth your skin is.' His penis was erect and impatient to enter Pascale; all night long he pleasured Pascale the way he did Nila.

The hot breath of Pascale burned Nila all night long.

From Five to Seven

The following week, Benoir came to Nila's at five every evening and left by seven. He had to because he was having dinner with Pascale, playing boogey-man with Jacqueline and some days he had to take them out or they had a dinner invitation.

Nila stayed at home all day. She had nowhere to go. She spent the whole day waiting for Benoir to come at five o'clock. After he left at seven, she spent the rest of the evening and night guarding his touch, his smell on her body. On Friday evening when he came and tried to kiss her as usual, she moved away.

'What's the matter, what's wrong with you?'

'Is this how you kiss Pascale?'

'Why are you asking me all this? I didn't hide anything from you. You knew I was married.'

Nila couldn't deny that. She couldn't deny that even after knowing everything, she had surrendered herself. But when he leaned towards her, she moved away and asked, 'Do you do all this with Pascale?'

Benoir threw back his arms and lay flat on his back. His blue eyes were shielded by the eyelids. Just the red eye of the penis stared at the sky.

Nila waited for his answer.

'Don't you know that I married Pascale for love?'

'I know.'

'Then why are you asking me all this?'

'I hate having to share you with someone.'

'Nila, you are so selfish.'

Nila was silent.

'Just think of Pascale! She loves me too.'

'You also love her, don't you?'

'Listen Nila, I don't lie. Any other married man would tell his lover that he hates his wife and loves only her. But Nila, I have given this a lot of thought, and truly, I love both of you.'

'Is that possible?'

'Why not?'

'I cannot imagine loving another man, sleeping with him.'

'Some truths can't be visualized until one faces them.' The red eye leaned towards the window. 'You wouldn't understand, Nila. You didn't marry for love, you don't have children. It's not possible for you to understand.' Benoir got up, naked as he was, and took out his wallet from the pocket of the trousers lying on the floor. He took out four photographs from it: Jacqueline and Pascale, the daughter kissing the mother, Benoir hugging Pascale from behind while Jacqueline sat on her lap, Pascale and Benoir and the last one was of Jacqueline alone, two years ago. Nila saw them, but Benoir took even longer over them. The red eye drooped.

'Isn't Jacqueline just like me?'

Nila stared hard, but couldn't find the slightest similarity.

'Her nose is the exact replica of mine.'

'Is it? Her nose is short.' Nila spoke softly.

'It is. But it'll grow as she grows. Just look at her ears.'

Nila didn't say anything; surely, Jacqueline's ears, when she grew up, would be just like Benoir's.

'Your hair is blonde. Her hair seems to be reddish.'

'That's because Pascale has red hair. But she says Jacqueline's hair is not so reddish any more, it is turning blonde gradually.'

'Oh!'

'Isn't she an amazing child?'

Nila took the photograph: a few strands of red hair on her head, her face marked by red boils, the gums exposed in a huge smile and two rotten teeth.

'Yes.' Nila's voice held no warmth.

'There's no child in the world prettier than her.' Benoir held the photo to his heart and smiled contentedly. 'Jacqueline is my raison d'être. She is the only meaningful part of my life.'

Suddenly he got up and asked, 'Don't you ever feel like seeing her?'

Nila didn't know what to say. Jacqueline was like any other child to her. She often saw a bunch of kids going to the museum with their teachers. Jacqueline could be any one of them.

'Jacqueline is a part of me, Nila. If you love me, you have to love her too.'

Nila spoke coolly, 'I have never seen Jacqueline. Love does not fall from the sky. Any relationship needs some time to grow.'

'Shame on you, Nila, you can't love an innocent child! It's easy to love any child and you are actually jealous of Jacqueline.'

'Rubbish! Why would I be jealous of her?'

'That's what is surprising; she hasn't done you any harm. You should be able to love a child quite easily, right?'

'I can, if the child is a genius.'

'How do you know Jacqueline isn't one?'

'I didn't say she is not. Perhaps she is a brilliant girl and we will be great friends; maybe I will love her a lot. I'll love her for who she is and not because she is your daughter. That would be false. Love, of all things, can't be enforced.'

'If you had a daughter, wouldn't you want me to love her, like my own daughter?'

'I would, but I wouldn't have forced you.'

'You'd have been pleased if I loved her, right?'

'Yes.'

'So then, why don't you understand that if you love Jacqueline, I will be happy. We should try to do things that'll please each other. You've decorated your house in light green because it's my favourite colour, right? No one forced you there.'

Nila left the bed. She felt Benoir's next wish would be that she love Pascale because she was his wife, and if she didn't, it'd make her a very selfish, sordid person.

Benoir reached out and drew her close. He placed her head on his chest, took in the smell of her long dark hair and said, 'Don't you want a child, Nila? A baby who'll play in this room and we'll watch, pretty, lively? Your life would be complete, giving birth to a child, an innocent child.'

Nila closed her eyes. A pretty, doll-like, golden-haired, white baby came running to her calling, 'Ma, Ma.' She picked up the child and Benoir hugged the two of them. Nila wanted to lie on his chest like that forever as he whispered about children in her ears, weave dreams around her.

'Do you want a son?'

Benoir said, 'Either one, girl or boy.' He kissed her.

'But what will be the child's identity?'

'The child of our love—isn't that enough?'

Nila looked at the window. 'We are not married.' There was just bright daylight outside the window.

'You said one day that you didn't believe in marriage, only in love. Why are you suddenly leaning towards marriage today?' Benoir turned her around to face him, 'You said that you hate Indian orthodoxy. And now you are angling for that?'

Nila's voice broke. 'Why do you love me, Benoir? You have a wife, a child, a happy family; what's the point . . .'

'I thought I loved only Pascale. But something happened deep inside. You appeared in my life like a flash of lightning. Now I need you, I have no choice, I love you. I think of you all day. At night I wake up suddenly, dreaming of you. This morning Pascale said I called out your name in my sleep.'

'So she knows all about me?'

Benoir sighed, 'Yes, she knows. She finds it very difficult to accept, though she doesn't say anything to me. She never asked me a second time about you. I feel for her too. But what can I do? I can't do without her, she is the mother of my Jacqueline. And I can't do without you, because you are my unbridled passion. Without you I am a dead soul.'

Nila got up and went into the kitchen.

The wilted, crinkled red eye hung limply at his thighs when Benoir came and stood behind her in the kitchen. 'What's the matter? Why did you come away?'

'To make some tea.'

'Don't you have anything to say?'

'Benoir, I feel our relationship is becoming very complicated. I really cannot understand whom you love, who you want to spend the rest of your life with. Of course, you say you love both of us, you need both of us. Tomorrow if another woman comes into your life, what will you do? You would want her in your life as well, won't you?'

Benoir's tone was listless. 'I won't ever love anyone else.'

'But you said that to Pascale before you met me, didn't you? You must have said she would always be your only love. But what happened? You said you love me. I don't know if this is true love or you don't want to let go the chance to enjoy another body. By hook or by crook . . . fooling a stupid girl . . .'

'For shame, Nila!'

Benoir shrank back from her, went into the bedroom and got dressed. When Nila came in with the tea, he was tying his shoelaces.

'Are you leaving? I have cooked for you—Bengali food. I bought some good wine too, the kind you like.'

'You have it.'

'Won't you eat? You must be hungry. Did you have lunch?'

'Sandwiches.'

'That's all? Come and eat.' Nila pulled him by the hand.

Benoir pulled his hand away and said, 'Eating is no big deal to me, it may be to you. There's nothing more valuable to you than rice because half your country starves to death.'

After he left, Nila took a chair into the balcony and sat there. She felt the joy that had come into her life was receding, going out of her reach.

At night she picked up a huge book and sat on the sofa. She didn't want to think about Benoir that night. She had no answers to the complex questions in her life. Homer Wells was a far better alternative. He began his life in an orphanage, the strange and curious Homer. Nila felt she was like him, an orphan, no one wanted her and no one took her in.

Late in the night the phone rang and Nila leapt up. The book rolled to the floor.

'Je t'aime, Nila.'

Nila arrested the 'Moi aussi,' on her tongue.

'What were you doing?'

'Reading.'

'Reading what?'

'Nothing much; just some strange things happening in a house where they make apple cider—'

'Do you know what happened tonight?' Benoir sounded as if he'd announce that he had left Pascale.

'What happened?' Nila was excited.

'I didn't eat dinner.'

'Oh.'

'I wanted to have it with you.'

Nila picked up the book from the floor. She glanced through the last page and shut the book.

'Do you love me, Nila?' Benoir asked.

'Don't you know?'

'I do. But I like to hear you say it.'

Nila had to say je t'aime because he liked to hear her say it.

The next morning she woke up to his touch. She wanted to tell him to go away. She'd spend her lonely life alone. But when his tongue searched for hers, went deeper, searched for the cherries and found them like discovering untold wealth, when his sunburnt body desperately sought her cool waters and drank it up like a thirsty man, and when Nila was completely covered by his lithe body, her desire to be alone vanished. Nila felt even if Benoir loved a hundred women and not just Pascale, it was all right. It was enough if she got one out of hundred parts of him. Beggars were not choosers. She knew she didn't deserve to have Benoir all to herself.

Benoir was to spend the whole day with Nila because Pascale had gone to a friend's house for the day. She had taken the car and Benoir had come by metro. Benoir felt it was silly to spend the day inside when it was a bright day outside. So they went out. They would go to Quartier Latar first and then they would roam around. Who lived there? Jean Jacques. He was in Paris for just a few days; he lived in Marseilles. He was a very talented man. This country had no dearth of talented men and so Nila didn't ask anything more about this Jean Jacques. They took a taxi, went to a six-storeyed house in Quartier Latar on Rue Pierre et Marie Curie and when it was exactly five minutes past eleven by Benoir's watch, they went upstairs. A man with long hair and a beard opened the door a crack, stared at the visitors and shut the door on their faces. A few minutes later another man, with a smile on his face, opened the door wide and invited them in. Benoir introduced himself. Nila assumed Benoir didn't know who Jean Jacques was. The smiling man invited them into the room. Benoir held Nila's hand tightly and his palms sweated in her grip.

She didn't get a chance to ask him anything. The man passed two empty rooms and led them into a small, dark room with two stools and one sofa. He sat on the sofa and his nose didn't look half as red in the dark. He stopped smiling and spoke in sombre tones, 'You are Benoir Dupont, aren't you?'

'Yes.'

'Born in Orléans?'

'Yes.'

'October, 1979?'

'Yes.'

'Quite healthy, even as a child?'

'Yes.'

'Met this girl quite suddenly?'

'Yes.'

'You love her.'

'Yes.'

'But you have a wife.'

'And a daughter.'

'She is very small?'

'Yes.' Benoir's voice was mechanical.

'Jacqueline has a disease, doesn't she?' Jean Jacques picked up a pen and chewed the top. His eyes were keen. Suddenly a bright green light came on, above Benoir's head. He had beads of sweat on his brow.

Jean Jacques spoke again, 'Quite an old affliction?'

'Yes, ears.'

'She is a little hard of hearing, right?'

Benoir said, 'Yes, that happens sometimes.' He looked anxious.

'What is your wife's name? Fabien? François? Pascale?'

'Pascale.'

Jean Jacques turned towards Nila. 'This girl—yes, it'll work; go ahead. She is from India. Indian women are sensible, they don't act on impulse—ha, ha, ha.'

Jean Jacques laughed and the light over Benoir's head went off. The room was dark and there was a sharp sound. 'Tell me, what is the problem?' The lights were back and this time it was red.

Beneath those lights Benoir looked like a ghost and his voice became more mechanical. Nila took one of his hands into hers. It was ice cold.

'Alcatel is downsizing, right?'

'Yes.'

'You've also considered taking a job with Ericsson?'

'I have applied.'

'But you want to stay on at Alcatel?'

'Yes. I am due for promotion here.'

'But there are no signs of it yet, right?'

'Yes.'

The man fished out a pack of cards from his shirt pocket. He shuffled them and placed them face down on the table. Benoir had to pick up one. His hands trembled as he picked out the six of spades. He held out the card to Jean Jacques and the lights went off. The room lay in silence. Benoir's breathing was the only sound in it.

Nila said, 'What is all this. Let's go.'

Benoir gripped her hand tightly and said, 'Shhh.'

This time a different light, neither red nor green, came on. It wasn't over Benoir's head but at Jean Jacques' feet, between the cracks in the wooden floor. The room was full of the scent of incense. Nila felt very uncomfortable.

Benoir wiped the sweat off his brow and looked a little calmer.

Jean Jacques looked him in the eye keenly and said, 'This evening, take one kilo of corn and scatter it in some woods. Two weeks later do the same with two kilos of corn. Are you thinking a wood in Paris will do? No, that won't do; you'll have to go outside the city.'

Benoir gave the man two thousand francs and came out of the place. Once at the stairs, Nila burst into laughter.

'Why are you laughing?'

'You went to an astrologer?'

Benoir took the stairs quickly with Nila close on his heels.

'Why were you giggling over there?' Benoir was irritated.

Nila hid her smile and said, 'You believe in all this?'

'Of course.' Benoir was solemn.

Nila laughed, 'You are joking.'

'No Nila. Many people have seen this man and they've had results.'

'You believe that if you scatter corn to the winds, you won't get sacked from Alcatel?'

'Perhaps.' Benoir began to walk.

Nila barred his way and asked again, 'You are going to do this?'

Benoir sidestepped her. 'Sure.'

Nila stood there as her scarf came loose and fell off her neck. Suddenly she realized that Benoir had walked on ahead. She ran up to him, took his hand and asked, 'Where are you going?'

'Come, I'll show you the Panthéon.'

'Fine. I thought you were off to scatter corn.'

Benoir didn't answer. But he said, 'You are so careless!' when a man shouted 'Mademoiselle, mademoiselle,' and ran after her with her scarf held between two fingers.

Panthéon! In 1744, when Louis XV escaped death narrowly, he was so glad to be alive that he decided to build a church for Sainte Geneviève. The French architect Jacques Germain started the work twenty years later, in the neo-classical style and it took twenty-five years to complete the church. The revolutionists left this one intact and made it the Panthéon, where famous Frenchmen would be laid to rest. They dug up the graves of Victor Hugo, Emile Zola, Voltaire, Rousseau, and Madame and Pierre Curie. Napoleon declared it a church again in 1806. The Panthéon had to wait another eighty years to be a pantheon again. From the dome a huge pendulum dangled, to which the French physicist Leo Foucault had pointed to indicate that the earth moved in its orbit.

Nila stood beside Madame Curie's coffin and said, 'This is the pride of Poland, not France.'

Benoir said she was the pride of France because she had lived here and it didn't matter where she was born.

Nila spoke slowly. 'I live here. If I were to make a great discovery, would I be called a pride of France?'

Benoir didn't answer.

Nila said instead, 'Yes, I would. But until then, I'll be an Indian, poor, starving, pauper, an immigrant here to destroy French culture.'

Nila laughed loudly. Benoir warned her that it wasn't allowed to laugh so loudly here.

Loud, mock sobs: 'Is it okay to cry here?'

'No.'

Nila stood before Voltaire's statue and said, 'Does that coffin hold Voltaire's remains?'

Benoir laughed. 'It'll be a few bones by now.'

Nila also laughed. 'That's true. But you know what I feel? I feel there's nothing of Voltaire here.'

'Of course there is.'

'But as far as I know, Christian fundamentalists stole his body, and dumped it in the rubbish heap. Of course, they preserved the heart in the bibliothèque and the brain was auctioned many times over and has disappeared since.'

Benoir laughed her story off.

They came out of the Panthéon and he said, 'I don't think Voltaire was all that great.'

He didn't go into why he thought that way, but he felt Descartes was really something. He reeled off stories about Descartes's amazing mathematical prowess and his geometric theories. Nila still mused about Voltaire.

'Cogito ergo sum.' Benoir repeated it twice.

'What's that?' Nila asked.

'Descartes's famous Latin phrase.'

Nila didn't know it. Benoir explained, 'I think therefore I am.'

Nila said, 'Descartes believed in God, didn't he?'

Benoir regurgitated, 'Everything in this universe is created by

God. The human mind is like Him, it thinks. Man has form and God does not. Man dies, his brain stops thinking and God is eternal, His thoughts remain and He doesn't depend on the creator for his existence.'

Benoir's eyes went heavenward. He loosened his grip on Nila's hand and asked, 'Don't you believe in God?'

Nila laughed and said, 'I believe in François Marie Arouet.'

'Who is that?'

'A Frenchman, born in Paris.'

'Are you in love with him?'

Nila laughed, 'Yes, for a long time.'

'What does he look like?'

'Handsome, slim, lithe body.'

'Have you slept with him?'

'No, not yet.' Nila slipped her fingers into his.

Benoir asked, 'Is he older or younger than me?'

'Older,' she thought for a moment, 'Not much, about two hundred and eighty-five years older than you.'

Benoir laughed. Nila joined him.

'So, why do you believe in him?' He was eager to know.

'Many reasons. François suffered a lot in his lifetime. He critiqued the French government in his poetry and the government imprisoned him in the Bastille for eleven months. After his release, he began to write. Then once, he insulted someone, a powerful man in society. He had to be punished for it. Either the prison, or exile. François opted for exile. He went to a neighbouring country, I won't say which one. He lived there for thirty years and came back to Paris and wrote a book in praise of that country. It was an old enemy of France . . .'

'I know, England. Who is this man? Dreyfus? Alfred Dreyfus?'

'If you were two hundred and eighty-five years younger than Dreyfus, you wouldn't be born yet. And England doesn't have an island, a penal one, where Dreyfus lived. Anyway, the French government wouldn't take it. François was to be punished yet again. He went into exile again. This time he didn't go too far from France. At least he didn't cross an ocean.'

'Did he go to Belgium?'

'No.'

'Italy?'

'No.'

'Spain?'

'No. He wrote many books in his exile, against ignorance and for reason. When he returned home at the age of eighty-three, he received a grand welcome. He died in Paris. But he couldn't be buried in a church because he was quite pronouncedly against religion. Eventually he was interned in an abbey of Chopin. He was brought back to Paris towards the end of the eighteenth century, with great honour of course.'

Nila noticed that Benoir's attention had wandered. He pointed to a fairly large building and said, 'Look at that building, it is my school, École normale supérieur. It's the most famous school in France and it's a great honour to study here. If you can get in here, you'd receive ninety thousand francs a year. I got it too. Many people have studied here and gone on to take the Nobel Prize. Have you heard of Louis Pasteur?'

Nila nodded.

'Michel Foucault? Jean Paul Sartre? Romain Rolland? Henri Bergsson?'

Nila had heard of them too.

'They were all graduates of this school.' Benoir pulled her towards him. He looked very contented.

Benior wore a light green T-shirt and khaki shorts. Clothes were all the better if they were shorter in summer. Nila wore a short skirt, with half her thighs exposed, and a tight black top. She wore high heels and still felt short. Nila was always conscious of her slight paunch. But Benoir told her it looked good on women. These days women were so keen to reduce any flab, that they fell sick and didn't have any breasts or thighs to speak of. His words gave her courage. Now she could wear such short clothes and go out quite comfortably. Nila noticed that French men looked at women's heels and legs more often, if at all. Indian men would gaze at the breasts first. Women's legs, however smooth and pretty, were not attractive to Indian men.

Nila found it very strange. In India Nila was considered too thin and in Paris she was seen as quite a healthy woman. In fact Catherine had told her she could reduce a few pounds.

They had lunch at a brasserie in Quartier Latar. Nila asked for a salad.

'What's the matter, do you want to be like those anaemic women?'

It wasn't entirely untrue. She had seen obese women in the streets. Most of them, Nila noticed, were alone. Perhaps one day Benoir would say, 'You've put on so much weight!' Nila was sure Pascale weighed at least five kilos less than her.

She had her salad and said, 'You have studied in such a good, modern school and you believe in the occult? The man is a fake.'

'Don't label someone without knowing anything, Nila. How did he know my age, Pascale's name and about Jacqueline's illness?'

'He must have found out.'

'No. The sister of a friend of my colleague's brother went to see him. My colleague never went there. He just got the address for me. And his brother or his friend don't know me from Adam.'

'They must have given your name at the time of taking the appointment. So the man must have gathered information from your name.'

'There must be a few thousand Benoir Duponts in Paris. Jean Jacques isn't even from here. Didn't you notice, he spoke French with the Marseilles accent?' Benoir corrected her.

'They have informers, don't you know that? Those people find out everything about the people who come there. And speaking with an accent is no problem at all.'

Benoir shook his head, unconvinced. After leaving the restaurant, he surprised Nila by buying one kilo of ground corn, going to the Bois de Bologne outside Paris, and scattering it in the woods.

At home, Nila headed for the foamy bathtub, to get rid of the day's surprises. Benoir joined her. There were two glasses of wine placed on the corner of the tub. The lights were switched off and the magic candles were lit. They soaked in the soft glow and sipped the wine. Benoir poured some liquid soap on the handtowel and brushed it over Nila's body. Nila began to enjoy it and the day's events that were bothering her, began to recede into the background. Her body lay hidden by the foamy bubbles and only the cherries peeked out. Benoir leaned forward to lick the cherries, but they dipped down. His tongue and the cherries played hide and seek. Benoir's body rose in response. It touched Nila all over, her breathing became shallower. He picked up her feet from the water and gazed at them in wonder— the smooth brown legs. Benoir's body rose and fell on Nila's body, keeping time with Beethoven's music, until the demonic sound of the mobile pierced the tranquil haven.

Benoir left at eleven in the night. As he left he delivered the last surprise: he wasn't coming back the next day or for the next ten days, for that matter. He was going to the Riviera with his wife and daughter, for a holiday, to sunbathe. What was Nila supposed to do here? She could think about him, think how much she loved him, think that wherever he was, Nila was always in his heart.

When Nila had shut the door, the windows, switched off the lights and the Beethoven, drowned herself in the silence and listened to her own sighs, there was a knock on the door.

Benoir had come back from the foot of the stairs to ask her a question.

'Who was that François of yours?'
'Voltaire.'

Love in This Foreign Land

Benoir returned from his holiday and took Nila out. They went to the Versailles gardens. In the beautiful garden on two thousand acres, designed by La Notre, she sat down beside the grand canal, face towards the palace, half wet from the fountains.

'Would you like to see the palace? The Sun King's room, Queen Marie Thérèse's room?'

Nila broke off a stalk of grass, bit it and asked, 'Why did the king and queen have separate bedrooms?'

Benoir said, 'It's a huge palace. No point crowding into one room.'

Nila touched the grass to his lips and said, 'Or was it because your Louis spent his time with his three mistresses?'

Benoir kissed Nila and said, 'Our Louis also married his mistress.'

Nila lay sprawled on the grass, looked up at the sky and said, 'After marrying her, he must have given that wife a separate bedroom too.'

'Drop it. Now do you want to go inside the palace?' Benoir rushed her.

Nila still lay there and said, 'Forget it. I shudder when I see all that glittering, shimmering wealth.'

'But why?'

'I feel like a poor, distressed subject, like I'm being whipped by the kings, for no reason.'

Benoir leaned on his elbows, lay back and said, 'Let me at least show you the Hall of Mirrors, famous for the Versailles Treaty.'

Nila took his left hand in hers and touched the fingers to her cheek. The gold ring on his ring finger, the symbol of his bond with Pascale, touched her cheek.

'What's the point of seeing that room? The Versailles Treaty didn't bring any peace. On the contrary it paved the way for another world war.'

Benoir sat up and said, 'Don't talk rubbish. Just say you don't feel like getting up from here.'

Nila's hair blew in the wind. It covered her face, her breasts. She sat up, swiftly wound her hand through it and tied it into a bun as she said she wanted to go to number twelve, Rue de Châtiere instead.

'What is that?'

'It's not a palace. It's a hovel where a poet once lived. A great poet.'

'What is his name?'

'Madhusudan Dutta.'

'What kind of a name is that? It's not a French name?'

'Neither is Oscar Wilde, or Gertrude Stein or Henrik Ibsen. Do you find these names strange?' she asked. Then she said, 'No you don't. Madhusudan Dutta was a Bengali.'

'Oh, so that's it. A Bengali.'

Benoir heaved a sigh of relief. Not knowing a Bengali poet's name and not knowing the name of a tiny insect in the Amazon was the same. It didn't really matter. Why should he know of Madhusudan, one of the greatest poets of Bengali literature? Instead he knew of Sai Baba, Deepak Chopra, Swami Prabhupada!

Although Benoir showed no interest in Madhusudan, Nila told him his story: Madhusudan was the son of a zamindar and he felt terribly drawn to European art and culture from a very young age. He wore European clothes, wrote poetry in English, converted to Christianity. He hated his own race so much that he said, 'God has sent the Anglo-Saxons to this world to save the Hindus, to civilize them and to convert them.' When he was in Madras, he married Henrietta, French girl. His father threw him out. Madhusudan came to England and became a lawyer. He spent his days in great hardship here in Versailles. Friends sent money from Calcutta to keep him going. At first he was happy in France because here he wasn't called a damn nigger, like in England. Instead, if he saluted the French emperor and empress, they saluted back. Gradually his dream of becoming a great writer in a European language dwindled, his infatuation waned. He remembered his past, the banyan tree by the river, the legends and tales, epics of ancient India. When he was in Versailles, he wrote some sonnets, inspired by Petrarch, the Italian poet. Petrarch and Madhusudan had a few things in common: Petrarch's father too was a lawyer and he made his son become one, but Petrarch gave it all up and dived into the world of art and letters. Madhusudan was the same. The difference was that Madhusudan didn't write sonnets only about his lover. He and Baudelaire also shared some traits: they were both bohemians and given to liquor and other addictive pleasures. Madhusudan went back to Calcutta from Versailles and thank god for that or Bengali literature would have been deprived of some of its grandest poetry. Nila stood in front of the house at number twelve, Rue de Châtiere and looked at the stone slab:

LE POÈTE INDIEN
MICHAEL MADHUSUDAN DUTTA
(1824–1873)
À DEMEURE DANS CETTE MAISON DE 1863 A 1865 ET Y A
COMPOSÉ EN BENGALI DES SONNETS ET DES FABLES

She went down on her knees and touched a bit of the dust to her brow. Benoir laughed, 'Why did you do that?'

'I saluted Madhusudan.'

'Was that to Madhusudan or the soil of France?'

'I did it because Madhusudan had once walked upon this soil.' Nila walked indifferently as she answered.

'But since then so many others have walked upon it, so many Louis, Phillipe, Valerie . . .'

Nila took the words from his mouth and said, 'So many Benoir, Pascale, Jacqueline . . .'

She changed the subject and said, 'So how was your holiday?'

Benoir didn't answer. He sighed when he got into the car, and said, 'You have changed a lot, Nila.'

'What makes you say that?'

'You always walked holding my hand. Today you didn't.'

Nila denied his allegation and reminded him that she took his hand as they sat in the Versailles gardens and she had noticed how snugly the gold ring fit his lovely white finger.

Benoir's voice was faint, 'Nila, you are fooling me.'

How can I fool you, I am weak, poor, common and feeble!

They stopped at a roadside café for some coffee. Benoir was grumbling about the thirty per cent of one's income which had to be given to the French government as tax, and how happy the people in Monaco were because they didn't have to pay tax. If he were in Monaco he'd have saved that money. They parked near the Pont-Neuf and walked towards the Notre-Dame, towards the bridge, which gave a clear view of all of Paris. Nila wanted to stand on that bridge and look at the Seine. Whenever she did that, she saw Joan d'Arc's ashes floating in the water. She was sure she caught a fleeting glimpse of Joan d'Arc's image in the water. Suddenly a question flew into her mind like a feather: did the Ganga and the Seine have anything in common? The water in the Ganga was also muddy. Then she looked at the bridge instead and her mind flew back to the Ganga. No! The Ganga was unbridled and the Seine was like an aquarium; one couldn't spend one's life with the Seine. All the waters in the world were not the same. Her mind drifted to Catherine Grand who had also stood here once, just like Nila. She was also from Calcutta, the daughter of a French official in Chandannagar. She was breathtakingly beautiful and the youth of Calcutta lost their night's sleep because of her. Such a beauty was married off to an elderly English officer, Francis Grand. The French Revolution was still in the future. A French youth, Phillippe, fell madly in love with her, scaled the walls of her house and went into her bedroom at night. Everyone came to know of it. Francis sued him and made him pay a heavy fine. It was a huge scandal and Catherine had to become the mistress of her French lover. She changed hands and her fate didn't improve when she came from Calcutta to London and then to Paris as his mistress. She must have been as old as Nila when she came there. She stayed in the Hôtel de Ville and one day she walked to this very bridge and stood there like Nila. A lout pulled at her clothes and a few others stood and laughed. Catherine changed hands again and again and finally rolled into the lap of Talleyrand as his mistress. At the time Talleyrand was the foreign secretary. But it was Catherine who conducted most of his business with the foreign ambassadors. That too became a scandal in Paris and finally Napoleon pulled him up. Then Catherine pulled a fast one over her lover. She bowed to Napoleon and declared that she was carrying Talleyrand's child in her womb. Napoleon was crazy for an heir then and he was even considering giving a divorce to Josephine, his dear wife, and marrying Marie Louise. Immediately he commanded Talleyrand to marry his mistress and his command had to be obeyed. Eventually, the girl who spoke French with a Calcutta accent became a minister's wife at a ripe age, after spending many years as different men's mistress. But if she hadn't played that little trick, she'd have died a mistress. Nila felt that after two hundred years it was Catherine again who was standing with her on the bridge.

Benoir's touch brought Nila back to her senses. He said, 'It looks like bad weather. Let's go home.'

Nila looked at the storm clouds in the sky and danced for joy. 'This is great weather. Why do you call it bad? Let's get wet in the rain.'

Nila wanted to get drenched but Benoir wasn't born under the scalding hot sun and rain was no welcome shower to him. When they reached home, Benoir wanted sex and Nila poetry. She picked up Baudelaire's *Fleur du Mal*, sat on the sofa and asked, 'Why did Baudelaire write about the Malabar woman?'

Benoir took the book away, hugged Nila and looked into her eyes lovingly as he said, 'Because Baudelaire fell in love with her. Do you know what he did to her?' A hot kiss fell on her lips. Benoir had brought warmth from the south, all the heat of the sun so that he could burn her up.

She picked up the book again and said, 'But Baudelaire never went to Malabar.'

Benoir snatched the book away again, smiled sweetly and said 'Who has told you that?'

'Did he go there?'

'Yes.' He nodded.

'No, he didn't. In 1841, on the 9th of June Baudelaire's stepfather forced him into a ship bound for India. When the ship was near Mauritius, Baudelaire jumped off; he didn't want to go to India. The following year, in February, he came back to Paris. He never set foot in Malabar.'

'You seem to know a lot about our Baudelaire.'

Nila spread out her silky black hair and lay down. Perfume wafted from her body and it was driving Benoir crazy; he wanted to write restless, manic love poems deep inside her. Nila took the book from his hands and began to turn the pages. Benoir asked, 'Is Malabar in India?'

'You don't know where Malabar is?'

'No.' Benoir's answer came without a trace of regret, almost with a sense of pride at his ignorance.

Nila said, 'Strange!'

'Why strange?'

'Strange because you have never wondered where this Malabar is, about which your poet has written, or wondered if he saw the Malabar woman in Malabar or in his dreams?'

Benoir got up and sat on the other sofa. He hadn't thought of all this because he had other things to think of.

It was on the tip of her tongue to ask, 'Pascale, Jacqueline?'

Suddenly, without any preamble, Benoir asked, 'Do you know when the Notre-Dame was built?'

'In 1334.'

'No, even before that.'

'The work started in the twelfth century and ended in 1334.'

'When in the twelfth century?'

'I don't know.'

Benoir flashed a smile and said, 'You only have that one Taj Mahal. I didn't see anything really ancient in India. There's the Victoria Memorial in Calcutta, but that was built by the British.'

Nila sat up and asked, 'Have you heard of Mohenjodaro and Harappa?'

'What's that?'

'It's a civilization. It flourished in India, two thousand five hundred years before the birth of your Christ.'

Benoir shrugged. He wasn't supposed to know all this.

Nila said, 'Don't think because it's about India you don't have to know it. This is history.'

'And why do I have to know history?' Benoir got up from the sofa noisily, walked around, heaved a loud sigh and shouted, 'Do you think everyone has to know everything? I know about things which interest me. You think you know it all. You are very arrogant, Nila.'

Nila laughed and spoke softly, 'Is that a bad thing? If you have the knowledge, why should you cower? You should proudly say yes, I know.'

Benoir pulled her up from the sofa, threw the book on the floor, dragged her to the study, slapped the computer and said, 'The world revolves around computers now. If you are so proud of your knowledge, then tell me the true value of ten base two terminator? You don't know? It's five hundred Ohms. How many i and q are there on the keyboard? You don't know, it's five. How many bytes in the Mac address? I know you don't know; your knowledge is useless. There are six bytes.'

He held her in a tight grip, dragged her back to the drawing room and threw her on to the sofa again.

Nila laughed. As she laughed, she said, 'Please pick up that book for me?'

Benoir was breathing heavily. He wouldn't do it.

Nila asked, 'Who threw it, me or you?'

Benoir said, 'I did.'

'Then pick it up like a good boy. You are not a naughty boy that you have a God-given right to throw things around, or are you?' Nila was laughing.

Benoir screamed, 'Why are you laughing?'

'Because I have the God-given right to laugh.' Nila lay down on the sofa as before, spreading her hair and perfume around. Benoir sat on the sofa behind her. He lowered his voice and said, 'Nila turn around and look at me. I have to talk to you; it's urgent.'

Nila spoke slowly, gently, 'First, please pick up my book for me; I feel like reading a poem and it is urgent.'

'More urgent than listening to me?' Benoir sounded surprised. Nila said, 'Yes, much more.'

'You just want to show off! This is what happens. People come into our country and they become obsessed with our art and culture.'

Nila looked out into the sunny evening and said, 'I am obsessed because poetry is in my blood.'

'In your blood, ha, ha, ha.' Benoir laughed strangely.

'Our poets wrote poetry even when your France was a land under snow. Just imagine, while your ancestors were fighting over a piece of raw flesh, my forefathers were spouting poetry.'

Benoir moved like lightning, picked up the book and threw it outside the window, 'You and your blood and your pride. Read, for all I care.'

He left. The tranquil woman laughed sweetly and shut her eyes. A dream flew in and perched on her eyes. She saw herself on the Malabar coast, the wind blowing in her hair, in her sari, as she laughed with all the colours of the sunset on her body. She ran barefoot and played hide and seek with the water as it touched her beautiful body and the wind whispered in her ears, '*O Malabar woman . . .*'

She wafted in the warm breeze, walked into the nearest bookstore and looked for *Fleur du Mal*. The glass display case showed off Baudelaire, Rimbaud, Paul Eluard, Paul Valerie. She leaned forward, opened the shelf and asked, 'Why are they locked inside?'

'It's the Poetry Week.' The shopkeeper was indifferent.

'Isn't every week, every day meant for poetry?'

He smiled, 'The days of poetry are numbered, mademoiselle.'

Nila had never felt that in Calcutta. Every day, every minute was for poetry. It was the poet who grabbed everyone's attention on the stage, whom every person on the streets saluted and whom everyone gave a second glance. Every youth wrote poetry, whether they fell in love or not, whether it rained or not. A drunken lout would be forgiven all his sins if he was a poet. Some said there were more poets in Calcutta than crows. When Nila fell in love with Sushanta, she also wrote poetry. She had thought France was the home of poetry, but here they had to declare a week especially for it, to sell poetry books and print them. Nila clicked her tongue and felt sorry for the country. As she returned home with the book clasped to her heart, she wished Molina would open the door to her, sit her down and feed her her favourite dishes. She'd fan her gently, brush aside the stray hairs on her brow and say, 'Eat up, you've grown so thin. It's been ages since you ate my cooking.' Nila's mouth watered. She walked home in a stupor and knocked on the door. No one waited for Nila. She had to let herself in. As she called, 'Ma, Ma,' the sound of her own voice startled her.

The Chimera Days

Nila was in a trance, in Malabar, and the room was bathed in a dim glow. Sushanta, bathed and clean-smelling like an Epicurean husband, reached for her aroused nipples. Drowning in languorous pleasure, Nila acquiesced to their lovemaking. Sushanta lay spent and tired after an orgasm.

The clouds parted and Nila's illusion shattered; the piercing eyes of the wolf tore her to bits. She shivered, cold. When she tried to draw up the sheets at her feet, they were snatched away by the wolf, as if her fingers were being snatched away by a maniac. Nila screamed. It was Sunil in front of her eyes.

'You have a high fever; don't cover up.'

Slowly she buried her head in the pillow and spoke feebly, 'What are you doing here?'

Sunil laughed his peculiar laugh.

Nila lay in a foetal position, tense, as she heard him say, 'Do you keep in touch with Kishan? He has spoken to the lawyers about a divorce.'

Sunil spewed out many more words that fell randomly around the foetus; he wasn't getting along with Chaitali and so he was quite upset these days. They slept in the same bed, but scarcely touched. Chaitali could understand that this was no way for a man to live. He paused and then continued in his thin voice, 'Actually it was a mistake marrying her; she is very different. She is angry that I have stood guarantee for this house and she doesn't want me to look for a job for you. She says I shouldn't neglect them so much and shouldn't pay so much attention to you; all this jabbering all day long . . . Ouf . . .'

There was a sound at the door. Quickly Sunil got dressed, threw a sheet over the foetus and opened the door to Benoir. A warm hand touched the foetus. Meanwhile Sunil waved goodbye and walked out casually. He kept Nikhil's letter from Calcutta on the table.

Benoir had brought her a gift, all wrapped up, and a single red rose.

Nila's voice came from a great distance, 'That man raped me.'

Benoir gathered Nila, all the heat in her to his bosom and burst into sobs. She wiped away his tears and said, 'I don't know, perhaps I wanted it . . . I wasn't thinking straight.'

'But I know, you were just angry with me.'

Benoir's voice was brimming with emotion as he said, 'I am beside you now and I won't let anyone touch you. I'll give you everything, everything.'

'Really? Promise?' She looked dishevelled, as if she'd weathered a sandstorm and needed help, begged for it.

Benoir promised her he'd never leave her.

When she untied the ribbon and unwrapped the package, out came all the books of Baudelaire's poetry. Nila's chapped, burning lips were drenched with kisses. She wanted to drown, to plunge into deeper waters. But Benoir said, 'Get well first.'

Nila took his hand and placed it on her brow; she wanted it to stay there, wanted him to say how high her fever was. Nila wanted Benoir to fuss over her the way Molina had when she had had fever, to put a cold poultice on her brow, to wrap a towel around her neck, bring her to the edge of the bed and pour cold water on her head. Nila wanted him to bring a bunch of grapes and sit on her bed and feed them to her one by one.

Benoir took his hand away from her forehead and asked, 'Are you feeling ill?'

Nila said she was fine. She quelled her wishes and asked, 'Do I have a very high fever?'

'I don't know. Do you want to check? Let me get the thermometer for you.'

He brought it from the bathroom and came towards her. Nila instinctively opened her mouth. He gaped at her open mouth and handed her the instrument with a smile that said, with this I lay my life at your feet. Nila noted the smile, put the thermometer in her mouth and gulped down the desires that almost popped out of her mouth at the same time.

The same night Benoir went and packed two suitcases and came back to Nila. She meant everything to him and this was his final decision.

'What about that other relationship?'

He said he'd wind it up slowly.

She didn't want to ask him how slowly. Benoir coming away to her like this made Nila tremble more than her fever did; she trembled with joy. It was obvious that Benoir loved her. She had nothing more to ask of him. Nila lay on his chest and closed her eyes in deep satisfaction. It had been worth it to have spent so much on this house. She had dreamed of living in it with Benoir and now the dream was close at hand. Her days of uncertainty were over. Nila could walk with her head held high now. Kishan's meanness, Sunil's pity, could all be discarded in one fell sweep. She had Benoir. He was hers and she wasn't his mistress. So what if he didn't bathe her head or feed her grapes, he loved her—this was the Western way of loving— bringing her the thermometer was no less than doing all that.

Benoir cooked some meat from a can, heated the contents and poured it on a plate. He sliced up the baguette, lay the table with silverware, poured them some wine and called Nila when it was ready. She looked at his smiling face in the candlelight. She found the lamb smelly and didn't feel like eating it although Benoir licked his fingers with apparent enjoyment. Nila agreed with him and picked at her food, because she didn't want to disappoint this new, domesticated Benoir.

Benoir talked about his childhood. Nila was absorbed in the stories. When he was six, he had gone to Italy with his parents by rail. They'd walked on the crowded streets of Rome. There had been a festival. A small boy stood leaning against a pillar and he had pulled Benoir's hand and said, 'Come, let's go to see the fireworks.' Benoir hadn't gone, but later he always felt he should have. He saw the fireworks from a distance and felt sorry he didn't go.

The next night he talked of his childhood again and told her the same stories.

Living together often meant hearing the same stories again and again and it gave her some sort of pleasure too, hearing about his childhood and adolescence. He told her about when he was praised by his teachers, when he hit a friend on the nose and confessed to the priest at the church in Orléans. His younger sister, Valerie, wasn't as good at her studies as he was and so was always jealous of him; when they were children she often tore up his books and buried them in the ground. Even now she envied him. She was married and had a child, who, she claimed, was better behaved than Jacqueline.

At night Benoir came to bed, naked. He frowned at Nila, fully clothed. 'How can you sleep with so many clothes on?'

'I can. I am not used to sleeping in the buff like you.'

Suddenly Nila felt it was a hint and Benoir wanted to fondle her naked body. But he held her close and told her the story of Saint Exupéry's little prince well until midnight and his penis hung limp on his tranquil body. The next night he told her stories of a fox and a tiger. When the story ended, he went and stood at the window.

Nila asked, 'What's the matter?'

'Nothing.'

'There must be something.'

Without taking his eyes off the window, he said, 'Jacqueline must be missing me a lot.'

'Why don't you go there and meet her tomorrow?'

He came back from the window, kissed Nila with bright eyes and said, 'Really? Can I?'

'Sure. If you feel like it, why shouldn't you?'

'That's true,' he said, 'Why shouldn't I?'

Nila's fever shot up in the night and she moaned all night long. The next morning, when the fever subsided, she asked Benoir to fetch her some amoxycillin from the pharmacy nearby. No, that wasn't possible unless the doctor prescribed it. Nila went into the kitchen after Benoir left for work and found he had washed and left the place spic and span. She spent the whole day looking at the clock, waiting for him to come back home. As she waited, Danielle called.

Despite the fever, Nila couldn't contain her excitement. She told her about Benoir coming to her for good. She repeated again and again that she was no mistress.

'Come home some time, Danielle, see how happy I am.'

Danielle had no interest in coming to witness Nila's joy.

'At least come to see me because I am ill? It could be typhoid.'

'There's no typhoid in this country; it must be something else. What's the point of coming now, when you are sick? Get well and I'll come one day to chat with you.'

Nila came to her senses. This wasn't India where people dropped in on you when you were sick. Get well, get lively, overflow with life and I'll come and drink some off you. And if you fall sick and die, I'll come to your funeral in a black dress, drink to you and dance a little. That's it.

Nila finished talking to her and opened the envelope that Sunil had left. She read Anirban's letter first: 'I suppose you can guess what I am feeling when Kishan told me everything. I am sure you are doing whatever you fancy in that foreign land, but one day you will come to your senses and then it'll be too late. Many of your compatriots have shared your fate. So please change your ways when there is still time. If you do not want to resolve things with Kishan, come back home immediately. There is still time to mend your ways, come back to India and live a life that won't have so many people point fingers at you.' Nikhil's letter was quite the same.

At seven Benoir called to tell her that he had gone to Rue de Rennes from his office. He was taking Pascale and Jacqueline out to dinner. He'd reach them back home, tell Jacqueline some stories, put her to bed and then come back.

Benoir returned home with a happy face. He had a happy little puppy with him, that looked like the stray puppies of Calcutta. There were two dogs in that house and he had brought the one that was more attached to him. The dog saw Nila, barked and jumped up on the bed. She raised her hand and said, 'Take it off the bed; it's messing up my bed.' Benoir came running, 'What are you doing.' He hugged Wanda close, held up one of her paws towards Nila and said, 'Shake my lover's hand, Wanda.' Nila welcomed the third member of her home.

Wanda was not a puppy. She was just small in size. These dogs were more expensive than the bigger dogs. Benoir undressed and came to bed like every other night, as he described in detail what were Wanda's favourite foods, when she went out, what she liked doing and when she woke up. He kissed her and said, 'Jacqueline didn't want to let me go. I have told her about you. She wants to meet you.'

Benoir kissed her again, smiled and said, 'Do you know what else she has said?'

'What?'

'She said she wants a brother.' Benoir's eyes were brimming with feeling, 'Won't you give her one?'

He placed Nila's hand on his erect penis and said, 'Let's sow the seeds of dreams today.'

Nila was about to ask, 'Whose dreams? Yours? Mine? Or Jacqueline's?' But she didn't because she was scared he'd say, 'Shame on you; you are so narrow-minded. You are jealous of a six year old?'

But she touched the erect penis and didn't feel a wave of awareness. Her nipples didn't rise to her lover's touch or his kisses. Benoir said, 'Get well and then we'll do it.'

Nila was afraid to leave Benoir unsatisfied. If her body was the only attraction for him, then she wanted him to enjoy her and still love her. Nila held out her body for his gratification. Benoir sowed the seeds of Jacqueline's dreams in it. Wanda jumped up on the bed and watched her master propagate.

He hid his face in her breasts and said, 'Sorry, I came early.'

'No, that's okay.'

'You are not upset?'

'Why?'

'Because you didn't come?'

Nila smiled sweetly, 'It's just one day, it doesn't matter.'

Benoir sat with a guilty look on his face until late in the night because Nila didn't have an orgasm and he explained over and over, 'Actually I've had a stressful week at work; probably that's the reason, or because I have gone without it for a long time.'

The last statement brought relief to Nila. At least, she thought,

he didn't make love to Pascale after putting Jacqueline to bed. She
was also taken aback to see a man so conscious of his partner's sexual
gratification. In India she had never heard of such an awareness. When
she had sex for the first time with Sushanta, her lover, he had never
asked her if she had felt the same exciting thrill that he had. Most
people in India believed sex was mainly for the man and all that the
woman would get out of it was children.

After three days of fever, Benoir took her to the doctor. He prescribed
medicines for her and when Nila came home with the medicines,
she saw the bottle was etched with trees and plants. Benoir explained
that these were herbal medicines. These days no one, except fools,
had any chemicals. People usually went for herbal treatment. Nila's
head started throbbing, not with the fever but with this revelation. In
Calcutta she had seen the illiterate, uneducated people have these
medicines, those who went to quacks, got cheated and died painfully.
Nila, the champion of logic and reason in the Western world, was
amazed to see that here people were looking elsewhere for succour;
the eyes of the educated upper classes were turned towards the dark,
irrational. She threw away those bottles when Benoir wasn't looking.
Nila's fever subsided on its own in seven days.

Once she was better, Nila turned her attention to her new home. She
cooked all day long, showered, dressed and waited for Benoir, her
eyes and mind stuck on the clock. Then Benoir called to tell her that
Pascale had invited him and he was going to her place for dinner—
Nila shouldn't wait for him.

'But I have cooked many things for you.'

'Why didn't you tell me earlier! Now I have promised Pascale
and I'll have to go.'

Nila had to agree. After all, Pascale was his wife and she had
more rights to Benoir's time than Nila.

Nila drifted around the house, alone. Benoir had arranged the
computer table to his liking with a few files and two framed
photographs of Pascale and Jacqueline. Nila picked up Pascale's photo
and looked at it closely. She didn't find her plain from any angle at all:

red hair, shapely pink lips, sharp nose, high cheekbones, green eyes—
Nila saw no reason for Benoir not to love this beautiful woman.

All day long Wanda had screamed the house down. Her master
came home late, picked her up and crooned to her, 'Oh sweetheart,
oh my pet.'

Nila wasn't asleep, but she pretended to sleep.

'Oh, you are sleeping. Okay, I won't disturb you.'

Nila acted like she'd just woken up and said, 'Oh, it's you! Have
you just come back?'

'It's been quite a while. I didn't wake you because you were
sleeping.'

Nila glanced at the clock and yawned, 'It's pretty late; I couldn't
wait any longer . . .'

Benoir's voice was fresh, 'There were many bills at the house
and I took care of them.'

Nila spoke sleepily, 'You could have just stayed over.'

Benoir spoke as he took his shoes off, 'I thought as much. But it
was Pascale who said, go on, Nila must be waiting for you.'

Nila wasn't sleepy now, 'Why does she send you away to another
woman? Does she love you or not?'

'Of course she does.'

'Then, doesn't it bother her that you are living with me? I wouldn't
have been able to say, go to your other lover. How can she do it?'

'She is a very good girl, Nila.' Benoir was firm, 'I haven't seen a
better woman in the whole world.'

'Then why have you left her?'

'You know why, don't you? It's for you.'

'And what is your wish? Where do you want to live and with
whom?'

'I am doing just what I want to do.' Benoir sat on the chair. He
looked into Nila's eyes. He sat in the dark and the light from the
small bedside lamp was on Nila.

Nila said, 'I feel you are still unsure about what you want.'

'I have told you many times what I want. I have said I cannot live
without you.' Benoir's tone was gentle.

'Why won't you live? Will you stop eating, sleeping, drinking or working? What in your life will come to a stop?'

'Perhaps I'll do everything, but it wouldn't be the same. I'll be like the living dead. Don't you believe me? Don't you know how much I love you, how much love it takes to leave a happy family and come away? I have never had a fight with Pascale. I told her all about you and she has accepted it; I didn't hide anything from her. She is my best friend, Nila. She loves me very much and because she loves me, she doesn't stop me from doing what I want to do. Have you seen a greater sacrifice for a loved one? Only Pascale can do it. I love her and respect her. I have left the people I love the most, my Pascale and my Jacqueline, all for you and that doesn't make you happy?'

Nila held up a book in front of her eyes. Benoir's voice was harsh, 'Keep that book away, I can't see your eyes.'

'Why do you have to see my eyes?'

'I am talking to you. Answer me. Aren't you happy that I have left my wife and daughter and come to you? Tell me.'

Nila kept the book in front of her face and said, 'Why do you say you have left them? You haven't. She is still your wife. You talk on the phone everyday and you go to her often. This is not leaving. The ring symbolizing your love is still on your finger, her photo is on your desk.'

Benoir got up, sat in front of Nila, snatched away the book with his left hand and said, 'Tell me what you want! Do you want me to go back there?'

'If you want to go, sure. I won't stop you. I didn't ask you to come here. You came on your own. When you were in that house, our relationship wasn't bad. Where's the difference?'

Benoir heaved a sigh and said, 'If it was another man in my place, he'd have said there's work pressure, a meeting or a working dinner and so he was late. I don't hide anything and tell you the truth. This is how you reward it? I can't understand why you are so narrow-minded, Nila.'

Nila spoke calmly, 'My mind isn't narrow, it's quite broad and that's why I'm telling you to go and stay with Pascale. Live happily with her, the way you always did. You haven't left her. You'll never leave her and you know why? Because you love her.'

Benoir pressed his elbows down on his knees and lowered his head onto his hands.

Nila placed a hand on his shoulder and said, 'I know you tell the truth. And I feel for Pascale. If you were my husband and you left me for another woman, I can imagine how much pain I would be in. Don't make her suffer any more. Don't give yourself so much pain. I will suffer a little when you go but I am used to it. My mother was also used to suffering.'

Benoir got up and switched on the bright lights. Nila's heart thumped loudly; any moment now he would start packing his suitcase. Any moment now her only succour would walk out, leaving her alone. Benoir sat on the bed, facing Nila and said, 'Tell me honestly, do you really mean these things? Do you really want me to go away?'

Nila didn't answer.

Benoir smiled. 'I know you don't mean them. You can't. You love me and you don't want to lose me.'

A lump of misery came and lodged itself in her throat. Nila bit her lips and tried to swallow it. Benoir hugged her close and swayed, right and left, saying je t'aime, je t'aime, je t'aime.

Nila knew what it was to be alone. If Benoir left she'd trip over her own shadow in that house. No one would hug her, hold her or say je t'aime. Her lover was surrendering himself to her; she, at least, didn't have the strength or the courage to push him away.

Benoir said, 'The day I threw your book and left, I thought our relationship was over. I even said sorry to Pascale. But every time I imagined my life without you, I felt stifled. You are my life Nila. That's when I knew. I knew that we were created for one another. I had wanted to kill myself. I even toyed with a knife. Then Pascale took me to a doctor.'

'What kind of doctor?'

'Psychiatrist.'

Nila was aghast. She untangled herself gently from his embrace, looked into his lowered eyes and asked, 'The doctor advised you to come here with Baudelaire's books and one rose?'

Benoir smiled bitterly. 'Do you think I didn't want to come here, that I came here because the doctor told me to?'

Nila was afraid, perhaps one day the doctor would say to Benoir, 'Go and live happily with Pascale,' and that's exactly what he would do.

Benoir asked, 'What's the matter? Do you think I am not stable enough?'

Nila laughed. 'Not at all. I think I am crazy and I need to see a doctor very soon.'

'Why, what's wrong with you?'

Nila said, 'I feel short of breath quite often.'

Benoir woke Nila slowly and whispered in her ears, 'Do you want to go some place with me?'

'Where?'

'Tell me if you want to go first.'

'At this time of the night?'

'Yes. If you agree, I'll take you there right away.'

'All right. Now tell me where.'

'To the seventh heaven.'

Benoir took her to the seventh heaven; she flew like a feather. Nila thought no one would ever be able to give her the pleasure that Benoir gave her.

She imagined her future in Benoir's harem and felt contented.

Their tour of the seventh heaven ended and so did the night. Nila's tired body had hardly drowned itself in sleep when Benoir's alarm clock dragged them up. Wanda jumped up on Nila and she shot off the bed. With the horrid smell of the dog in her nose and the radio yelling away in her ears, Nila flew to the fourteenth heaven in an instant. She made coffee for Benoir and set the bread, butter and jam on the table. He just sipped the coffee and rushed off.

'What's the hurry?'

'I have to take the metro.'

'Why? Where is the car?'

'Oh, I didn't tell you. I gave the car to Pascale; she'll use it.' Benoir's tone was calm and collected.

Nila set the water on the boil for her tea and asked, 'What will *you* use?'

'The metro and buses for the time being.'

'And later?'

'Actually, Nila, I prefer the metro and buses. You know how difficult it is with a car in Paris; parking is hell and you get a ticket for every little thing.'

Nila nodded. She knew where the problem was. She clicked her tongue and said, 'So Pascale will have a bad time with the car.'

'She needs it more than I do. She has to drop Jacqueline to school and pick her up again.'

'Oh.'

Benoir threw her a sarcastic glance, 'I guess you are not happy to hear this?'

'You have told me and I have heard. That is all. There's nothing to be happy or unhappy about.'

Benoir pulled on a T-shirt over his blue jeans. He seldom wore ties or shirts. He said he'd wear the shirts Nila gave him when they went out somewhere. The ties lay unused. The eau de cologne too. He wore Aramis because that was the name of one of the three musketeers.

He doused himself in perfume and stood before Nila and said, 'Listen carefully: I have told you before that although I have left Pascale, I have to bear her expenses. She was not able to give Jacqueline enough time because of her work and so I had asked her to quit her job in Strassburg. So she did. I have to pay for the expenses of that establishment. Pascale and Jacqueline are entirely my responsibility; is that clear?'

It was.

She wanted to say, 'I don't work either. Who is responsible for me?'

But she reined in the words yet again.

After Benoir left, Nila went into the study and picked up J.M. Coetzee's *Disgrace*. The title of the book drew her; she hadn't read anything by the same author. As she read, her glance slipped to Pascale's photo again and again. She fixed her gaze on the book, on every letter in it and finished nearly half the book when she realized her mind was on Pascale and not on the book. She went to the balcony and took some deep breaths. She wasn't living with Benoir alone, she was living with his whole family; it was too crowded.

Benoir called, 'Have you fed Wanda?'

'No.'

'Why?'

'It slipped my mind.'

'What do you have on your mind these days! Anyway, feed her the way I have told you . . . she's a small dog and . . .'

'And what? I am jealous of her too?'

'No. I thought she must be suffering.'

Nila hung up and poured out three kinds of food from three cans into the bowls in front of Wanda and filled the water cup with water.

She went to the balcony again and breathed deeply.

A little later Benoir called again and asked, 'Did you feed her?'

'No.' Nila's tone was cold.

Benoir sounded worked up, 'Why?'

'I didn't because I have eaten up all her food.' Nila sounded cool and normal.

'What are you saying?'

'I am telling you the truth. I come from a poor country and I'm not used to giving such good food to pets; we don't get to eat such things ourselves. I couldn't help myself; I ate it up.'

Click.

Along with the telephone's click there was the sound of breaking glass. Nila went to check what it was about and she found Wanda standing on the desk, wagging her tail and Pascale's photo frame lay in pieces on the ground. Nila didn't pick it up. She left it like that and walked out. She bumped into the police, taking out a corpse from the flat next door. It was Madame Suzanne Duget's. Nila and Madame Duget used to wish each other bonjour whenever they met on the stairs. One day Suzanne had taken the conversation further and asked her if it bothered her that she listened to music until late in the night. Nila had said it didn't bother her at all. Madame Duget told her that it was impossible to while away her time if she didn't have music to see her through. Nila spoke to the police and found out that Suzanne had lain there, dead, for a few days. The concierge got a bad smell when she came to clean the corridor and called the police. They broke the lock and found Suzanne's decomposed, swollen corpse. Nila looked at Suzanne's deformed face and shuddered. She leaned against the walls with her eyes closed for a long time before running out into the George Brassein Park, beside the lake and lying face down on the grass.

A couple of hours later she went out into the city and wandered around aimlessly. In the evening she returned home with a new photo frame. She put Pascale's photo into it, swept away the glass and cooked some duck—Benoir was fond of duck.

Benoir returned from work in the evening and said he had spoken to his mother that day. He had promised them he'd bring Nila to meet them soon; if possible, that day.

Nila felt as if he was going there to seek his parents' approval on his choice of a bride. She dressed accordingly. She did her hair, her face, wore high heels, a black dress and left the house holding Benoir's hand.

From Gare d'Austerlitz to Orleons. Benoir talked all the way for that one hour; he said that if he wasn't serious about Nila, he wouldn't have taken her to see his mother. He repeated what he had said earlier, that he wasn't unhappy in his family life before; on the contrary, it was a very happy unit and his friends often said they'd never seen a more perfect couple before. Pascale never crossed him; she loved him like a dutiful wife and did everything to please him. So there was no reason to think that he was unhappy with his wife and gone to another woman. Benoir's story was not like other people's; it was different. Nila's sudden appearance in Benoir's life, like a lightning flash, changed everything. But Benoir wasn't so heartless that he'd forsake Pascale completely. His whole month's salary would go from his office directly to Pascale's account; he'd just keep a little bit for his own expenses. He was making this sacrifice for Nila's sake. And the following weekend he'd have to stay over at Rue de Rennes because

Pascale and Jacqueline wanted it.

Nila sighed, 'I'm trying to understand.' She had gathered enough breath in her lungs and could spare a sigh or two, here and there.

Benoir's father waited at the station with his car. He picked up both of them and drove home. There, Benoir's mother welcomed Benoir and his lover: kisses on both cheeks. Nila almost called her 'Ma', mistaking her as the mother-in-law; she changed it to Madame Dupont in good time.

Madame Corinne Dupont was plump, jolly and middle-aged. She had been a factory worker once, now she was retired. Monsieur Dupont made Nila sit next to him and told her his life story; he was one of the baby boomers of the forties, a result of what the soldiers did to their wives in Europe once they returned from the Second World War. When he was fifteen, he also entered a factory like Corinne. Then he quit it because he didn't like it and went to Marseilles where he worked in a ship for two years. He drove a taxi for some time, then he cultivated grapes in the Alsace and eventually joined the police force. Now he was retired because his back caused him some trouble from time to time. He was contented, eating, sleeping, playing solitaire on the computer, smoking his pipe and dreaming of buying a Porsche. He poured out four glasses of wine and fetched a shoebox full of old photos. He showed her photos of his grandfather, great grandfather, scores of relatives and eventually of Benoir as a baby. Benoir had come home after two and a half years. He left home when he was thirteen. He studied in a Catholic school and then he passed his baccalauréat. Since then the government paid for his education. He kept in touch with his parents mostly through letters. He came home after he started seeing Pascale. They liked her very much. They came here once again after Jacqueline was born and now again with Nila. It was just an hour's journey from Paris and yet Benoir didn't have the time to visit his parents, not even on holidays.

Life was very discrete. No one wanted to dwell on the past. Monsieur and Madame Dupont had their own lives; their children were grown up and their duties were over. If the child was physically and mentally fit, he was supposed to bother you less. If there was good news, they'd be happy to know it by a phone call or a letter.

Benoir's new love was also good news for them. Benoir brought them the news personally. They weren't here to judge how Nila looked or how she behaved. Whatever she was, if his son was happy with her, they wanted nothing more. They didn't poke their nose into other people's lives, like Bengalis did. His parents told her stories of Benoir's childhood and they missed the last train to Paris and had to stay over. In Benoir's old room, the bed was small, the table and cupboard were small in which, tiny clothes still hung neatly. Benoir spent the night on that bed with Nila, reminiscing and romancing. Nila felt their cries of orgasm would disturb the other two people in the house. Benoir didn't bother about it.

The next morning they left Orléans, the city of Joan d'Arc's memories and the lively Duponts. Nila looked out of the windows from the train and saw the neatly ordered villages, the farmlands, homesteads and the healthy looking cows. Farmers sped by in fast cars, beer cans in hand, joyous, celebrating. No one grazed cattle; machines sowed seeds, harvested the crops and gathered them. Whenever Nila left Calcutta she saw emaciated cows harnessed by emaciated farmers, who sowed seeds by hand and reaped the harvest by hand. After working hard all round the year they seldom got two square meals a day. And here the government gave farmers lots of money *not* to farm, or raise cattle, sheep or pigs. They had so much that the markets overflowed. In this country it was cheaper to buy produce from other countries than to produce it themselves. A farmer could tweak his moustache and say that on his land, if he farmed, he would earn so much money and the government would say I'll give twice that if you don't farm.

Suddenly Nila laughed.

'Why are you laughing?'

'Sometimes I find it very funny, Benoir. People's situations can be so different in two parts of the world. Here there's a surplus of wealth and there a total lack of it. Someone struggles while others have fun. The whole thing is a joke.'

Nila was lost in thought.

Benoir nudged her thoughts and said, 'What are you thinking?'

'Nothing much.'

'Tell me.'

'Not much to tell.'

'Still . . .'

Benoir's tone was demanding, the demands of a lover. Being his lover meant sharing her thoughts as much as giving her body to him.

'I'm thinking of Sartre,' Nila said.

'Our Jean Paul Sartre?'

'Yes, your Jean Paul Sartre.'

Benoir laughed, 'And I thought you're thinking about your poor farmers.'

Nila was silent. A little later she said, 'Sartre said life is pointless but it has to be made worthwhile. How does one do that? A girl or a boy is born into a poor family; he doesn't get an education, suffers from starvation, works hard all day long to get himself one square meal. Perhaps he had the talent to be a great scientist or a great writer or philosopher. But how would he use that talent? Where is his chance to make life worthwhile? If he doesn't have food to eat or clothes to wear, what is life if not a series of pain?'

Nila thought of Molina. Did Molina have the capacity to make her life more meaningful? She had been a prisoner in her husband's home; she had had invisible chains on her mind and body, the chains of society, and she hadn't known how to break free. There were millions of such Molinas the world over, who didn't know how to set themselves free.

Benoir laughed again. 'What nonsense! Everyone doesn't make their lives worthwhile the same way. My life is worth it for Jacqueline. My parents weren't rich and they struggled a lot; in their lives I brought meaning, wealth. Besides, one can reap the harvest of this life in the next. Why would life be pointless?'

Nila laughed loudly.

'Why are you laughing?'

She was still laughing as she said, 'You believe in life after death?'

'Sure. Don't you?'

'No.'

Benoir said, 'But why? You have heaven and hell in your religion too.'

Nila laughed and said, 'Long ago a Bengali author said, "Where is heaven and where is hell—who says they are far away? In the midst of man resides heaven and hell, both".'

Benoir sat up straight and asked gravely, 'Don't you believe in God?'

Nila was firm. 'No.'

Benoir leaned back. 'Strange.'

He told her that he had always known India was famous for its spirituality. It was as ancient as the country itself.

Nila said, 'Did you read about India's Charbak school of philosophy in your books? In those days the most popular philosophy was the Lokayat. These Lokayits didn't believe in the soul or in God, or heaven and hell. For many years India was ruled by the British. They wanted to make us believe that we were very mediocre people, not equal to them in knowledge, sophistication or anything and we were fit to be slaves and nothing else. Of course, this wasn't true. It was said just to fool the people of India. So, when the freedom movement started, some fundamentalist pundits wanted to glorify the Indian past. They dug up Indian history to prove how great we were. To oppose the rationalism or materialism of the West, they began to claim that ancient sages had said life was temporal, illusion and maya. This was entirely to revoke a self-esteem that we had lost and the Westerners took this to be the true image of India.'

At this point Nila was afraid Benoir would ask, 'If India really believes in materialism, then why is the country still so poor? Why are most people below the poverty line?'

Nila formulated an answer to this possible question: 'That is because two hundred years of British rule has crippled the economy.' Question: 'They left fifty years ago.' Answer: 'Fifty years isn't long enough to build a nation.' Benoir could point out that after the Second World War Germany was nowhere. Fifty years later it was the richest nation in Europe. Nila would raise the question of America's Marshall plan.

Nila's head was spinning. The fear of Benoir's questions crouched low in her head. She felt something was wrong somewhere. Her country lay there alone, like Molina's sick and withered body.

There was no one to nurse her. Nila turned into a bird and flew there, she rained over the sunburnt, drought-stricken lands. Nila began to feel she, too, was chained. If only she could unshackle herself and bow low before her country! She didn't know why she was living in this cruel, foreign land. The more she saw this country, the stranger it seemed. What would this country give her? Security? Of what— happiness or life? Sometimes Nila felt there was no point in living! There was no point in happiness.

Benoir stroked her fingers and said, 'So you want to tell me that you don't believe the Lord has designed us for one another?'

Nila didn't take her eyes off the window. 'No.'

The End? Not Yet!

The following week passed like that of an ordinary housewife for Nila. At seven in the morning Benoir's alarm clock woke them both. Once she said to him, 'The radio bursts like a bomb and I jump out of my skin. I don't get enough sleep.' He said, 'You sleep too much. It's not good. It'll make you fat.'

Nila was scared of growing fat and so woke to the radio every morning and went into the kitchen. She made a different breakfast every day, so he wouldn't get bored. Once he kissed her on the lips and left for work, she cleaned the house, bought his favourite things from the store nearby and cooked them, watched the clock and jumped when the phone rang. Benoir would ask her what she did all day, Nila described her day in detail. Finally he'd ask her if she loved him and she'd say yes. Benoir needed this reassurance quite a few times in the day. In the evening when he came back from work, he kissed her; then he sat before the TV and came to the table when she called him for dinner. One day there was a documentary on India and Benoir jumped up, 'Come quickly, it's India.' Nila had to see a sex workers' procession in Sonagachi. The film was basically about their fight for rights. Benoir saw it and said, 'Gosh, there are so many prostitutes in your country?' Nila tried to distract him, 'I've brought mussels for you today.' Benoir said, 'Mmmm, mmmm,' even before seeing it. Nila played a Hariprasad Chaurasia album in an effort to confound Benoir with the beauty of Indian classical music. But he said, 'Nila, please don't mind, but I am changing this.' He played a French music CD instead.

'Didn't you like Chaurasia?'

'Well Nila, its not my cup of tea.'

Of course, he drank his French cup of tea alone. One day when he saw Nila use her fingers to eat, his eyes became round with surprise as if he was looking at a savage. Embarrassed, Nila quickly washed her hands and picked up a knife and fork. Benoir consoled her and said, 'Oh, go ahead, don't feel shy. We too have picked up the fork only recently. Our ancestors used their fingers, like you. Say a thousand years ago, there was no silverware.'

Every night Nila set the table with Benoir's favourite dishes and he praised them. He liked the mutton curry Nila made one night and so she repeated it. In bed, Benoir drowned in Nila's body. He began a new game. The entire time they made love, Nila had to speak in Bengali, saying I love you, I want you, deeper within me and many more sexual innuendoes. He couldn't understand any of it but it sounded different and that's what he enjoyed. In order to please him Nila began to say them and her own voice sounded strange to her because she wasn't used to saying these things in Bengali. Nila tried to overcome her ineptitude and she practised while dusting, cleaning, cooking or cleaning the window. Benoir often said, the Indian woman's body was more mysterious; it had a different feel to it. And this difference gave him a pleasure that Pascale never could. Nila was glad to hear she could at least give him a taste of difference, which Pascale couldn't. After their stormy love making, Benoir kissed her goodnight. At dawn the radio's riotous wakening brought another kiss. Nila took some time to learn the different kisses for the different times of day. This was the least one could do when one had a French lover.

One evening they went to the Picasso museum and the Pompidour. Nila didn't show any excitement over Picasso's work. When Benoir asked her, she said except for the one with two girls running by the seashore, she didn't like any of them. Benoir said one had to have the sense to appreciate them. Nila didn't have the sense and so she had just gaped at Picasso's work.

'Such a great artist, a great man, Picasso . . .

Nila said, 'He may have been famous, but as a person he was nothing great. Françoise has written what his life was like. He protested against Spain's civil war and yet had a warring household himself: Olga, Marie Thérèsè, Dora, Françoise, Jacqueline, he cheated them all.'

'You seem to know a lot about our Picasso.'

'He is not yours, he is Spain's.'

'Oh, all the same; the West's nonetheless.'

Nila realized she was from the East, the exact opposite of the West. When she saw the modern art at Pompidour, Nila couldn't believe they were called works of art. The first work she came to was a dress made of beef. The meat was sliced thinly and sewed together to make the dress. There was even a photo of a girl wearing the dress. There was a torn piece of paper with some scribbles on it which was framed and hung up as art. Old, torn cloth, broken radios, torn tyres, empty cigarette packets and much more were picked up from the rubbish heap was gathered there and called 'art'. Nila stood before a blue canvas and tried to figure out if there was a single brush stroke on it, or even a dot. There wasn't. But it was 'art'. She asked Benoir how this could be art when there was nothing on the canvas. Benoir said it must be art or it wouldn't be here. Nila couldn't make sense of it. She lost faith in modern art and felt like going back to the Louvre to see more classical art. The next day she went there and feasted her eyes on the art of Egypt, Greece and Africa. Nila said, 'Now there is no colonialism. Why don't they return these precious pieces to their respective countries!'

Benoir said, 'These things have survived because we have preserved them. In their own countries they wouldn't have lasted.'

Nila asked, 'What would have happened?' She mused that they'd have dug up the pyramids and brought them here.

One evening Nila and Benoir had dinner with Morounis. She lived in the posh area of Avenue de President Wilson. The house was a gift from her French father.

On their way back, Benoir said, 'Morounis is very lucky.'

Nila said, 'Luck isn't everything. She made it because she had the talent.'

Every evening Pascale called. When Nila answered, she said, 'This is Pascale. May I speak to Benoir?' Nila gave the phone to Benoir. On Thursday evening, after her call, Benoir went to Rue de Rennes and informed her at night that he was staying over.

He came back the next day. After some desultory conversation Nila asked, 'Didn't you sleep with Pascale last night?'

'No.'

'Why?'

'What do you mean, why?'

'You love her. Why wouldn't you sleep with her?'

'Since the day I fell in love with you I have only slept with you, not with her. I haven't touched her since we returned from the Riviera.'

'But you said you loved me even when you went there.'

'Nila, why are you complicating everything? Do you want me to have nothing to do with Jacqueline?'

'Of course not. All I want to know is what's your problem in having sexual relations with two women? You believe in having sex if you love someone; that's why you slept with me.'

'I didn't sleep with Pascale because you wouldn't like it.'

'You have curbed your desires because I won't like it?' Nila clicked her tongue sympathetically.

'Besides, Pascale also doesn't want to sleep with me.'

'How do you know that? Did you ask her? You wanted it and she said no, right?'

'Nila, you talk too much.'

'Not too much. Answer my question. What would you have done if she had said okay? You held back because she said no, but if she wanted it you'd have made love to her, wouldn't you?'

'No, I wouldn't because I know you wouldn't like it if I slept with her.'

'Suppose I like it?'

'What?'

'I would like it if you sleep with Pascale tonight, have sex with her.'

'How is that you want that suddenly? You can't even stand her, you are so jealous of her.'

'You have suffered enough thinking I am jealous of her. As of now, I am like the Indian woman of your dreams, patient, tolerant, competent and generous to a fault.'

Benoir sat there glumly for a while and then left silently. He came back with two bottles of wine and a bunch of roses. He gave them to Nila and spoke softly, 'I love you and that's the greatest truth.'

Nila smelt the flowers and said, 'In this country flowers don't have a scent; they just look good. In India the roses smell terrific.'

'These are hybrid varieties. All the scent goes away in the process.' Benoir ran his fingers through her hair and said, 'There is nothing contrived about you. That's why I love you more every day.'

He made Nila sit beside him and slowly told her about his conversations with Pascale the night before. He had said that after much soul searching he'd realized his love for her was that of a friend and his everlasting passion was for Nila. He realized he shouldn't have spent the night there. He had not wanted to hurt her at all. Pascale had told him to stop dallying and choose one of the two relationships. Although it was a very difficult decision to walk away from a neat and beautiful family, Benoir had chosen Nila. Now he'd have to go for a divorce with Pascale on mutual consent. In this country divorce took some time to be effected and both parties' lawyers would have to work out the details. They could resolve the matter of dividing their possessions quite easily. Sometimes Benoir and Pascale would have to interact about Jacqueline. Pascale said she'd find a job and until then, she had to depend on Benoir, much against her wish. He would have to be responsible for Jacqueline as her father, since that was the rule in this country. But she would grow up pretty soon and once she was fifteen she'd leave home and be on her own.

He didn't leave it at that. He picked up Pascale's photo from his desk, dropped it into an empty suitcase saying he'd return it to its owner one of these days.

That same week, on Friday, Nila got a letter from Kishanlal by registered post: it was a legal notice initiating divorce proceedings. She sat holding the letter and listening to the hammering of her own heart for a long time. For a while the lights dimmed and flickered before her eyes. Benoir steadied them again, 'Don't you have faith in me?'

He took Nila's hands in his and said, 'Nila, no one will love you the way I love you, no one.' Nila's hands looked too black against Benoir's.

'I have given you everything, Nila, including myself. What else do you want!' Benoir's blue eyes were as deep as the ocean.

The hammering of her heart stopped. Benoir turned her face towards him and the insignificant stalk of grass gazed in awestruck wonder at the massive tree.

The night she received the letter, Nila called Calcutta for the first time since she had left home. She wanted to let them know about the divorce, acknowledge receipt of Anirban's and Nikhil's letters and let them know that she was alive and well.

'You? Has the sun risen in the west today?' Nikhil exclaimed when he heard her voice.

Nila said, 'The sun doesn't rise in the east or the west. It stays put in one place and makes everyone else dance to its tune.'

'So tell me, how are you? I heard you are living with a foreigner?'

'Did Sunil say that? He must have given you my phone number and address?'

Nila informed him that the paperwork for her divorce with Kishanlal was already under way. She was happy with the foreigner and they were getting married soon. So let no one spread rumours in Calcutta that Nila was a fallen woman.

'How are you, dada? Are you getting married soon?'

'We are seeing some girls. Last month we saw five.'

'Did you like anyone?'

'No way.'

'Why?'

'All five were dark. My luck!'

Nila said, 'But you are dark.'

'It doesn't matter if a man is dark.'

Nila said to herself, 'That's true. It doesn't matter if the man is dark, ugly, grotesque, corrupt, a lout, a rascal, a monster or a debauchee.'

A Big Day

Nila wanted to celebrate Benoir's twenty-sixth birthday in style. She drew up a list of invitees for that day's dinner party.

1. Morounis
2. Frederique
3. Danielle
4. Natalie
5. Nicole
6. Michelle
7. Rita
8. Mojammel
9. Mojammel's friends (3 or 4)
10. Sanal Edamaraku
11. Babu Gogini
12. Babu Gogini's wife
13. Tariq
14. Odil
15. Chaitali
16. Sunil

Morounis and Frederique said they would come. Danielle said she had to go to school on Tuesday evenings and so she wouldn't be there. She had recently joined a new school where she had classes three days a week, learning 'how to be a writer'. Natalie was going to the solarium and so she wasn't free either.

What was a solarium? It was where they took in artificial rays to tan their bodies. Of Nicole, Michelle and Rita, two were not in Paris and the last one said she was supposed to have coffee with a friend on that day and this rendezvous had been fixed for the last four months and so it couldn't be called off. Mojammel jumped up when he got the invitation, 'Didi, where were you all this while? We have missed you! I even looked for you at the box-factory.' He was even more excited when Nila extended the invitation to his friends as well. Sanal said he'd come. He also said Babu Gogini and his wife were in Hyderabad. She got hold of Tariq's phone number and was told that Tariq and Odil would try to come. Although she had thought of Chaitali and Sunil at first, on second thoughts she cancelled those two names. All together her guests were seven in number. When she asked Benoir whom he wanted to invite among his friends or relations, he said no one stayed in Paris in August. Paris was empty. Pascale was going to the Canary Islands. Benoir also wanted to go there but this time he wasn't going because of Nila.

She got busy organizing the party. Mojammel called her and offered to help her with the shopping and the cooking by coming a little early. Nila agreed.

On the big day, Mojammel and Jewel arrived by afternoon. Nila had met Jewel in Kishan's restaurant; he had a childlike face. Jewel began to chop the onions. There was no ginger at home and Mojammel ran to fetch it. He came back with the ginger and a gift packet for Benoir. Jewel was petite, fair and childish. He chopped the onions and the garlic painstakingly and asked if he should go ahead and cook the meat. Jewel worked in the restaurant and knew how to cook. Nila fried the fish. She had arranged for a huge menu. The three Bengalis enjoyed themselves in the kitchen, as if it were a picnic. They swayed to the beat of Rabindrasangeet as they cooked and time flew. Close to evening, Tariq called to say that his son's schizophrenic fits had increased and so he didn't feel like coming.

'There's so much food.' Nila hung up.

Mojammel said he had recently met a boy called Modibo and asked if he should invite him. Mojammel scratched his head and said, 'But he is black.' Modibo had recently arrived from Mali. The poor boy stayed underground for fear of the police and he often didn't eat very well.

Nila was in a generous mood. 'Why just Modibo, call Jodibo, Sodibo, everyone.'

Benoir got dressed in time, in a new shirt gifted by Nila and a tie.

Nila wore a Baluchari sari. Once the guests arrived, champagne flowed and Tracy Chapman's *Revolution* played in the background. Benoir was the centre of attention. It was customary here to open the gifts immediately. Sanal gave him an Indian statuette in the Ellora-Ajanta style of erotic sculpture. Mojammel's packet revealed a Brut. Benoir exclaimed over each gift delightedly and thanked everyone though Nila knew that the eau de toilette, Brut, wasn't Benoir's cup of tea. Nila's gift was the smallest, wrapped in a red paper. She asked him not to open it right then. There was loud laughter in the room and Sanal winked. Nila gave him a dry kiss, not French but Bengali and said, 'This kiss has a little less slaver and lust.'

Sanal expressed his view on birthdays. 'It's a very sad day because it reminds you that you are one year closer to death.' On his birthdays Sanal mourned, he was the sole invitee and he sat in a room with all the doors and windows shut. The rules of gaiety were that you had to fast all day, keep the phone off the hook and lose your TV remote. Modibo, with his large, pitch black, illegal, immigrant eyes and rounded nose, stayed in the background like Tracy Chapman. He held a glass and even when the champagne was over, his mouth was shut. Nila studied Modibo. Sanal spoke in crisp Hindi. 'Who has invited this monkey here?' His comment brought a gust of laughter from Mojammel and Jewel. Nila poured more champagne in Modibo's glass and said, 'I have.'

Benoir claimed Bordeaux wine went well with Bengali cuisine. One bottle after another was finished. The evening was cheerful. Around midnight, Morounis, Frederique and Sanal left. Before going Sanal congratulated Nila because her French had come a long way.

Nila answered him with a merci beacoup. There was a round of applause from all present.

Nila held the fort with Mojammel, Jewel and Modibo even after Benoir retired to bed. Mojammel told her about Bachhu, the cook. He didn't get his papers in France and so he was off to Italy. He had to pay the agent a hefty amount to get his papers for Italy. The agent told him what to do, when to run and when to jump. Just before entering Italy, Bachhu had jumped off the train in the dark—as was the rule. Once the train was gone, he was supposed to run on the tracks and

hide in the bushes if another train came along. He did all this and
went some way but he was accidentally hit from behind by another
train and that was the end of him.

Nila felt a shiver run down her spine.

She poured more wine as they heard Jewel's story of arriving in
the country. He had gone to Moscow from Dhaka. From Moscow he
stowed away on a truck carrying vegetables to a city in Romania and
from there he crossed the border to the Czech Republic and crossed
over into Germany over snowy mountains. Jewel's brother Rubel
was with him. Neither of them had seen snow in their lives. Rubel
took his shoes off thinking he could run faster that way. But he fell
into the snow and it was over . . .

Nila came back to reality when she heard Benoir call her. He lay
in the bedroom, his brow crinkled.

'Who are these people? Why are you talking to them for so long?
Can't you see I am lying here alone?'

Wanda sat on his chest. Nila said, 'You are not alone; you have
Wanda.'

Benoir stared at her nastily. Nila said, 'Come to that room.'

'Why should I go there? You are talking in a strange language.'

'Bengali. I haven't spoken Bengali for ages and I am enjoying the
taste of it on my tongue.'

'But you don't speak Bengali when I ask you to.'

'You don't understand Bengali, Benoir. You are not a Bengali.'

'So you should have told me earlier that you've arranged for a
Bengali chat session.'

If that was it, why would she invite Morounis, Frederique and
Sanal, leave alone Modibo? He doesn't even know there's a language
called Bengali in this world. Nila didn't reply and went back to the
other room to hear the rest of Jewel's story. The police came and
picked up Rubel. He had to have both legs amputated since the blood
circulation had stopped and gangrene had set in. The German
government treated him and then sent him back home. He had sold
their land, collected lakhs of rupees and left Dhaka with dreams of a
golden future and he came back there, physically, economically and

mentally crippled.

Mojammel said, 'Rubel was twenty years old.'

Jewel ran with his shoes on and so he escaped the frost-bite and the police. He ran away to France from Germany. The police could pounce on him any day and deport him; his life was uncertain at best. If he had to go back, he only hoped, it wouldn't be as a cripple.

Modibo was also there to build his future. He had grown up beside the Niger river in Timbuktu. His thick lips hung like his uncertain future. He was living in dark, rejected housing estates, on food donated by the church and with the fear of the police haunting him every moment. He had strength and courage, but these were also growing more and more frail as each day passed.

At this point, Benoir walked out of the house, leaving everyone dumbfounded. Nila ran after him. 'Where are you going, so late in the night.' But before she could reach him, he was off at the speed of light.

Modibo had to end his story early and they had to leave. Benoir's abrupt departure left a heavy atmosphere in its wake, which affected everyone.

Benoir called after fifteen minutes, asked if the men had left and then came back home.

'Did they plan to stay the whole night? Your chatting session showed no signs of ending. The whole day is spoilt. Pascale wanted to treat me to dinner and I refused, for your sake. This was the first time Jacqueline saw I wasn't there for my birthday. Pascale has missed me all day today and wept for me. And I was subjected to this joke of yours.'

Nila said, 'I didn't ask you not to go there.'

'You didn't but you don't like my going there either. If I go, you'll ask me if I've slept with Pascale. That's all you have on your mind.' Benoir poured himself some wine, sat on the sofa in front of the bed and drank it.

'And I don't understand you sometimes. What is this you've given me? What's this key for?' Benoir threw the key at Nila.

Nila handed him the piece of paper from the dealer that said Reno, Model authentic 14, 139G/Km, five doors and she said, 'Go and pick up the car any time tomorrow.'

Nila went to bed. She was tired.

Perturbed

'What do you know of cars? Why did you buy it on your own? You should have told me.' Benoir screamed at her all day.

'Why? Is the car a lemon? Doesn't it run?'

'You could have bought a better one for this price. You were cheated.'

Nila laughed and said, 'Benoir, I have been cheated all my life. I am used to it.'

She hugged him and asked, 'Aren't you happy?'

He disentangled her arms, went and sat at a distance and said, 'Listen, don't ever do this again, don't invite strange people into the house without asking me first. Paris isn't what it used to be.'

Benoir had ten days' leave. He didn't know what to do with it. He called and asked about his wife and child twice a day. They had reached the islands and were swimming in the sea and staying in a good hotel.

Paris was deserted and so was Benoir. He had never spent the August holidays in Paris.

Nila said, 'Let's go to the Mutualité, there's a function there.'

'Oh no, feminist functions. They'll merely crib in their smooth voices, we want this, we want that; they can never be satisfied. Just a bunch of gay and ugly women getting together.'

That day's agenda was that advertisements should not use women's bodies with sexual intent and no commercial organization should tickle the people's fantasies through their ads; those organizations and their brands would be banned by the attendees at the function. Nila didn't find the whole sexual thing unattractive at all. Since there was more sexual freedom, Nila felt, sex crimes were less here. The ease with which women could walk around here, was impossible to find in India. Nila could dress as she pleased. If she wanted to be naked, why shouldn't she have the freedom? Even if women covered themselves, even if ads were sexless, men would get aroused. It was more important for people to respect one another. Nila thought if only Mithu's lifeless body could be placed at the Mutualite today, if the audience could be told about Molina's life! No one had taken Molina or Mithu for sex objects. No one had reached for them in lust! Yet, they had spent each moment of their lives in an indescribable pain. Nila felt sexuality was a kind of asset. It was because sexuality existed and because she could give him that gratification, that Benoir loved Nila. Without that, Nila would have had to spend her life in the vacuous loneliness of Molina or end her life like Mithu. Benoir would have rather caressed Wanda than Nila, if the latter didn't have breasts and thighs and if he didn't get immense pleasure in her pelvic circle. Nila was hungry for love and sexuality was important to get that love. Suddenly she saw Sunil's face in her mind's eye and felt like throwing up.

'I am supposed to attend this meeting. If you don't come, I have to go alone.'

'You want to go alone? And I am supposed to waste my leave, sitting at home all alone?'

Nila didn't go to the Mutualite.

The day passed in heavy silence. The next one was no better. The day after that Benoir went to his place at Rue de Rennes, to collect some papers he said. At home Nila felt lonely and walked out. She wandered around and went into the Catacomb.

When Benoir came back, she looked at his unhappy face and said, 'Let's go to Italy.' Benoir said he didn't have the money to go abroad. He had spent a lot in sending his wife and daughter to the Canaries.

'That's no problem. I have money.'

'So you go to Italy.'

'How could you think I'll go alone?'

Benoir sounded downcast, 'I'll go when I have the money.'

'But that wouldn't be the same as going now, together.'

'Nila, it's my dream: we'll go somewhere far away and lose ourselves, just you and me with no known face around. We'll stay lost in each other day and night. I want nothing more than that. But dreams don't come true.'

Nila looked into his dreamy eyes and asked, 'Don't you feel I am close to you? Why do you differentiate between my money and yours? I don't. I can never think like that.'

Benoir smiled wanly. 'All right, since you are so keen, let's go.'

They looked up ads for dog sitters in a magazine and placed Wanda in the care of one at the rate of fifty francs per day. The whole of this month, business boomed for dog and cat sitters.

Nila held the carte bleue. Benoir's yellowed teeth smiled wide when a pair of tickets for Paris, Rome, Florence and Venice dropped into his hands.

'Italy, Italy bleu, bleu. Oh Nila, you really love me so much! I am really lucky to have your love.'

A spate of French kisses took their toll on Nila.

From the airport they went into a suite of the five star hotel Galleo in old Rome. They ate at Cuisino Italiano, toured the Colosseum, saw the markers of Roman civilization or uncivilization, threw coins into the Fontana de Trevi. Benoir stood on the Spanish Stairs and wondered if he had stood just there when he was a child. In the church of Vatican Benoir bowed his head and crossed himself. He dragged Nila away from the Sistine Chapel to show her more wondrous ruins all over Rome. They came back to the hotel and Benoir sat enjoying his Chateau Margot as he looked at Nila, just out of the shower, and said, 'You look like a virginal beauty from heaven.'

Nila said, 'I am a non-virginal, non-beauty of this earth.'

Benoir pulled her on to his lap and said, 'Oh gorgeous damsel, won't you taste this heavenly liquid? If you only knew what you are missing.'

Nila drank in the intoxicating blue eyes and said, 'I don't care if I lose Chateau Margot, as long as I don't lose you.'

Benoir kissed her lips, her chin, breasts and nipples. He held Chateau Margot in one hand and Nila in the other and looked deliriously happy.

Nila was terribly excited when they went to Florence. She could gaze upon 'David' to her heart's content, David of her dreams.

They finished the Uffizi and then Nila went round Michelangelo's 'David'. She spent hours looking at him. Benoir rushed her, 'Why are you taking so long? Let's go.'

'Have you noticed something—David is not flawless. Look at his right hand; it's too large.' Nila didn't take her eyes off David as she spoke.

Benoir said, 'That happens. My penis is also comparatively too large. You've said yourself that you really like that in me.'

Nila laughed as she said, 'So I did.'

After they left the museum, Benoir said, 'You just wasted the whole day here.'

He took the driver's seat of the rented car, heaved a long sigh and asked, 'So, where would madame wish to go now?'

'Wherever you wish.'

'My wish hardly ever matters. Tell me where you want to go.'

'Your wish hardly matters? Didn't you want to visit the museum?'

'I don't really like all these museums. I went because you like it.'

'So let's go wherever you'd like to go.'

'No, there isn't any time.'

'If we had the time, where would you have gone?'

'What's the point of talking about it? Tell me Nila, why don't you drive?'

'I don't know how to drive.'

'But you said you have a car in Calcutta.'

'We do, and the driver drives it.'

'You are very rich, aren't you?'

'It's a poor country. Whoever has a car, hires a driver. It doesn't cost much.'

'You said there are maids in your house. You must be terribly rich.'

'It's the same—maids don't cost much either. Almost everything is very cheap there.'

'Humans too, possibly. Do you have slavery there?'

'No.'

'So, you've hired me as your driver. Tell me where you want to go and I'll take you there. There's the map and we can look up any address there.'

Nila didn't speak.

Benoir drove around aimlessly and said, 'Nila, you want to buy love with money.'

'I don't know. Perhaps I think of you as a gigolo.'

'Don't be vulgar.'

'I spend money because I love you. Are you afraid thinking you'll have to give something in return? Don't be. You don't have to give anything.'

Benoir's jaws hardened. 'You are very selfish. You have come on a holiday to Italy and you've brought me along to drive you around. You don't love me Nila, you are using me. It's just I who love you, insanely.'

They spent the next two days in Florence in an uncomfortable silence and then they went to Venice. There she didn't hire a car, there was no need for one. There was water all around. Nila was relieved to note that at least Benoir would no longer feel the humiliation of being a driver. What now? Let's take a gondola. They went by gondolas and saw the Venetian palaces, ruined buildings, prisons, everything. There were no Venetians in Venice—they had all gone to Padova or to villages nearby. The escalating prices in Venice made life difficult for them. The Americans and rich people from Japan had bought most of the houses in Venice. These houses stayed locked all round the year except for a few months when they wanted to float around in gondolas.

Nila halted on the Bridge of Sighs. 'Do you know, Wordsworth has written poetry about this Bridge of Sighs. The prisoners sighed upon this bridge as they were led away from the palace and into the prison; they looked at the blue lagoon for the last time.'

Nila exclaimed again among a hundred pigeons as she stood on the square behind the palace and the pigeons flew away.

'Why are you shooing them away? Let them eat.'

'I'm shooing them away because I am jealous.'

'You envy the pigeons too?'

'Yes, I do.'

'Why?'

'Because I can't fly like them.'

Benoir walked away to a café, alone. Nila stood there amidst flocks of pigeons flying back down, alone.

That night, lying in the hotel room, Nila explained a unique Bengali word called '*abhimaan*' which couldn't really be translated into any other language. Did it have a counterpart in French?

Benoir didn't get a chance to reply—his mobile rang. It was Pascale.

He finished his phone call, came back to Nila who was almost asleep, and drank his fill of a different brand of liquor, a different body, different colour, different gestures, different waves.

Benoir covered her body with his, played the games of hide and seek and tag, and suddenly heaved himself forcefully, deep into Nila's mysterious difference.

'Do you feel me? Can you sense me?'

Benoir brought his mouth close to Nila's and said, 'Tell me you love me, tell me, tell me you love me a lot, insanely. Say je t'aime à la folie, say à la folie. Say I am everything to you. Tell me you can't live without me, you won't ever love anyone else. Tell me, Nila, tell me.'

Nila pulled away. Benoir's mouth smelt of dead rats. His mouth often smelt like that; only, Nila had never found it odious before. Or, perhaps, Nila thought, she may even have liked the smell once.

This is the End

Nila went to see a doctor because she missed her period that month. The doctor checked her and said she was pregnant. He even did a DNA test and informed her that Benoir Dupont was the father of her child.

Benoir went wild with exhilaration. He hugged Nila close and covered her with kisses in full view of the hundreds of people in the hospital corridor. He kissed her all the way back and said, 'My life is complete; my dreams have come true.' At home he picked her up and rocked back and forth. He held her close and spoke with great emotion, 'Je t'aime, je t'aime, je t'aime. Je t'aime à la folie. There isn't a man on this earth happier than me, more fortunate than I am.'

Nila's empty eyes were fixed on the window.

Benoir turned her sad face towards him and said, 'What are you thinking? Names for our son? You want him to have a Bengali name, right?'

Nila said, 'I'm thinking I need to find a job. The money I had is all over.'

'Don't worry about it. I'll take care of that,' Benoir said as he kissed the smooth brown skin on her stomach.

'I can't afford this house any more. I'll have to give it up next month.'

Benoir looked up with a smile of satisfaction, 'You know something? I'll put you up in my own house. Pascale can rent a place somewhere else. Won't that be good?'

Nila brushed away the few strands of golden hair that fell over Benoir's eyes and said, 'You will live in that house with Pascale.'

Benoir jumped off the bed. 'What are you saying? Do you think

I love Pascale more than I love you?'

Nila said, 'No, that's not what I think.'

'So then you know just how madly, passionately I love you.'

Nila's voice was strangely calm. 'No Benoir, you don't love me.'

In one swift motion Benoir pulled her up from her supine position, 'What the hell do you mean?'

Nila took his hand off her arm and said, 'I know what I am saying.'

'So you are still jealous; you can't take it if I speak to Pascale for a few minutes. You think I love her still.'

Nila fixed her deep, black eyes onto his and said, 'Benoir, you don't love Pascale.'

Benoir's eyes, his eyelashes trembled, 'So who do I love?'

'You love yourself, Benoir, your own self. No one else.'

'Don't be a moron,' Benoir shouted.

Nila laughed, 'Does the truth hurt? Do you know something, Benoir? I have realized one thing by now: you are no different from my father Anirban, my lover Sushanta, my husband Kishanlal and that Sunil. Of course, you appear to be different from them, you speak sweet words of love, kiss me every now and then, you say "ladies first" and make way for them or hand them a flower or two, help in the kitchen, push the pram on the road; but deep inside, all of you have some things in common.'

Benoir drew her close to his heart and said, 'Nila, you are carrying my child. Can't you see how happy that makes me?'

Nila extracted herself from his arms and said, 'You need a Madame Butterfly, don't you, Benoir? But I have no desire to be her.'

'Why are you saying this?' Benoir was shaking with rage; Nila couldn't tell if it was from fear or wrath.

'I have given you a taste of the different for a long long time. You have had your fill of the exotic, enough in fact. I had no self-esteem or self-confidence and that's why I came this far for your love. Now you must let me go. I cannot spend the rest of my life in tears. I won't let you have that pleasure at least! You would love to watch the fun, the love and tragic grief of a stupid, silly eastern woman. Finally suicide! No, I am not ready for that.'

Benoir's breathing was shallow. 'I will marry you Nila. You will be my wife. I'll divorce Pascale tomorrow; come, let's get married. Please believe me, I'm going to marry you. No one else but you.'

Nila placed her hands on his shoulders to stop him from trembling. 'I believe you—you *will* marry me. But I won't marry you.'

'Nila, you are pregnant. We will live together, we'll have a happy family with our son, a happy family forever.'

'No, this child will not be born.'

'What?'

'It will not be born. I will have an abortion.'

Benoir burst into tears. He went down on his knees and wept. Nila's feet were drenched in his tears. Benoir spoke in broken mumbles, 'Please don't leave me. Don't be so heartless.' He wailed loudly, knocked his head on the walls, once, twice, thrice. His forehead was cut and blood gushed out. He screamed, 'Please take your words back.' He knocked his broken brow on the floor and said, 'I cannot live without you, Nila. Cruelty doesn't suit you.'

'Does it suit you?'

Nila raised him from the floor, sat him down on the bed and said, 'Don't be so crazy; it is senseless.'

Benoir hugged her and said, 'You are mine, only mine. You cannot leave me. I have given you my all, all the love I had to give. I have loved you and known the meaning of true love, true emotion. I have never loved anyone so deeply; please don't hurt me. You are getting me wrong. You don't understand that if you leave me, my life loses all meaning, I'll kill myself. I have seen many women, but none like you. No one is as good, as honest, generous, loving, patient and selfless as you. You are the greatest woman on earth; nobody can be like you. You are incomparable. You don't know just how great, how noble you are; I know it. You have brought light into my mundane, modest life and I cannot bear to lose you. I have love and it is all for you, no one else. Keep me at your feet, but don't leave me.'

Nila laughed out loud.

'Benoir, you are out of your mind. You are talking utter nonsense.'

Benoir stood up in a flash, pointedly took his gold ring off his finger and threw it out of the window. 'You will be my wife, Nila, tell me you will marry me.'

Nila shook her head, she wouldn't.

'Why don't you understand me? What have I done? Where have I gone wrong? Tell me, and I'll correct myself. If I have wronged you, please forgive me.'

Nila said there was nothing to forgive, nothing to correct.

'Then why?' Benoir counted on his fingers, 'I have done things for you from that very first day. That day I reached you to Gare du Nord in my own car. I have taken you around to various places in Paris. I didn't spare any time for myself but gave it all to you. You wanted to rent a house and I took you around to various places. I have dropped my work and come to you whenever you called me. I trusted you so much that I have never used a condom with you. I took you to the doctor. I have cooked for you, served you, cleaned the house, vacuumed it, brought you water, made you tea. When that Bengali friend of yours raped you, I offered you security, I helped you chase away the demons.'

Nila stopped him half-way and said, 'Don't count on your fingers; this is a strange habit you have. You are so practical and you don't know this simple fact?' Nila held up her hands in front of him and said, 'If you count on your fingers, you'll only have ten chances, but use the divisions in them and you'll have thirty, including both hands.'

Benoir snapped at Nila, 'I took you to meet my parents. I left my Pascale and my darling daughter for your sake and began to live with you. I have considered divorcing Pascale and marrying you. I have hurt Pascale and deprived Jacqueline of her father's proximity. You wanted to go to Italy and so we did. I have taken you wherever you wanted to go.'

Nila said, 'I know Benoir, you have done a lot for me.'

'Then why can't you accept that I love you?'

Nila laughed.

'Are you in love with someone else?'

Again, Nila laughed.

'That night, when you spent half of it chatting with those men, did something happen? Have you fallen in love with one of them?'

Nila laughed and said, 'Yes, I quite like that Modibo.'

'Oh, you thought black men have bigger penises and so you are lusting for more. Have you touched his penis?' He pulled her hand and placed it between his thighs, 'Bigger than this? Bigger than mine? This is ten inches long and eight inches wide—is it bigger? That savage from the woods, can he give you the kind of pleasure I give you? Does he have any finer feelings?'

Nila pulled her hand out of Benoir's strong grip. She spoke calmly, 'Benoir, please collect your belongings from this house and leave immediately.'

'Do you really mean that?'

'Yes, I do.'

'Do you know you are making a very big mistake?'

'No, I am not.'

'You don't love me?'

'No.'

'Are you aware of what you are saying?'

'Yes.'

'You are ending our relationship here, today?'

'Yes, I am.'

Benoir stood up. His eyes brimmed over with hatred.

Nila leaned against two pillows and sat with her knees raised up.

'You have toyed with me all this while, Nila. You have had fun at my expense. You have fooled me. You are a greedy, selfish, horrid, lowly, rotten woman. You speak of Pascale, but you cannot even hope to measure up to her. You are a big zero, a vacuous being. I have seen many people, but never one like you. You have sucked me dry, burnt me alive, ruined me, ruined my family. I was such an ass that I loved a lousy woman like you. You are worse than the worst of them. I shudder to even look at you. You are ugly, dirty and revolting. Loving you was the biggest sin I ever committed. I hate myself for it. You are a murderer; you are about to kill an innocent child. I have never laid eyes on a murderer like you.' Benoir spat at Nila.

Nila laughed, 'I'm telling you again, use the parts between your fingers to count, it'll help you. After all, it's a long list you have.'

Benoir went on. 'What do you think of yourself? You think you are quite something. You know nothing, absolutely nothing. What are you so proud of? You have nothing to be proud of. Even my Jacqueline knows more than you. There's nothing but a truckload of shit in your head. I pitied you; no one else would have spared you a second glance. You think you are great in bed. Ha! You don't even know anything there. You are a piece of dead wood. You are an object of ridicule, Nila, just ridicule. You are a lesbian, a disreputable character. No one can make a home with you. Your husband threw you out because you are unfit to live with. Sunil raped you? Lies. You slept with Sunil and lied to me. I was so crazy that I didn't see you for what you are. Your world is limited to the three inches below your navel. That's all you know. You are a slut and I don't know what else you have done to me; perhaps I have contracted AIDS from you— who knows! Tell me, how many men have you given your sexual disease to? You wanted to fool me into marrying you! Thank goodness I could unmask you before it came to that.'

Nila didn't utter a single word. Benoir packed his things into his suitcase, his clothes, shoes, photo frame, gifts, Aramis [cup of tea], Brut [not cup of tea]. As he walked to the door, Nila said, 'Leave the keys behind.'

Benoir turned around, 'You want to get rid of me and live happily, don't you?' He put the suitcase down and began to throw around the things in the room. He crushed the CDs under his boots and broke them, smashed the tape deck on the floor, smashed the vases to smithereens, kicked the TV and broke it and took a hammer to the computer and shattered it. He tore up the books on the bookshelf and threw them out of the window. He ran and fetched the knife from the kitchen and slashed at the sofa, the beds, opened the cupboard and slashed at Nila's clothes. A storm raged inside the room. Nila gazed at it in silence.

Then Benoir grabbed her by the throat, 'You miserable creature, I'll kill you.'

Nila could hardly breathe. She used all her strength to unclasp his fingers. Benoir pushed her down on the floor. She fell face-down and he kicked her with his hard boots. He picked up the meat cleaver and raised it on her chest. Nila went cold with fear. She closed her eyes and listened to her heart beat. The knife fell bluntly against her back.

'I won't dirty my hands by killing a worm like you. You'll rot here by yourself.'

Benoir walked out. Nila's French lover walked out, her handsome man with his blue eyes, blonde hair walked out. She lay on the floor for a long time. She could hear nothing but the sound of her own heartbeat. Her whole body ached. When she got up, she did four things.

One, she took in deep breaths in the pure air. She stood at the window and looked out at the greens, reds and yellows of nature, at the festival of flowers beneath the blue of the sky, the white of the clouds. Nila had never seen such a pretty autumn before, had never seen nature in such gorgeous costumes. Was this her own country? Nila knew this land, decked up in such a beautiful autumn, was not her own land.

Two, she called Danielle and said she needed to get an abortion done and asked if she could help in any way. Danielle said, 'Certainly. So, what happened?'

'Nothing much. I fell into the trap of love and came out of it myself.'

'I knew it,' Danielle said in an I-told-you-so tone of voice and added, 'I warned you earlier. I told you not to waste your time on this man.'

Nila said, 'Danielle, time is never wasted. This time was spent in acquiring wisdom and I needed it. Or I would have spent my life under a misconception. I feel men, of whichever country, whatever society, are all the same.'

Danielle was bursting with curiosity. 'So what are your plans? Are you going back?'

Nila asked, 'Where?'

'Where else? To your own land?'

'Do I have a land of my own? If your own land spells shelter, security, peace and joy, India is not my own land.'

Danielle said, 'Then stay here. Didn't you once say everyone has two motherlands, one his own and the other France?'

    'Danielle, do women ever have a land of their own or a motherland? I really don't think so.'

It was in Paris that Simone de Beauvoir had fought for abortion in the fifties. She had rented a small house in the sixth arrondissement and helped women abort illegally. Her battle resulted in the legalization of abortion. Nila felt happy that she was going to enjoy the fruits of that revolution in the same city.

    Three, she called Mojammel and asked him how Modibo was doing, whether he had a phone number and where did he live? Mojammel told her the little he knew about Modibo. Finally he said Modibo was desperately seeking a French woman to make her fall in love with him and marry him, so that he could get permission to live here. The good news was that Modibo had found a French girl.

    Nearly four thousand years ago the fair Aryans came from Central Asia and drove the dark Dravidians further to the south of India. They sang in praise of the fair, who were better and the dark worse, the fair were the masters and the dark the slaves, fair was greater, the higher caste, that was their society, their faith. It was a conviction embedded deep in their blood. Two hundred years of British rule had strengthened that belief: white was better, more learned, the masters. Nila's blood had also carried that belief, every brain cell felt it and even if she tried to shake it all away, a little bit remained somewhere. She knew it wasn't easy getting rid of that tiny bit, but she was happy to have achieved it finally.

    Four, she called Morounis and asked her to send someone to help her get the house in order.

    A Philipino girl, Marilu, who charged fifty francs an hour, came to her house that same evening. She put the broken junk into large bags and threw it in the garbage outside. It took her about three hours to get the work done.

    Then Nila made Marilu sit down and heard the story of her life.

    Marilu had come from the Philippines to this city six years ago. She had other relatives in this city and they were the ones who had helped her come here. She was a student in the university of Manila. Her subject was sociology. She quit her studies, her homeland and came to France. Since then she had worked as a cleaning lady and earned money. Many of her relatives worked in garment factories. Marilu was learning tailoring in Sandani, at her relative's place. Very soon she'd get into a factory too.

Nila asked, 'Can I get a small, cheap room in Sandani to rent?'

'Sure.'

But Marilu warned Nila that Sandani was not a good locality.

'How bad is it?'

'People are unemployed, there's robbery, theft, drugs, murder; it is chock full of black people.'

'Look at my skin—is it very white? In a way it's black. Is it only the unemployed people who rob and steal? Those who have jobs, get fat salaries, don't they steal? So what if it is chock full of black people. Don't the white people do drugs? Murder? Tell me, is there a good place on this earth? Where would you say there is total safety? Aren't there addicts in Manila? Robbers, murderers? There is poverty, sorrow and superstition there, as it is here. This country has racism, so does India. Women are raped in Calcutta, and it's the same here. This Rue de Vouyere, where only white people stay, do you think murders never happen here? Of course they do. One could have happened just today!'

Korean Women
and God

WOMEN FROM THE MARGINS

An Orbis Series Highlighting Women's Theological Voices

Women from the Margins introduces a series of books that present women's theological voices from around the world. As has long been recognized, women have shaped and continue to shape theology in distinctive ways that recognize both the particular challenges and the particular gifts that women bring to the world of theology and to ministry within the church. Their theological voices reflect the culture in which they live and the religious practices that permeate their lives.

Also in the Series:

Grant Me Justice! HIV/AIDS & Gender Readings of the Bible, Musa W. Dube and Musimbi Kanyoro, editors

Korean Women
and God

Experiencing God in a
Multi-religious Colonial Context

Choi Hee An

ORBIS BOOKS

Maryknoll, New York 10545

Founded in 1970, Orbis Books endeavors to publish works that enlighten the mind, nourish the spirit, and challenge the conscience. The publishing arm of the Maryknoll Fathers and Brothers, Orbis seeks to explore the global dimensions of the Christian faith and mission, to invite dialogue with diverse cultures and religious traditions, and to serve the cause of reconciliation and peace. The books published reflect the views of their authors and do not represent the official position of the Maryknoll Society. To learn more about Maryknoll and Orbis Books, please visit our website at www.maryknoll.org.

Copyright © 2005 by Choi Hee An.

Published by Orbis Books, Maryknoll, New York 10545–0308.
Manufactured in the United States of America.
Manuscript editing and typesetting by Joan Weber Laflamme.

Library of Congress Cataloging-in-Publication Data

Choi, Hee An.
    Korean women and God : experiencing God in a multi-religious colonial context / Hee An Choi.
        p. cm.
    Includes bibliographical references (p.   ) and index.
    ISBN-13: 978–1–57075–622–1 (pbk.)
    1. Women and religion—Korea (South) 2. Women—Korea (South)—Religious life. 3. Women—Korea (South)—Social conditions. 4. Patriarchy—Korea (South) I. Title.
    BL458.C46 2005
    200′.82′095195—dc22
                                                                2005011091

For my family

Contents

Acknowledgments

When I was young, I lived with many people. Thirteen of us from three or four different families occupied one house. And there was only one bathroom outside. Every morning, a long line formed in front of the bathroom. There were always some people who simply could not wait their turn, so there were also bad smells. One day I was playing in the dirt in front of another family's room in our house. A mother, father, and son lived there together. The woman came out of the room and sat down with her son. I greeted her and she smiled at me. She brought out some grapes, and she and her son started to eat them. I did not know what kind of food it was, but it looked delicious. They looked so happy and satisfied. I stopped playing, and I think I stopped breathing too as I watched them eating. Somehow she dropped a grape. It rolled along and fell into the dirt where I was playing and finally stopped right in front of me. I swooped like a hawk and popped it into my mouth. Some dirt was mixed with the grape in my mouth, but I didn't care. All I wanted to taste was that grape. It remained in my mouth for no longer than a second. What happened to my treasure? I looked up in anger and saw my mother with tears in her eyes.

I did not know what poverty was and how it affected my life. I never complained about not having grapes or of having only one bathroom for thirteen people. I just lived with it. However, there was always some unexplainable fiery anger and feelings of pain in my heart. Eventually, when I met God, I felt that I had found someone with whom I could talk. I decided to get to know God.

When I began my studies, I learned that God is the God of the wounded and powerless people, of the marginalized. However, wherever I looked, I saw hate, poverty, and war, and later I became aware of sexism, racism, classism, colonialism, elitism, heterosexism, ageism, ableism, and other discriminations. In fact, God seemed to be the God of the oppressors, the powerful people, and the people in the center. It seemed that God was usually on their side. However, I also realized that there were many poor and marginalized people, especially women, who still confessed God as their God. Despite their poverty and struggles, they still believed in God. They did not stop trusting God. Why? Why do people still believe in God? Does this God really exist? How do people keep their faith? How does this God transform their lives? How can I understand this mystery?

My life is being lived trying to answer these questions. As a Korean woman, I want to see *my* God, not the God of others. I want to find the God who lives and breathes with women, the poor, the oppressed, the marginalized, and the powerless. During my journey I have met many women and men who have answered my questions and shared their faith. They have showed me their God and taught me how to find the God I seek. I thank them from the bottom of my heart.

My heartfelt gratitude belongs to the entire community at Chicago Theological Seminary, especially my dissertation committee members, Dr. Lee H. Butler, Dr. JoAnne Marie Terrell, Dr. Robert Moore, and Dr. Laurel C. Schneider, who greatly encouraged me to seek answers through my doctoral studies. I could not have continued on my academic journey without the help of my mentors, Dr. Susan Brooks Thistlethwaite, Dr. Ken Stone, Dr. Tat-siong Benny Liew, Dr. Julia Speller, Dr. Seo Bo Myung, Dr. Mary Farrell Bednarowski, Dr. Kwok Pui-lan, Dr. Rita Nakashima Brock, and Dr. Yang Seung Ai, along with the community of the School of Theology at Boston University.

As an international scholar, I still struggle with doing academic writing and thinking in English. I have great appreciation for my editor, Susan Perry, who has given me incisive organizational and editorial assistance and helpful suggestions for every chapter of this book. I also want to thank my dearest friend,

Sharon Hunter-Smith, who spent endless time reading my drafts and encouraged me to maintain a continuing dialogue. I am also indebted to my friends Sarah Marhevsky, Kelly Jane Rider, Gay Harter, Kathy Deacon-Weber, Kim Jin Kyoung, Yoo Yeon Young, Rinnie Orr, Rev. Ann Marie and Donald Coleman, Rev. Dr. Christine E. Reimers, Rev. Belva Brown Jordan, Dr. Kim Nami, and Dr. Shin Eun Hee. Their beautiful friendship has continually motivated me and taught me both hope and love.

I am also most grateful to my persistent supporters, my mother, Choi Yang Ja, and my father, Choi Jong Kil, who never stopped believing in me and loving me. Their prayers guide me in this journey. Their tears lead me to hope and power. I also owe much to my sisters, Choi Jae Yeon and Choi Kyung Hwa, who support me with their whole hearts. I thank my entire family, Rev. Chae Hyo Min, Chae Jun, Choi Hang Ja, Choi An Ja, and many others, and especially my parents-in-law, So Dong Wook and Jang Rye, for their consistent prayers and encouragement.

Most of all, for being my unflinching hope and unlimited love, keen critic, astute editor, and patient counselor, I thank my husband, Rev. So Kee Boem. He has been there for me in every step of this journey. His warmth and tenderness, his peace and composure, his smile and happiness, his intelligence and knowledge are at the center of my life.

Thanks be to God!

Introduction

Knowing God
as a Korean Woman

One day, when I was young, I had a strange dream. In the dream I saw myself in the mirror. I knew that it was I, but I could not see my face clearly. It was a blur. When I woke up, I felt very uncomfortable. I ran to the mirror and looked at my face very carefully. I tried to memorize my face, so that I would not forget it. However, after a few hours, I realized that I could not remember my face. I went to the mirror and memorized it again. I closed my eyes and tried to remember my face. At that moment I could imagine my face in my memory, but as soon as I turned around, I forgot it again. I thought about other people's faces, and I realized that I clearly remembered their faces, but not my own. I was very frightened. Something was wrong with me! I could remember every face except my own. I asked my mother whether she could remember her own face. My mother smiled at me and said, "No one can remember one's own face." As soon as I heard her, I was very relieved. It was a natural phenomenon, I thought. However, I could not understand why people could not remember their own faces.

When I studied in America, I shared this story with my friends and asked them whether they remembered their faces. Without any doubt, I expected that they would not. However, I was very surprised. Many women answered that they did not remember their own faces, but many men and a few women said that they

1

could remember. I was stunned. I thought that not remembering one's own face was a universal phenomenon. My mother, sisters, and many Korean women I had known could not do this; however, I discovered that it was not true for all people. It was a great awakening moment for me.

Remembering my face was not only an inability on the part of my brain to memorize something. As I pursued my theological studies, with a strong emphasis on women's theologies, I realized that remembering my face, my voice, my body, and my soul were all connected. It was the process of recognizing my whole self. We recognize other people from their faces, smells, voices, body shapes, and personalities. However, when we try to recognize ourselves, many of us do not experience our own smells and voices. When we look at ourselves in a mirror, most times we see ourselves from the perspectives of other people because we are concerned about the way we look in the eyes of others.

So, my question is, How do we learn to recognize ourselves? How can we recognize our own being? How, especially, do we as women know our selves? There are many ways to approach this subject, because we are created out of many layers of individual and communal experiences, past and present, that have not been built from only one period within our lives. We have been formed in various historical, social, political, cultural, and religious contexts, as well as through unique individual experiences. Therefore, recognizing our selves requires us to use a multidimensional approach.

My task in this book is to use the reflections of some Korean women on how they understand God as an entry point into such a multidimensional analysis. I demonstrate how this approach can help women reevaluate their selves, assess their power, and reconstruct the reality in which they believe. Using the personal and communal experiences of Korean women, I show how their understandings of God's attributes can damage, embrace, or recreate Korean women and their self-images.

This process requires two different and important steps. The first is to evaluate the attributes Korean women ascribe to God and to explore the origins of these attributes. The second part of this step is particularly important because Korea is a country heavily influenced by patriarchal tradition and by the legacy of colonialism. Evaluating attributes of God reveals the reality of women's lives.

A second step is to reconstruct these understandings of God, if necessary, to help women use their own power to find ways to transform and heal their hearts, which have often been broken by the circumstances in which women find themselves. Reconstructing the attributes of God is a process of finding something that has existed in Korean women's lives but has not yet been recognized in Christian theological discourse. It is not merely a concern of Korean women but a possible channel to transform all of Korean society.

At this point I would like to introduce my understanding of a healthy woman. Although I have a particular perspective on women's health, I do not hold that there is a single image that will promote women's health. Each woman should use her own power to promote her self-image and total health. However, I propose that three significant elements are important.

First, I believe that healthy women love themselves. Remembering their own faces can be one aspect of showing this love. Women should love their physical bodies regardless of their age or their body type. They should be proud of their physical bodies. Women also should love their psychological strength and their warm hearts. They should listen carefully to what they need and want psychologically and spiritually as much as to what their bodies need and want. In this way they will understand who they are and who they want to be.

Second, healthy women live their lives with joy and happiness for themselves. They do not forget to celebrate their own happiness. In many women their joy comes not from their own being but from their children, husband, and others. They accept other people's joy as their joy but easily forget or ignore the joy in their own lives. Therefore, I think that women need to practice enjoying their lives without guilty feelings or self-disrespect, so that they can share their lives with others in joy and happiness.

Third, healthy women can express themselves. As we will see later, many Korean women are socialized to listen to others, not to themselves. They are not supposed to talk about their feelings and pains. Their feelings remain deep inside, because they do not know how to express them. Learning how to express their feelings, pains, and experiences with their own voices is a most important step in the development of healthy lives. In this way women can connect to their self, feel their own power, and relate to others with mutual respect and equality.

In many cases I have a hard time finding these three characteristics in Korean Christian women's lives. Because of religious teachings, hierarchal social norms, and patriarchal community-oriented culture, Korean Christian women are taught to sacrifice themselves for others and to deny their own needs as a noble cause. Loving themselves and enjoying their lives for their own happiness have been defined as selfish acts. Others' needs and wills always come before their own needs and wills, even in the family. Therefore, expressing their own feelings is not appropriate on many occasions.

These women's feelings and struggles are called *han*. Even though *han* does not belong only to Korean women, it certainly represents their experience. *Han* is a fundamental feeling of defeat, resignation, the tenacity of life, unresolved resentments, or grudges.[1] In the understanding of Andrew Sung Park, *han* is expressed as frustrated hope, the collapsed feeling of pain, resentful bitterness, and the wounded heart.[2] It has become deep "inner wounds" in Korean people's souls.[3] According to Chung Hyun Kyung, *han* comes from the sinful interconnections of classism, racism, sexism, colonialism, neocolonialism, and cultural imperialism, which Korean women experience every day.[4]

Han is not just the product of a certain cause. It is the suppressed, accumulated, and condensed experience of oppression caused by the carrier of a message from the collective unconscious in Korean historical and social structures. Most efforts to explore *han* in *minjung* theology are concentrated on the socio-economic dimension of *han*, which is identified as the subjective experience of those who have been oppressed politically, exploited economically, and marginalized socially by powerful and wealthy oppressors. *Han*, as a symbol for the cry of oppressed people, has become a political metaphor. But while Korean *minjung* theology, which is rooted in Korean experiences of life and culture, considers *han* to be the central theme of its theological enterprise, unfortunately, it is still very androcentric. Even though some *minjung* theologians such as Suh Nam Dong define women's experience as *han*, generally women have not been *minjung* theology's subjects, because *minjung* theology does not take seriously Korean patriarchy as the oppression that needs to be abolished, not only for women but also for men. Most *minjung* theologians as well as other Korean theologians do not want to talk about women's oppression. They simply avoid and ignore women's experience as an important part of *minjung* suffering.

Therefore, I take women's experience seriously as a subject of doing theology and ask whether current *minjung* theology is truly *minjung* or rather a patriarchal *minjung*. I show women's struggles and lift up the importance of women's liberation, empowering these unknown voices. In doing this, I seriously analyze the different dimensions of Korean multi-religious society and colonial hierarchal history, because *han* is the Korean women's psychological reality as an individual and communal phenomenon. It is a part of Korean women's epidemiological daily identity. It is woven into their lives. Thus the transformation of *han* is the most important theological subject for Korean women. Their liberation starts with this process. Transforming *han* means the transformation of their lives, empowering them and liberating their whole beings.

In order to transform women's *han* and envision the images of healthy women, I employ several important methodologies in this book. First, I recognize women's experience as the primary source for doing theology. As I mentioned earlier, women's experiences are ignored and avoided in most circumstances. Korean women's experiences are barely considered seriously by any religious or sociocultural discourses. Their experiences tend to be hidden, and their lives are forgotten. Therefore, I want to examine women's experiences as the main significant subject of theological as well as sociocultural discourse. The hidden and forgotten women's experiences within Korean colonial history need to be recognized and honored. Chapters 1 and 2 provide these sources by focusing on selected aspects of women's social roles and religious practices. Chapters 3 and 4 analyze these sources by focusing on women's psychological and spiritual lives relating to their faith in God.

Second, I examine Korean religious history as well as its colonial political history in the light of colonial, post-colonial, sociopolitical, and cultural perspectives. Korean religious history tends to present a male-articulated monologue regardless of multidimensional situations and women's experiential perspectives, but most Korean religions have been woven with women's religious devotion and sacrifice. In order to understand women's religious history in the contemporary context, it is important to note that behind the male monologue, women have helped to establish Christianity in Korea. Therefore, it is important to analyze the "Koreanized process" along with the multidimensional approaches to religious history. Chapter 1 brings these processes together by employing the four main Korean religions: Shamanism, Buddhism, Confucianism, and Christianity.

Third, in order to understand women's experience I selectively address feminist psychologies as examples for evaluating women's lives and reconstructing women's selves with critical consideration of Korean patriarchal attributes, because feminist psychologies can be helpful to Korean women as they seek to see their own psychology through their own eyes. However, as feminist psychologies try to understand Western women's struggles and experiences, these feminist psychologies are undercut by the limited Western perspective that presumes the universality of women's experience. Therefore, feminist psychology itself cannot support Korean womanhood without critical understanding of Korean patriarchal colonial history and religions. For this reason I must locate my perspective on psychology in Korean women's struggles and in their own experiences. With careful consideration of contextualization I provide an example of the creative transforming process of healing for Korean women.

Fourth, even though I present Korean religions as the most abundant resource for Korean women, as a Korean Christian woman I think about these issues within the context of Christianity. Inasmuch as Korean Christian women's unconscious and conscious identities have been influenced by multiple Korean religious cultures, understanding these cultures is helpful in understanding

Korean Christian women's selves. I consider these other religions as forming an important sub-identity of Korean Christian women, whether they are aware of this or not. This pluralistic religious understanding opens Korean Christian women to the broader view of their own multi-religious colonial and social structure so that they understand the psychological, spiritual, and somatic senses of their whole beings. This does not mean that Korean Christian women are pluralists, but it does mean that Korean Christian women have abundant resources for understanding God and rich resources for reconstructing their selves.

Employing these methods, I explore how the attributes of God have influenced Korean women's lives in both positive and negative family relations and in other social historical contexts. I show the process of how women's own transformation can overcome their lives and history. In addition, I examine the prominent pastoral practices in the Korean Christian context and suggest three significant pastoral theological issues that, if addressed, will help Korean women transform their *han* in church contexts.

PART I

KOREAN WOMEN'S
EXPERIENCES OF GOD

People's concepts are formed by sociopolitical, historical, and psychological realities. As people seek God, selectively sorting through their experiences consciously to collect their understanding of God, factors of which they are unaware also shape this understanding. Through this complex process, they grow to understand God and develop their faith. In the case of Korean women, the characteristics they attribute to God have been and are shaped by Korea's colonial history, religious history, sociopolitical situations, and over centuries by the cultural philosophy of the East. And, of course, the four predominant religions of Korea—Shamanism, Buddhism, Confucianism, and Christianity—have influenced how women think about the attributes of God in everyday life.

1

The Tradition of Shamanism

Shamanism is an indigenous religion that existed in the Korean peninsula well before the tenth century B.C.E. during the Bronze Age.[1] Over time it has developed a certain cultural consciousness and sense of identity and has represented the most basic reality of religious experience in Korea.

CHARACTERISTICS OF SHAMANISTIC GODS

The nature of Korean Shamanism reveals several characteristics of the religious mind-set of the Korean people. First, Korean Shamanism is polytheistic, with more than eighteen thousand gods.[2] The gods have various forms, which include female, male, animal, nature, and supernatural deities. For example, on Cheju Island, Korea's largest island, located on the south side of the Korean peninsula, approximately three hundred shrines have been constructed and named for the different gods.[3] Each province also has its own names for the gods. Sometimes Shamanism has a hierarchal structure, and sometimes it does not.

Historically and culturally, the Korean people are polytheistic. When people think about God, whether they are Christians or Buddhists, there is often more than one God. While they may confess one God, both consciously and unconsciously they think of God in the plural. This portrait of an abundant collection of coexisting multiple gods brings new possibilities for diverse and rich understandings of God, and these gods can be much more comforting to people than one heavenly God.

In many cases gods are female, and female deities are worshiped equally with male gods. In the following creation myth, the creator is a giant grandmother god.

> She made all mountains and oceans. Her urine became rivers and her dung became small mountains and islands. When she brought some soil in her dress and put it in Cheju Island, it became Mt. Halla, which was the highest mountain in South Korea.[4]

Another female myth tells the story of a wise woman who made day and night and created all the stars in order to make north, south, east, and west. She created all of the world order.[5]

Female creator myths exist beyond Cheju Island. While female creators have different names in each province, regardless of their names they are all giant grandmothers with very strong powers.[6] Many of these stories are compounded with the myths of San Sin (the mountain god), since some of these creators make mountains and also become mountain gods. Because 69 percent of Korea is surrounded by mountains and each mountain has its own god with independent power, there are many mountain god stories.

Likewise, because Korea is a peninsula, there are a lot of Hae Sin (the sea god) stories. According to a survey, some forty sea-god shrines still exist on Cheju Island. These gods, generally called Grandmother or Grandfather of the sea, are petitioned for safety on the sea.[7]

Sam Sin (the god of birth) is the most powerful and famous female god in Korea. Sam Sin shows very independent power and strong character even within Korea's patriarchal culture. It is believed that Sam Sin brings into existence all human beings on earth and protects babies from diseases and bad spirits for one hundred days after birth.

Animal myths and worship, especially those centered around the snake god, are quite popular in rural areas, and women are a central part of their narratives. Two well-known snake gods are

Yodured-dang (eighth-day-shrine) or Chilsong (seven star).[8] The myth about the snake god begins with the only daughter of a noble family who became pregnant through the magic of a monk. She was thrown into the sea in a stone basket and drifted to an island where she became a mother snake, or Bat-chilsong, and supposedly lived on a bundle of straw in the backyard.[9] Women worshiped these snake gods as gods of fortune or wealth in a family. For example, if an accident occurs, one worships the snake god immediately to appease it, because a failure to show favor to the snake god is believed to have caused the accident. This belief still persists today in some provinces.

Whether male or female, most shamanistic gods are closely connected with women's living spaces. Every house has its own spirit uniformly throughout the country, even though the names and the form of the house shrines differ. Song-Ju (the god of the household) includes within its meaning three ideas: the god protecting the house from evil, the god fostering the fortune of the house, and the god safeguarding the head of the family. These gods usually live in a corner of the wooden floor or hallway. Cho-wang (the god of the kitchen, or the fire god) is an important god for housewives. In Honam Province, in the southern part of Korea, the first thing women usually do after daybreak is to show reverence to Cho-wang with an offering of a bowl of pure water at the kitchen altar. Other household gods include Toju, the god of the site of the family residence; Chae-suk, the god of storage; Op, the god of fortune; and Su-mun-jang, the god of the gate.[10]

These gods are believed to live in the places where they are in charge. They have their own particular functions in their various locations, with no practical connections with one another or hierarchal relationships among them. Women as well as men believe that these gods help protect people from negative occurrences and bad fortune, and sustain their lives as long as they treat these gods favorably. It is worth noting that in many cases women practice the worship of these gods.

The shamanistic gods are also close to the common people's working culture. Because Korea has an agrarian culture, there are gods of wind, agriculture, longevity, water, and rain that are worshiped by farmers and other working-class people and are closely associated with their lives. These gods are connected with religious rites that aim at healing diseases and enjoying wealth and long life. They are not universally present with the same face, but they penetrate the whole of people's lives, manifested through different names and characteristics. They live with and in people and lead and guide them. These are not abstract or ethereal gods, but beings who are alive through their regular, everyday presence. While they are not regarded as omnipotent, they do help sustain people's lives and keep them persevering day in and day out. These gods are familiar to and comfortable for people throughout their lives.

Some shamanistic gods evolve from ancestors, as spirits of the dead become gods. These shamanistic images are deeply associated with Korea's Confucian culture, which is discussed at a later point. However, one myth well illustrates the ancestor-related understanding of gods in the shamanistic context:

> Koryosa [the history book of the Koryo Dynasty] records the myth of three ancestral families, the Go, the Yang, and the Pu. According to the myth, three gods emerged from the earth, hunting and eating flesh, while three goddesses entered the island in a boat, bringing with them the seeds of five grains, calves and ponies. They wedded the three ancestral gods and became the progenitors of Cheju Island. The Three Holes, about ten centimeters in diameter, from which the three gods are believed to have emerged, are worshipped as a sanctuary in Confucian rituals.[11]

The myth is initially a song about the shamanistic gods. It is believed that the Three Holes originated as totems of serpents and then became the ancestors of people. These gods bring Korean people's understandings of God into a familiar closeness, like that of family members. Generally, Koreans respect their ancestors in the same manner that they worship gods, and they love their gods as they love their own kindred. Gods are like their family, their mothers and fathers. It is interesting to note that after women die, they are respected equally with men. In this sense shamanistic gods can be both men and women.

Shamanistic gods are strongly associated with the roles of benefactor and protector. People believe their gods protect them from bad fortune, bad weather, harmful ghosts, evil countries, and so on.[12] Thus, they become not only protectors from evil but also bring about worldly blessings and foster social harmony. These attributes of the gods are found not only in Shamanism but also in Buddhism and Christianity. Because of continual poverty and the threats of colonialism, the Korean people traditionally have had a strong need for both spiritual and psychological protection. This explains why all the shamanistic gods are closely connected with every aspect of the people's daily lives: they provide both protection and stability.

KOREAN WOMEN AND SHAMANISM

Although the gods are protectors and benefactors, they have both negative and positive functions in Korean women's lives. Unfortunately, women devote themselves to these gods in the same manner that they worship their so-called human protectors, who are often oppressors and colonizers. Hence, women hesitate and examine themselves carefully to determine whether they are "good enough" to please their gods—just as they do with men and others in power. Because their lives are not in their own hands but are controlled by their protectors, they feel powerless. Instead of seeking their own strength, they have been taught that they need someone to protect them from others. When women worship the shamanistic gods, they often have this same feeling. They try to please the gods by whatever means are necessary. Usually, these gods are not generous but are easily angered and irritable, similar to the human beings who are supposed to be women's protectors. They live in an inevitably dependent reality and, because of this unhealthy mechanism, are in danger of permanently losing their own sources of strength.

However, these gods also comfort women and help release their repressed feelings. The gods serve to sustain their lives. Korean women believe that the gods work with them and act with them and protect them against unreasonable and unjust occurrences. They look to the gods for support as they try to overcome their miserable reality and hope for a better future. When the shamanistic gods are developed or reinterpreted in a positive manner, they can redeem wounded people and heal shrunken spirits.

Finally, the shamanistic gods can bring reconciliation and peace between individuals, between individuals and the community, and between communities, challenging hierarchal powers on all levels.[13] These gods tend to bring blessing and foster harmony. Whenever people participate in a shamanistic ritual, it eventually brings about reconciliation and peace within families, among relatives, within villages, and even among nations. Whenever a fight occurs between family members, villagers, and even strangers or dead people, these gods lead people to solve the conflict and reconcile. One of the reasons Korean Shamanism has survived is that these images of gods provide people with the power needed to reconcile themselves and intermingle their lives. These gods do not allow the destruction or domination of others but lead people to undo their pain and *han*, showing that life continues and that they can flourish together.

SHAMANISTIC RITUALS

Various rituals are used to call upon the powers of the shamanistic gods. One of the most widely known rituals is *Kut*, directed at the reconciling gods, when an individual or place finds itself in trouble. While certain shamanistic rituals are performed only at certain times and locations, *Kut* is open to every person and every home at any time. A female shaman performs *Kut* for people who may be sick or near death. Wearing a beautiful costume, she dances into a state of mild euphoria, possessed by the people's gods. Sometimes she honors *han*-filled ghosts who have been abandoned and ignored, blaming the household that ignores them. After consoling the ghosts, she asks their forgiveness and reconciles the people with them.[14] Other times she may discover a hidden conflict or secret between people. Again, she consoles them, makes them reconcile with one another, and redeems their pain. Sometimes, with heavenly authority, she challenges social oppressions and taboos in order to bring about reconciliation, speaking something unspeakable and revealing something unimaginable in their culture but real in their lived reality. The shaman's gods help her to find the hidden, unbearable *han* that destroys people, and it is these gods that want to bring peace among people and undo their oppressive *han*.

One of the unique characteristics of Korean Shamanism is that it represents the voices of oppressed people.[15] Using forms of Shamanism, oppressed people can satirize their oppressors and caricature their oppressive reality. Shamanism has been and is sometimes called the religion of Korean women, because most shamanistic rituals have been practiced exclusively by female shamans and most myths and stories have been handed down by women throughout the generations.[16] Korean Shamanism calls female shamans to learn how to communicate with the earth, the gods, and the universe, and to lift up their voices through these practices. However, not only female shamans, but also most Korean women perform shamanistic rituals in their everyday lives. Shamanistic rituals and storytelling provide women with a cathartic release from their oppressive reality and empower them to share their pain. Hence, in shamanistic practices, women tell their *han* and share the reality of their lives.

Within society at large, however, female shamans who have spiritual power have been viewed as polluting, dangerous, mystical, and unclean.[17] They are usually socially marginal people who come from a low caste/class. It was not always this way. In the Koryo period (918–1392) some shamans were even considered upper class. However, with the founding of the Yi Dynasty (1392–1910), the situation changed. Shamans were relegated to the lower class of merchants, artisans, butchers, and entertainers. Eventually their freedom was restricted as they were forbidden access to political power and were prevented from carrying out ceremonies and rituals out-of-doors. During the Yi Dynasty, Shamanism was practiced less frequently than any other religion, even though it was certainly not eradicated from people's minds. Gradually, Shamanism was treated as the religion of uneducated women and as little more than superstition. After the coming of

Christianity in the nineteenth century, Shamanism was viewed as no more than old-fashioned superstition and heresy, and its gods were driven underground. Nonetheless, the gods were not forgotten or lost; in fact, they still communicate with women in the present time.

SHAMANISM IN THE POLITICAL CONTEXT

Shamanism is the religion that typically represents indigenous people's beliefs and ideas about God, the community, and the cosmos. It presents primordial concepts of the images of God through myths and rituals that reveal a complex system of beliefs and practices encapsulating significant notions of household, family system, religious belief, and social structure. Understanding Shamanism is vital to understanding ancient and modern Korean society.

Because of its centrality to the Korean people and society, the ruling class often controlled, or attempted to control, Shamanism for its own purposes. By manipulating storytelling and creating politically charged myths, the ruling class planted its own ideologies into the minds and thoughts of the common people. Shamanism was then no longer able to represent the voice of the marginalized and powerless. Instead, when appropriated by the power structure of ancient Korea, it was used as the religion of and for the ruling class.

A good example of this ambiguous functioning of Shamanism is found in scholarly debates over the story of Tangun, the Korean birth myth. According to several modern Korean historians such as Yi Nung Hwa, Choe Nam Son, Shin Chae Ho, and Choe Tong, the origin of Korean shamanism was intimately connected with the myth of Tangun.[18] However, there is also a number of Korean historians, such as Im Sok Chae, who disagree with this view.[19] He contends that even if the myth of Tangun has the form of ancient Korean Shamanism, its content has been deeply shaped by a political ideology. Moreover, he says that it may be possible that there is no connection between the myth of Tangun and Shamanism. Rather, by using the forms of Shamanism, the ruling class sought to legitimate its political power and national authority.

The Tangun Myth

The earliest and most fundamental form of creation mythology is the myth of Tangun, found in the *Samguk Yusa*,[20] which reveals the paradigmatic structure of a people's world view:

> Tangun was the son of Hwanung, a son of Hwanin, the heavenly lord, and Wungnyo (which literally means a "bear-woman"). Hwanin had a bold, wise son called Hwanung (literally meaning "heavenly male"). Hwanung was interested in ruling the human world and his father granted his wish. As he looked down upon the earth, the young prince's gaze fell upon the green hills of a beautiful peninsula between two great seas. He chose it. His father allowed him to descend to earth with three thousand servants to help him rule the land, and with three powerful ministers: Pung-Beg, U-sa, and Un-Sa—Lord Wind, Lord Rain, and Lord Cloud. They were to govern health and sickness, harvest and season, good and evil.
>
> One day, a bear and a tiger anxious to become humans asked Hwanung to fulfill their wish. He ordered them to stay in a cave without sunlight and to eat garlic bulbs and mugwort plants for a hundred days. The tiger failed but the bear fulfilled his command and became a woman. Then Hwanung married the bear-woman and begot Tangun. When Tangun died he became a San Sin (mountain god). He is never forgotten by the grateful people of Korea.[21]

Korean history has always emphasized the importance of the Tangun myth to the origin of the Korean nation. After the Paleolithic Age and Neolithic Age, Kochoson (2333? B.C.E.–107? B.C.E.), the ancient tribal community, opened the Bronze Age in southern Manchuria.[22] The title of Tangun was actually Tangun Wanggom, which meant that he combined political and religious functions in a single personage. This title itself suggests that the myth of Tangun is not a pure shamanistic myth but a political shamanistic myth, or a political myth in shamanistic form. While establishing Kochoson's legitimacy, this myth simultaneously revealed the religious perspectives of the Kochoson government. Tangun, who had descended from the heavenly lord, had divine origins. His origin and divine power enhanced the dignity and authority of his political leadership. He was not the human chosen by God, but the human who became God after he died, the God who protected Korea.

Because the ancestors of the Korean people were closely related to the people of central Asia, Mongolia, and Manchuria, the Kochoson government may have created this myth in order to stake a claim for Korean uniqueness. When the Han Dynasty of China invaded northern Kochoson in 109 B.C.E., a long history of colonial invasions of the Korean peninsula began.[23] The Kochoson government may have created this myth in order to support its own legitimacy. Whether or not it actually created the Tangun myth, however, the Kochoson government did use this myth to bolster claims for the uniqueness and legitimacy of the Korean nation in the eyes of its own people and of other nations.

The Tangun myth has functioned in the same way in later periods of Korean history. During the period of Japanese invasion and control (1910–45), Korean patriots again endowed this myth with special meaning, emphasizing the significance of the national origin of Korea and its unique identity. Resisting colonialism, Korean nationalists and patriots reinterpreted the Tangun myth as their original and genuine Korean identity.

Periods of national crises caused by colonial invasions, wars, and patriotic struggles engendered a strong patriarchal and military culture that despised women and powerless people. From the beginning, this myth itself appears to have been created in the midst of political struggle. Because of their loss of national independence, Korea's government officials and patriots linked male divine images with the image of Korea in order to gain their protection and as evidence of Korea's superiority to other nations and people.[24]

This is not the first time in history that religion has been called on to establish a national identity, at least within the ruling class, that affirms its connection with or support from God or heaven. One outcome of this political manipulation of the ideology of the Tangun myth was that "the Korean nation is ultimately the community of men, created by an extraordinary man, in which women exist only as its precondition."[25]

The Tangun Myth and Women

In this myth the woman was treated clearly as animal in origin and closely associated with the earth. All that was valued was a piece of her body, her womb. In order to be human, she endured all the suffering, but this was not sufficient for her to become a perfect human being. Her role was not ruling the land together with her husband or her son but merely begetting a "son." Her function in what became the national myth was to submit her body to men. Her animal roots prevented her from being close to or associating with men, who were divine. The transformation of a bear into a woman symbolized Korean womanhood, which would be filled with suffering and ordeals.

Throughout history, each ancient government of Korea chose a specific religion and supported it, creating its own national birth myths and religious stories, depending on its ideologies. However, unlike the myth of Tangun, many myths neither directly cooperated with the political dilemma posed by colonialism nor supported national patriotism. As can be seen in the female creator myth described earlier, some of the myths were expressed with humor and satire, resisting the ideologies of the ruling class and reflecting the common people's reality and culture. Because of the unique character of different provinces, myths reflected local culture and history. At the same time, they asserted, consciously and unconsciously, resistance against the national circumstances of colonialism and the patriarchal and hierarchal social structure. They arose from individual or village rituals and storytelling, practiced and retold in the private sphere of women, who continuously transmitted their essential structure without many changes over time. Even though the male-dominated colonial cultures disdained these stories and manipulated them, many of the myths and rituals still retained their power to express people's struggles and to lift up their voices against unjust suffering and ordeals.

Shamanism, which existed from the beginning of Korean history, has been practiced continuously by many generations of women from ancient times to modern times, even though since the seventeenth century strong Confucian and Christian influences have encouraged people to disdain shamanistic rituals and practices.

In conclusion, Shamanism provides an array of diverse understandings of God, despite political influences, that Korean people have created from their authentic lives. These understandings of God encourage women to envision alternative manifestations of God, unlike the Christian attributes of God that cling to a single vision of a male God. Understandings of God gained from shamanistic traditions, centered around reconciliation and peace, are often closely associated with women's lives as well as their cultures. Over time, these understandings of God have certainly helped and can continue to help Christian women transform their limited and narrow Christian God. However, because of the influences of Korea's hierarchal culture and of patriarchal Christian traditions, these attributes of God have been trivialized or overlooked in our historical and cultural memory.

2

The Tradition of Buddhism

Buddhism has had a great impact upon the Korean mind. It was introduced by China in the fourth century along with colonial power during the period of the Three Kingdoms: Koguryo (37 B.C.E.–668 C.E.), Paekche (18 B.C.E.–660 C.E.), and Silla (57 B.C.E.–668 C.E.). The right to the throne in Koguryo was secured in the time of King T'aejo (53–146?). Paekche first appeared as an aristocratic state in the reign of King Kun Ch'ogo (346–75), and Silla was consolidated as a confederated kingdom in the time of King Naemul (356–402). In the mid-seventh century the Three Kingdoms were united by Silla; this period is called Unified Silla (668–935).

Among the Three Kingdoms, Koguryo was the first to receive Buddhism.[1] As described in the *Samguk sagi*, Fu Chien, a Chinese ruler, sent a monk named Sundo with images of the Buddha and copies of several texts from the canon (372).[2] In 385, two Buddhist monasteries, the Songmun Monastery and the Ibullan Monastery, were founded. Furthering its growth, in 392, King Kogugyang ordered that his people practice Buddhism, and the religious movement attained secular benefits.[3]

The kingdom of Paekche admitted Buddhism in 384, twelve years later than Koguyo. The *Samguk Yusa* says that in the first year of King Chimnyu's reign (382), Marananta, who came from eastern China, introduced Buddhism. In 385, ten Buddhist monasteries were built in the new capital of Hansan. In the first year of King Asin's reign (392), Asin proclaimed that the people should believe in Buddhism and seek happiness.[4]

Silla was the last kingdom of the Three Kingdoms to accept Buddhism. During the reign of King Nulchi (417–57), a Koguryo monk, Mukhoja, went to Silla and secretly propagated Buddhism. Later, during the reign of King Soji (479–99), another Koguryo monk, Ado, also went to Silla. From this point on, the number of followers increased. Silla Buddhism developed quickly under King Chinhung (540–76). In his fifth year the king completed the Hungnyun Monastery and allowed men and women to be ordained.[5]

BUDDHISM—TO PROTECT THE NATION

After the periods of the Three Kingdoms and Unified Silla, the Koryo (918–1392) government adopted Buddhism as the national religion. In order to maintain a military structure and hereditary social classes, the government and the monks used Buddhism to gain worldly benefits for the nation. While the government helped the Buddhist monks to build monasteries, the monks had to do service and pray for national protection, and during war they served in the military as soldiers to protect their monasteries and the country.

From the period of the Three Kingdoms, Buddhism was supported by the governments as an agent of national protection. Buddhism was used by the ruling class to legitimate its ideologies and a military culture. The following legend from *Samguk sagi* illustrates how this was done:

> After ruling the kingdom [of Silla] for twenty-one years, the great king [Munmu] passed away in the second year of the Tang Yung-lung era. . . . Following the king's command, he was entombed atop a great boulder on the Eastern Sea. During his lifetime, King Munmu always said to his chaplain, Dharma Master Chiui, "After my death, I vow to become a great dragon protecting the kingdom. I wish to worship the Buddhadharma and guard the families of the

nation." The chaplain responded, "A dragon is an animal; how can this be an appropriate rebirth for you?" Munmu answered, "Since long ago, I have done nothing but disdain worldly glory. If it is my lot to be reborn as an animal, then that will suit me just fine." . . . A record in that Monastery [Kamun-sa] says, "Because King Munmu wished to suppress the incursions of Japanese pirates, he first began to construct this Monastery. Before its completion, the king died and was reborn as a sea-dragon. His son, Sinmun, assumed that throne and in the second year of Kai-yao (682), [the construction of Kamun Monastery] was completed. Under the stairway leading to the Golden Hall opened a cave that faced east. This made it convenient for the dragon to enter the monastery and move about. Alternately, it might be that, on the posthumous order of King Munmu, the place where the great king's remains were kept was named Taewang-am (Great King's Boulder) and the monastery was named Kamun-sa. Sometime later, the place where the appearance of that dragon was seen was named Igyondae (Auspicious Sighting Terrace)."[6]

King Munmu wished to become a dragon spirit that would guard the kingdom of Silla and protect it against the incursion of pirates. Dragons functioned as spirits of national protection and were believed to have strong powers. They moved between the terrestrial world of people and the ethereal world of spirits. At this time Korean Buddhism was strongly influenced by China; dragons were regarded as a symbol of royalty in China. However, in Korea, because dragons resembled snakes, dragons were believed to be either great snakes or spirits containing the magical powers of snakes. In agricultural societies snakes were worshiped as gods who were indispensable in controlling the waters. In this legend the dragon spirits were not simple water divinities but extraordinarily powerful, even wrathful, water spirits. To magnify the power of the dragon was to demonstrate the strong power of ancient Korea's own imperialism. The myth of King Munmu, therefore, used complex concepts of both Buddhism and Shamanism to support national protection, to encourage fervent patriotism in times of national crises, and to guard against intruders. Through this myth shamanistic cults and Buddhism were used in cooperation to produce an imperial ideology that supported the monarchy and the ruling aristocracy. Thus, both indigenous cults and Buddhism served the nation.[7]

THE DEVELOPMENT OF KOREAN BUDDHISM

In order to adjust to the Korean context Buddhism embraced both local cultic beliefs and Shamanism not only to collaborate in legitimating the ruling class but also to attract common people into Buddhism. Buddhism struggled hard to attract the common people. Even though many ancient imperial Korean governments supported Buddhism, in the beginning many common people rejected it. Because Buddhism encouraged people to leave this world, including their own family, it ran counter to the Korean tradition of placing value on the family.[8] Therefore, in order to implant itself as a Korean religion, Buddhism inevitably had to adapt to the Korean cultural and religious milieu and appear as a form of indigenous belief.[9] As it was "Koreanized," Buddhism became not just an abstract Eastern philosophy and religious doctrine but another type of folk belief. The Buddhist monasteries came to resemble shamanistic shrines, so that whenever people needed help, they went to pray and consult with the monks. Monks were considered to be shamans with thaumaturgic skills who were able to subdue demonic spirits through the use of spells and cure people with magic medicine. The monks were encouraged to provide therapeutic and healing services in behalf of the common people.[10] Many stories, such as the following, highlight this:

> During the third year of King Michu's reign [264], the duchess of Songguk was struck by illness, which neither incantations nor medical treatments could cure. Seeking out doctors throughout the entire country, the king finally located master Ado, who went to the royal palace and cured the woman's illness. The king was greatly relieved and offered

him a reward; Ado sought permission to build temples and disseminate Buddhism, which was granted.[11]

These stories implied that Buddhism was a means to conquer personal misfortunes, such as illness, and social disasters, including famine and flood. In some accounts Buddhism took the place of Shamanism, but at the same time Shamanism sometimes fused with Buddhism. Buddhism stimulated tremendous evolution within Korea's shamanistic culture, prompting cooperation and allowing the two traditions to influence each other in new and interdependent ways. The best example of this process is *Samguk Yusa*, a lengthy account compiled by Iryon (1206–89). Iryon, an educated monk, wrote these stories to interpret the traditional beliefs and practices of the illiterate non-elite according to the standards of their adopted religion of Buddhism. This is why indigenous spirits like demons and bears are usually presented as sinister in some way. Through shamanistic folk stories interpreted by Buddhists, Iryon revealed his agenda to embody Buddhism in Korean culture and everyday life.

Other Buddhist leaders and scholars also integrated Shamanism and Buddhism in the service of national protection. For example, Wonhyo (617–86), one of the great Buddhist scholars and a great teacher of the common people, established the metaphysical concept of *hwajung* (the harmonization of all disputes). According to Wonhyo, there are no actual distinctions between secular and sacred, right and wrong, or truth and falsehood. These distinctions only exist in one's mind. He wanted to attain oneness by overcoming dualisms. In many ways his interpretation of Buddhism was very similar to a shamanistic world view and shamanistic spirituality.[12] Not surprisingly, this shamanized Buddhism flourished in the lives of the common people.

DIVINE IMAGES IN KOREAN BUDDHISM

In surveying the historical background of Buddhism in the Korean context, two factors clearly shaped divine images held by women. First, even though Buddhism itself does not have a concept of God, Korean Buddhism inspires divine images. Korean Buddhists believe in Buddha and bodhisattvas (Buddhas-to-be) in the same way that other Korean people believe in their gods.[13] In the process of accommodating Buddhism to Korean culture, the images of Buddha and bodhisattva often overlap with images of the shamanistic gods.

The mountain gods serve as one example. These were originally shamanistic gods, but in Buddhist stories often both mountain gods and Buddha appear at the top of mountains. Sometimes mountain gods even replace the images of Buddha, or their images overlap. The following story provides such an example:

> During the reign of King Chinpyoung [579–632], the bhiksuni Chihye, who excelled in her religious practice, resided at Anhung Monastery. She planned to repair the Buddha Basilica at Anhung Monastery, but was without resources. She dreamed of a female Transcendent of modest demeanor, who was wearing a headdress adorned with pearls and kingfisher's feathers. She appeared before Chihye and consoled her, saying, "I am the divine mother of Mt. Sondo (Transcendent Peach Mountain). I sympathize with your desire to repair the Buddha hall, and wish to donate ten *kun* [catties] of gold to help with it. Take the gold out from beneath my pedestal and adorn the three principal images of the hall with it. . . ." Startled, Chihye awakened. Leading her followers, she went and dug a hole under the pedestal. There she found 160 *yang* [taels] of gold, enough to complete her project. All of this was possible due to the commands of the divine mother.[14]

This myth was closely connected with another myth, the legend of the Holy Mother of Transcendent Peach Mountain, which was part of the foundation myth of the Silla kingdom:

> The divine mother was a Chinese princess, named Sha-su, who gave birth to a child out of wedlock. Because of her indiscretion, she was set adrift on the ocean and eventually

landed on Korean shores. She became the mountain spirit of Transcendent Peach Mountain. It was her child who became the founder of Silla, King Hyokkose. Mt. Sondo is a tall mountain northwest of Kyongju, the capital of Silla. During the Silla period, it was of special importance as the abode of the mountain god who guarded the capital. As the spirit of that mountain, the divine mother was widely revered throughout the land.[15]

The legend of Chihye relates tales of indigenous deities within the overall story of Buddhism. Despite Chihye's devotion to Buddhism, it is apparent that the people did not have much faith in Buddhism since they were unwilling to contribute money to help restore the shrine. To raise the money, Chihye needed help from the divine mother who was the mountain god and who indirectly supported the Buddhist religion as well. In the end, this divine mother, an indigenous deity who helped Buddhism to flourish, was portrayed as divine in this Buddhist story.

After Buddhism was introduced to Korea, the mountain gods overlapped with the bodhisattva, and people often treated the two as identical.[16] People honored the bodhisattva in ways similar to those used to worship their own shamanistic deities, such as the mountain gods.[17] Buddhism grew to be recognized and treated like their indigenous faith. This form of Buddhism was promoted not by its profound philosophy but by the shamanistic needs of the common people, and particularly the needs of women.

Many common religious women helped Buddhism to grow in Korea. They manifested an intense spiritual devotion to Buddhism. They participated in morning services, one hundred days of prayers, and daily meditation, and they supported Buddhist temples with different kinds of offerings. Before Buddhism was recognized as an acceptable religion, or before it was recognized by political power, Buddhism had to synchronize with Shamanism and be taken up by the common people, especially the women who would practice it every day. While Buddhism was introduced and taught by male monks and had patriarchal religious structures and rituals that were led by male monks, most religious

Buddhist rituals and services were practiced and supported by common female seekers. As women practiced their daily devotions in a shamanistc context, they did the same in Buddhism. They not only had similar images of gods in Shamanism and Buddhism, but also similar attitudes of fidelity and loyalty to both religions.

Thus, while Buddhism was introduced by China, it evolved in unique ways through its interaction with the indigenous mountain and ursine spirits that women worshiped. Before any political involvement occurred, Buddhism was understood as a part of indigenous belief. Buddhism and the indigenous shamanistic cults benefited from mutual coexistence, enriching the entire religious life of the Korean people.

BUDDHISM'S APPEAL TO WOMEN

A second factor that helped shape women's images of the divine was Buddhism's unique concept of equality: all beings are equal. Buddhism presents the possibility of both male and female divinities. Women were able to see female divine power in themselves and dream about transforming freedom. Although women were not equal in this world, through Buddhist faith and practice they could escape this painful world and transform themselves as equal beings. These teachings led women to enlightenment and allowed them both freedom and equality. Female images of the divine gave women opportunities to see transforming power in themselves. It is interesting to note that art from the period of the Three Kingdoms and Unified Silla reveals that a popular figure was not a male Buddha but bodhisattvas who had both male and female characteristics.[18] Despite Korea's patriarchal culture and traditions, many worshipers believed and depicted these bodhisattvas as their divine images.[19]

As an example, in Paekche (18 B.C.E–660 C.E.), a popular image of Buddha showed Buddha seated on a dais with one foot on the floor and the other crossed over the knee.[20] This image was believed to be Maitreya, who was in the form of a bodhisattva, not a Buddha. Usually the center figure of Maitreya was believed to be Buddha, but in Paekche the seated figure of Maitreya was depicted as a bodhisattva, the future Buddha who often appeared in both male and female forms.[21] It is possible, therefore, that the image of a female bodhisattva was introduced to Korea through Korean Buddhist art.

However, because of the influences of the patriarchal structure of Buddhism and Korea's hierarchal structure, people were rarely taught about female divinities or bodhisattvas. Because of Buddha's historical appearance, Buddha was always pictured as male. Not only Korean Buddhists but other Buddhists as well consciously and unconsciously accepted Buddha as male, and so over time the female image of the divine was hidden. Even though Buddhism was non-theistic, with no gendered Absolute or Supreme Being, and even though both female and male divine images existed in Korean Buddhist art and history, the female image of the bodhisattva was barely known to Korean women.

Although the images were barely known, from the beginning numerous women's stories were told in Mahayana Buddhist writings in the tradition of wisdom in which the images of bodhisattvas, Buddhas-to-be, were often reborn in both male and female forms.[22] A Chinese collection of Jatakas (Buddhist tales) includes "three tales of previous female existences of Gotama (two as a woman, one as a mother swan) and one of a female existence of the next Buddha-to-be of our world system, Maitreya Bodhisattva."[23] There are also several Mahayana sutras that have female bodhisattvas as heroines. The most fundamental and influential Mahayana sutras, the Perfection of Wisdom Sutras, affirm that all the apparent characteristics of beings are deceptive and illusive, for everything is in and of itself nothing. All is empty. There is no distinction between female and male. If Buddha should not be distinguished by physical condition or earthly appearance, it is impossible for Buddha to be male.[24]

The Vimaladatta sutra includes a famous story about a female bodhisattva:

Vimaladatta, the heroine, is the 12-year-old daughter of King Prasenajit of Kosala. She had accumulated great merit in previous existences and now engages all the major male bodhisattvas and disciples of the Buddha in extremely subtle debate on dharma. She bests them all, thus demonstrating her profound comprehension of emptiness, *sunyata*. Nonetheless, a spokesman for the views of the conservative elders (this time it is Mahamaudgalyayana) accuses the princess of not having understood the bodhisattva way because it is known that no one can attain perfect enlightenment with a female body. She says, "If I shall truly become a Buddha in the future, let my body change into that of a young boy." This change occurs and the Buddha announces that Vimaladatta had long ago aspired to attain perfect Buddhahood and she will do it. Still disgruntled, Mahamaudgalyayana asks Vimaladatta why she hadn't changed her female body to male long ago, if she was so wise. She replies that true enlightenment cannot be attained with either a female body or a male body; that is, such distinction-making has nothing do with the perfect enlightenment of the Buddhas and those who have truly embarked upon the path to that goal must leave all identification with gender and with sex-based roles behind.[25]

Generally, the female images of the bodhisattva are very wise. Even though to be Buddha, Vimaladatta changed her gender, many sutras such as the Diamond Sutra and other Prajnaparamita sutras claim that all distinctions of worldly forms are extraneous. Any being can be a bodhisattva if that being sincerely aspires to do so.[26] As the sutra demonstrates, the enlightened woman is more insightful and wiser than the male. The prejudiced male follower clings to his maleness, but the woman, who does not worry about changing her gender, is enlightened and able to demonstrate the meaning of emptiness. She is transformed and becomes a source for revealing the truth. She becomes the teacher of male followers. Gender itself should be eliminated in order to be enlightened. In fact, changing gender is illusory; both men and women have to abandon their gender and became genderless in the teaching of Buddhism. The concept of emptiness, *sunyata*, incorporates this teaching within its androgynous images of bodhisattvas as well as within Buddha.

Although such images appeared in ancient Buddhism in Korea, in the course of Korea's colonial history "Koreanized" Buddhism became allied with the hierarchal political structure and lost the androgynous aspects of its religious balance. Women lost the ability to imagine themselves as equal human beings with men, and they no longer believed they could transform themselves into enlightened beings. Rather, they saw themselves as deserving of pain and suffering from the sins of their past lives, which they would have to endure until they died in this life. They did not expect enlightenment until they finished their karma as women. In Korea, these concepts were interpreted and accepted by the political, social, national, communal, and individual ideologies as teachings of Buddhism. Women were caught between egalitarian Buddhist thought and the social and political interpretations of Buddhism by Korea's ruling authorities.

Even though Korean society was a strong patriarchal society, Buddhism did not severely discriminate against women's religious practices as Confucianism later did. Rather, near the end of the Koryo Dynasty (918–1392), women were actually encouraged to participate in Buddhist practices because of a national crisis. The weakened Koryo Dynasty built many Buddhist temples and encouraged people to perform Buddhist rituals to protect their country from a Mongol invasion.[27] It relied on Buddha's paranormal power and asked the people to pray for their country. Buddhism, deeply mingled with Shamanism, was believed to protect the Koryo Dynasty. Shamanized Buddhism was practiced at the national level but also in Buddhist temples by individuals, mostly women. At this local level Korean shamanized Buddhism supported women as actively involved with religious rituals and prayers for both their families and the nation.[28]

At that historical time, shamanized Buddhism, the national religion, was coopted by political power and it led people to be overly dependent on supernatural powers. As a result, a new group that arose to take over the country chose Confucianism as its new ideology. Korean Buddhism was then merged with Confucian ideologies, which had stronger patriarchal and hierarchal structures. However, because of women's religious devotion to shamanistic Buddhist faith and practice, Buddhism and Shamanism did not disappear despite political oppression. Rather, they have remained alive in the lives of Korean women and have been communicated and understood as the religion of women. Even today, women, as the main supporters and propagators, lead and sustain Buddhism and Shamanism financially and spiritually. Even though most Buddhist institutions in most countries do not support women's ordination into a formal order of nuns, Korean women struggled against this discrimination and gained a historical victory in 1982 when the full ordination ceremony for the nuns *(Bhikshuni)* was allowed. Many Buddhist nuns whose ordination was not possible in their countries, such as Tibet, Thailand, and Sri Lanka, traveled to Korea to receive ordination.[29] As lay people and as nuns, women actively participate in Buddhist practices and even gain official recognition. It is evidence of their devoted faith and strong spirituality.

In its development from an aristocratic ideology to the religion of common women, Buddhism has had a great impact on Korean history. In Korea both Shamanism and Buddhism, closely intermingled, are intimately connected to women's lives and encourage women to talk to God every day through their religious practices. Because both religions have the possibility of providing alternative non-patriarchal understandings of God, women have found room to imagine their own God. Because both religions teach the equality and freedom of all beings, women can learn to exercise their equal relationship with others and imagine freedom from their patriarchal reality.

3

The Confucian Tradition

Confucianism was introduced into Korea earlier than Buddhism. It began to be recognized in the later Koryo Dynasty (918–1392) and became the main ideology for the Yi Dynasty (1392–1910) when it prospered. During the early Yi Dynasty, Buddhism as well as Shamanism were strongly criticized by the ruling group.[1] However, even though they were without political power, Buddhism and Shamanism were not forgotten in women's lives. The number of shamans increased, and every town had a chief woman shaman. Even while the government disdained Shamanism and persecuted it severely at the national level, a few government-appointed shamans had great power and presided over shamanistic rituals in cases of political crises or natural calamities.[2] Nonetheless, Confucianism became recognized not only by the ruling group but also by the common people, and it has been strongly valued by Korea's traditional culture ever since. Part of the reason for this is the congruence of Confucian values with the values of the Korean family system and its easy incorporation into the already existing political hierarchy.

During the Yi Dynasty, Confucian teachings became increasingly emphasized, and eventually Confucianism was adopted as the national religion. As the state adopted a continuing policy of spreading Confucian principles, Buddhist influences were actively suppressed. Political and cultural strife between Buddhism and Confucianism was a major issue at the time of the change of dynasties from the Koryo to the Yi.[3] After the founding of the Yi

Dynasty, Confucianism, or more specifically neo-Confucianism (Chu Hsi learning), replaced Buddhism as the official orthodoxy. All writing, teaching, and scholarly efforts tried to explain the significance of the Korean adoption of neo-Confucianism and to legitimate the founding of the Yi Dynasty through Confucian ideologies.[4] This was an exclusively political and economic choice. The Confucians expelled previously powerful Buddhist elites and monopolized political power solely on the basis of Confucian teachings, and the founders of the Yi Dynasty built a new structure-based Confucian ideology.[5]

Originally, Confucianism was based very heavily upon the values of order and harmony. In the Confucian view, heaven and earth exist as essentially life giving. They continually bring new life into being, cherish and uphold it, and bring it to its completion. Life is good; in fact, it is the most precious gift. In order to sustain life, both reproduction and prosperity are important values. This respect and appreciation for life forms the basis for ancestor worship.[6]

However, every culture has a system that awards prestige. In many cases this system is rooted in the male-dominated, public sphere of social life. It provides collectivity, judicial order, and social cooperation, all of which are organized primarily by men. In the case of Korea, Confucianism was used to support the prestige system. Since the Yi Dynasty, Confucianism has been more strongly exercised than any other religion or political structure. It became a hierarchal social organization that maintained social, institutional, and political order and that functioned as the primary system of classification in Korean society.

WOMEN'S ROLES IN CONFUCIANISM

In the Korean context, Confucianism, which was built around reproduction and familial bonds, has been particularly constraining to women. Heaven, husband, king, parents, and men are in the superior, higher position, while earth, wife, servant, children, and women are in the inferior, lower position. This hierarchy is seen by Confucianism as indispensable to maintain the cosmic

order. While persons in the inferior positions should be obedient to their superiors, persons in the superior positions are obliged
to use their power to take care of their inferiors. Each seems
patterned to work for the good of the whole, but when Confucianism weds the ruling ideology, it serves only to legitimate the
power of those in the superior positions.

Under such social conditions and Confucian teachings, women
learned their designated roles and duties. Even though they played
an important role both in economic production and in management, their sacrifices were never recognized.[7] Rather it was believed that sex differences and sexual discrimination were an essential part of the Confucian cosmic order, necessary in order to
maintain universal harmony. For example, during the Yi Dynasty,
Confucianism had two major principles governing the interac-
tions between the sexes: *namnyo-yubyol* (sex difference) and
namjon-yobi (honored men, abased women).[8] According to the
Five Classics, "the female was inferior by nature, she was dark as
the moon and changeable as water, jealous, narrow-minded, and
insinuating. She was indiscreet, unintelligent, and dominated by
emotion. Her beauty was a snare for the unwary male, the ruin-
ation of states."[9] Thus women had to obey their male family
members in order to be saved from their own stupidity and inferiority. As daughters, they had to obey their fathers and brothers;
as wives, they had to obey their husbands; and as daughters-in-
law, they had to obey their parents-in-law. There was no room
for women to be equal with men. Women's entire lives were designed to follow male orders and provide male genealogies.

Two important duties were expected of a Confucian woman.
First, a woman's most important duty in Confucianism was to
produce a continuous male genealogy. In order to maintain a
pure male bloodline, women's bodies belonged to their husbands'
families. If women lost their chastity by rape or other experiences, they were compelled to commit suicide in order to maintain the family's honor. To produce a pure male bloodline, it was
obviously expected that a woman should give birth to a son. Without a son, a woman had no identity whatsoever. The women who
did not have sons were treated as nonhuman beings who were
invisible in their society.[10] A woman's life goal was to produce a

son. In contemporary Korean society, even though many from the younger generations have challenged this tendency, the expectation is still strong.

A woman's reputation was determined not only by her chastity, but also by her capacity to look after her husband and his family. Filial piety to his family was upheld as the essential value in Confucianism, at least in Koreanized Confucianism. Women had to maintain this fidelity their whole lives and even after death. Once they were married, they had to serve their husbands' families and children, whether their husbands were alive or not. These ideologies have been enormously influential in Korean society and have been practiced and enhanced throughout generations.[11]

CONFUCIAN RITUALS

The second essential duty for women in Confucianism was remembering and preparing Confucian rituals, particularly ancestor worship. Preparing ancestor worship was the first responsibility a married woman had to assume. Once married, wives had to remember every special day and the varying styles of rituals. For every ritual they had to prepare different food and serve it with special silverware.

Traditional ancestor worship had three main ritual services: (1) *ki-je*, a ritual service at home on commemoration day; (2) *charae*, a ritual service at home on a holiday; and (3) *si-je*, a ritual service at the grave.[12] Performed at midnight, *ki-je*, the ritual service on commemoration day, was the most important ceremony of all ancestor worship. This ritual lasted several days and involved the whole family. The eldest son and his family had to fill their minds with good thoughts, and they neither left the home nor slept with each other. The housewife carefully prepared the food for the ritual, but she was not allowed to participate in it. The men performed all the rituals and enjoyed the meal, while the women prepared and served the meal after the service. Women did not enjoy the meal until after the rituals, when the relatives had departed. Other ritual services were semi-annual festivals.

Generally, they were held on New Year's Day and on the fifteenth of August by the lunar calendar.

People generally performed these rituals for ancestors going back four generations. While ancestor worship was the most important duty of any offspring, a woman's duty was to remember and prepare the whole ritual process. It was believed that whole families could receive good blessings or bad fortunes depending on how carefully women prepared the rituals. Even though household shamanistic gods have disappeared in modern times, ancestor worship is still performed in both public and private, and it is sustained by the hidden work of women. Thus, using women's labor and diligence, ancestor worship strongly developed and supported patriarchal and hierarchal structures and reinforced Confucianism as the ideology of a patriarchal culture.

The goals and identities of most Korean women have been determined by Confucian ideologies. In the name of Confucian "harmonious order," women have been oppressed and disdained. Even though Korean modernization has legally given women freedom and equal rights and has disputed some Confucian practices against women, it has done little to change the patriarchal and hierarchal social structures. Instead, the components of the patriarchal Confucian structure have become more subtle and operate in the culture under the guise of high moral values.

Confucianism in Korea is not recognized as a religion today but rather as a cultural social structure that provides the norms for Korean people's social behavior. Confucian teachings lead people to respect their elders and protect the values of community. The purpose of these teachings is to maintain harmony and a respect for life. Even though Confucianism can create space for better community life, because it was used as a political ideology in Korean history and misused as a tool for legitimating abusive power, its effects have usually been toxic. Women, in particular, have suffered from an extreme emphasis on male genealogy and patriarchal community values, both of which have reduced the value of their existence. Misused Confucian ideologies accentuate the need for women's obedience and at the same time ignore men's abusive power. These misused ideologies have been the primary cause of women's *han*.

When modernization came to Korea through the Western powers, particularly through Christianity, Confucian ideologies, along with Buddhist and shamanist cultures, merged quite smoothly into colonial Christian traditions, and they helped Christianity build strong patriarchal church systems and educational institutions.

4

The Entry of Christianity

Catholicism was the first form of Christianity introduced into Korea, with the baptism of the Korean scholar Lee Sung Hun in 1784. In 1785, Lee Beuk, Kwon Chal Sin, and Chung Yak Chun gathered and began the *Kang Hak Hae* meeting, in which they called Christianity "Western Study." At first Christianity was understood not as a religion but as a part of Western culture. However, in studying the Catholic church, they eventually became Christians. They believed in the Christian God without the influence of colonial Western power.

THE MISSION ENTERPRISE

In 1875 the American government invaded Korea and treated Korea as its colony. When Roman Catholics founded a Korean Catholic parish in 1831 and the Protestant church officially started in 1884, Christianity brought both Western colonialism and Western ideologies into Korean society. Because of this tense political situation, Christianity functioned as the religion of the colonizer. The Korean people strongly believed that Christianity destroyed the spirits of the Korean people because it did not respect the Korean culture, people, society, or gods.

The first hundred years of Korean Christian history was a history of martyrs' blood because of the Catholic church's persistent rejection of ancestor worship. In the cases of China and

41

Japan, the Catholic missionaries first tried to understand and absorb Chinese and Japanese culture and then they tried to create Catholicism within Chinese and Japanese culture, honoring ancestor worship and recognizing their indigenous gods. However, in the case of Korea, the missionaries insisted on obedience to the Christian God alone. They rigidly interpreted ancestor worship as the worship of pagan gods. They disdained Korean culture and tradition and treated the Korean people in an imperial, superior manner.[1] Because of this imperial manner, many Koreans resisted accepting Christianity as a legitimate religion.

In 1884, in the aftermath of approximately one hundred years of severe conflict between the Catholic church and Korean culture, Protestantism was introduced to the Korean peninsula. At this time the overemphasis on strong patriarchal Confucian principles, the oppressive foreign power dynamics, and the military growth of Japan caused extreme confusion and led to the fall of the Yi Dynasty. In the midst of this confusion, the first Protestant missionaries, Methodists and Presbyterians, concentrated not on direct evangelization, but on education and healing.[2] Justice among human beings, liberation from oppressors, and the vision of a new kingdom in another world were invigorating ideas, and they were attractive to people who were oppressed. However, Korean Protestant Christianity was basically inherited from the conservative, fundamentalist theology of early American missionaries. The ethnocentric, colonial attitude of missionaries resulted in a poor quality of pastors for the Christian community and affected the nature of Korean Christianity.

Christianity was called JesuKuo (the religion of Jesus) by the Korean common people, because in the Korean context, the term *Christ* was unknown. The Korean language did not have the word *Christ*, even though the shamanist and Buddhist contexts contained many stories with divine savior images. So Christianity was known as JesuKuo, and Jesu represented Christianity *and* Western power. JesuKuo was a symbol of Western religion and also a tool for killing Koreans' spirits. The Korean people believed that Christianity was a religion of ignorant and vulgar people who were not aware of Korean spirituality and did not understand Korean experiences of God.[3]

While Jesu was taken negatively and *Christ* was an unfamiliar term, the Christian term *God* was seen as equivalent to the Korean term *Hanunim*. *Hanunim* means sky-god. The word *Hanunim* is *han* plus *nim*, the suffix for respect; therefore, *Hanunim* is *Han*-God.[4] *Han* has different meanings and functions in the Korean language. The concept of *han* in *Hanunim* includes concepts similar to *han* in Shamanism, Confucianism, Taoism, and Buddhism. It lies in "its non-orientability and absence of boundaries."[5] *Han* is one, but it also includes many; it overcomes all segregation and separation. It signifies the definite reality. "*Han* transcends the world, but also it is immanent in the world."[6] Therefore, to Korean people, *Hanunim*, their God, is one of many and many of one. God and human beings, people and people, human beings and nature—all are connected ontologically. God is simultaneously immanent and transcendent. In this sense the Christian God already existed in Korea in the form of indigenous gods because their *Hanunim* always had been with them.

Through its struggling early stages in Korea, Christianity unconsciously was absorbed into the multiple religions of its environment. Many other religions in Korea protested that Christianity was a Western colonial religion, and the religious battles between Christianity and other religions are still extremely intense in this post-modern century. In the midst of these struggles Christianity itself has influenced and been influenced by other Korean religious traditions. The best example is found in worship styles and attitudes in Christian communities. Most churches have a daily morning service around five or six in the morning, similar to the Buddhist daily service or the shamanistic rituals. Korean Christians clean their bodies before they go to church, just as they do before praying to the household gods or the heavenly god, *Hanunim*, in front of a holy tree or shrine.

Christianity was finally recognized and accepted as a Korean religion during the colonial period of the war between Japan and Korea (1910–45) when Korean Christians and American missionaries worked and fought together against Japanese oppression. The prophetic tradition of Christianity combined with Korean spirituality seeks justice, freedom, equality, and human rights, and Christianity offered a powerful moral force for the independence of Korea. Christianity resisted a politically distorted Japanese authority as well as the authority of the colonized Korean government. It was here that Christianity came into Korean people's lives and spirits intimately and was recognized as a friendly and supportive religion for Korean communities.

KOREAN WOMEN AND CHRISTIANITY

Christians compose 25 percent of the Korean population, and 70 percent of Korean Christians are women. Women have been the main supporters and propagators of Christianity, because throughout Korean history Christianity has encouraged women to liberate themselves from the influence of oppressive patriarchy. The Christian teachings of justice and freedom empower women to overcome their reality and to seek freedom from the hierarchal culture. Christianity released women from the cultural suppression of Confucianism, offered women the chance to go outside the home to participate in worship services as well as in other roles in church, and expanded their educational opportunities. Korean women, who until then were locked in the house, tasted a new and liberating life. It was a great revolution both for women and for the patriarchal society.

However, because Christianity itself includes Western colonial patriarchal thoughts and structures, it dismisses other religious practices as sinful and distorts the abundant possibilities for understanding God that other religions embrace. Also, through the process of becoming Koreanized, Christianity operates within the parameters of Korea's hierarchal culture and patriarchal religious traditions. Christianity has become a part of these structures of prestige and has become multi-religious itself.[7]

Korean Christian women have formed their "selves" in the tension between these two contradictory characteristics of Koreanized Christianity, freedom and oppression, which have coexisted in Korea's colonial religious history. In the midst of these conflicting dynamics and their ongoing individual and communal struggles, Korean women must find their own place.

PART II

THE SOCIAL ROLES
OF WOMEN IN KOREA

Christianity and Korea's other religions have surely influenced how Korean women have defined their roles and their lives. In the familial context all women are expected to be good wives, sacrificing mothers, and modest daughters and daughters-in-law. In varied economic contexts they are used as cheap labor and as a secondary source of income for their families. In the national or political context women and their bodies have been treated as national goods or resources. In each role women bear different responsibilities, and each role implies a different dimension of human interaction. However, there is one constant: the position of women remains secondary, regardless of their role. This secondary position has been and remains an unchangeable part of their duty as women.

In the midst of Korea's many transitions—cultural, historical, social—the position of women is believed to have changed for the better. While women's work is now easier, the expectations for women in modern society are greater than ever before. For example, today women are required to be perfect mothers *and* confident career women; they are expected to be "superwomen" in any given situation. The fact is that the systems of patriarchy and hierarchy have not truly changed. Instead, these systems have become stronger and operate in more hidden and ingenious ways to ensure that the strong patriarchal value of family is still passed down from generation to generation in an unbroken chain. While women's positions remain secondary, their social roles have become more complicated.

Comments made during a number of conversations with several women who are part of my life clearly describe the sociopolitical and cultural reality of Korean women. While my academic interests guided these conversations,[1] the women spoke freely about the dissatisfactions and satisfactions of their lives, including some of their psychological and spiritual struggles as well as their financial situations and their social relations. The women come from different provinces such as Seoul,[2] Kyoung Ki Do,[3] Chuwg Chung Do,[4] Jun La Do,[5] and Kyoung Sang Do.[6] Most of the women are full-time mothers and wives who comes from lower-class or middle-class families.[7] The majority have semi-arranged marriages.[8] The range of their academic backgrounds is largely from middle school to college; very few have either no education or a graduate education. The religious background of the women is Protestant Christianity and, in fact, they are mostly Presbyterians and Methodists. Some women used to be Buddhists, shamanists, or atheists, but they converted to Christianity for various reasons, while others have been Christian from birth.

Their ages vary. Those who are mothers, wives, and daughters-in-law are usually in their late thirties to their early sixties. In the case of daughters, their ages range from the early twenties to the middle thirties. In the cases of mothers, I did not talk with any women who had only one son or only sons. Most of them had only daughters, daughters and one son, or daughters with sons born later on. Thus, all of the women had specific concerns about having a son and often wanted to talk about their experience of being son-less mothers.

Among the daughters I talked with women who have an elder brother(s), younger brother(s), or only sisters. Some are married, and others are not. The daughters-in-law I talked with had or currently have the experience of living with their in-laws. Usually the eldest daughters-in-law are obliged to live with their parents-in-law and, depending on the situation, other daughters-in-law may have to take care of their in-laws as well. Even though women have many roles within the family, I focus on four—daughter, wife, daughter-in-law, and mother—to describe the dynamics of a Korean family and the sociocultural influences on women.

5

Women—Always Daughters

The identity of a Korean woman is built around her role in the family unit. Her value is ultimately measured by how faithfully she performs as wife, mother, daughter, and daughter-in-law. A woman is taught how to fit into these roles from early childhood as she responds to the demands of her family, culture, society, and nation. However, even when responding to these demands, women often feel that they are not good enough. Some of the interviewees expressed this feeling as follows:

I am a zero mother. Because I am so foolish, my children are fools. They cannot enter the university. Maybe because I have a lot of sin or karma, my innocent children have to suffer.[1]

Because I am a daughter, my parents do not like me. Even though I am smarter than my brother in school, my parents never give me equal attention. But I understand, because my brother is a man and I am a woman. If I get married, that is it, but my brother has to take care of my parents whether he marries or not. I am so ashamed that I am a daughter.[2]

I have been married four years, but I have only three daughters. I have no face to my husband's family and my husband. I am so ashamed. I will try again.[3]

I married my husband through the arrangement of our parents. But he did not love me. He thought that I was too ugly. . . . I knew. . . . I was so ashamed. Because I was so ugly, he blamed everything on me. Because I was ugly, he could not get a job. Because I was ugly, he could not go any place with me. I did not know what to do, but I knew that it was all my fault. I was so ashamed.[4]

I did not know how to make rice and side dishes. Before I married, I was a student. I was too busy. So I did not have time to learn how to cook. The first time I made a dish, my mother-in-law threw my food into the garbage can. My husband just watched her without a word. And I did not feel anything. I did not even feel ashamed. I did not think I was a bad cook. Maybe she was right. She said that I could not be married if I had been born in ancient times.[5]

Because they are daughters, because they do not have a son, because they cannot cook well, because they think that they are ugly, these women feel both responsible and ashamed. They are trivialized by their husbands, their families, and even by themselves. Their existence as women is denied. Many Korean women have internalized patriarchal values so thoroughly that they have become not only important and permissible but even desirable. Such internalization starts with their experience as daughters.

All women are daughters. While the role of mother, wife, or daughter-in-law can be a choice, being a daughter is not a choice. It is fate. It is the case that some women in Korea have been known to abort fetuses when they are determined to be female in order to prevent potential daughters from being born.

Young Hwa, one of my interviewees, told me about her life-threatening experience when she was born.

My mother had expected a boy as soon as she was married. My father was the eldest son in his extended family so the whole family expected her to have a boy. My mother said when I was born, she thought that I would be a boy because her doctor said so. He had shown the ultrasound picture to

Mom and said that I was a boy because I had a penis. (Later after I was born as a female, he said it must have been my finger.) My mom was relieved and decided to have me. Otherwise, she could have had an abortion. I was born because of her doctor's mistake. That was God's mercy. Otherwise, I would not be here to see this world. But when I was born, my mother cried so much. She surely believed that I would be a boy, but I was a girl. . . . I wished that I were a boy so my mom would not have to cry and suffer so much.[6]

Young Hwa's life-threatening experience started before she was born. Because of patriarchal values, her being was disdained and demeaned from that moment on by her own family and by society. She was ashamed of herself as a woman. In her endless self-doubt and self-hate, she did not know what she could become. Sometimes she and her sister were left alone until their mother returned from the field. She still remembers the darkness of the house. To get attention from her parents, she worked very hard and tried to show her ability in school by being an excellent student. She wanted to be recognized as a good daughter to her parents. From childhood on, she always worried about her mother and father, trying to help her parents financially and physically, and saving all her money for family emergencies.

Deep in her mind, she knew that she would never be good enough for her parents because her very existence was a mistake. Her whole being was humiliated and shamed. Whenever her parents fought over their lack of sons, she felt very vulnerable and was frightened. She begged them to calm down and said that she was sorry, ultimately taking on herself responsibility for her parents' fighting. Her guilt was immense.

Her internalization of the negative character of being a daughter made her feel vulnerable and less competent in everything. Even though she was an excellent student, she believed that she was not good enough to do anything other than to stay inside and take care of her family. She wanted to be a good daughter to her parents and a good wife to her future husband, but the more she wanted to be a good daughter, the more she hated herself as well as her mother. She became frail and deeply depressed.

She thought that God had given her a chance to live, but that she had failed God. She was angry at herself and often cried that God could not be satisfied with her whatever she did.

God is like someone who gives me life. I could not be born without God's will. God changed the ultrasound picture of my mom's womb and saved me from evil. God was good. But I disappointed God. God loves me like my parents but I am never good enough for God or for my parents.

For Young Hwa, God was similar to her parents. She believed that God loved her the way her parents loved her. In the same way, God was equally disappointed with her. Whatever she did was not sufficient. When she was young, she prayed to God to be a son, but God did not change her. On the one hand, she was thankful to God that she had been born. She existed because of God's mercy, so surely God had a plan for her. But on the other hand, she felt that God had made a big mistake. She should have been a son. God's mistake made her life miserable. Nobody wanted her. Her parents needed a son, not her. God was cruel to her and enjoyed her suffering. Because of God's mercy and cruelty, her faith and love for God were conflicted. She was afraid of God, and at the same time, she loved God.

In her memory her parents never stopped fighting over the issue of a son, which always made her feel guilty. Whenever her parents fought, she became extremely anxious, feverish, and even broke out in a rash. Her parents reminded her constantly that she could not take care of them after she married. She would leave with her husband. She was frightened that they hated her because of this. She felt that they had treated her as an outsider since her childhood, as someone who had never belonged to this family, as someone who was only passing through.

DAUGHTERS AND MOTHERS

Daughters are regarded as an outsider group who never really belong to their birth families.[7] In the words of an old Korean saying, daughters are the others and potential enemies. From their earliest years, through childhood and adolescence, women internalize these inferior images of daughters. Their negative roles in their families lead to guilt and other unhealthy and even harmful states of mind.

Such feelings by women are very common in Korea. The old Korean saying, "The parents who have a daughter are sinners," is still popular. Daughters often feel they must apologize continually to their parents for being daughters. Generally, they experience sorrow and guilt throughout their lifetimes. These feelings of guilt most affect the relationship between daughters and their mothers, because the mothers bring their own guilt into the relationship by having given birth to a daughter, a guilt much greater than a father would feel.

This relationship between mother and daughter has been explained, although outside the Korean context, by psychologists, including feminist psychologists. According to feminist scholar Nancy J. Chodorow, the mother-daughter tie in East London, Java, and Indonesia is extremely close. In Java and throughout Indonesia, women have more power than men within the family. A daughter learns her identity and role from her mother in a relationship of companionship and mutual cooperation. Daughters develop a strong sense of self and self-worth that continues to grow as they get older and take on a maternal role.[8]

In terms of companionship and mutual cooperation in the work of the household, the relationship of a Korean mother and daughter is similar. They are companions and set the boundaries together for their roles in the household. Daughters are seen as allies by their mothers. Based on their mutual understanding of being women, they develop relationships of attachment to and identification with their mothers as well as with other adult women. However, despite the strong ties between mothers and daughters in Korea, their relationship is usually tense.[9] Many daughters feel separated and isolated from their mothers. Young Hwa said:

From my early childhood, my mother kept saying that I was the other. I could not belong to my family forever. Because I was a daughter, I had to leave. I could not stay in my room or my house. My father said that he would never let me go, but my mother yelled at my father that he should let me go and not make me confused. That was the message I always heard from my mom. I knew that she loved me so much and she sacrificed for me. But when she said that, I really hated her. I was really hurt.

Throughout Korean history mothers have cried for their daughters and daughters have cried for their mothers. They cry for their lives, their sorrows, and the *han* they share. That guilty feeling reaches its peak when a daughter gets married. On the day of the wedding, a daughter's parents cry, their faces showing many feelings and struggles. They think that they are losing their daughter, that their daughter is no longer their own and now belongs to another family. The daughter's status also changes. She always feels sorry for her parents but also worries about her own family life. She sees her parents' *han* and bears her own *han*. However, she knows that the best way for her parents is to be a dutiful daughter-in-law and wife in order not to ruin her own family's reputation.

DAUGHTERS AND BROTHERS

When women have brothers in their family, their experiences of discrimination are even more explicit and severe with very material, physical, and psychological dimensions. The following stories were told by several women:

My mother always gave him good food and eastern restoratives that my sister and I could not eat. When my mother bought a box of eastern restoratives, she kept those in a closet we could not reach. She gave him these restoratives everyday. One day, I saw one pack of a restorative on the table. I ate it before my brother came. My mother asked me where it was. I told her that I ate it. She said that it was OK, because it had gone bad anyway so she wanted to throw it away. I was dumbfounded. I wanted to vomit it. It was absurd. I could not believe that she was my mother![10]

I did not want to eat wheat. When I was young, I ate wheat instead of rice, while my father and my brother ate very warm and smooth white rice. I always wanted to eat that rice, but my mother never gave it to me.[11]

I wanted to study. I was a good, smart student. I jumped two grades. I passed those exams by myself. But because my father did not want to give me money for tuition, I almost could not graduate from middle school. On graduation day a friend delivered my middle-school degree, because my teacher paid for me. I really wanted to go to high school. I borrowed a school uniform from my friend and went there, but my father found out. He tore the clothes and beat me. He said that if I went again, he would throw me out. But he sent my four brothers to college, even though they were not good students. Just two of them graduated from college.[12]

In many cases daughters' relationship with their mothers cannot be discussed without also considering their relationships with their brothers. Women who have a brother or brothers live with different psychological dimensions than women who have none. Often daughters with brothers do not receive any attention from their parents. This lack of attention comes especially from their mothers, who from very early childhood project anger and resentfulness toward them.

Traditionally, girls with older brothers know that they are not important in the family. A girl in this position must obey her brothers as well as her father and mother. If a daughter has a younger brother, she is blamed because she was not a boy, and later she must take care of her younger male sibling. Her childhood often disappears as she serves as his "little mother," spending her time taking care of him, nurturing him, and protecting him until he grows up. Even after his childhood, she may still sacrifice herself to support his time at college so he can secure a good career. Many mothers have asked daughters to do that for their brothers and sometimes, even after marriage, sisters still have to support their brothers financially. Needless to say, these sacrifices and unequal situations are rarely recognized or appreciated. While daughters and mothers might cooperate in the kitchen, in the living room daughters have to know their place.

THE DREAMS OF DAUGHTERS

A woman, as a daughter, has always been the other and never belongs to her family. Even as adults many women may remember being consumed by fear and anxiety about their parents' resentment, especially the resentment of their mothers. Years of being treated as eternal failures within their families result in enormous pain and *han*. However, many daughters as women show great strength to overcome their *han* through their lives. Despite unbearably unjust circumstances, they survive, live, and succeed in their pain-filled world. Even though they understand their mothers' lives as women, they do not want to follow in their mothers' painful footsteps. They seek to be free of this unjust reality. While some women want to deny themselves as women and daughters, others recognize themselves as women and daughters with honor and dignity.

Some women seek a new family, through marriage, that they will not have to leave and within which they will always be included. Some also seek a new God, one who understands them and loves them in light of their needs. They dream of the realm of God as their new family and long for God to be like parents who never let them go, who are there for them forever, and who say they are fine as they are. This God, whom many daughters desperately seek, represents a new family that does not discriminate against daughters but instead loves them. They seek a God who does not ask them to sacrifice for their brothers, a God who will support them as God's children. As children of God, these daughters dream of this new family to which they could belong.

In modern times, with the coming of feminist movements, some daughters can see their dream coming true, even though very slowly. Many younger generations of women try to make a difference in their position as daughters by working to overcome the traditional roles of daughters and create new models of family. With those new visions and dreams in mind, they strive continuously to turn these possibilities into realities and to begin to recognize themselves as daughters and women with a dignity and pride given by God.

6

Women as Mothers

The most important and respectful role for a Korean woman is to be a mother, and the most honored mother is the one who has given birth to a son. There is no respected place in society for the unmarried, widowed, separated, divorced, or barren woman, or for the single mother. A woman's whole worth and value is tied to being the mother of a son.

To be the mother of a son changes a woman's whole life in relation to family, social position, and economic circumstances. For the first time she is recognized as an insider, a person of status. In order to maintain this recognition, she becomes an agent marking boundaries within the hierarchal social structure and a perpetuator of the values of patriarchy. This is a communal process of experiencing both social inculcation and retribution. The mothers of daughters do not fare so well; they suffer greatly from inside and outside pressure. Sun Ja, the mother of five children— four daughters and one son—shares her experience.

My son is the youngest child. To have a son, I prayed every day, morning and night, for seven years. Before I had a son, my mother-in-law persecuted me severely. My mother-in-law asked me to divorce her son. My mother-in-law looked for another woman for my husband. My mother-in-law encouraged my husband to beat me. But when I had a son, my mother-in-law could not persecute me or make me leave any more. My mother-in-law gave me power to manage the household and our ancestor worship. Not only my mother-in-law but also the whole family recognized me as a daughter-in-law, wife of my husband, and mother of my child. Other neighbors did not recognize me as the poor woman who had four daughters, but as the mother of my son. They did not laugh at me any more.[1]

Even though the Christian scripture notes that women's salvation comes through giving birth (1 Tm 2:15), in Korea, a woman's salvation comes from giving birth *to a son*. Because of the absolute power that comes from having a son, mothers are prouder of their sons than of any other person or any other thing, even their husbands. They devote their lives to their sons and try to protect them from anything perceived to be bad, such as disease, bad ghosts, bad luck, or bad karma. Their ears have to hear every breath that their sons breathe, their eyes have to see every movement, and their presence has to be with their sons all the time. Everything must be focused on these precious sons.

THE CASE OF JIN-A

Jin-a is the mother of three daughters and one son. Whenever she was pregnant, she prayed for her baby. She asked God to give her the baby as a son. She prayed with every step she made. She prayed every morning and evening. She promised God that she would serve God with her whole life if God gave her a son. When she finally got her son, she was sure that God loved her and cared about her. And then she quickly transferred God's love for her to God's love for her son. "I know that God cares about my son and loves him, because all my prayers were answered. He is God's child. God loves him. All I have to do is love him and let him go in God's way. He is God's present for me. I love him more than anything. He is my hope to live in this world. He is the evidence of God's love for me. He makes me alive. Because of him, I work very hard with a happy heart. I have prayed for him before I had him in my womb. I will not exchange anything for him. He is my heart and everything. God loves me, because God gives him to me. I have no desires any more. God has given me everything I need. God loves me."[2]

Despite terrible poverty and her situation, Jin-a thought that God was good because she had given birth to a son. Even though she knew that her husband did not love her when she married, she said that it didn't matter because she believed that she was "as ugly as an old pumpkin" and she felt lucky to be married. While he did not come home or love her, she thought that was acceptable, as long as she was his legal wife.

Many women love and have great affection for their sons rather than for their husbands. Within the relationship of mother and son, a woman feels love and hope. Her son is the first man who loves her and respects her and listens to her. She feels her *han*-filled life redeemed by and through her son. Because of him, other people recognize her for the first time. Her husband and in-laws lose their power to expel her. Her husband cannot ignore her. Her own parents are proud of her. Her sisters-in-law and brothers-in-law recognize her as a member of the family, and thus her life becomes easier.

Because of this, mothers sometimes become obsessive, never letting go of their sons throughout their lives, because they are the only men whom they can control. As women, there is little they can do or be, but through their sons women have power to enter into the world and actualize their wishes. As long as they hold their sons in their arms, they can taste power, and so they want to hold on to their sons forever, even though they know they cannot.

The multi-religious influences and patriarchal colonial structure of Korea encourage the delusion that a son is a woman's power, her hope, and the symbol of God's love for her. As long as women have sons, their existence as women is forgiven. Their stupidity and desires are overcome and conquered through their sons. Sons also represent the power of the nation, and thus the whole society makes women proud when becoming mothers of sons.

In these circumstances women believe that God gives them sons to better their lives but also to transform the whole world into a better place. They think that sons are their hope but also the hope of God. God's will is to be completed through their sons, and they are being used as God's tool to bring hope to the earth.

THROUGH THEIR SONS' EYES

Most sons would describe their mothers using words such as *sacrificing love, self-denial, warmth, gentleness, endless patience, hard work*, and *modesty*. Throughout Korean history, literature, myths, and even television dramas have projected these attributes as the primary traits of motherhood. These attributes are not just ideals for they are often manifested as lived experience and truth in the lives of sons. In sons' reality, mothers are more generous, forgiving, gentle, and sacrificial than fathers. When sons describe their God, it is often in terms of such mother-like qualities. Mothers are the unconditional and constant lovers whom sons always miss and ultimately long for. Mothers are revealers of God's love.

However, because of these social circumstances and the endless sacrifices of mothers, some sons depend on their mothers even after they grow up. This unhealthy dependence can cause difficulty within their married lives. Because they are so dependent on their mothers, as husbands they may be incapable of shaping their own lives with their spouses.

On the other side, the mother of a son has a huge crisis of identity and emotion when her son gets married. She experiences a mixture of anger, exhaustion, anxiety, love, emptiness, jealousy, and guilt. Oftentimes she feels threatened by her daughter-in-law. So, with her power, she sets out to supervise the lives of her son and daughter-in-law. She violates their boundaries intentionally and consciously and often exercises her power over her daughter-in-law.

This unsuccessful transition is a common and unhealthy situation in Korea. It is the product of the patriarchal ideology of motherhood and the hierarchal cultural attitudes of sonhood.

These social pressures produce immature relationships for both mothers and sons. Because of these relationships, in many cases daughters-in-law become scapegoats. The strong power of patriarchal cultures and societies manifested in both the obsessions of mothers and the immaturity of sons has caused the *han* of daughters-in-law. These triangular relationships often carry with them unhealthy and excruciating anxiety, and this proceeds from generation to generation.

THROUGH THEIR DAUGHTERS' EYES

Daughters generally would describe their mothers in less generous terms.[3] However, to put into perspective the relationship between mothers and sons, I want to summarize briefly the dynamics of the relationship between mothers and daughters.

For daughters, an ideal image of mothers hardly exists. Mothers are not lovers but rather enemies and companions at the same time. For a daughter, a mother's house is not a comfortable home but instead a shelter to which she wants to return for a while and then prepare to depart on her own journey once again. Paradoxically, mothers are simultaneously their daughters' kind supporters and friends as well as their dreadful stepmothers and persons to be feared. Therefore, daughters are caught in between—they want to separate from their mothers and be independent, but they also cry for them and identify in love with who they want to become.[4]

Mothers also have a very hard time loving their daughters. They cannot love their daughters as they love their sons, because daughters are not theirs forever. They fear the pain of losing their daughters, so they sometimes seek consciously to stop loving them. This action causes pain for both. A mother's life in relation to her daughter is in tension between the close bonds of love and unavoidable separation. In the eyes of mothers, daughters are long regrets and big sighs.

I want to stop loving my daughter because I deeply love her and am involved with her so much. She is my companion and friend, but she is the one who has to leave. If I love her more, it makes it harder for us to separate. Sooner or later she marries and leaves. I have to forget her. I want to ignore her before she leaves, so I can let her go . . . so I do not have to have enormous pain in my heart when she really leaves. Daughters are a pain in their parents' hearts. From birth, we mothers know we have to let them go as our mothers did to us. Daughters are strangers in this world. "Daughters are always the others." Forever others. We cannot be, never can be on the same team.[5]

Because of toxic patriarchal environments and ideologies that deeply damage women's lives, mothers and daughters remain victims of a vicious circle that has been passed down from generation to generation, caught in the conflict between loving and hating. Throughout Korean history mothers have shed tears for their daughters and daughters have felt pathos for their mothers, lamenting for each other, their lives, and their shared *han*.

MOTHERS AND SACRIFICE

Regardless of the different psychological and cultural factors at work, most mothers sacrifice themselves for their children, and most sons and daughters would agree that their mothers do this with no hesitation. In this sense mothers represent home, the place to which their children always want to return.

Because of these expectations, mothers do not have lives of their own; they are always busy taking care of their children. As the primary caretakers of their children, they feel they are responsible for everything. Indeed, because it is commonly believed that being a mother is natural, normal, and the right thing for women to do, many Western and Eastern psychologies and some feminist psychologies hold mothers responsible for their children's total psychological, social, and cultural experiences. Some basic assumptions of these studies are that mothers have absolute power over their children and thus can become the object of children's anger and desperation. Mothers intentionally and viciously can constrain, control, and oppress their children. Helpless infants may view them as all powerful and fearsome.

Other feminists maintain that this results from patriarchy rather than from individual evil intentions because patriarchy rends mothers powerless rather than powerful.[6] However, such a theory presumes or implies that if the patriarchal system is eliminated, then the mother should be perfect.

These perspectives all appear to assume that mothers should be perfect and totally responsible in terms of childbearing and child-raising. They also assume that a perfect mother is self-sacrificing and giving. When psychological theory and/or cultural ideology finds fault with mothers for the inevitable frustrations their infants and children experience, it implies that women as mothers are not making enough sacrifices for their children. Korean women in particular live under the authority of the sociocultural expectation of this perfect-mother myth.[7]

However, in fact, such "perfect" mothers would be women who do not fit the models of human development as described by some Western male psychologists. In her book *In a Different Voice* Carol Gilligan demonstrates that since many male psychologists have set up the male experience as the standard for the experience of human development, female psychological development has often been excluded or treated as abnormal and unhealthy. Even though mothers are expected to be perfect, women are given the message that they never can be perfect, because they are women. This psychological dilemma causes frustrations for women and also creates unhealthy social expectations.

For Korean women who try their best to be perfect mothers, such devotion to perfection has physical and psychological manifestations, but it also affects their spirituality and their sexuality. In order to have a son or to keep a son, women who are nonbelievers become believers and non-churchgoers become churchgoers. Their spirituality becomes centered around this desire to have and to keep a son. Women will fast for forty days. They will partake in morning fasts and prayers for one hundred days, night prayers for twenty-one days, and participate in all kinds of other wish offerings and rituals. It is interesting to note that before sons are born, wives as well as husbands pray and attend church together. But after they have sons, in some cases, only women, as wives and mothers, continue to attend church, and they do so in order to retain God's grace and mercy.

Women continuously obey God so as not to lose or bring harm to their sons and families but to let them be under the care of God. This is true not only for Christian women but also for Buddhist and shamanistic women, who pray every morning and evening in order to have a son. The son is the symbol of God's love or the ancestors' mercy, since it is believed that having a son is the only way women save themselves from their sinful nature. The son is their safety net and their future. Sometimes sons take on greater importance than God for mothers. Even though they might be willing to give up their belief or faith, they would never give up their sons. Because of their sons, they experience God and God's love. They give not only their breasts and wombs but also their hearts and spirits to their sons. Motherhood is believed to redeem women from women's inferiority and sin. The Buddhist understanding of karma, the shamanistic idea of retribution, the Confucian hierarchal order, and the Christian tradition of misogyny have combined to present motherhood of a son as atonement for being a woman.

THE RELATIONSHIP BETWEEN A MOTHER'S *HAN* AND POWER

The connection between having a son and having power is very hard to break in the reality of Korean women. This has been their faith, their belief, and their reality throughout the generations, and it has been the only way that they have been recognized by their patriarchal society. However, because of modernization, the younger generation of women does not desperately long for sons as their mothers did. Not only does having a son not give them power in the way it did in ancient Korean agricultural society, but they realize as well that being a mother itself is a blessing to be enjoyed. As daughters, they have honored their mothers and shared their pain; however, as mothers, their feelings have changed. They do not want to generate *han* for their daughters; rather, they want not to cause them pain. Many young mothers today want to recognize their children for who they are. These young mothers struggle to move themselves away from the burdens of patriarchal motherhood by breaking the cycles of historical, social, and psychological patriarchal violence. They seek respect, not because they have sons but because they are mothers. They want new goals in life that center around themselves as well as around other family members, and most important, they desire new models of motherhood that will change their lives and their society.

7

Women as Wives

Being a wife is supposed to be a woman's natural duty in Korea. In ancient Korean traditions, prearranged marriages were popular, and many people married without seeing or knowing each other first. Because the real goal of marriage was to have children to carry on the family, love or affection was not necessary. In modern society most marriages are not prearranged and love can be a precondition of marriage, but the expectations of marriage have not changed. A woman is expected to devote her whole life to her husband as long as he lives and even after he dies. Her reputation is determined by her capacity to look after her husband and children.

Hee Suk married when she was twenty. She has two daughters and two sons. She has to make a living for her family. Sometimes she sells some vegetables on the streets and in the marketplace. Sometimes she works to help make dishes and to clean house. She says that in her life she never sleeps more than three hours a day. Her husband does not do anything for his children or her. He has never had a regular job in his life. But she cannot complain to him. Rather, she has to be careful not to hurt his pride. Before she goes to work, she cooks food for her husband and family. She knows that he will not cook but would starve himself and the children. When she has a payday, she brings all the money she earns to her husband. She never spends any money on herself, even though he throws away all the money gambling. She cannot blame him but begs him not to do that again. "I know that he is just not lucky. Even though he does not have a job, it is not his fault. He does not have enough education. I cannot blame him. God loves him more than me. He is the father of my children and our household. God gives him the right to have authority over the family. Even when he and I have different opinions, God is on his side, because God has ordained him to be head of our family. I cannot be over him, because God does not allow me to do that. If I do that, our children will not respect their father. That is a real sin. . . . If he decides the wrong things, God will change his mind. I have to wait until God changes his mind. That is the wisdom God gives me."[1]

Hee Suk strongly believes in the hierarchal order in her family. Many Korean women like Hee Suk are taught by Korean society that they have to listen to their husbands and obey them without question. Sometimes, if they know that their husbands are having an affair, they pretend not to know or do not want to know about it as long as their husbands are not caught outright. Even if a wife catches her husband in an affair, instead of blaming her husband or being jealous of another woman, she may go to church and try to forgive him. She probably feels that it is safer to continue in marriage than to get divorced.

Although not unique to Korea, the most important virtue in marriage is not love but this kind of loyalty. In reality, this rule of loyalty applies to one side only, even though it is thought that the relationship between husband and wife requires mutual loyalty and fidelity. For women, loyalty to their husbands and families requires sexual purification and submission of their whole being sexually, economically, psychologically, and even spiritually. Wives-to-be must be chaste, and wives are to maintain chastity throughout their marriage. Virginity is essential for marriage. Even though many young women and young men have premarital relationships today, the Korean Christian church expects unmarried women to be virgins and innocent about sex. If women are not virgins and tell about any previous relationship with another man, they are disdained and treated as prostitutes. Women's chastity and virginity are the most important conditions for marriage in Korea's Christian churches.

Wives must be well educated, "decent," middle class, and proficient in daily household skills, for it is these wives who can maintain strong households and provide good care for children. *HuyngMoYaungChu* (wise mother and good wife) has been the ideal image of a Korean wife.[2] A wife is not seen as a sexual being, but it is still expected that she should be good-looking by Korean standards. Women as wives should also be wise, proper, submissive, passive, and enormously patient. They should silently support their husband's reputation in society and raise his children to be successful citizens.

After marriage, a wife's place is at home, where she often waits all day for her husband and serves her in-laws. Even in modern times the tendency is still encouraged and expected that women as wives and mothers will tend to the home and be ready to welcome their husbands. Loyalty to the family means two different experiences: husbands have the right to ask for time to do what they need, while wives show their loyalty by staying at home all the time.

In the past, Korean society expected women to quit their jobs before their weddings. Until the mid 1980s, most Korean companies could legally fire women after they married.[3] The latest possible time for women to quit their jobs was when they became pregnant; this practice lasted until the mid 1980s, although some women still follow it today. This was the decent and noble thing for women to do. Even if they had to work for financial reasons, when they had enough money they would quit their jobs and stay home. Even today, the most important thing for good wives is to provide good food and a restful place for their husbands and the family, so that their husbands can recover from the stress of the work place and their children will have mothers to watch them and play with them all the time.[4]

In marriages in Korea there is no emphasis on romance between husbands and wives or on communicating with and understanding each other. Love means sacrificing by wives for their husbands, and by mothers for their children. Women are expected to wait on their husbands and children with endless patience, and wives do not expect gentle or tender encouragement from their husbands. Because they are expected to give everything, sometimes more than they have, many Korean women are exhausted by their continual sacrifice and giving.

WIVES' *HAN* AND POWER

From their subordinate position, God also seems very authoritative to wives. For Hee Suk, whose images of God have been distorted by the male-dominated family structure and culture, God is abusive and on the side of her husband. God works for her family only through her husband because God has given her husband the authority to rule over the family. Even though her husband is a failure as a husband and father, she does not want to hurt him by taking action. God is the one who tells her to wait and endure. God is the one who asks her to love and obey him. In the end, her husband becomes like God to her.

In her understanding, God is enormously gracious and merciful to her husband, but harshly unjust and unfair to her. Even though Hee Suk believes that God is there for her, God is powerless and silent in the midst of her suffering. She hardly touches God's ongoing intentions for herself, and her total devotion to her family appears not to be recognized by her husband or by God.

However, she does not give up her fight or her faith. She has strength to wait and believes that it is God who gives her this strength. In fact, it takes strength and wisdom to survive in her reality. Even though she still sees God as an oppressive and violent supporter of her husband, she also may perceive a God of her own, a God who is as powerless and oppressed as she, one who bears her husband's violence or abuse together with her. God is her silent companion and her partner, giving her strength.

Many wives see God through the eyes of their husbands and other family members. They understand God within the cultural expectations and ideology of traditional Korea, and these social and cultural expectations become expectations for God. Such cultural ideologies become God's will for them, and all the religious and traditional norms and values become God's commands. As wives, women envision this God as their husband, so they obey and serve this God as they do their husband. This God is like their husband, who does not love or understand them. Women may know and worship this God, but they cannot believe or trust this God.

Han-filled women ask God to recognize their need for a different God, a God whose eyes can fill with tears. They need a God who lifts up the beaten and broken lives of women. They need a God who cares and loves and who stands up and takes on the abusive world. Wives do not need their husbands' God but their own God, one who understands and fights alongside them.

Today, knowing a God who can suffer with them, many wives begin to assert their need for love, which they deserve. As they witness their mothers' relationships with their fathers, they are now beginning to protest against abusive husbands and to refuse to submit to patriarchal authority. They want to create a new home for themselves. They are learning that their unconditional loyalty is not for the sake of their abusive husbands but for reciprocal love and care within the family. They have learned wisdom from the sacrifice of their mothers and by listening to the voice of their hearts. They have learned to struggle to protect themselves and their new family. They are beginning to see God not through their husbands' eyes, but with their own eyes. They envision their own God, who will help them seek ways to find and communicate with their husbands. This God gives women strength to stretch their limits and transform their uneasy reality. Through this new understanding of God, they learn to taste the happiness in their lives and to enhance their relationships with their husbands. This God can be a transforming force in their difficult lives.

WOMEN AS DAUGHTERS-IN-LAW

Becoming a daughter-in-law is an enormous transition for a woman. A woman's complete identity is changed as she moves from being a daughter to being a wife and a daughter-in-law. Her family now becomes her husband's family, and it is this new family that shapes her life. By use of humiliation and shame, young wives are trained to learn new roles and responsibilities. In the past, many young women have faced atrocious and merciless treatment at the hands of their husbands' families. As Korean Confucian society was strictly structured under the principles of patrilineality and hierarchal order, especially in the period of the Yi Dynasty (1392–1910), little protection was offered to women by their birth families. Under such conditions women had only one choice: to endure and survive within their husbands' families and to accomplish their objectives through and for their sons.

The following tale of an aristocratic family in traditional Korea illustrates the practice of daughters leaving their birth families:

> The family had produced a great scholar in the middle of the dynasty, and around the same period, one of the daughters also produced a famous scholar-official. She delivered the child at her natal home. A famous geomancer told the family that the house site was predetermined to produce three great men, which implied that there was only one more to come. In order to prevent a son of their daughter from taking away the *ki* (spirit) of the house site, the family established a rule prohibiting the daughters from delivering babies in this house.[5]

In many cultures, as rivalry and competition among the lineages intensified, a daughter was often given to establish peaceful relations or in exchange for favors.[6] They were also traded for housework or farming labor. Many experienced severe poverty and political pressure within their husbands' families. They served as the boundaries between the two families, while paradoxically being treated as outsiders by both groups. This ambivalent position made their lives even harsher.

In Korea, the lives of daughters-in-law were clearly marked by this ambivalent position. On the one hand, they bore affection and concern for their birth families; on the other hand, they had to show greater fidelity and submission to their husbands' families. Their natal families and their husbands' families both treated them as outsiders. Therefore, in order to become part of their husbands' families and to overcome their emotional attachment to their natal families, daughters-in-law had to demonstrate absolute loyalty to their new family.

In an old Korean saying, when a woman marries, she has to serve her in-laws for nine years; the first three years as dumb, the second three years as blind, the last three years as deaf. During these nine years as a daughter-in-law, she has to learn new family traditions and a new family culture, she can have no opinions, and she must do nothing other than obey her in-laws and her husband. And, of course, as previously noted, she must bear a son and bring good fortune to the family.

The following tale exemplifies the way a woman should show filial piety as a daughter-in-law:

A wife of a poor *sonbi* (a generic term for a scholar who was preparing for the state examination and was expected to be concerned only with public virtue) attended her grand-father's funeral. That night she happened to overhear her father and a geomancer discussing a possible burial site on a hill. The geomancer told her father that the site seemed to be in an excellent location that would surely guarantee the prosperity of the family. However, he added that an on-the-spot survey was required in order to make certain that the place was not too wet. The daughter, being covetous of the site, climbed the hill and walked back and forth pouring water on it all through the night. The next morning her father and the geomancer were disappointed to find that the spot was wet, and they had to find a new burial site. After the funeral the daughter asked her father to give the deserted burial site to her, to which he readily agreed. Later, she buried her husband [her father-in-law, in another version] there, and her husband's family became prosperous. She produced many sons who became high public officials, and her descendants were abundant.[7]

This widely told story served to indoctrinate women into un-yielding loyalty to their husbands' families instead of to their natal ones. As a daughter-in-law and wife, a woman is to devote herself and demonstrate her fidelity to her husband's family. Her fidelity is to be built around the production of a son, the management of the household, and obedience to her husband and her husband's family. The household has to be managed as efficiently and re-sourcefully as possible, even with severely limited resources. A wife/daughter-in-law internalizes this role as her life goal to the extent that this role becomes acceptable and even desirable.

The Case of Hyun Jin

Hyun Jin is a mother of three daughters and three sons. Her marriage was arranged by her parents. She married the second son of a poor family. He used to help with his father's farming, but when he married, he went out and tried to do new things. So Hyun Jin had to work in the field instead of him. When she gave birth to her first daughter, she was in the field. She had great pain. For a long time she endured the pain and kept working. When her water burst, she ran to the house and asked her mother-in-law to help. After she gave birth to her first daughter, her mother-in-law asked her to finish her field work. She went outside and finished the field work. After she returned from the field, she remembered that she was hungry, so she went to the kitchen and made a simple dish for herself and ate it. Then she prepared supper for the rest of the family.

She thought that her mother-in-law was brutal to her, but she felt that she should understand her mother-in-law rather than blame her mother-in-law. "It was not right to blame someone, because God always listened to every word. God does not like to blame anyone for any reason. God is good. God loves everybody, even my mother-in-law. And also we have to understand and respect how fearful moth-ers-in-law are. We have to respect them. We cannot blame

them. God watches us. God wants us to love everyone, because God loves even me."[8]

Traditionally, the relationship between a mother-in-law and a
daughter-in-law delivered much *han* to the heart of the daughter-in-law. Mothers-in-law and mothers-in-law-to-be often attempt to persuade and convert their daughters and daughters-
in-law to follow patriarchal virtues. They themselves believe and
teach other women that this is the only way women can be comfortable and safe in their world. Because of the cultural obsession
with having sons and the immature dependence of sons who then
become husbands, a daughter-in-law can be caught between a
powerless husband and a fearful mother-in-law, an odd and po-
tentially dangerous situation. She must bear her suffering and
give up her own happiness to be with her husband and to make
her own life within his family. She may have to endure her mother-
in-law's harsh treatment and her husband's apathy. It is not surprising that in modern times marriages occasionally end in divorce.

Hyun Jin's case is a good example. Hyun Jin received very harsh
treatment from her mother-in-law. She remembered how harsh
it was, but she did not want to blame her; rather, she wanted to
let her mother-in-law experience God's mercy. As a faithful Christian, she obeyed her mother-in-law and tried to understand her
life in the light of her Christian faith and Korea's traditional virtues. As a daughter-in-law, she took care of the inner household
work and the outside farming while she raised six children by
herself. She did not ask anything for herself in her life. Even
though she did not have rice to feed her children, she said that
she always thanked God for what she had in her hand, because
she believed that God gave her everything she needed. She showed
enormous faith in God under extreme conditions of poverty. She
believed that everything was under God's control, so she would
wait until God was ready to show her blessings.

She did not recognize her needs but constantly denied herself,
trying to live by the teaching of Korea's cultures and religions and
hiding herself beneath her circumstances and faith. However, she

did respond to her own needs through her image of God. She wanted a God who did not blame anybody, who loved without condition. Her God embodied the reflection of her ideas about love and justice. It was this God who was her only hope and who sustained her life. Even though she could not express her anger and pain aloud, she expressed her pain and anger in talking to God. Even though she had been taught to obey and endure, her faith in God did much to transform her wounded heart.

With her inner strength and power, she changed her anger and pain to love and peace. Instead of blaming her mother-in-law, she sympathized with her and had mercy on her. Instead of regretting her life, she forgave her mother-in-law and tried to understand her mother-in-law from a woman's point of view. Her enormous faith wanted to feel God's merciful love through her mother-in-law. While the battle between tradition and her true self continued in her, she held up her life as whole. She wanted to recognize her life in God's love. Even though she was trapped between a situation of silent, traditional Confucian virtue and Christian doctrine, she recognized her life as beautiful and valuable to God.

In modern times being a daughter-in-law is still not an easy role, but modernization has brought more conjugal forms of family life. Many daughters-in-law no longer have to live with their in-laws. Mothers-in-law try not to exercise their power over their daughters-in-law and learn to let go. Both daughters-in-law and mothers-in-law strive to find a way to communicate better. Even though it has been one of the most difficult relationships between women, women in both of these roles have learned from their mothers and struggle to bring mutual peace to their family. Work has begun to create new models of family relationships and more harmonious community life.

Women and the Family

Women can be disliked by their children, disdained by their in-laws, and demeaned by their husbands. Even though their sons and daughters may appreciate their mothers' sacrifices, they can still criticize their mothers for numerous reasons. In-laws hold their daughters-in-law responsible for everything negative that happens after the new wife enters the house, while husbands require them to obey absolutely their mothers-in-law. Women as daughters, mothers, wives, and daughters-in-law absorb accusations and blame and often, despite all their sacrifice and work, still feel that they are not good enough.

Because of these conflictual relationships, women have a hard time trusting other women within their families. Unconsciously and consciously, they have difficulty communicating or establishing strong bonds with one other. Even though mothers and daughters have compassion for each other, they have difficulty working through their conflicts. While daughters-in-law and mothers-in-law have the same path and experience, they are not taught to work together to understand each other. Because of historical and social influences, women often live in an atmosphere of distrust. The influences of a patriarchal and hierarchal society on family relations, education, the media, religious training, finances, and national history, policy, and economics all engender humiliating attitudes toward women. Because of these exclusive conflicts and pressures, many women struggle with self-denial, self-hate, and self-distrust. They feel frustrated and depressed, often without knowing the source of the enormous powers that dominate their lives.

Nonetheless, women as daughters, mothers, wives, and daughters-in-law have survived. Despite colossal burdens and struggles, Korean women have not given up their lives or forgotten their own voices. Many Korean Christian women express these voices in their faith. Faith keeps them alive and images a God who hears them. For them, God is the one who controls Sam Sin (the birth goddess) and JeoSung SaJa (the death ghost); God is also the Sustainer who controls good and bad luck over their children and the rest of their families. Christian women as daughters, wives, mothers, and daughters-in-law may start and end each day by praying for their families. With the power of prayer, they struggle to transform their family relationships and imagine a new life. They believe that God is their provider, nurturer, endless giver, and silent supporter. Because of their situations, women choose to believe in God, creating their own attributes for God and transforming reality to the extent they are able. As women—daughters, mothers, wives and daughters-in-law—they try to bring hope and faith into this world with their God.

8

Women and the Nation

The economic development of South Korea is one of the exciting stories of the post–World War II era. In the early part of the twentieth century Korea encountered the streams of modernization and globalization flowing through the world. Korea's crucial position in northeast Asia located it in the midst of complex political and economic contexts. Colonial manipulations, imperial politics, modernization, the growth of multinational corporations, and globalization all required enormous amounts of cheap labor. Most of Asia, including Korea, responded. Seeking to build a new nation on the land decimated by the coercive colonization that took place during World War I, World War II, and the Korean War, South Korea adopted Western capitalism and its accompanying economic ideologies.

South Korea jumped into a new form of colonialism, whether voluntarily or not. South Korea's acceptance of foreign economic support from the United States and its ability to supply a cheap labor force composed of working-class people and women served as the main springboard to economic growth. Since incorporating itself into international politics and accessing foreign capital and technology, an economic boom has come about in Korea, but this has not benefited all equally. Korea's industry is characterized by low pay for workers relative to business profits, poor working conditions (especially at smaller factories), and the longest average work week in the world (about fifty-four hours). The workers have shown great forbearance in the face of such hardships, which were especially prevalent in the 1960s and early 1970s.[1] For the past forty years low labor costs have been South Korea's main economic resource in the international market.

When workers began to demand better working conditions and more freedom in the late 1960s and early 1970s, the Korean government put in place labor laws to oppress and persecute any union activity. Women and lower-class people were ruthlessly put down and even killed.[2] Their demands and rights were dismissed, and they faced unimaginable sexual harassment and menacing military violence. In the name of national economic growth and political independence, powerless working people were killed or disappeared without explanation.[3] The dictatorships of Presidents Park Chung Hee, Chun Doo Hwan, and Roh Tae Woo in the early 1960s to the 1990s proudly linked patriotism and nationalism and used military violence as a legitimate force against innocent people in the name of national security and economic growth.

While women generally are more likely to be abused within work structures, women from many parts of the world are also repressed by cultural demands. According to Korean traditional culture, women working outside the home do not conform to the acceptable version of Korean womanhood, since virtuous women stay inside the household. However, throughout Korea's long history of wars and invasions, women without the support of men have cared for their families by working outside the home. They do their housework as well as field work and factory work. Work outside the home is done quietly and invisibly, because Korean culture has taught them to take care of their family without ruining the pride and dignity of men. This tradition is exploited to benefit South Korea's economic growth, although it presents a complicated dilemma for women. "Filial piety, family loyalty, acceptance of the Korean government as a representative agent in the development of society, a respect for status and hierarchy, and social harmony"[4]—all these concepts push women to work outside the home secretly to provide food for the family and to work for the good of the nation. While the Korean government and the foreign powers cultivate a partnership among male elite entrepreneurs, the wages of women and working-class people are kept low to maintain a comparative advantage in the international labor market. Today's Korean nation has been built on the sacrifices of poorly paid women and factory workers.

In recent times, although women have recognized possible new roles for themselves in the modern world, women who work are still viewed in a negative way and their roles are quite limited. Many women work in factories run by transnational companies that can be exceedingly abusive and also in the workshops of sub-contractors.[5] Their jobs are characterized by low pay and extreme insecurity. Despite increasing political power for women, their job security and welfare are given no priority by national policy and are in extreme jeopardy in times of economic crisis. Ironically, in response to the strength of the international women's movement and to aid foreign policy, the Korean government officially supports women's rights and gender equality while in actuality promoting the status quo.

This lack of support for women's concerns is demonstrated by government policies for a system of welfare for women who are heads of households and support of family planning. Welfare benefits providing temporary residences, minimum living expenses, and basic job training are supposed to support underprivileged women such as single mothers and female heads of households.[6] The government's intention is to support the women themselves and their dependent family members. However, this intention falls far short of its goal, because in reality the government does not provide enough basic support and as a result fails to provide women with independent living. Moreover, this policy excludes prostitutes from receiving aid; the intention seems to expose these women as deviants from the middle-class norms of femininity. Its aim is not training women to become self-sufficient wage earners but preventing "deviant women from going further astray, seeking to redeem their fallen or lost femininity through having them perform feminine tasks."[7]

Family planning has been officially encouraged in every five-year economic development plan since the early 1960s with the intention of reducing the birthrate, at times coercively.[8] The Korean government created a two-child family policy in order to slow population growth and support economic prosperity. The campaign for the two-child family was visible throughout Korea on billboards and in the media from the 1960s to the 1980s. This policy changed the structure of the Korean family from an extended family to a nuclear family. "Total fertility fell from 6.0 children per woman in 1950 to 1.6 children per woman in 1990."[9] Here, national economic growth is given far greater importance than the bodies of women, especially those of lower-class women. The policy, which evokes a preference for the birth of male children, stimulates patriarchal values. While Korean military governments maintain that these laws demonstrate their concern for women, undoubtedly in order to achieve international recognition and prestige, the laws also control and manipulate women with patriarchal and colonial ideologies.

WOMEN'S JOBS

Most working women hold manufacturing and industrial jobs and are usually low-wage-earning laborers. Most factories employ young single women because they require full-time employees who work regularly; subcontractors prefer married women who can work cheaply at home.[10] While American women earned almost seventy-six cents for every dollar earned by American men in the 1990s, Korean women earned forty-two cents for every dollar earned by Korean men in the 1980s and fifty-two cents for every dollar in the 1990s.[11] Even though the employment rate for Korean women has increased since the 1960s, it does not mean that the social status of women has improved. Women are used as cheap labor, and their social economic status is still very low.[12]

Many young single women work in factories for ten to twelve hours a day. Their jobs are usually in manufacturing itself or in simple secretarial work; they do not receive promotions or benefits. They are exposed to extremely exploitative and vulnerable situations, particularly those involving sexual relationships with their bosses. In many cases these relationships are initiated through rape and sexual harassment, but because women employees are threatened with layoffs, these incidents are rarely reported.

Another kind of discrimination against young women at work stems from the hidden message within Korean family life, where traditional values lead young women to quit their jobs after marriage or childbearing. In the early 1980s many companies fired women when they married. After the age of thirty, women are teased by co-workers because they have not married or had children, and sometimes they are treated as abnormal, old, hysterical women who have failed as women. To have professional careers, women often have to choose to reject marriage and to endure social scorn. Divorce is also an obstacle for women who want to have a career. Divorce is generally viewed as a sign of women's characteristic problems and lack of judgment, and divorced women have to tolerate social scorn their entire lives.

After working women marry, their situations often became more serious than those of young single women. Listen to the stories of two working women:

> When I was married, I did not report my marriage to my company, because at the moment they knew of my marriage, I would have to leave my job. So my husband and I decided to delay our wedding, and we hid our marriage. After three years, they discovered my marriage. They fired me. After that, I did not have to hide my marriage any more. My husband provided food and money. After my son is four years old, I will start to find work. Maybe I will work for a domestic factory or a milk delivery.[13]

> When I had three children, I needed a job. But without skill or a college degree, it was not easy to find a job. Fortunately, because my friend introduced one subcontractor to me, I started to work. The job was to make something with beads. I put beads onto a string and made three hundred strings a month. The subcontractor paid me 10,000 *won* (US $10) for one hundred strings. During my kids' school hours, I worked at home, and after my kids slept, I worked more. I worked more than eight hours a day. I earned 30,000 *won* per month. My husband worked for a small cloth factory. He worked from eight in the morning to ten at night.

He was paid 400,000 *won* (US $400) a month. That is not enough for our family. I just try to help my husband and family make some extra money.[14]

The percentage of married women in the paid work force is lower than the percentage of single women because married women are usually self-employed or work part time for subcontractors. In the latter case, subcontractors offer only piece-rate payment with no benefits. They persuade women to see their work as secondary to their role as wives and mothers. While men's primary identity in Korean culture is as rice-winners and providers, women are satisfied to accept even a minimal payment as a secondary source of income.[15] Ideal womanhood, the primary identity of women, is achieved by mothers and wives with legitimate marriages and not by workers, despite rapid modernization and globalization. Women are collectively and consciously oriented toward the view that working is either a secondary role or a deviant choice of economic necessity. This is true regardless of income or education. In terms of industrial employment, married women represent the most marginalized class.[16]

It is no surprise, then, that in such a patriarchal culture women are the last people to be hired and the first to be fired. The laws of gender equality and equal employment are rarely practiced; they are, in fact, counter to Korea's cultural traditions and Korea's national policy of stimulating economic growth. However, because these laws exist, women feel guilty when they cannot get a job and are ashamed if they are fired. To maintain employment, women make many sacrifices as they totally devote themselves to work. Absent an analysis of Korea's patriarchal structure, the dilemma of working women is often seen as the problem (inadequacy) of an individual woman.

In addition to manufacturing work and piece work for subcontractors, women have one more employment possibility. This is to work in the sex industry. In cooperation with the Western post-colonial powers, the Korean government has done much to stimulate this industry. From the early 1960s to the 1990s, the former Korean dictators proudly and publicly used women both as cheap production workers and as sex laborers.

ANOTHER FORM OF COLONIALISM— PROSTITUTING WOMEN'S BODIES

During its long periods of colonial domination, Korea tried to establish a national identity distinct from that of its colonizers. One way to construct a national identity is to "demonize" the other. To make Korea distinct from other nations and to develop a Korean consciousness and identity, the government created anti-colonizing movements that showed people how to overcome colonial influences and create their own culture. Those movements and thoughts were usually diametrically opposed to values of the colonizers. During the Japanese colonial period (1910–45), Koreanness and its independence represented the most important Korean value, and it countered the Japanese concept of *HwangKukSinMin* (New People of the King's Nation), which tried to eradicate the national identity of the Korean people. Likewise, in the Western post-colonial era (1945–present), the Korean people have strongly emphasized Korean community consciousness and contrasted it with Western individualism, which has been interpreted as selfish thought.[17]

The concepts of oneness and national identity stem from the long anti-colonial struggles of Korea. The greater the possibility of encroachment by foreign powers, the more Koreans emphasize the homogeneity of their people.[18] Geographically and culturally, Koreans form a homogeneous society. It is believed that all Koreans should affirm a unified identity and hold tight to the belief of one blood (one race) and one nation. Koreans are taught that if one person suffers, all Koreans suffer. If one person wants to fight, all people must fight together. In the same manner, every individual must fight and sacrifice in order to save all people. Therefore, individual sacrifice may be part of one's duty. This logic has been exercised over and over again, especially by Korea's dictators, who have forced people to sacrifice for their nation while in actuality the sacrifices are needed to maintain their dictatorships. It goes without saying that it is usually the poor and marginalized people who are compelled to sacrifice, while a few people with power and money benefit.

This orientation of community consciousness conforms well to Confucian patriarchy as well as to Buddhist practices of transcendence and selflessness. For example, primary Korean virtues are to show loyalty to the nation *(chung)* and filial piety to one's parents *(hyo);* these concepts are equally important in both Koreanized Confucian and Buddhist practices.

Unfortunately, these virtues have been employed in ways that have been disastrous for women, including persuading women into prostitution. Using the concepts of Confucian and Buddhist sacrifice, the Korean nation legitimated prostitution as a sacrifice women could make for their families and their nation. Such sacrifice, it is maintained, is the only method of survival by which women can contribute to national freedom and independence.

The twentieth century was marked by two major instances when the bodies of Korean women were treated as national goods and raped. The first is the provision of "comfort women" for the Japanese military. The second is uncomfortably and indecently recent: the provision of *yanggongju* (women who work for American soldiers).[19] While the historical and political contexts differ, the victimization of poor women is strikingly similar.

Korea's Comfort Women

During the period of Japanese colonialism (1910–45), Korean women as well as other Asian women were kidnapped and forced into sexual slavery by the Japanese military government. Thousands of women, an estimated 80 percent of them Korean, were victims of this sexual slavery. The issue of the "comfort women" remained buried for half a century. However, in the late 1980s, women's groups in Korea and Japan tried to bring this tragedy to light. Kim Hak Sun, the first former comfort woman to share her ordeal in public, addressed the Japanese government's responsibility. Then many other women stepped forward to testify to their unforgotten and unforgettable experiences. Their testimonies revealed how this officially organized system of rape happened, how it was hidden and then forgotten by the imperial Japanese forces and by their own governments.

On December 6, 1991, several former comfort women gathered in the Tokyo District Court and demanded compensation and an apology from the Japanese government. On August 4, 1992, after a long struggle, they won a victory. For the first time, the Japanese government admitted its use of deception, coercion, and official involvement in the recruitment of comfort women. However, even today, the Education Ministry of the Japanese government does not allow any reference to comfort women in the nation's textbooks.[20]

After World War II many former comfort women could not return to their countries. They were basically forgotten, being neither war prisoners nor military personnel. It was as if their existence itself had been erased. Neither the Korean government nor the Japanese government raised any questions about them. They simply wandered in foreign lands as strangers and had no choice but to live there without any identification or national protection. Many women died or were lost through suicide, illness, or hard work.

Some women were eventually able to return. However, they felt too ashamed to tell what had happened to them. They hid their past from their families and relatives and tried to erase their memories. Most ran from their fear and shame for the rest of their lives. Here are brief accounts of two comfort women:

I have looked forward only to death, without telling anybody my story. My tribulations remain buried deep in my heart. Now I have reported to the Korean council, and I take part in its various activities. But I am anxious in case anyone recognizes me. I have a husband and children, so I cannot bewail my life and be so resentful in public. If, by any chance, my children's spouses and their families discover I was a comfort woman, what would become of them? Who would be able to guess what inner agony I suffer with this awful story buried in my heart? My story, as hidden as it is from those around me, will follow me to my grave.[21]

After having poured out what I had to say for so long, I felt that half of my problem was solved. I told my son about the whole thing, and he wept uncontrollably, saying "Mother, you have lived so courageously, even with such a rough past. I am proud of you." But the wife of my youngest son became despondent, and even my son is disheartened. I feel very sad and guilty when I see them.[22]

Every step of their lives has been bathed in worry and guilt. They live every day of their lives with hearts heavily burdened by this horrendous nightmare. Even though they are the victims of war and a structure of colonial power, their society has judged them culpable and without honor.

Korean women's bodies were used by the Japanese not just to satisfy the sexual needs of the soldiers but also as a way to humiliate Korea's men. Using the concept of oneness, the Japanese raped the women to show their power over Korean men. Even though the Korean's concept of oneness never fully encompassed women, both the Japanese and Korean societies made use of it. For the Japanese, it became a symbol of power, and for Korean men, a symbol of humiliation. The end result was that women's sexuality became nationalized, and it symbolized Korea's powerlessness at the hands of a controlling power. The damage done to the bodies of Korean women symbolized the national shame and the powerlessness of Korean men, as well as the national pride of Japanese men. It is interesting to note that when women's chastity was regarded in the patriarchal order as a property, once it had been destroyed by Japanese males, "the comfort women issue was no longer between Korean women and Japanese men, but between Korean men and Japanese men."[23] The women themselves were unimportant; this was a matter to be resolved by men.

For Korean men, the existence of comfort women was an embarrassment that revealed their anger, frustration, and shame. It appeared that their concern was not so much for the women themselves as for their national shame and the dishonor of Korean males. This is why the Korean government tried to conceal this issue for fifty years. And while the issue concerned national pride and superior power for the Japanese, the Japanese, having lost the war, had nothing to gain by revealing the atrocity. It took much courage on the part of the women to bring their stories to light.

Once the issue of the comfort women began to be discussed, the Korean and Japanese governments both dismissed the credibility of the comfort women and never recognized them as human beings, but as bodies—or property—that had been violated. Their lives and deaths became topics of public discourse by men. The women cowered under the burdens of blame and humiliation, and most remained buried in silence. They seek justice, but both patriarchal societies still deceive and ignore them.

Even today many comfort women remain marginalized and isolated and struggle from lifelong depression and deep wounds. Justice has been very slow in coming. The following testimonies of Korean comfort women demonstrate their pain:

> I felt so ashamed. In this society, people still talk behind our backs. I would feel humiliated, even if I was to receive compensation. But then, I would feel mistreated if I did not get any compensation. Whenever I think of those years, my heart pounds and my whole body is racked with pain.[24]

> Of course Japan is to blame, but I resent the Koreans who were their instruments even more than the Japanese they worked for. I have so much to say to the Korean government. The Korean government should grant us compensation as well.[25]

Most comfort women have lived in fear that they would be stigmatized by Korea's traditional society as defiled or promiscuous women. Many have lived for half a century carefully guarding their past in bitter shame and silence.

However, they have not stopped their fight. Despite terrible individual situations and unimaginable social pressures, they have not given up their lives, their rights, or their search for justice. They have taught this world to see human stains and to hear God's cry and to taste Christ's tears.

Korea's *Yanggongju*

Following the Japanese colonial period the Korean government again became involved in the sexual slavery of Korean women. Since the Korean war, the United States has dominated Korea's economic, military, and political capabilities. The reality of US superiority has not changed essentially since the 1950s, even though many adaptations have been made. For the convenience of the armed forces, the US military has required Korea to provide several local businesses near its bases, including prostitution. Korea's military government forced women to serve the sexual needs of the American soldiers stationed there. Thus Korean women's bodies became part of the colonial relationship between the United States and Korea. With the support of the Korean government, American troops still patronize Korean prostitutes today.[26]

This prostitution results primarily from US militarism and imperialism as well as from Korean nationalism. The American military's need for sexual substitutes imposed voluntary sexual slavery on Korean women, and it also forced the Korean government to treat and employ Korean women as national resources to be exploited. While the American military did not physically force individual Korean women into sexual service, as did the Japanese government, it did manipulate the Korean political situation through its overwhelming power. With the cooperation of the Korean government, the end result was voluntary sexual slavery for many Korean women.

While most Koreans morally censured these women for selling their body to non-Koreans, the attitude of the Korean government toward these women during the two postwar decades (the 1950s and 1960s) was ambivalent. While expressing concern for women's poverty, the government legitimated the practice of prostitution by invoking Korea's multi-religious concepts of women's sacrifices for family and country. Again, as with the Japanese, women's bodies became instruments of foreign policy, national economic development, and security enhancement. The Korean government has exempted itself from taking responsibility for the betrayal of these women. Thousands of poor girls and women put their bodies to work selling sex to US soldiers to save their families and their country.

Throughout the decades they have experienced extreme sexual violence and poverty. For most, the pattern of abuse and violence, which involves both physical and psychological injuries, in the sex industry is unimaginable. Burns, broken bones, internal bruises, damaged organs, and brutalized faces are common and often lead to lifelong physical and psychological trauma. Today these women are also in danger from HIV/AIDS. It will take much more than the removal of US military bases or the praise of the Korean government to restore their feelings of dignity and self-worth.[27]

Many of the former comfort women do not want to be associated with the "morally decadent" or "trashy" women who "voluntarily" entered prostitution.[28] Yet, given the critical perspective of Korea's colonial context, "camptown" prostitution should not be condemned as voluntary prostitution. Although it could be assumed that these prostitutes had a free choice to sell their bodies for sex, just as others chose their occupations (even though such a choice seemed immoral), for most of these women, prostitution was not a choice made with individual freedom; it was not one of many options available.[29]

Prostitution has always been closely connected to Korea's colonial history. Indeed, the Korean people have paid a high price for their independence. It cost the lives of many innocent people and some incredible sacrifices on their part. The prostitution of Korean women was part of the "trading" that took place leading up to Korean independence. It continues today as part of the presence in Korea of American troops and also as a product of economic domination. The Korean and American governments cooperate in its perpetuation today. Both have actually defended it as a necessary institution. Whenever the term *choice* is used in connection with prostitution, the economic and political contexts must be carefully scrutinized and critically evaluated.

THE *HAN* OF COLONIZED BODIES

To reenter Korea's "noble society," women who have been engaged in prostitution have to hide their past as deeply as possible. Comfort women and all women engaged in prostitution have struggled with long nightmares their whole lives. They are followed by the shadow of their past, from which they try to hide or run away. Many disdain and hate themselves for what they have done or become. Suk Young, a Christian woman, is a former prostitute:

I ran away from home when I was fifteen. When I was young, I liked my father a lot, because he was my father. But whenever he was drunk, he always hit my mother, my sisters, and me. One day he beat my mom horribly and tried to beat me. I ran away. I did not come back for ten years. I did not finish middle school. I did not know what to do. I started to be engaged with prostitution. I met one nice guy. He was my customer. I lived with him for a while. But things did not go well. My pimps found me. They forced me to pay my debt. They said that I had a lot of debt from the brothel. But at that time I was too sick. I had serious physical diseases. Also, I did not want to live like that. Even though they knew I could not work, they did not let me go. I called my mother after fourteen years of running away from home. My mom waited for me. She prayed for me every day. She was a very sincere Christian. My mother paid my debt to them. I was free to go home. I lived with my mom and sisters. My father lived with another woman in another place. I worked for the nail shop. Nobody knew my past. I met my husband. He did not know my past. He thought I was innocent and a virgin. I pretended that. My family and I agreed that we would carry this secret until we died. He was a good Christian, so if he knew my past maybe he would not want to see me any more. He surely believed that I was the most beautiful and innocent girl he ever met. I could not break his heart. He wanted to marry me in the church. But I could not. Fortunately, we could not find any church for our wedding, because many couples were getting married at that time. We were married in the citizens' building. Sometimes when I walk on the street, I am afraid to meet someone who knows my past. Even when I see someone who looks like one I knew from the past, my heartbeat goes very fast and I try to find someplace I can hide. I believe in God. God forgives me and loves me. As long as I do not go back there again, God loves me. Now I am a new person. When I was baptized, I was born anew. I did not want to look back. But sometimes I feel that I am still a sinner before God. I cannot be innocent and clean again. I still repeatedly remember what I did. What I did was not forgivable. Even though God forgives me, I cannot forgive myself. I know this is a bigger sin. . . . I do not think that my husband and my children would forgive me if they knew my past. I believe that God also lets me keep the secret from my family as well as myself. I do not want to think about it. I do not want to remember anything. . . . I am safe now. I am happy. I am normal. . . . I am normal.[30]

By Korean standards a "normal" woman is a person who is a daughter of her father and marries a decent man, who has a husband and children, who stays at home and takes care of the children and the housework, who provides a comfortable home, and who waits for her husband. A "normal" woman has never engaged in sexual activity with anyone but her husband. A woman's virginity and chastity belong to her husband.

Many women do not expect a "normal" life after they have engaged in prostitution. Very few ever marry. Sometimes they have children by mistake, but they and their children live outside of society. To enter into a "normal" life, they must bury their memories deep in their hearts and never let them surface. They cannot tell their secrets to anyone, even God. Clergy are the last people they would want to confide in, and church communities would be the last places to which they would turn. However, many have learned how to act like good Christians in front of others. Many former prostitutes become aggressive, restrictive, and conservative Christians, who rarely forgive other people who have done wrong. Internally, however, they struggle mightily with everything from physical diseases to psychological illness.

In Korea, because female identity is so closely linked to bodily chastity, women who cannot meet this norm usually suffer from deep psychological wounds that leave them feeling unclean and soiled. Some never emerge from these shadows of secrets and unresolved pain. Failing to face their pain often mutes their inner voices. Keeping secrets divides their lives and prevents integration within their psyches and bodies. Estranged from their "selves," they are unable to trust and unable to love. And they feel unworthy of another's love. Sometimes the more they yearn to be "normal," the more they feel isolated from who they really are. Guilt and shame always accompany them.

Suk Young, whose story was just told, thinks that God could perhaps forgive her, but she knows the church communities and the society to which she belongs would not. If they knew her past, they would always think of her not as a good Christian but as a former prostitute. She also senses that if she were to expose herself to her family or to her church, her whole life would be destroyed. Instead, she constructs herself as a loving mother and wife as well as a faithful Christian woman—and she buries her past. She loses her self-respect and makes it impossible to regain her self-esteem.

She is likely to seek continuous forgiveness from God, needing God's forgiveness more and more, and sacrifices herself over and over again to win favor. She needs endless forgiveness but is unable to forgive herself. Because her inner self is lost, her spiritual hunger is not filled. Undoubtedly she wants to escape this circle, but she does not know how, because traditional doctrine and theology have marked her as an eternal sinner.

KOREAN WOMEN'S SEXUALITY AND POWER

Korea's patriarchal religions of Christianity, Buddhism, and Confucianism all fall short in offering salvation to women: Buddhist concepts of body have esteemed men's bodies more than women's; patriarchal Confucian concepts of women's roles have abused women; and Christian traditions have portrayed women as unclean and iniquitous. Patriarchal ideologies permeate all of Korea's religious traditions and deeply wound not just comfort women and *yanggongju*, but all Korean women. The misogynist ideologies of Korea's multi-religious traditions suppress and oppress women's bodies and their spirits. Even the stories of Shamanism, such as the Tangun myth, have been manipulated by patriarchal political influences. Comfort women, *yanggongju*, and women who are daughters, mothers, and wives often have been and still are treated only as wombs and bodies that need to be controlled by men. Their bodies have serviced not only colonial male power but also the power of their fathers, brothers, husbands, and sons, while their own sexuality has been disdained and demeaned. In the past, under the patriarchal power of colonialism, their bodies were raped and their spirits tortured; today, held in check by the power of Korean patriarchal traditions, their sexuality must remain hidden and their spirituality smothered.

Korean women, however, have not hidden or run away. The daughters of Korea have faced up to their past and survived. Despite their oppression, they have struggled to create ways to overcome their situations. Creating their own understandings of God—even though they do not correspond to the traditional patriarchal attributes of God—is one of their methods. Through this process, Korean women are exercising the power they find within themselves to transform their own reality. They seek a God who gives them power to free themselves from their society, and they believe in a God who can liberate them, a God who forgives and forgets their sins. As they embrace God to rediscover themselves, they find a God who heals their wounded hearts, who tells them, "I love you whoever you were and are." With this God women can transform not only their own selves, but also their culture and society.

PART III

THE TRANSFORMATION OF *HAN*: KOREAN WOMEN REINTERPRET GOD

Korean women as daughters, mothers, wives, and daughters-in-law have lived and struggled in a multi-religious and multidimensional society in which the burdens of women's social roles have not diminished but grown heavier. Korean patriarchal Christianity and Korea's other religions have not brought women freedom but instead have asked for even more obedience by asserting the authority of a patriarchal interpretation of God. The colonial, political, and economic contexts of Korea have never protected women; rather, their bodies have been exploited and their spirits have been psychologically and spiritually denigrated.

Such circumstances leave women in a life without options. Generally, women are controlled by circumstances that can nearly crush their lives and destroy their identity. Despite their *han* and constant suffering, women have survived, and many women live by their faith. Their faith seems to be a living energy that helps get them through their daily experiences. Their prayers and rituals are actions that create hope in their lives. Their sufferings do not stop; neither do their prayers. And they struggle all their lives to understand their God.

Minjung theologians have tried to interpret the people's *han* and their struggle to transform their *han* within the Christian faith. They have used the paradigm of Israel's struggles and suffering to explain the Korean people's lives and faith in relation to God. While other Korean Christian theologians assume that people's suffering is God's punishment for their disobedience, *minjung* theologians strive to see the people's suffering as God's suffering in this unjust world. *Minjung* theologians are aware of the people's *han* as part of the reality of economic poverty and political powerlessness. Working from the abundant cultures of the Korean people, they try to demonstrate how Christian faith can transform the Korean people's *han* through social justice movements and grassroots people's movements.

However, most *minjung* theologians fail to recognize or address the reality of women. They do not acknowledge the patriarchal nature of Korea's religions, especially Christianity. Even though they protest the injustice of the colonial structure of prestige and hierarchy, they rarely identify the injustice of patriarchal cultures and the asymmetry of gender. They want to support the *minjung*, the common people, but they do not think to include women. Women's issues are only secondary issues. Hence, women's freedom and equality are rarely discussed in the theological circles of male *minjung* theologians.

I believe that addressing women's experience is a theological priority, as is analyzing Korea's multi-religious cultures and colonial history. By lifting up the unflinching faith that has sustained women's lives, regardless of their circumstances, I find that women have found transforming power by forming their own understandings of God. Although women have been taught many attributes of God by their society, they have reworked these attributes into a God who empowers them.

Three understandings of God, in particular, can sustain and transform the lives and faith of Korean women: God as family, God as liberator, and God as friend. I believe that analyzing these attributes of God helps reveal how Korean women can reconstruct their faith, find their "selves," and ultimately transform their *han*. Although I do not believe that reconstructing the attributes of God is the only way women can transform their *han*, I believe that at the very least it is essential for us to identify how various understandings of God can help women empower themselves and envision other possibilities that will assist in their transformation.

Even though understandings of God are selectively formed by people's circumstances and affirmed by their decisions, both consciously and unconsciously, many attributes of God are designated, controlled, and manipulated by those in political power as well as by cultural traditions. In a hierarchal and patriarchal society such as Korea, such concepts, often legitimated by authority, are consciously or unconsciously internalized by women. When patriarchal or colonial authorities control concepts of God, they also invade women's spiritual lives. That understanding of God, however distorted, will become their understanding of God. This presents a constant struggle for Korean women as they have been taught to believe in a patriarchal God but at the same time they have experienced a different God.

It is important to analyze how various understandings of God affect the reality and the spirituality of Korean women in both positive and negative ways. The three understandings of God to be examined—God as family, God as liberator, God as friend—are closely tied to women's personal, familial, and social relations as they have struggled with the colonial history of their lives. Even the use of the term *Father* to name God can be based on different experiences within women's lives *and* differing experiences of God. It seems that women's understandings of God can change the path of their journey through life. Similarly, it seems possible that new understandings of God can help women to become aware of and value what they have in their own lives and also enable them to see new horizons, to change their paradigms of struggle, and to transform their *han* with new hopes and new possibilities.

9

God as Family

In Korea, there is no stronger concept of community than family. Going back centuries, the Korean agricultural lifestyle created a strong bond in family relationships. Family became the primary economic unit. Despite the modernization movement that began in the 1950s, changing Korea's communal agricultural lifestyle to an industrial capitalistic lifestyle centered on the individual, the concept of family as the unit of life has persisted. Surviving many wars and periods of colonialism, whether military, political, or economic, the family continues to exist as the core of Korean daily life.

For Korean women the family has been and continues to be the main focus of their lives. They live with and through their family. Unlike Western women, they rarely live by themselves. Even after college or graduate school, they live with their parents until they marry. After they marry, they live with their husbands and husbands' families. If a woman never marries, she lives with her parents until her parents pass away. Even if women happen to live by themselves for study or work, they feel obligated to return to their families to help support them.

Women are always surrounded by family. For them, family is as essential as air and is a concept they cannot separate from themselves. It is not surprising, then, that the nature of their family relationships shapes their understandings of God. More than anywhere else, women feel God in their family. They understand God as they understand their family. They feel God's presence as they feel their family's presence, and God exists as their family exists. God is part of their family.

Because the patriarchal social structure creates a strong bond among family members, many women experience God in terms of patriarchal family relations. In many cases this experience has restricted the possibilities for God. At the same time, it is also important to recognize that women have struggled with these patriarchal understandings of God and tried to transform them. Often a battle rages between women's patriarchal and non-patriarchal understandings of God as women search for God through their mixed experiences and messages.

GOD AS FATHER IN CHRISTIAN HISTORY

God as family includes many aspects of family relations. However, within the Christian tradition and throughout two thousand years of human history, God understood as Father and Son has triumphed over all other attributes of God. Even though God as Spirit has been recognized and affirmed in the Eastern Christian traditions, particularly the Orthodox tradition, the images of Father and Son continued to dominate throughout the Christian Far East. Despite the importance of the role of the Spirit (and of spirits in Eastern religious traditions), the Spirit has never been viewed in Korea as having the same importance as the Father or the Son. In addition, male theologians—female theologians have played a significant role only in the second half of the last century—have generally projected a patriarchal image of Father unto God. They have also used the ideals of the strength, the omnipotent power, and the unforgiving justice of the God of the Hebrew scriptures to reaffirm, intentionally and unintentionally, the patriarchal and hierarchal systems imbedded in their traditions and cultures.

The Father God leads men to legitimate male superiority. Men project their understanding of the Father God onto their own understanding of fatherhood. For example, in the theology of Karl Barth, God as Father is completely independent of all God's creatures.[1] Such an interpretation leads men to believe and to behave as if a father can also be independent from his family. If God does not depend on God's creatures, a father does not have to depend on other family members. As God and God alone controls everything and everyone, so a father should control other family members and the family's resources. Because God knows all, a father knows every need of the family members without a need to listen to them. God's way is beyond human ways, and a father's decisions should be beyond question. While God's sovereignty and omnipotence might be covered at times with rhetoric, this is the God believed and loved in Korean Christianity, because this God fits into Korea's patriarchal family system and hierarchal multi-religious structure.

However, as this God does not really explain anything or relate with anyone, this God is alone. This God does not touch people's lives. Such a Father God does not care about people's suffering and is beyond human suffering. This God can become a form of dictator who rules people without relating to them. If this God appears to choose and support the rich and powerful and legitimate their authority, what God is present for the people who are powerless, marginalized, and abandoned? Faced with this kind of God, how do we understand the meaning of the goodness and love of God? Where is the God of love and faithfulness, the God of sinners and the outcast?

Many classical Christian attributes for God, especially the trinitarian formulas, explicitly demonstrate patriarchal family relationships between Father and Son, leaving no room for other family relations. Even though Spirit is understood as female in some interpretations of trinitarian teachings, emphasis has often been placed on the Spirit as supporter or sustainer of the Father and Son rather than as Mother. God's love and justice arise only within the relationship of Father and Son. Without Father and Son, there is no salvation. The trinitarian formulas of Jürgen Moltmann and Wolfhart Pannenberg, which have strongly influenced Korean Protestant churches, along with the theology of Karl Barth, shed much light on the nature of Korean Protestantism.[2]

According to Moltmann, God relates to the world as the Father, the Son, and the Spirit. God wants to love the world; God affects and is affected by the world. Unlike Barth, Moltmann brings God into relationship with the world. God is not totally independent from God's children. God loves them and feels their pain. In the understanding of Moltmann, this divine love starts from an event between the Father and the Son, and the cross becomes the core experience of this love. Therefore, the model of love is the love between Father and Son. God experienced this world as Father and Son and expressed love only through the relation between Father and Son.

Moltmann developed the role of Spirit as the divine source of life. Even though he tried to reject the subordination of the Spirit to the relationship between Father and Son and to give attention to both pneumatology and Christology, he could not overcome this asymmetrical balance because he defined the role of the Spirit based on God's experience as male. This God appears to relate to the world of men but not to the world of women. The divine source of life was a divine male experience. This God has suffered as the Son but has never suffered as the Daughter. This God has cried as the Father but not as the Mother. God loves God's children as Father but never experiences them as Mother.

In the view of Pannenberg, a disciple of Karl Barth, God's love in the relationship between the Father God and the Son Jesus is the only foundation of love for neighbor. God is eternally the Father revealed in the Son. Jesus the eternal Son correlates to the Fatherhood of God. Therefore, the Son receives all power in heaven and on earth from the Father until God's rule becomes universally victorious, when the Son will return the power to the Father.[3]

This interpretation also explains the logic of the patriarchal family. From generation to generation the son becomes the father and keeps the father's name and power. Within this patriarchal family the mother does not beget the son, since only the father can truly beget the son. The father begets the son through sacrifice, religious doctrine, ritual, or practice. In Nancy Jay's term, this is the action of "remedy for having been born of woman."[4] Both males legitimate the structure of intergenerational continuity through various ideologies and rituals. They transcend their absolute dependence on women's reproductive powers by the father generating the son. This patrilineal descent is socially and culturally organized and legally and religiously legitimated. The patriarchal line from father to son passes on the power to rule people and the world. Other relationships, which are secondary, require only submission and obedience.

In a patriarchal family, as is true in Korea, dominant males such as fathers and sons are responsible for providing all things. They are omnipresent and omnipotent. Others just depend on them. This is the social, historical product of the Father God. The Father God has been the most dominant image in Christianity for two thousand years. This dominant patriarchal Father-Son relationship does not leave much room for other relationships. Other images of God are seen more as accessories. The Father God, as head of a patriarchal family, oppresses all the other rich understandings of God and seems obsessed with power and authority. Because of this distorted interpretation, the Father God has been misused and abused. This has negatively influenced both people's understandings of God and their understandings of themselves. If a patriarchal church or a patriarchal society affirms only this Father God, it risks imprisoning or limiting God.

GOD AS FATHER IN KOREA'S CHRISTIAN CONTEXT

Korean patriarchal society has had no difficulty accepting the Father God presented to it over the past one hundred years. Rather, these concepts actually support the building of a patriarchal Christian society within Korea's multi-religious society. In consequence, Korean Christianity has built a God on the foundation of Korean patriarchy, Western Christianity's patriarchy, nationalism, colonial capitalism, and victimhood. Because a patriarchal God already existed in Korea's multi-religious contexts, the Father God allowed Western Christianity to meld more smoothly and quickly into Korea's patriarchal culture. Through Christian doctrines, sermons, and Bible studies, Christianity continues to affirm this God. The teachings of Western male and colonial theologies continue to be spread and repeated by Korean male clergy every day and every week. These teachings encourage women to memorize understandings of the patriarchal God, and eventually the teachings are inscribed in women's minds. Such a Christianity gives men power to rule over women and other powerless populations. It thus can become a religion for a powerful country and for men, not a religion for people who need and seek liberation.

Not surprisingly, many Korean women have had a very hard time accepting the Father God as their own God. Because Korean women as daughters, wives, daughters-in-law, and mothers have deep and painful problems within the relationships in their families, they cannot imagine a Father God who would listen to them or seek to understand. They show great reverence to Father God, but also have great fear because the Father God is the God who commands them. Father God does not listen to daughters but orders them. Even though they worship this God and confess their belief in this God, as they have been taught to do, women cannot believe in this God without the dreadful trepidation that comes from their relationships with their fathers and the broader patriarchal society.

This God is cold and strict. By calling God Father, women as well as men have been instructed in how they can relate to this God.[5] As women are trained to embody the virtues of sacrifice and obedience, they are expected to relate this God with sacrifice and obedience. It is not surprising that this God has failed to heal women's pain and suffering; rather, this God seems to encourage women's suffering and accelerate women's sacrifice.

GOD AS FAMILY
BEYOND PATRIARCHAL RELATIONS

Despite the heavily patriarchal thrust of the family, the church, and society, women still experience God within many different aspects of family relationships. Several women shared their experiences of God with me.

Even though I call God the Father, in my mind my God is thought of as Mother. The Mother who is always there for me and loves me. If I were educated differently, maybe I would call God Mom. That is what I feel for God in my life.[6]

When I think about God, God is like a grandmother who has very keen eyes and very prophetic wisdom.[7]

When I feel God, God is a very close person like [those in] my family, who live together and share pain and feelings. God lives with me and is always there for me.[8]

God is my ideal of a father who can listen to me and understand me. My real father never communicates with me or with anybody. He does all the speaking. Nobody can speak but him. I want to have a father who never beats my mother and me and who wants to know about my woundedness. I believe in a God who listens to me and cares about me and my family a lot. God is my father.[9]

Even though Korean women have been taught to believe in the Father God, their experience of God has been not only father but also mother, grandmother, sister, brother, and other family members. Throughout Korea's colonial history many women experienced the absence of a Father God who was almighty and omniscient. In their reality this God did not exist. The almighty God was with their oppressors; their God shared their powerlessness and hopelessness. Their God was immanent, part of their living family. Their relationship with God was born from their suffering and *han*. The discrepancy between the teaching of the Korean Christian church and their living experience caused them to reshape their understanding of God.

Even though they could not totally ignore the image of the Father God, many Korean women allowed their living experience to transform patriarchal teachings, leading to images going beyond the Father God. Family, which is one of the most significant models created to honor both the teaching and women's own experience, has provided the most powerful understanding of God. Because family relationships are the closest relationships in most women's lives—and this was especially true during the colonial period—women experience this God in everyday family life. The lessons of colonialism taught women that they cannot trust any nation or anyone but their own family. Faced with cruel poverty and oppression, the family held together and provided an absolute ground of trust and faith. God shared their poverty, suffering, and oppression as family. God as Family is compassionate and merciful. God is there with and for them every day and night. God shares their every tear. God dies with them and revives them from poverty, colonial oppression, and male violence. God and women are together every day.

This attribute of God is very similar to the shamanistic understandings of the God who was present to their ancestors. This God dwells with them. This God exists in every place women live, such as the inner room, kitchen, garden, or well. This God works when women work. This God keeps an eye on women wherever they go and whatever they do. However, this God is not an omnipotent or almighty God who rules over all; rather, this God is one with them so they can be together, struggle together, and share their pain and life together as a family. Even though they call this God Father, they sense this God as Mother, Sisters, Brothers, Aunts, Grandparents, Daughters, and so forth. They relate to this God as a member of their family who understands and supports them. When they go to the kitchen, they talk to this God. When they go to work in the field, they ask this God for help. This God listens, and this God understands. This God is the most comfortable and gentle family member that they can have.

Korean Christian women seem to adapt this shamanistic, friendly understanding of God and adopt it as their own. Even though many Korean Christian men and women do not consciously want to relate their God with any shamanistic sense of God, many Christian women unconsciously know their God in the same way that their grandmothers and ancestors understood their traditional gods. Many shamanistic concepts of God were rejected by Christian missionaries simply because the missionaries trivialized Shamanism as superstition, but the understandings of the Christian God that women have re-created surely are an amalgamation of the attributes of the shamanistic gods that were affirmed through women's religious lifestyles, experiences, and traditions. This confluence makes it possible for them to transform Father God to Family God.

GOD AS MOTHER

When God is understood as loving and gentle, God is seen very much as the traditional, gentle, sacrificing Korean mother who is believed to have unlimited love. This attribute of God as Mother has become popular in women's theological discourse. In many traditions this God is called Creator and Sustainer and is usually involved with creation and reproduction. This Mother God brings about abundant life and the safety of progeny. Instead of God as Father, many Korean women seek and worship this Mother God in order to have an abundant life and to protect their children. However, because many daughters have mixed feelings for their mothers, they can become confused by the understanding of God as Mother. On the one hand, Mother God promises the happiness of life for their family, and it is the actual mother who feeds them and protects them. On the other hand, daughters may feel hatred toward their mothers while, at the same time, they may admire and sympathize with their mothers' sacrifices throughout their burdens of poverty, housework, and the struggle against violence. However, in the midst of this confusion, as daughters grow older, their understanding of their mothers increases.[10] When they themselves become mothers, they understand why their mothers cried for them. Then daughters and mothers become more like sisters and friends. The older daughters become, the more closely they draw to their mothers. Finally, through the understanding of a Mother God, daughters and mothers can communicate with and show sympathy for each other. They can listen to and understand each other. The Mother God helps them share their suffering as women and saves them from their isolation and marginalization. Women who have been abandoned by others can still cling to God the Mother-Woman, a protector God who can see women for the first time through women's eyes. That is the God whom women seek as their God.

GOD AS DAUGHTER

In thinking about other familial attributes, God as Daughter is a unique concept within Korean female traditions. God as Daughter is not found in Western Christian traditions, but it does exist in traditional shamanistic beliefs and is expressed in women's religious rituals and faith. God as Daughter is unique not only in the sense of gender but also in the sense of how it reflects women's lives. The Daughter God sees and listens to women's experience as a daughter. The myth of BaRiDeGi demonstrates this well. This myth is found in a group of texts known in Korean folklore as narrative shaman songs. In this song BaRiDeGi shows how a woman as a daughter survives, lives, and is transformed into a god through dramatic declaration, song, and dance. The performers of this myth are female shamans, known as *mudang* or *mansin*.

Once upon a time, a king named Ogu married Byong-On. They had many children, but they were only daughters, seven in all. The seventh was abandoned because the baby was not expected to be a girl. Her name was BaRiDeGi, which means a deserted or abandoned child. She was raised by animals and an old couple.

Meanwhile, her parents, Ogu the Great and his wife Byong-On, were dying in bed. Despite the best doctors and medicine, they did not improve. Finally, they consulted a fortune-teller who told them, "Since the disease of the king is the punishment of heaven for abandoning his daughter, the chosen one, he cannot be healed with any medicine made in his country. Only spring water from the west can cure him."

So Ogu the Great called his six daughters and asked them to bring the spring water for him. They all refused to do this. So he ordered his servants to search for the princess BaRiDeGi. After bidding her stepparents farewell, she was brought to the palace. When she learned that her parents were dying, she was sad and wept. Even though they had abandoned her as an infant, she agreed to travel to the west for the spring water that would cure them. She went through the west, mountains, and hills.

Whenever the princess BaRiDeGi asked directions, some work was required of her. But she did not give up. Buddha and Amitabha gladly gave her directions and gifts of three bunches of flowers and a gold stick. With the aid of the gold stick, she crossed the river, riding on a rainbow.

Before finding the spring water, she met a fearful-looking giant, the god, Peerless. He asked her to work for him. So BaRiDeGi worked for the giant for nine years. But the fearful giant still demanded more of her. He told her that if she married him and bore seven sons, he would then accept her will. There was nothing else she could do but marry him and bear him seven sons. After all this, BaRiDeGi could finally take the spring water and return to her parents.

While she was searching for three colored peach flowers, the giant decided to go with her. As they returned, they saw a boat on the water with no anchor and no light. On it were the bodies of dead women—those who did not have children when alive and those who died during childbirth. These women were still wandering around after death. Then BaRiDeGi prayed for them and blessed them. Finally she reached the human world. When she arrived home, her parents were about to be buried. She stopped the funeral march and let her parents drink the spring water which she had brought. They revived. BaRiDeGi and the giant were formally married before her parents and lived happily thereafter. After the death of BaRiDeGi, she became a goddess. Her story has been handed down for generations.[11]

In this story BaRiDeGi is the victim of a patriarchal family and society. Abandoned and left alone from birth, she was helped by heaven and raised by animals and stepparents that heaven sent for her. In this myth the Heaven God supported a daughter. God stood where a daughter stood and saw the world with the eyes of a daughter. This god did not abandon her but instead punished her parents. The Heaven God allowed her to live and helped her through the difficult process. In the end she was transformed into a goddess who shared power with the Heaven God. The daughter was allowed to become equal with God's self. In Korea it is maintained that the first ancestor of Shamanism was BaRiDeGi.[12] The first human being to become a god was a woman, not a man, and a daughter, not a son. The Heaven God chose a daughter to be like God.

The Heaven God also gave her power to transform her family and this world. Her redemption was not limited to just her family. She saved not only her parents, who were abandoned by God, but also all lost souls who had been abandoned by society and lived in hell. She even redeemed the monster, who became her husband. Her love and forgiveness were key to the redemption of others. Because the Heaven God transformed her *han*, her parents and others realized the nature of their patriarchal sins and the sufferings they imposed on others. The whole structure of patriarchy was shaken and its vicious circle stopped. BaRiDeGi became their savior and their god.[13] This well-known myth demonstrates in the end that the Daughter God understands the lives of daughters and can overcome their victimization and marginalization. She gives power to daughters to redeem and unite their families and the world.

The understanding of God as Daughter supports not only women but also other marginalized family members as well as marginalized members of society. Family members and members of society stand as equals in a relationship that is neither hierarchal nor patriarchal. This God as Daughter does not divide women's family relationships according to sexual discrimination or marital status. As a married daughter, BaRiDeGi still has status in her family. This Daughter God sees women as redeemed children and gives them new models for family to bring into everyday life.

DIFFERENT EXPERIENCES OF GOD AS FAMILY

Understanding God as family can involve concepts of family different from those of a nuclear family or a patriarchal family.[14] As discussed above, women also experience the multi-generational extended family, the single-parent family, a family of homosexuals, a family without children, and so forth. While the traditional patriarchal family model emphasizes the relationship between father and son, the model of God as family can be much more open, encompassing may different kinds of family members.

Women experience their family first as daughters. They may also become mothers, sisters, daughters-in-law, and so forth. In many cases they may experience their family through the eyes of the marginalized and excluded. Some women will lead their families as single mothers, perhaps experiencing poverty and war together. Sometimes, women will live together to help each other, without concern for creating a maternal line or perpetuating their name; their concern may be simple survival, and family will then be composed through relational experiences with others rather than by shared blood. The Korean concept of family involves "living together" physically, emotionally, and intellectually, whether the family members are happy or undergoing difficulties.[15]

For women, and especially women whose lives are difficult, the family includes the people who share their everyday lives, the people who communicate, understand, cry, and laugh together. Living together with God as family, women have healed their brokenness and redeemed their wounded hearts. God as family can sustain women's lives without terror or fear about intimate violence. God as family can also empower women to overcome the patriarchal world, bringing peace to their lives and hope for abundant life. It is not surprising, then, that an understanding of

God that makes sense for Korean women is that God can be their family in all the meanings of the word: ancestors, grandparents, parents, spouses, sisters, brothers, children, aunts, uncles, in-laws, and neighbors. God in this form is always with them.

10

God as Liberator in Korea

When America and the United Kingdom invaded Korea with Christianity in the nineteenth century, they compelled Korea to change what they saw as Korea's "savage" culture. In the heyday of the missionary movement of the late nineteenth century, many fundamentalist and evangelical missionaries came to Korea and taught that their Christianity was the superior and absolute "truth." Christian missionaries attempted to destroy the other religious traditions that already existed in Korea and throughout other parts of Asia. Along with their Christian beliefs, the missionaries also introduced a new patriarchal system that was part of the colonizing movement.[1] Colonial Christian missionaries treated Korean culture as idolatrous and Shamanism as pure superstition. The European and North American imperial narratives were the only acceptable narratives in Christian discourse. People's indigenous narratives were forbidden. In the name of divine power, colonial Christianity muted other truths, other norms, and other narratives. Because of Western Christians' high-handed imperial style, many Korean people viewed Christianity as a tool of Western colonialism and refused to accept it.

However, during the Japanese colonial period (1910–45), Christianity was officially recognized when Christianity helped Korea win independence from Japan by organizing and supporting Korea's independence movement. Christian churches hid and protected Koreans who were involved with this movement. In addition, by using biblical stories, Christian schools were the key institutions that taught about liberation and independence.[2]

During World War I, World War II, and the Korean War, Korean Christians believed that God would save them from the terrible oppression of war and liberate them like Israel. The story of the Exodus was a very popular and hopeful source for many Korean Christians who proclaimed Israel's God as their God. It was not whether the Christian God existed that was in question, but how Koreans could discover this God in the core of their reality.

During Korea's independence movement the Christian liberator God was lifted up as the Korean God. The God who liberated Israel from Egypt would set the Korean people free from Japan. Such a liberating God was a most appealing image for the many Koreans who sought and longed for liberation. As they read the story of Exodus into the Korean colonial reality of suffering, Koreans discovered a God who empowered them with hope and faith. Therefore, when this previously unimaginable dream, Korean independence, came true, Korean Christianity was recognized as a powerful religion. Many nonbelievers joined churches and began to worship this liberating, transformative God. With this living experience of liberation, the God of Israel became their Liberator God.[3]

This transformation occurred because Korean women and men experienced the Christian God from their own reality. They became confident enough in themselves to ask what this God meant to them, and they looked for the meaning of this God beyond doctrine. They saw God not within abstract Western colonial doctrines or theologies, but from their colonial reality, from their experience of ruthless military violence and the poverty caused by war. This was a God who was there with them.

This Liberator God did not disappear after Korean independence but became stronger. In the end, Korean independence brought neither real independence nor enough food. Rather, because of the two opposing ideologies of Western democracy and communism, the Korean people now began to kill one another. Families were separated as a border was drawn between

North and South. The land was devastated, turned into an endless mound of ash, and the people were exhausted, their spirits broken, and plagued by hunger and poverty. Everyone seemed powerless, even the nation as a whole. Family members were dead or missing. All the survivors knew was that they had survived and would have to struggle to remain among the living.

THE LIBERATOR GOD IN JESUS

In the midst of such suffering, Korean Christians looked for God and connected with God through the image of Jesus.[4] They saw Jesus as a true comrade who would work with them for their equality and freedom, who would lead them in their quest for liberation, and who believed in women as equal children of God.

As in Israel, where Jesus acted against political, colonial, and imperial authority, Koreans struggled against colonial power as well as their own military governments. The Liberator Jesus grew even stronger for Korean Christians. They looked at the cross of Jesus, and then, in the resurrection of Jesus, they found their hope, their own possible resurrection, because they were carrying the cross together with Jesus.[5] The oppressive, toxic power could not capture them by death. Instead, they found power in the cross; death would neither stop their struggle toward liberation nor suppress their resurrection for justice and freedom.

Even though patriarchy seems to say that Jesus is the savior of the world, but not necessarily of women,[6] and even though colonialism says that Jesus is the savior of the world, but not necessarily of colonized peoples, Korean women felt that the Liberator Jesus could be their savior as well. Jesus became their eschatological hope for justice as Jesus revealed an always compassionate God of love.

The resurrection of Jesus can liberate every place in the world that has been oppressed, and every person who has been hurt, broken, or wounded. Hope comes alive in the resurrection of Jesus. The resurrection brings hope and the power to transform a hopeless reality and even overcome death. Jesus brings hope that justice and wholeness are indeed possible.

Korean women believed in the Jesus who constantly resisted the exploitative forces of colonialism, fought against oppressive patriarchy, and stood firmly with them against militarism. They identified their suffering with Jesus' suffering. Their suffering was shared by and with Jesus. Korean women saw Jesus' cross as the end of their suffering and as a judgment against patriarchal society. They shared death with Jesus and then were raised up with Jesus to experience liberation and freedom.

GOD AS THE LIBERATOR OF KOREAN WOMEN

During the period of Japanese colonialism the Korean people experienced physical oppression as the Japanese military took over Korean land. In the face of this tangible oppression, Korean women and men joined in solidarity to work for Korean independence, enduring the struggle together. But after Korean independence was won, women were left behind and denied equal liberation. The male culture of Korea revived and instinctively began to oppress women anew. Women's abilities were ignored as they were pushed back again into the box of patriarchy. When a visible outsider was the enemy, women's gender roles were relaxed. Once the enemy was gone, women were put back in their "original" place.[7] Moreover, in the post-colonial era, described in the previous section, Korean men sent women into industry as a source of cheap labor and women's bodies became national commodities. From that point on, women, burdened with the two patriarchal systems of culture and religion, needed to resist the intrusion of a foreign power and needed to refuse traditional gender constructions.

Even though Japan's defeat in World War II officially brought liberation to Korea, colonialism still posed a real threat to Korea's political, economic, and cultural independence. Under the powerful influence of America and Russia, Korea was exposed to other neocolonial powers. Even though they did not appear to include a geographical conquest like that of Japan, they implied that Korea remained subjugated in every way. While the American powers remained firmly "convinced of their good intents even in the face of overt violence,"[8] this new neocolonial threat had a devastating affect on Korean society, and particularly the situation of women. Women's bodies, turned into a cheap labor force, became a vital national economic resource, a means to gain economic strength; women's bodies, turned into sexual resources to be exploited by the American military, became a means to placate the colonial powers.

THE LIBERATING GOD
FOR KOREAN CHRISTIAN WOMEN

As Korean Christian women struggled for freedom even while incorporating the beliefs of Western, patriarchal missionaries, a male patriarchy took control of Korean Christianity and, despite women's devotion and sacrifices, excluded women from leadership positions in the churches. However, this had not always been the case.

In early Korean Christian history, women served with men not only as lay people but also as missionaries and church leaders. Women offered their homes as churches, delivered Christianity into people's inner rooms, and propagated God's love and justice to grassroots people. Many Christian women devoted their lives to Jesus and to spreading the Christian message.

Many women struggling with patriarchal culture and violence found Jesus through the message of other women. As widows, abused wives, abused daughter-in laws, and women from the marginalized classes, they sought new avenues for their lives and found Jesus in the middle of this search. In 1895, Jun Sam Duck was the first Korean woman to be baptized. At that time she was married, and her husband had many women. She had to serve her in-laws with total obedience. Despite persecution from her husband and his family, she began to believe in Jesus and walked seventy miles to go to church as she searched for the meaning of life. She went on to found nine churches and one school before she died in 1932.[9]

Many other women met Jesus and changed their lives. They did not surrender to patriarchal oppression or stop asking the meaning of their lives as women. Through Jesus, they found new meaning in their existence. Through Jesus' eyes they saw themselves as independent human beings. Lee Kung Sunk, a widow, became the first Korean to teach at EHWA Women's University, Korea's first educational institution for women in Korea, founded in 1887. Choi Naomi, who had been oppressed by her husband and in-laws because of her failure to have a son, became the first overseas missionary. Jululu, a shaman's daughter who had lived in shame and poverty, was a great preacher in HeaJu province.[10]

Because Western missionaries were not able to reach people who lived in the countryside and deep mountains, they encouraged Korean women to go out and preach the good news to these people. During the nineteenth century, missionary work was led by these lay women, who were called Bible women, and mission and church services depended on them. After meeting Jesus in their lives, they enthusiastically worked as Christian missionaries, not hesitating to go to marginalized places and start new churches. Their devotion to the church was powerful. According to one Bible woman's report, she visited 6,730 women and sold 4,491 bibles in one year.[11] Indeed, the Bible women sacrificed themselves for the church and became the leaders and teachers of the church and friends to the marginalized peoples.

However, from the beginning, women received but a brief period of education and were trained as assistants, while men received a long-term education with ministry-training courses to prepare them as leaders. Christian education for women and men was segregated by gender as Western missionaries and Korea's patriarchal culture manipulated church structures and suppressed the leadership of women. In spite of their desire and devotion, women were not accepted as church leaders. Even when some women graduated from the same school, taking the same courses and achieving the same degree as men, women could not become ordained.

Because of its patriarchal structure, Korean Christian churches ignored women's devotion and leadership ability and forced women to conform to traditional roles within patriarchy. A male clergy took over all authority, including worship and leadership. Within the church structure, men decided church policy and financial matters. They designed worship services and church programs. Women were asked to take responsibility for children and to provide food services. Within theological education, Korean Christian leaders adopted Western patriarchal theologies and condemned women's bodies as unclean. Male superiority was asserted as women were denied ordination and leadership positions.

Many Korean Christian women were also abused and exploited by male hierarchal churches and were forced to forget that they were included in God's promise of liberation. And such patriarchal discrimination was adopted in the name of God—it was seen as "God's will." Christianity, which Korean women initially saw as a liberating gospel for their *han*-filled lives, actually bound Korean men tighter to God, once it was colored by patriarchal ideology and colonial discourse. Many Christian women became so subservient and inert that they lacked the ability to even dream of a better way of being human or being church in God's world.

In subsequent years, however, women did not completely forget about their Liberator God. Their continuing desire for women's ordination demonstrated that women had not lost their calling from God as they determinedly struggled against patriarchal Christianity.

WOMEN'S ORDINATION
AND THEIR LIBERATING MINISTRY

The ordination of women in Korea has been a long journey that began with the Methodist Church. The Methodists accepted women's ordination in 1931, but women could not get into the educational system leading to ordination until 1955. In 1955, two Methodist women, Jun Mil La and Mung Ha Lung, were the first to be ordained. In the Korean Presbyterian Church, the struggle lasted much longer. After thirty-nine years of struggle and discussion, the Presbyterian Church in the Republic of Korea finally approved women's ordination in 1974, although this denomination had allowed the ordination of women elders in 1956. In 1977 Yang Jung Shin was finally ordained in this denomination. The Presbyterian Church of Korea (another Presbyterian denomination) accepted women's ordination in 1995 after rejecting applications for sixty years.[12] This was a fulfillment of women's faith that had been previously expressed in tears and sorrow. Christian women continued to evidence their faith in God and their belief in a Liberator God, rather than in a God who oppressed women.

The Korean Christian women's movement started with their struggle for ordination but became a larger struggle for equality even beyond the church. This issue led Christian women to see other violations of women's human rights under Korea's patriarchal structure. They opened their eyes to look at other forms of women's oppression and colonization. The power of God in Jesus gave them strength to survive and to resist the forces of oppression and colonization. The presence of God the Liberator empowered them not only within church walls, but outside the church as well. They tried to establish solidarity with other social-justice movements: the antiwar movement, the anti-sexual-tour movement, the peace movement, the anti-militarism movement, the movement to revise laws affecting women, and so on.[13]

Sometimes, when women and other marginalized people supported the anti-militarism movement, they were accused by Korea's dictatorial governments of being Communists or radical activists. Sometimes, when they proclaimed justice in demonstrations of the peace movement against former dictators, they were arrested and tortured by the police and/or military forces. Some were abandoned by society as well as by churches that remained silent. Some church leaders who believed that politics and religion should be separate felt such oppression had nothing to do with faith. Many conservative churches pretended not to hear stories of the oppression of women and the poor, or the reality of life in Korea. Women who worked for liberation from those discriminations were labeled evil and dangerous.

Many Christian women, however, listened to the voice of God in the oppressive reality of the poor and powerless rather than turning to scripture or church doctrine. They saw God in the middle of these struggles and believed that God walked with them in their peace demonstrations. They confessed a God who worked for the liberation of all people throughout history. Korean Christian women fought against Korea's military governments and helped political prisoners and their families. They supported the female workers' movement, the farmers' movement, and the poor people's movement. In the midst of hostility and apathy from within the church, they did not lose their faith in God, because their God the Liberator was working with them.

Korean Christian women believe that this Liberator God does not continue the liberation movement only within the church sanctuary or within Christian traditions. Rather, this Liberator God participates in all social-justice movements and is in solidarity with them against poverty, sexism, racism, nationalism, and colonialism. Korean women, including Korean Christians, have struggled against all kinds of discrimination and segregation with powerful energy, desire, pain, sorrow, sighing, moaning, and ceaseless love.

Sometimes they feel God's love in the places of their work and struggle rather than during worship in church. Sometimes they feel God's joy singing with the political prisoner rather than with the choirs in church. Many Korean Christian women see and experience God as Liberator not only for Christians, but for all people whom God created and has loved. Their God is the God of justice and love who should not be boxed in by patriarchal Christianity. They believe that God the Liberator wants to change society and create a good and equal community for all human beings beyond the boundary of religions. Since Korean Christian women have moved with this God, they have learned how to be interdependent and interconnected with one another, seeking relationships of equality, establishing solidarity, and celebrating difference.

11

God as Friend

Human beings are relational creatures whose lives include multiple layers of complex relational dimensions. Most religions, including Confucianism, Shamanism, Christianity, and Buddhism, suggest that everything in life is relational. Human beings, animals, heaven, earth, nature, and even ghosts all interact. However, the power of these relationships is not equal. Human beings always attempt to play the superior role in these relationships. Moreover, within human relationships there are always power issues connected with sexism, racism, classism, nationalism, colonialism, ageism, ableism, heterosexism, and so forth. And human relationships contain much discrimination.

In Korea, people's relationships are very hierarchal, with most relationships defined by people's age, sex, social position, and personal/official relations. These relationships are structured in complex ways, and each functions in its own unique manner. Relationships also fit like perfectly meshed gears with the Korean language system.[1] Except for the relationship between friends, horizontal relationships rarely exist. Because of the hierarchal system, the relationship between friends has a very special position; it is the only relationship in which Korean people experience equal power.

However, there are two necessary conditions for friendship in Korea. First, the friends must be the same age, whether they are women or men. A person one or two years younger or older cannot be a friend; such a relationship fits into the category of an older-younger relationship, as with older brothers or older sisters. The second condition is that friends must be of the same gender. A man has a male friend, and a woman has a female friend. Today women may have a male friend or a man may have a female friend, but even though they might call themselves friends, they do not think about their relationship as a friendship; rather, it is a relationship of acquaintances. Especially after marriage, almost no relationships of friendship exist between men and women. While these two conditions hold for both men and women, men and women build their friendships in different ways.

WOMEN'S FRIENDSHIPS

In Korea, when people discuss friendship, they usually think immediately of male friendship or male bonding. Even in modern times many dramas and films describe true friendship or powerful friendship as a relationship entered into only by men. Most people would be quite skeptical of friendships between or among women. It is thought that when women gather, they waste time chatting about nothing. There is an old Korean saying, "If three women gather, the dish is broken." If women gather to talk or catch up on news, they are not paying attention to their housework. Moreover, it is believed that women's friendships end after they marry while male friendships continue for a lifetime. Male friendship is viewed as strong, deep, big-hearted, and nonjudgmental, while female friendship is generally viewed as shallow, garrulous, and judgmental. Korea's male culture generally scorns women's gatherings as meaningless time spent in idle chatter.

However, despite male derision, friendships are often at the center of women's happiness. Women experience these living relationships with friends from early childhood to death, weaving their lives together. While all other relationships are tinged with obligation and necessity, relationships with friends have an essential power that lies in freedom, reciprocity, equality, and responsibilities not connected to the power structure.

For Korean women the most important component of friendship is communication. A friend is the person who understands and shares a woman's feelings. When women exist to serve husbands, parents, in-laws, and children, and to listen to their commands and needs, there is no reciprocity between them. Women bear the *han* of these hierarchal and patriarchal burdens in silence. But with friends, women do not feel the constriction of these burdens. Women can talk freely about their husbands, children, families, jobs, religion, and everyday lives. Friendship with other women is the only way they can put aside the obligations of hierarchal relationships. They feel equal and they learn about the freedom and richness of human relationships. They can use their own voices and express their own opinions. Unfortunately, in Korean society, opportunities to make choices and to have reciprocal responsibilities are available only within this relationship.

Because of the military culture and colonial history of Korea, many male friendships are based on making others "the enemy." Many strong male friendships are formulated in the context of military training or violent male bonding. Especially after the Korean War, relationships among the military became the model for friendship. Such friendship did not include mutual understanding or reciprocal sharing. It was based on a common project and usually generated violence under the name of national security. It required the existence of demonic "others" and entailed strong political and social subjugations.

However, for women, friendship has a different context. Through the colonial experience and the Korean War, women built their friendships based on survival. Women friends were survivors who lived through pain together. These were friendships for a lifetime. Therefore, the first characteristic of friendship between women is that it is not a contest to win or lose but a relationship between "I" and "Thou."[2] During the colonial period women quickly saw that they could not exist alone and that they needed more than family, particularly if their family was heavily weighted to the male side. They learned that they had a need to live in harmony with other people to have satisfying lives. Through friends, they tasted the richness of life and the world despite the harsh reality of each day before them. "I-Thou" friends always have relationships as whole and equal beings, and such friends are never objectified or made subservient. Such friendships do not require that people share the same opinions, beliefs, or political agendas, but rather that they have the same experience of life and death. Because it is about people, not a project to win, women do not desire to make "others" of their friends. The goal of the relationship is friendship and equal sharing. It is about people who genuinely love one another and choose to be together.

A second characteristic of women's friendships is that they begin with recognizing each other's difficulties and differences. Sharing their different situations and difficult pains, they learn to open their hearts. The relationship is about people and mutual understanding and sharing and the empowerment of each other. This requires openness to themselves as well as to others. It is about inclusivity, making room for diversity and difference, creating harmony, and providing common space for understanding and sharing. For women, friendship means neither sameness nor comradeship. Friendship does not imply having the same goal; it is willing to disregard differences. Diversity and difference can empower voices and increase mutual understanding. Furthermore, through friendship, women see themselves as beloved. They realize that they themselves are worthy without the demand for endless sacrifices and service. Such relationships encourage self-respect and self-love and can make women feel alive and joyful.

A third characteristic of women's friendships is that their lives become interdependent and fully connected. Women extend their love to others and receive love from others with complete freedom of choice. Their lives are sustained and abundantly lived through this relationship with others. Others become non-others; unknowns become knowns. In the middle of their struggles to survive, such relationships prove that they are not lonely sojourners but common weavers of their lives.

Women's friendships have a unique place in Korea's highly structured culture. While family relationships are built on obligation, friendships are built on freedom, personal choice, equality, and reciprocity. Friends can call one another by their first names, and this is about the only time such familiarity is allowed. Even within families, name calling is governed by rules. For example, an older sister can address a younger sister by her name, but the younger sister must address her older sister only as Older Sister. The ability to call a friend by her first name creates warm intimacy among the friends. They are free to define themselves and grow in confidence. Because of their unique nature, women's friendships are marked by a certain fragility and nurtured in a special manner. They demand mutual effort on the part of the friends. These friendships also suggest possible ways of relating to God that are non-hierarchal and non-threatening.

GOD AS THE FRIEND OF WOMEN

Even though Christianity introduced God as Abraham's friend in Genesis, the understanding of God as Friend is not prominent in either Korean or Western society. Because of the prevailing image of God as Father, and other hierarchal images of God, such as king and ruler, Friend has not often been seen as an appropriate name for God. People know in their heads that they can call God Friend, but in their subconscious minds they are not comfortable thinking of God as Friend. God is a Higher Being, not an equal being. It is believed that thinking of God as Friend lowers God, making God less divine, and this would not be acceptable to God. However, it may not be God who feels this way, but rather a hierarchal system that requires a hierarchal God.

Despite Korea's hierarchal culture and patriarchal practices, Korean women have established a relationship with God as Friend, believing God is their Friend despite hierarchal religious teachings. God was their friend in their indigenous beliefs as well as in other religious traditions in Korea. The rituals of Shamanism maintained a tradition in which women communicated directly with God in their everyday lives. Without fear, they talked to their Friend God about their husband, family, and everyday problems and experiences, much as they would to their women friends. They met this God not with fear but with mutual respect and comfort. The practices of Buddhism taught them to see the possibility of enlightenment as the way that they could experience God and understand God's wisdom and feel God's presence. In the performance of Confucian rituals as well, women have shared communion with God. They feed God and share their food and love. But it is particularly in the Christian tradition that women have affirmed that this God is alive as their Friend. With these abundant cultural resources, women have exercised their freedom to create a new understanding of God as Friend, a more suitable companion for them than the hierarchal and patriarchal God.

Even though God does not fit into the Korean category of friend or into the paradigm of hierarchal relationships, these rich cultural resources enable women to imagine their friendship with God. They believe that God wants to be Friend to them. God does not treat them as would a ruler or conqueror. God does not give them orders but wants to communicate with them. Friend God communicates with them, not just through hearing confessions of their sins or praise of God's almighty power; instead, this Friend communicates with them by listening to their feelings, their concerns, their unsolved pain, and even their wishes. This God does not live apart from them up in heaven but with them in their very earthly, everyday lives. Friend God talks with them with openheartedness, inclusive sensibility, companionship, reciprocal interdependence, and mutual advocacy. This friendship encourages them to lift up their different voices and gives them opportunities to explore their uniqueness. This God and Korean women sustain each other and help each other in weaving their common life together as friends. Even though God does not need to depend on human beings, Friend God is willing to depend on them because they are God's friends. In this way human beings and God can have a mutual, equal, interdependent relationship.

Under the reality of colonialism Korean women have invited this Friend God into the dialogue with their unspeakable and unbearable suffering and pain. This God calls them not from outside but from inside. Even in their deepest suffering they remain hope-filled, because they know in their hearts that they have a Friend who understands their silent screams and struggles together with them. This God is there for them, and this God is in them. God supports and redeems women with friendship.

From this relationship women learn to exercise and benefit from their interdependency. It gives them an opportunity to practice their freedom and power with mutual trust and empowerment. When women accept God as Friend, they accept themselves as who they are and are better able to sustain their lives. God becomes the source and sustainer of life, and giver of life after death. This God is their co-sufferer, wounded healer, attentive listener, and comfort provider. Even if Korean culture and traditions are not listening to women, their *han*-filled hearts are heard by their Friend God.

Such a friendship can be called love of the same height. When God is on the same level with women, God can be neither above women nor beyond women. It also implies that God views the hierarchal world from the position of women. God does not rank women unequal or inferior partners but rather shares reciprocal power with them. The relationship between women and this God is mutual, trustful, and horizontal. God as Friend shares the burden of the patriarchal and hierarchal discrimination of an unjust world, yearns for justice, and offers hope and endless strength.

GOD AS FAMILY, LIBERATOR, AND FRIEND

According to Ahn Byung Mu, one of the founders of *minjung* theology, God lives in the middle of screaming life with people.[3] According to several *minjung* theologians, such as Suh Nam Dong, Ahn Byung Mu, and Song Ki Duk, God is with the *minjung*, among them, and in them, and God becomes one of them.[4] As Family, Liberator, and Friend, God moves beyond traditional boundaries and understandings. This God who seeks to overcome the unjust reality of oppressed people must be the God that minjung theologians also seek.

I believe that women's experiences of God as Family, Liberator, and Friend are some of the most important theological resources in the Korean context. These three understandings of

God are derived from aspects of the life and experience of God that the *minjung* have endured throughout the ages. As such, they can help men as well as women expand the possibilities available to them for finding meaning in their lives.

Korean women keep hold of their own lives and other people's lives through their hope manifested in God. I believe that understanding God as Family, Liberator, and Friend is just one of many possible ways women have explored and will pursue to name God. Through their own process of reconstructing the various attributes of God, they can find strength, hope, and the power to transform the reality of their lives. In finding and confirming their own experience of God, women can share in God's love for intimacy, justice, freedom, and equality. This can be a path toward justice and the endless strength of love needed to transform and redeem this wounded world.

PART IV

NEW UNDERSTANDINGS OF GOD—THE POWER TO TRANSFORM

For more than two thousand years Korean women have adapted and adjusted their understandings of God to fit their circumstances. While these understandings have been greatly influenced by Korea's history of colonialism and patriarchy, women have always sought a God in whom they can believe and trust, and on whom they can build their faith. Their own understandings of God have been a tremendous source of strength and survival for Korean women. Experiencing a God they can trust has provided healing for their wounded lives.

However, even though women practice this transforming process as part of their daily lives, it has not been recognized by the church or the wider society because of the all-pervasive influences of patriarchy. By its very nature this process has remained hidden, rarely discussed even within theology and the church, and even less frequently written about. Yet there are several concrete practices within most churches and other religious bodies that could benefit women and strengthen their faith by being sensitive to their particular needs.

12

Pastoral Landscapes within Korean Churches

Several theological and ministerial practices are exercised in Korean churches, including regular Bible study, preaching, worship, and pastoral care and counseling for members of the congregation. Because Bible study, preaching, and worship are much more exercised than other pastoral practices, such as pastoral care and counseling, many Korean women scholars and theologians have focused on biblical reinterpretation and liturgical re-creation. They have challenged the patriarchal nature of theology and liturgy and developed various ways of seeking God within these practices.

However, in the case of pastoral care and counseling, very few women scholars and theologians have given attention to the pastoral needs of women or attempted to discern the psychological and spiritual directions appropriate for women. While there are several reasons for this, two seem particularly significant. First, counseling itself is not a familiar act for most Koreans; indeed, there is a general fear of counseling in Korea's culture. This holds true for both women and men. While going to the hospital for physical sickness is nothing to be proud of but is acceptable, going to the hospital for nonphysical illness is considered shameful. It is a sign of disgrace. Counseling in such circumstances is reserved for "crazy" people, and "crazy" people are to be avoided at all cost. Such beliefs today are remnants of shamanistic and traditional folk beliefs that the mentally ill were cursed by heaven or possessed by ghosts. They are equally rooted in early Christian beliefs that the mentally ill are possessed by demons or bad spirits. Whatever the belief, it is thought that such people need a shaman or an exorcist, not a counselor. Because counseling is understood as the management of insanity or possession, many people will not seek counseling but instead suffer in secret.

Second, in church settings the concepts of pastoral care and counseling are quite unfamiliar to most Korean Christians, although today many Korean pastors are learning this vocabulary in the seminary. Unlike courses in biblical studies, many seminaries do not emphasize pastoral care and counseling as essential courses of study; instead, homiletics and biblical studies are viewed as the most significant. As pastoral care and counseling are being introduced as new areas within practical theology, most seminary courses on pastoral care and counseling are heavily based on Western theories of psychology, which, in turn, are strongly influenced by male psychology.[1] These courses include, among other, the theories of Sigmund Freud, Carl Jung, Erik H. Erikson, Howard Clinebell, and object relation theorists.

However, these theories and practices have often created a conflict even for women in the West, as many Western feminist scholars have pointed out. In the eyes of classic Western psychology, the goal of human development generally is believed to be individual independence. It is about detachment, separation, autonomy, individuation, and individual rights. To achieve this independence in the real world requires gaining total control and power within the given structure, which tends to be overwhelmingly patriarchal and hierarchal. Considering the criticisms of many feminist psychologists such as Carol Gilligan and Jean Baker Miller, in the view of this male psychology women's psychological development of interdependence is seen as "elusive mystery."[2] Women can never complete the cycle of psychological development because they cannot fit into the categories of complete detachment and separation. Their inability to do so is understood as psychological immaturity.

In the case of minority women this male-oriented psychology becomes even more problematic. It is assumed that the psychological underdevelopment of minority women is unfixable, given their racial inferiority and sexual impotence. Their interdependence, therefore, is understood as a lack of confidence and determination. The unavoidable powerlessness caused by racism and sexism doubly charge them as permanent psychological failures. Without consideration given to the effects of racism, sexism, and classism, minority women are relegated to a lower rank within society.

In the case of Korea the concept of independence is even more complex. Western independence is founded on concepts of individual freedom, economic independence, and national sovereignty. To achieve the ultimate in human development requires individual, communal, financial, and political freedom, rights, autonomy, responsibility, and power. Whoever lacks one of these elements loses the capacity to be independent. From the logic of Western psychology, Korea's colonial history and its resulting level of post-colonial dependency mean that Korean people do not have the ability to obtain and keep independence of their own. Their complete psychological development must wait until they obtain complete political, economic, social, and national independence.

Following this logic, a people or a nation lacking the power or freedom of other nations cannot achieve the same level of independence. Only persons or nations with the strongest power and control can achieve the complete level of independence. In other words, only they can access the conditions to attain the ultimate level of human development. Independence then becomes the ultimate stage of freedom. As a consequence, Korean styles of living and community-oriented interdependence are considered to be signs of psychological immaturity, and the communal mentality of Koreans is regarded as a communal illness.

A Korean mind-set views such Western definitions of independence as selfish acts that threaten the community. Koreans understand individual independence to be an inhuman way of living because they have witnessed that Western independence (and colonization) has demolished their existence and cost many lives. Western individual independence is not the ultimate goal of human achievement but rather negligence of others. Instead of individual independence, the goal should be to gain trust so that people can live together interdependently. Many Korean people believe that interdependence is the only way of improving the quality of lives for all and for healing Korea's long history of colonialism and its longing for national oneness and wholeness.

Unfortunately, the conflict between these two perspectives has not yet been explored or defined, neither by Western psychology nor by Korean pastoral theology. Just as many theology courses have uncritically adopted Western theologies, most pastoral care and counseling courses in Korean seminaries have adopted Western biases and hierarchal frames for ministry. When Korean ministers meet the reality of churches, they usually have two options: the absolute acceptance of Western psychologies and practices, or their total abandonment. Because of a lack of critical analysis, it is impossible to design an appropriate foundation for these practices. As a consequence, they tend to be abandoned altogether, and many pastors have very little sense of their value.

PRIMARY PASTORAL PRACTICES

Pastoral practices exist in the Korean church in different forms. However, most Korean churches follow a pattern that includes three situations: pastoral home visits, funeral visits, and hospital visits, and each of these has a specific goal and/or nature.

Home Visits

Regardless of denominational differences, most Korean churches carry out a program of pastoral home visits every spring or fall. This annual event is very important for ministry. The visits are scheduled for all church members, not just those who need help. Pastors and members form teams to visit other members' homes during the day. They usually gather in the churchyard in the morning and pray for the success of their pastoral visits on that day. When they enter a member's home, they lead a short worship service, singing two or three hymns and reading from the Bible. One of the visiting team members prays for the worship and the family whom they are visiting. The minister provides a short sermon for the family. After the sermon, they sing one more hymn and end with a benediction. After the worship, they usually are served food. The minister or an elder or deacon organizes the order of visiting houses and decides in which house they will have tea or a meal. However, the hosts usually provide very good food, and etiquette dictates that the minister will bless the food and eat more than he or she normally would.

Pastors never go alone to visit church members' houses because the hosts of these visitations are usually women. The visit is not for the purpose of listening to people's stories or doing individual counseling. Instead, this visit is understood as a special worship service for each individual family and also as a chance to encourage people to increase their participation in the church.[3]

The symbolic meaning of the home visit is to bring the Holy Spirit into homes through worship. As each family receives a special service and a blessing, the people expect that God will bring good fortune to their family. Family members will often interpret the sermon as the vehicle for explaining God's special will for their family.[4] Therefore, although a pastoral aim of this visit may be to become aware of and understand people's life situations, both lay people and pastors understand the true purpose of the visit as an annual ritual to bring good fortune to that particular family. Because this is an annual occurrence, many people expecting a home visit clean their houses and prepare their best food, even food they cannot normally afford. During the home visit some women give money to their ministers as a sign of respect. The people generally expect pastors to exercise spiritual power to terminate bad fortune and ban evil spirits. In this respect the role of the minister is highly similar to that of the shaman.

Unfortunately, because most pastors are men and most people who are visited are women, the home visit is often used to exercise the power of the church, generally male and hierarchal, over individual women. However, given a different approach, this could be a good opportunity for pastors to communicate with women. After worship, as food or tea is being shared, pastors could listen to women talk about family concerns, problems with children and teenagers, difficulties in caring for the elderly, tensions with spouses. Even though women would not be likely to speak directly about their problems, they could reveal some of their feelings and struggles to their pastors through such a visit. Pastors could develop a better understanding of community life in the parish and develop bonds of respect and even friendship with church members.

Funeral Visits

In Korea's multi-religious context, when a family member dies, the funeral service usually follows the religious beliefs of the eldest son. However, often times, when many family members follow different faith traditions, the family attempts to organize the funeral using two or three different religious rituals. It is not surprising that many conflicts and tensions surface.

In the case of Christian funerals, pastors are usually in charge of organizing the service. When pastors hear of the death of a church member, they quickly visit the church member's home or the hospital to console the family and pray for them. In this first visit pastors try to learn how the person died and how the death has affected the family members. During a second visit the pastor organizes the time, place, and the worship service for the funeral. The service usually takes place two or three days later. The funeral service has four separate parts: a worship service at the deathbed, a worship service for placing the body in a coffin, the funeral itself, and a worship service for lowering the coffin into the grave.[5] Each of these services is similar except the funeral service includes a sermon. The order generally includes an opening hymn, prayer, a hymn, the Bible reading, the sermon (only at the funeral service), prayer, the Apostle's Creed, and the benediction, although this varies somewhat by denomination. Unlike Western funerals there is no viewing of the body or eulogy during the funeral service. The pastor tries to bring messages of God's mercy and the Spirit's consolation to the family.

However, because the services are led by the minister, with little or no family participation, they result in one-way communication. The pastor speaks, and the others listen. In such a hierarchal system as the Korean church, worship services, even funerals, can be used to demonstrate the pastor's authority and power over others. It is easily understood that only the minister has access to heavenly authority; only the minister can be the channel of salvation. The nature of Korean culture poses a second problem. It is often difficult for pastors to share the family's pain over the loss of a loved one, not because of any shortcoming on their part, but because of the cultural requirements of modesty. Even though the family members may be overwhelmed by their loss, the cultural need to maintain modest behavior demands that they not cry hard or talk too much. Feelings and emotions are supposed to remain hidden.

For women, the death of a male family member can be particularly devastating. When women lose their husbands or sons, they also lose their social status. Because women are often dependent on their male family members financially, psychologically, and even spiritually, such a death may force women to face cruel realities and spiritual depression. And women can be disregarded not only by society but also by the church. While women are undergoing social derision or even religiously veiled scorn, Korean pastors may remain quite unaware of these social and cultural dimensions and thus be unable to offer comfort or support. Once again, the patriarchal structure is reinforced.

The funeral service is understood as one of the most important rituals in Korea, and this is an appropriate time for pastors to share people's pain. It could be a time to listen to church members' sorrow and to console them. During the period after a funeral a special home visit would help members share the struggle together. If women's needs were considered with greater care and sensitivity, women could find healing in difficult circumstances and draw closer to the church.

Hospital Visits

Although Korean styles of pastoral practices rarely provide an opportunity for pastors to listen to women's stories, the hospital visit does provide one possible avenue. Even though these visits also include a short worship service, pastors and church members spend some time talking about real pain. Church members often try to find the meaning of illness in their lives and try to explain their frustrations and depression. Pastors listen and seek to understand their struggles. Chaplains are not readily available in Korean hospitals, so pastoral visits to members in the hospital are a very important opportunity for pastoral care and counseling.

Fortunately, such visits are strongly encouraged; unfortunately, free communication between pastors and church members is not usually encouraged. In some cases, instead of listening to people's pain, pastors are taught to have a worship service in the hospital and then to go to the "prayer house" to pray for their parishioners' health. The power of prayer receives much more emphasis than listening to the sick. In other cases, pastors regard illness as a sign of sins and faults. It is not surprising, then, that some hospital visits are turned into times for confessing sins and asking for forgiveness. Because shamanistic, Buddhist, and Christian faiths are all entangled in Korean culture, some Christians believe that this is true, that illness is a curse of fate or a punishment from God, and they try to identify their faults and confess their "wrongs" in front of God as well as the pastor. The hospital, sadly, lends itself to such behavior. Because many Christians are asked to think about the meaning of their sickness and convinced to confess their sins, their pain and its cause remain secondary.

For women, sickness takes on another dimension. Women's feelings of guilt go well beyond their own sickness, because women have traditionally taken on all responsibility for sickness, regardless of who is sick. Hospitals thus can reinforce women's stereotypical roles. Women often believe that it is because of their lack of care that other family members suffer. This is particularly true of serious illnesses and can lead to severe spiritual and psychological hurt and long-lasting guilt.

Because of the importance of hospital visits, pastors could use these times as opportunities for intentional communication with people. Instead of simply delivering a sermon or seeking reflection and confession, pastors could actively listen to and share worries and concerns in a reciprocal way. In the case of women, pastors would have to be aware of the spiritual and psychological burdens that women carry. A program of pastoral care and counseling that seriously considers women's social and cultural contexts and multi-religious influences could be healing for women and for society.

PASTORAL PRACTICES TO EMPOWER WOMEN

Given the nature of pastoral practices in Korean Christian churches, I would like to consider three preconditions highly significant for designing a method of pastoral practices effective for women in Korea's present context. First, Korean women's experiences must be understood in light of a history of patriarchalism and colonialism, which have both wounded women's self-understanding. These wounds have been and still are deep; they weaken self-concepts and cause women to develop a false sense of who they are. This, in turn, deprives them of vitality, self-esteem, and the capacity for genuine intimacy. As has been pointed out by theologians and scholars such as Albert Memmi, R. S. Sugirtharajah, Musa W. Dube, Andrew Sung Park, and Kwok Pui-lan, this is true of most colonized people. Patriarchal and hierarchal experiences can destroy women's capacities to enter into relationships of equality, and colonial experience can demolish their ability to seek freedom and justice. Such experience goes beyond an individual problem or a local issue to become a collective experience that is a genuine wound for all of society, women and men.

Second, the experience of Korean women must be understood within a religiously plural context that balances individual backgrounds, family traditions, and social relationships. The traditions of Shamanism, Buddhism, and Confucianism all color the religious mind-sets of Korean women and, while undoubtedly transformed, still influence Christian beliefs and practices. They should be viewed as enriching religious being. Generally, these experiences are not recognized within Christian churches. If they are, these multi-religious experiences are treated not as spiritual traditions that can contribute to an abundant life and strengthen faith but as pagan syncretism. Traditions of other religious faiths should be critically examined, carefully evaluated, and respected. They are part of who we are as Korean women.

Third, poverty must be considered not as an individual problem but rather as a communal circumstance. Throughout Korea's colonial history, many women led their households as single mothers and many were sacrificing daughters or daughters-in-law. Women, children, and poverty are tightly interwoven. Whenever there are wars and civil conflicts, women and children suffer more than others. Burdens of poverty never leave them. This issue is frequently forgotten or trivialized as an individual's own particular problem.[6] However, poverty in Korea has been a national phenomenon. As a small, powerless country, Korea still spends more money for national defense than it does to help poor people and women. Even though the economy of Korea has been developing rapidly during the last two or three decades, many single mothers, sacrificing daughters, and children have struggled to live in situations of extreme poverty with few possibilities of escape.

Building on these three givens—a patriarchal society, a multi-religious society, and a society impoverished by colonialism—three specific approaches can be explored that will establish programs of valid and effective pastoral practices with the power to counsel and transform Christian women in Korea:

- Give specific attention to the importance of listening to women's voices;
- Give importance to recognizing the special roles of women;
- Give importance to introduce new ways of understanding God that are more congruent with the sensibilities of Korean women.

Recognizing these three significant factors will aid in designing programs that will help women to start respecting themselves as whole persons and to develop a more mature faith. The goal should be to help women see themselves as having choices and to allow them to experience empowerment. Empowered Christian women, in turn, will know how to reach out to others and to the community in new ways. In the end, this will encourage and promote both individual and communal spiritual transformation and allow for continuous growth.

THE IMPORTANCE OF LISTENING TO WOMEN'S VOICES

According to many women scholars and theologians, listening to women's voices is the first step needed for healing. In the Korean church context, however, several barriers make this process difficult. The primary barrier is rooted in a common cultural assumption about women: Korean women are expected not to talk until asked to do so by others. They are taught to be silent and not to express anything about themselves or their opinions on issues. In church they are expected to listen to the sermons, opinions, and teachings of pastors or church authorities but not to comment on these matters or raise questions in public. In general, they are taught never to ask questions; they are instead trained to listen to others, especially men.

In addition to attending worship regularly, women's roles in Korean churches are restricted to providing church meals and babysitting services for small children during Sunday worship. Men are expected to serve as ministers, elders, and to hold other positions of leadership. Men lead worship and conduct church programs. Most Christian women are expected to prepare for and assist in any church event, yet they are not allowed to lead worship or to make decisions about finances or programs. Maintenance of the present system, strongly patriarchal in nature, grants women few choices and denies them their voices. Because this has long been the practice, their voices are often forgotten, and their eyes have been closed. When they want to talk about their feelings and their lives, they do not know where to begin, what is allowed and what is off-limits, how to express themselves, or what to feel. These patriarchal and hierarchal ideologies over time have become part of who they are. Therefore, in order to help women, pastoral-care programs must consider the ways in which women express themselves and attempt to engage in two-way or reciprocal conversation.

The Use of Silence

To hear women's voices it is necessary to be aware of the various ways in which Korean women show their feelings and express themselves. One of the most significant ways is to recognize women's voices in silence. In their roles as daughters, mothers, wives, workers, and simply women, they are supposed to have no voice. Silence, a noble virtue, represents women's obedient nature. However, it has been shown by many feminist psychologists and anthropologists that women's silence is not natural but is the result of their reality, which is often characterized by domination by others.[7] Women, on the other hand, have often used silence as a way to express themselves. Through silence, they can sympathize with others and even express their own anger. Silence can be the silence of fear under oppression, but it can also be the silence of rebellion against oppression that demonstrates will and strength. Silence is one of women's voices, but it is a voice that needs to be understood for what it is.

The Use of Art Forms

Women's voices are heard not only in speaking and in silence but also in their singing, dancing, and poetry. In some Christian churches Korean women are allowed and even encouraged to sing and dance in the form of "praise and worship." Christian women can express their passion for life and their belief in God through this channel. Traditionally, singing, dancing, and poetry have been used satirically by the ordinary people to describe their reality, laugh at its oppressive nature, and demonstrate their strength and wisdom to overcome that reality.[8] Singing and dancing are used to express what they cannot express with words. Women use these art forms at times to reveal their thinking, their lives, and their pain and brokenness. They allow women to be who they are and can free them from the heavy burdens of their social roles and duties. In churches women can use singing, dancing, and poetry to speak their faith to God and to transform silence into voice.

The Need to Build Trust

Persons responsible for pastoral practices must learn how to build trust. In many cases, especially those that involve intimate violence, women cannot or will not begin with the truth. Parts of their stories will remain hidden, sealed by lies that protect them as victims. In extreme situations they do not trust anyone, even God. If women's lives are associated with an abusive and authoritative father, husband, grandfather, or other male figure, their stories may be strange or disturbing.[9] Nonetheless, in their times of need women need to feel absolute trust. They want to be believed and acknowledged no matter what horrors lie hidden in their stories.

Absolute trust is the first step to healing women's wounds. In order to create and maintain this trust women should come together as a group. Healing does not take place in one encounter but requires ongoing care and empowerment. While a woman by herself is most unlikely to confide in a male or even in another woman, in a group women may have the courage to start this process and maintain it over time. As they continuously work together to create an environment in which they can listen to and understand each other, they can transform their silence into audible communication. Even though some women may have a hard time learning to trust even their women friends, most would still want to form a sisterhood or friendship with other women from their culture who share their spiritual needs. Despite the patriarchal ideologies within Korean Christian churches, women have struggled to share their lives and faith in order to learn to trust and to be trusted. In doing so, they can rediscover their own traditions and how to nurture relationships. Bringing women together in equal and horizontal relationships where they can learn to trust one another is key to women's transformation. Such relationships hold out the hope that women will learn to trust their own voices and imagine a new relationship with God, one quite different from the patriarchal ideology that has previously dominated their lives.

THE NATURE OF WOMEN'S GROUPS IN KOREAN CHURCHES

In Korea, forming a women's group within the church is not an easy or straightforward task. The expectation is that women's groups are formed to cook and clean and otherwise support church events. Thus women's groups meet the needs of the church and not the women. Women are not expected to pursue their own interests or their spiritual growth; male ministers are there to do this. Women are not expected to have relationships of their own, because they are supposed to provide continuous care for their families. Even today, many married women who are full-time housewives or even career women rarely go outside the home for several reasons until their children get married. Because they bear the responsibility for raising children, providing financial support for the family, and caring for aging parents-in-law and other family members, women do not have time to think about themselves or to build relationships with other women. If they do go out with their friends, it generally causes trouble within the family because "their families expect to be served by their women every second of the day."[10] Isolation makes them even more vulnerable and afraid of having relationships with other people.

In addition, forming a women's group requires the capacity to trust other women. Patriarchal ideologies have taught that women in general cannot be trusted because they are weak and wicked. As noted in an earlier chapter, women often have a hard time trusting their mothers, daughters, daughters-in-law, and mothers-in-law. In this complicated context they have learned to relate to one another out of duty and obligation rather than in trust. In the eyes of traditional society, women's groups are useless. Given this context, forming women's groups of trust can be a difficult undertaking.

However, Korea's indigenous agricultural traditions have provided a positive example for building women's groups. In the past, when most people lived in agrarian societies, women lived in close proximity and shared their lives with other women. Even though relationships were still deeply based within the family, other women who lived in the same town shared the same experiences. As women exchanged and shared labor on the farm and in the field, they became like family.

In the same sense, people in the same church can resemble a family. Even in the city a church can provide similar relationships to those of a rural society, although this will require effort on the part of both the church's leadership and membership. In fact, because more than 70 percent of Korea's church members are women, women's groups of fellowship and relationships should be an essential part of the church's reality.

As psychologist Carol Gilligan and her colleagues have pointed out, "making connections" with others can be recognized as sharing one's total self and strength. A women's group can be in itself a primary source of strength in a woman's life. Women as a group can support one another by forming a communication network to deepen their health and wholeness throughout their lifetime. Women's growing experiences of trust can make it possible for them to raise questions about God, the world, society's rules and traditions, and themselves. Women as a group can relearn to trust their own voices and those of others, enhancing their true selves and challenging their world. Women as a group can practice equal power in relationships and find freedom together. They can learn about new possibilities and interpretations of their lives that can lead to healing and transformation.

THE IMPORTANCE OF RECOGNIZING
WOMEN'S ROLES

As daughters, wives, mothers, sisters, and daughters-in-law, Korean women have existed for many generations without speaking aloud of the burden imposed by their roles. As daughters, they are outsiders who endlessly seek to be insiders. They bear enormous guilt and often regret their lives as daughters. As wives, women must devote their whole lives to their husbands with absolute loyalty and fidelity, even when that fidelity and loyalty are not returned. They must always appear subordinate and yield to their husbands for the sake of family harmony. They must support whatever their husbands do with complete trust. The role of wife directly and always connects to their roles as mothers and daughters-in-law. The three roles of daughter, wife, and mother are defined and expected by all of Korean society and culture. Acceptance in Korean society begins when a woman becomes a wife. However, being a wife or being a loyal daughter-in-law is not sufficient; they are simply steps toward motherhood. According to Korea's traditional values, all women are destined to be mothers. Motherhood, which is believed to be a natural desire given by God, is the final goal for their lives. Women are born not as individuals but as wives-to-be and mothers-to-be.

Because of such unambiguous role definitions from birth, women tend to perceive any threat to or disruption of these family relationships not only as a potential loss of a relationship but as something closer to a loss of self. The greatest fear of many women is that any challenge to these traditional roles will provoke trouble in their relationships within their families as well as in society.[11] It is not surprising, therefore, that even if women realize the burden of their roles and responsibilities, they are unlikely to challenge them.

Many pastoral practices in Korean Christian churches (and also in some churches in the West) emphasize that solving women's problems is not a process of listening to women's suffering and painful experiences, but rather a task of helping women return to their "natural" roles and find happiness in fulfilling those roles. This approach is more suggestive of indoctrination than it is of care. Mary Ballou and Nancy W. Gabalac call this process "harmful adaptation."[12] They suggest that women are born into a sexist culture that exists everywhere. Such a culture leads women to adopt patriarchal values as a legitimate narrative. This process starts at birth and continues throughout their lives. Without a form of significant intervention, it can be a ceaseless process. Ballou and Gabalac describe this as a five-stage process of humiliation, inculcation, retribution, conversion, and conscription.

The first stage, humiliation, the experience of being defeated and devalued, reduces one's sense of worth and negates self-respect. Humiliation experiences are a part of Korean women's daily lives.[13] For example, if a woman shows an assertive side or great intelligence, she is teased that she will not have any men in her life. Her character and intelligence are both devalued.[14] The second stage is inculcation. Women are supposed to internalize the positive valuing of "male aggression, the sex-linked dichotomization of human traits and abilities, and the inferior status and dependent roles of women."[15] In stage three, retribution, male violence is legitimated as a proper punishment for women who betray cultural norms. Its mechanisms are complicated and intricate. Even if a woman develops strength from her internal resources, her strength may be treated as madness and she may have to pay a high cost. Her struggle may be overwhelming, and she may give up altogether, accepting once again the patriarchal teachings, along with gender discrimination, pervasive devaluation, scapegoating, and physical punishment.[16] And such a reaction is characteristic of the fourth and fifth stages, conversion and conscription, which combine to conclude the process. These teachings pass from mother to daughter, from generation to generation. Over time, women adjust to their situations, even gaining some satisfaction from them, and then convince others to do the same. In this way a woman shows her loyalty to the hierarchal system and is able to cope without being overcome by acute depression.[17]

The theory of Ballou and Gabalac provides a helpful framework for understanding psychological struggle, although, given the definition of social roles in Korean society, the culturally specific ways in which Korean women move through the five-stage process are often more extreme.

Humiliation for Korean women begins even before birth. When it becomes known that unborn babies are female, some Korean women are still compelled to have abortions by their husbands' families and sometimes by their own choice. Some female children have to struggle to survive even inside the womb. This humiliation becomes more severe as they grow and are married.

Korean women usually have little recourse other than to accept the humiliation and to internalize cultural norms. Blame will be placed on them through parental favoritism toward sons, mothers-in-law's criticism of their cooking and the way they run the household, husbands' affairs, and children's failures at exams. And women continually receive double messages: they are to be aggressive as mothers and mothers-in-law, but obedient as women, wives, daughters, and daughters-in-law. By the time girls become mothers and mothers-in-law, the inculcation is already complete. Women are taught to accept inequality, humiliation, hostility, and domination as the natural order. They are taught to understand and endure male violence and harassment as a method of correcting their behavior.

The inculcation of Korean patriarchal values is usually accompanied by punishment. Retribution is a concept common to Buddhism and Shamanism. Even though their fate may be terrible or harsh, women accept that they must endure it to obtain salvation in the future; this is their karma. If they endure suffering with patience and obedience, they will be enlightened and move to a better stage in the next life. Therefore, it is a woman's responsibility to repress her anxiety and anger and to think happy thoughts. If she can do this, she has reached the stage of conversion.

If a woman becomes the mother of a son, she will also be converted and will move on to the stage of conscription, teaching others respect for cultural norms. If a woman does not give birth to a son, she remains vulnerable. She may struggle with overwork and lack of support, feeling complete emptiness and resentment. Korean mothers-in-law, women who have married and given birth to sons, reach a stage of relative power and play a major role in conversion and conscription, passing down rules and traditions to the following generations.

These carefully defined roles can coexist through women's lifetimes. Women can be daughters, daughters-in-law, mothers, and mothers-in-law within families at the same time and each role demands different, and often conflicting, feelings and thoughts. Some women do try to change this vicious circle, seeing themselves through their own eyes rather than through the lens of rigid tradition. From the sacrifices of their mothers and grandmothers, the solidarity of their sisters, and friendships, many young women have gained the wisdom and power to challenge this patriarchal structure and to turn from these abusive relationships.

In the middle of their struggles some of these young women realize that it is important for them to recognize themselves and also important for society to recognize their devotions and sufferings. After all, it is their roles, whether harmful or not, that shape a large part of their identity. Individual and social recognition is not their ultimate goal, however. They seek their own happiness and joy either within or beyond these roles. They want to learn to fulfill their roles in ways that foster interdependence rather than to deny their various roles and responsibilities in order to gain complete independence. One skill needed is the ability to express feelings and experiences of resentment, humiliation, or anger rather than simply obeying in silence, and this must be done without breaking down existing relationships. Young women in Korea today still struggle between generating traditional expectations and creating new practices.

Building new models for women's roles and relationships does not necessarily require abandoning old models. This can be part of the process of establishing happy relationships with others *and* of defining women's own needs. Despite the Korean church's significant collusion with oppressive patriarchal, cultural, and social forces, women have lifted up their voices in hope, faith, and love. By providing appropriate pastoral practices, the church can nurture and support this transformation.

13

Reconstructing Women's Understandings of God

In the Korean Christian tradition it is hard to think of God in any terms other than Father. Even though Jesus' calling God Abba was a revolutionary transformation at the time, over centuries the essence of Jesus' action lost its meaning in male-dominated Christian history.[1] As God was limited to Father, it seemed almost impossible to think about God with other metaphors. God was locked into a hierarchal image. Rituals and religious worship treated God as a powerful and higher Holy Being. The Father was also a warrior, almighty, omnipresent, and omnipotent.[2] God became unapproachable and inaccessible, a Being without feeling who judged all. This was a patriarchal and colonial God who was not interested in hearing Korean women speak of their pain and *han*. Rather, this God became a God of whom women were most afraid. It is very important, therefore, to challenge women to think of God using a different language. After all, the language and imagery for God can partially describe and determine the cultural reality of a people. According to Christie Cozad Neuger:

> How God is named, imaged, and conceptualized signifi-
> cantly affects how we understand ourselves, how we under-
> stand our purpose, how we order our social and familial rela-
> tionships and how we structure our culture. If we believe,

for example, that there is a natural order or hierarchy of value that God has ordained and that God represents, then we create cultural structures that keep that order in place. If we believe that God is male, and thus, that the male is closer to the image of God than the female, then, we value males more highly than females and we claim that males are naturally created to do more "godlike" things than are females. It is not just that this image of God is destructive for women and the social ordering of women's place in the culture. The core critiques of idolatry and irrelevance proposed by many feminist theologians have more recently been joined by those of male theologians looking at the religious concerns of men. Images of God that combine authority, power, rationality, protectiveness of others, kingship, dependability, righteous anger, maleness and fatherhood have a formative and normative effect on dominant definitions of manhood and masculinity. [3]

Reconstructing the attributes of God is one of the most important steps in reconstructing women's understanding of themselves and their lives; such attributes can provide a mirror reflection of the women themselves. Names and perceptions of God that emphasize patriarchal power entrap women in the prisons of patriarchal traditions and hierarchal cultures. Such understandings of God charge women to bear the burdens of their social roles, and they reduce women's spiritual and psychological power. Even worse, patriarchal attributes of God can prevent women from seeing other possibilities. According to Laurel C. Schneider,

> They [monotheistic cultures] seem more often to associate their monotheistic beliefs with boundaries of exclusion and imperialism rather than with indications of cosmic unity. The one God is understood to be not only superior to all other concepts and experiences of divine experience, but "He" exclusively opposes all others by colonizing and absorbing them, or by outright denying them. [4]

Conceptualizing God in new ways will help women to realize how deeply they have been indoctrinated, traumatized, and damaged. At the same time, it will encourage women to develop their own strength, to heal their wounds, and to evaluate their lives on their own terms. Reconstructing the attributes of God is not just about "releasing their pain";[5] it is also about developing their inner strength so they can find new meaning for their lives.

When women reconstruct attributes for God, they not only discover who they are, but also they are free to imagine who they want to be. They examine themselves not with patriarchal eyes but with their own eyes. They learn to look at the total picture of their world, confronting and reconstructing destructive forces in politics, cultures, and religion.

NEGATIVE IMAGES OF GOD

Several negative attributes of God have posed obstacles for Korean women. The first negative image of God is that of the nemesis: women see the oppression within their lives as resulting from their sin, and God is the one who seeks retaliation against sinners. This image of God is common in the Korean and wider Asian context as well as in Western society. Both Buddhist and Christian views of humanity have taught that women are sinful creatures who deserve suffering and punishment.

The Korean church interprets suffering as the judgment of God. This belief also coincides with Korea's multi-religious traditions, which generally accept retribution as justice. People suffer as they deserve. Their suffering may go far beyond their present sin. A Buddhist view would explain women's suffering as the karma of their past lives. A Christian interpretation might maintain that women's suffering is due to the sin of Eve. The sin may be original or it may be inherited or transmitted from one life to another. Both traditions accept suffering as "balancing the scales of justice" or "setting right a past wrong." Women are thus forced to accept suffering as the consequence of the sin.

God then becomes an abuser or enemy. God reigns over all, is overpowering, frightening, or even interested in benefiting from a privileged position. Women are often terrified by this God of revenge and unpredictable anger, and they feel obliged to love and obey this God out of fear. They never feel themselves close to this God but rather try to please God so as not to suffer or be punished. God, possessing unlimited power and the immense authority of a ruling judge, is clearly at the top of the hierarchy. With God as the dictator of their lives, women become submissive, passive, and obedient, living their lives in trepidation and fear.

A second negative attribute of God that affects women's lives is when women think of God as an eschatological savior. This image comes from both shamanistic and Christian concepts of salvation: God will save them, not in the midst of their suffering but when their lives end. God can retain all power, and sufferers can extend their hope to their next life. This attitude compels women to endure their suffering without protest, and it leads women to cling to false hope rather than seek to change their present reality.

God as eschatological savior does not care about people's suffering in the here and now. Even though the people's suffering is real and their wounds are actual, their relationship with God yields nothing in the present. God demands women's blind faith, although this God is in heaven, a place people never reach during their lifetime. In this sense the kingdom of God is not the place where ultimate justice and love are fulfilled, but a place where one escapes the present reality.

A third negative attribute of God is found when women think of their lives as full of mystery and of God as the "Enigma."[6] Both life and God are mysteries. In a positive sense, such an understanding can allow women to celebrate the joy of life and the mercy of God. It also can elicit thoughts of abundant life or an exploration of the mysterious union between God and humanity. However, when this God is defined by oppressive forces, the meaning of mystery changes. Mystery then becomes a tool that legitimates women's suffering and pain. Instead of seeking transformation, they accept reality as mystery. Moreover, the God of mystery is not necessarily trustworthy. God can intend anything for any reason and cannot be counted on when Christians walk "through the valley of the shadow of death." God might be a woman's friend this time, but next time God might cause pain and sorrow.

These understandings of God are widely accepted because God's attributes of power and mystery seem to explain to some degree the meaning of people's suffering.[7] These also provide a plausible rationale for the reality women face. Women feel not God's presence but God's absence, and such explanations make sense of God's absence. Women can justify their reality without losing God.

While these perceptions can be employed to explain unjust suffering and excessive violence, they also can be used by oppressors to legitimate their positions of power. These attributes of God also cause great inner conflict and tension for women. While their inner voices and resources might cry out that such suffering is unjust and that they should resist it, such cultural perceptions of God's power encourage women to do just the opposite—to accept their suffering.

Because the price of rebellion is extremely high, women want to close their eyes and ears and accept a patriarchal, all-powerful God. They are more familiar with being sinners than with being free; they are more familiar with suffering than with enjoying life. They are used to their lives as victims. They want to replace this oppressive God with a God of their own design, but at the same time, they are too afraid.

THE VALUE OF POSITIVE IMAGES OF GOD

Constructing positive attributes for God to replace the traditional negative attributes can open up real possibilities for Korean women and give them direction as they face the conflict between their inner and outer voices. Even if they give up the fight and retreat to their old selves and the old patriarchal understandings of God, the attempt to overcome can in itself change women's natures. The process of reconstructing the attributes of God is also a process of reorganizing their inner world as well as redefining the patriarchal reality of the past and the present. They are not likely to return to exactly where they were before, at least not with the same intensity of belief. The process of reconstructing images of God also involves reconstructing images of self.

As has already been noted more than once, Korean women have often lived as helpless victims with the reality of colonial oppression, war, and poverty threatening their lives year in and year out. Living as victims exposes women to inevitable wounds, which are the consequence of both sociocultural history and painful individual experiences.[8] For psychologically or physically traumatized women, those wounds penetrate their very being. Women, repeatedly defined as powerless and worthless, have been taught to believe that they are victims who are powerless and hopeless, whatever they do and wherever they are.

Despite all odds, Korean women and other women living in patriarchal cultures do survive such trauma and overcome their victimhood. Even though their experience has been manipulated by political, social, historical, and colonial ideologies, something within keeps them alive. Even though their unconscious and conscious collective resistance is not often allowed to surface and their possibilities for different kinds of faith in God are quashed, it seems to be their seemingly illogical and incredible faith in God that sustains them. Their faith, *their own spiritual transforming power*, does not die. Even when women are overwhelmed by their reality and shrunken by physical and psychological violence, they seem to want to tell the truth of their experience. Even when faced with the abusive power of hierarchy, women can "whisper the truth."[9] Even their silent voices cry out as they continue to seek *their* God.

It is difficult to understand why or how women maintain their power to survive and try to continue to be more than the way reality defines them. Yet countless women throughout countless generations have done exactly this. It seems that their faith in the God of freedom does not fade, that the struggle to understand God can bring new meaning to life. It helps women understand their true selves, the beings equally created in God's image. It also helps them learn critically to balance or harmonize their inner selves with their outer reality.

Through this process women can find the God with whom they are most comfortable and with whom they can best communicate. Many will rediscover the God who touches their lives and makes them alive. When women communicate with this God, they undo their *han* and find meaning in their lives for themselves as well as for God and for others. When women reconstruct a compassionate God of justice rather than a God of judgment, they also reconstruct their "selves," their self-confidence, and their pride.

As women evaluate their lives in relation to God and begin to communicate with God, they also open their eyes to the meaning of their own lives. They can ask God about their calling in this world and their relationships with others. As they see a clear picture of who they are as God's children and friends, they gain strength from their inner resources to fight against forceful oppression and unjust violence. They have the strength to face up to making new choices that will create better lives for themselves and their families. While new images of God may not diminish or dismiss their actual pain or problems, they can see a new context for their lives as beings created by God, worthy of God's love, and deserving of God's understanding and compassion. These are Christian women of faith who are thus empowered to transform their relationships, their church, and their society. While the transformation is not easy, with God's grace and their faith it is possible.

CONCLUSION

When I was young, my grandmother always cried for me and said that I should have been a son. My journey of questioning who I am as a woman started even before I recognized myself as a woman. Many women defined by others are forced to accept who they should be and what they should do. Christian women in particular are often taught to deny themselves and to disdain their traditional cultures and religions. Their rich religious resources of faith are believed to be evil enemies of their Christian faith. They are taught that their painful colonial history is their shame and dishonor. They often live and die as women, daughters, mothers, and daughters-in-law without recognition or apologies. They suffer in silence. With countless sacrifices and endless love, they live for others.

At the same time, they live their lives as women, daughters, mothers, grandmothers, granddaughters, and daughters-in-law with honor and grace. They overcome their struggles by their incredible courage, and they live with amazing love. Their silence has cried out to God, and their prayers have sustained Korean society. From this living journey they try to rediscover how beautiful they really are.

Each day I still struggle to remember my face. And I find myself to be a beautiful woman that God has created and pronounced to be good. Healing one's self is not a one-time event or a miracle. As women, we struggle every day of our life to rediscover the astounding courage, power, and faith that lie within. As Korean women we are emerging from a painful but honorable past. Each day we seek a more enjoyable present. We believe that we can be part of a hopeful, imaginable, and joyous future. We trust that God is and will be with us during this journey, encouraging and sharing God's vision of what it means to live in this world in justice and harmony and love.

Notes

Introduction

1. Suh Nam Dong, "Toward a Theology of *Han*," in *Minjung Theology-People as the Subjects of History*, ed. The Commission on Theological Concerns of the Christian Conference of Asia (Maryknoll, NY: Orbis Books, 1981), 58.

2. Andrew Sung Park, *The Wounded Heart of God: The Asian Concept of Han and the Christian Doctrine of Sin* (Nashville, TN: Abingdon Press, 1992), 15–19.

3. See Lee Jae Hoon, *The Exploration of the Inner Wounds—Han* (Atlanta: Scholars Press, 1994).

4. Chung Hyun Kyung, "Han-pu-ri: Doing Theology from Korean Women's Perspective," in *Frontiers in Asian Christian Theology: Emerging Trends*, ed. R. S. Sugirtharajah (Maryknoll, NY: Orbis Books, 1994), 52–61.

Part I: Korean Women's Experiences of God

1. The Tradition of Shamanism

1. Kim In Hoe, "Korean Shamanism: A Bibliographical Introduction," trans. Young-sik Yoo, in *Shamanism: The Spirit World of Korea*, ed. Chaishin Yu and Richard W. Guisso (Seoul: Asian Humanities Press, 1988), 12.

2. Kim Tae Gon, *The Study on Korean Shamanism* (Seoul: Jipmundang, 1981), 287.

3. Because of its area, population, and distance from the mainland, this island has preserved the old characteristics intact more than any other part of Korea. Now, even though it has been modernized as a tourist site, one finds that the old cultural types are still preserved. See Chang Chu Kun, "An Introduction to Korean Shamanism," in Chai-shin Yu and Guisso, *Shamanism*, 36.

4. Choi So Young, "Female Creators, Grandmother Gods of Korea, and Their Distorted Story," in *The Feminist Theological Perspective of Female God*

in Korean Indigenous Religions, ed. The Korean Feminist Researchers of Female God (Seoul: Korean Feminist Press, 1992), 14–22.

5. Ibid., 21–22.

6. Ibid.

7. Chang Chu Kun, "An Introduction to Korean Shamanism," in Chai-shin Yu and Guisso, *Shamanism*, 43.

8. Especially, the Yodured-dang spirit that is originally from Chollado in the southwestern part of the mainland.

9. Chang Chu Kun, "An Introduction to Korean Shamanism," 44.

10. Lee Kwang Kyu, "Family and Religion in Traditional and Contemporary Korea," in *Religion and the Family in East Asia*, ed. George A. Devos and Takao Sofue (Berkeley and Los Angeles: Univ. of California Press, 1984), 190–91.

11. Chang Chu Kun, "An Introduction to Korean Shamanism," 40–41.

12. Hahm Pyoung Choon, "Shamanism and the Korean World-View, Family Life-Cycle, Society and Social Life," in Chai-shin Yu and Guisso, *Shamanism*, 60–97.

13. Ibid., 88–97.

14. Chung Hyun Kyung, "Han-Pu-Ri: Doing Theology from Korean Women's Perspective," in *Frontiers in Asian Christian Theology: Emerging Trends*, ed. R. S. Sugirtharajah (Maryknoll, NY: Orbis Books, 1994), 54–55.

15. Chung Hyun Kyung, *Struggle to Be the Sun Again: Introducing Asian Women's Theology* (Maryknoll, NY: Orbis Books, 1990); Suh Nam Dong, "Historical References for a Theology of Minjung," in *Minjung Theology-People as the Subjects of History*, ed. The Commission on Theological Concerns of the Christian Conference of Asia (Maryknoll, NY: Orbis Books, 1981); Hyun Young Hak, "A Theological Look at the Mask Dance in Korea," in *Minjung Theology—People as the Subjects of History*.

16. See Kim Youngsook Harvey, *Six Korean Women: The Socialization of Shamans* (St. Paul, MN: West Publishing Co., 1979); Laurel M. Kendall, *Restless Spirits: Shaman and Housewife in Korean Ritual Life* (New York: Columbia Univ., 1979); Kim Tae Gon, "Regional Characteristics of Shamanism in Korea," in Chai-shin Yu and Guisso, *Shamanism*.

17. Kim Youngsook Harvey, "Possession Sickness and Women Shamans in Korea," in *Unspoken Worlds: Women's Religious Lives in Non-Western Cultures*, ed. N. Falk and R. Gross (New York: Harper & Row, 1980), 41–52.

18. Korean people romanize their names in many different ways, with no set standard way. For the convenience of Western readers, I am using one consistent form, for example, Choi Hee An, instead of Hee An Choi, Choi Hee-An, or Heean Choi.

19. Kim In Hoe, "Korean Shamanism—A Bibliographical Introduction," in Chai-shin Yu and Guisso, *Shamanism*, 13.

20. *Samguk Yusa* dates from the Three Kingdoms. Written by the monk Iryon (1206–89), it begins Korean history with Tangun. It is a book containing folk legends to be retold in a Buddhist manner. It empowers the people of Koryo (the kingdom that succeeded Unified Silla) to sustain their identity as a distinct race, and it gives force to the concept of their descent from a common ancestor. It shows the deep respect the authors felt for the traditions and legacy of their past history. See Carter J. Eckert et al., *Korea Old and New: A History* (Cambridge: Ilchokak Publishers, 1990), 103.

21. This myth has several different versions. This is my own translation of one version. See James Riordan, *Korean Folk-Talks: Oxford Myths and Legends* (Oxford: Oxford Univ. Press, 1994), 1–3; Moon Seung Sook, "Begetting the Nation: The Androcentric Discourse of National History and Tradition in South Korea," in *Dangerous Women: Gender & Korean Nationalism*, ed. Elaine H. Kim and Choi Chung Moo (New York: Routledge, 1998), 40–41.

22. Lee Ki Baik, *A New History of Korea* (Seoul: Ijjogak, 1989), 9.

23. Even though Korea was an official Japanese colony from 1910 to 1945, Korea had lived under the strong imperial power of China from the beginning of Korean history until the Japanese colonial period. The relationship between Korea and China was a king/subject or big brother/little brother relationship. After World War II, Korea has lived under Western, especially American, post-colonial influences. These Korean colonial experiences have had and still have a great impact on the Korean people's physical reality and their psychological and spiritual mind-sets. I will show how these unconscious and conscious influences have damaged women's lives through an analysis of their understandings of God.

24. Moon Seung Sook, "Begetting the Nation: The Androcentric Discourse of National History and Tradition in South Korea," in Elaine H. Kim and Choi Chung Moo, *Dangerous Women*, 40–42.

25. Ibid., 41.

2. The Tradition of Buddhism

1. Kim Tong Hwa, " The Buddhist Thought of Koguryo," in *Introduction of Buddhism to Korea: New Cultural Patterns*, ed. Lewis R. Lancaster and Yu C. S. (Berkeley: Asian Humanities Press, 1989), 79-108.

2. *Samguk sagi*, vol. 18. *Samguk sagi* is the history of the Three Kingdoms. This book, which is Korea's earliest remaining historical work, lists several titles such as *Haedong kogi*, *Samhan kogi*, *Kogi*, and *Tangun ki*, which were clearly national histories. It reflects "the common desire of the rulers of the Three Kingdoms to display the sovereign dignity of their centralized aristocratic states to the contemporary world and to posterity." See

Kim In Hoe, "Korean Shamanism: A Bibliographical Introduction," trans. Young-sik Yoo, in *Shamanism: The Spirit World of Korea*, ed. Chai-shin Yu and Richard W. Guisso (Seoul: Asian Humanities Press, 1988), 15; and Carter J. Eckert et al., *Korea Old and New: A History* (Cambridge: Ilchokak Publishers, 1990), 37.

3. Ahn Kye Hyon, "A Short History of Ancient Korean Buddhism," in Lewis R. Lancaster and Yu C. S., *Introduction of Buddhism to Korea*, 1-3.

4. Ibid., 2.

5. Ibid., 3.

6. Hideo Inoue, "Reception of Buddhism in Korea," in *Introduction of Buddhism to Korea*, 44-45.

7. Ibid., 44-49.

8. Hahm Pyoung Choon, "Shamanism and the Korean World-View," in *Introduction of Buddhism to Korea*, 93.

9. Chang Chu Kun, "An Introduction to Korean Shamanism," in Chai-shin Yu and Guisso, *Shamanism*, 36.

10. Hideo Inoue, "The Reception of Buddhism in Korea and Its Impact on Indigenous Culture," in Lewis R. Lancaster and Yu C. S., *Introduction of Buddhism to Korea*, 36.

11. Ibid., 37.

12. See Hahm Pyoung Choon, "Shamanism and the Korean World-View," 60-97.

13. A bodhisattva is a Buddha-to-be. A bodhisattva is reborn in many different forms. In some cases the appearance is female. See Nancy Schuster Barnes, "Buddhism," in *Women in World Religions*, ed. Arvind Sharma (Albany: State Univ. of New York Press, 1987), 116-17.

14. *Samguk Yusa 5, T.* 2039.49.1011c12-22.

15. Hideo Inoue, "The Reception of Buddhism in Korea and Its Impact on Indigenous Culture," 62.

16. Ibid., 61.

17. More than 75 percent of Korea consists of mountains. Often Buddhist monasteries are located on mountains. Therefore, geographically, the overlapping of images between Buddha and mountain gods are an inevitable process in the Korean context. See Hideo Inoue, "The Reception of Buddhism in Korea and Its Impact on Indigenous Culture," 61-68.

18. Ahn Kye Hyon, "A Short History of Ancient Korean Buddhism," 7.

19. Hideo Inoue, "The Reception of Buddhism in Korea and Its Impact on Indigenous Culture," 33.

20. Lee Ki Baek, "Early Silla Buddhism and the Power of the Aristocracy," in Lewis R. Lancaster and Yu C. S., *Introduction of Buddhism to Korea*, 169.

21. Ibid., 170.

22. Nancy Schuster Barnes, "Buddhism," 115.

23. Ibid., 118.

24. Nancy Schuster Barnes, "Changing the Female Body: Wise Women and the Bodhisattva Career in some *Maharatnakutasutras*," *Journal of the International Association of Buddhist Studies* 4, no. 1: 24-69.

25. Nancy Schuster Barnes, "Buddhism," 120.

26. Ibid., 120-22.

27. Carter J. Eckert et al., *Korea Old and New*, 92.

28. See Kim Yong Chung, ed. and trans., *Women of Korea: A History from Ancient Times to 1945* (Seoul: Ewha Women's Univ. Press, 1977).

29. Lucinda Joy Peach, *Women and World Religions* (Upper Saddle River, NJ: Prentice Hall, 2002), 68.

3. The Confucian Tradition

1. See Cho Song Whan, "Ideological Change and Social Stratification during the Transitional Period from the Koryo to the Yi Dynasty," in *Sohoehak Yongu*, Sociological Studies 1 (Seoul: Deyoung-sa, 1984).

2. Kim Yong Chung, ed. and trans., *Women of Korea: A History from Ancient Times to 1945* (Seoul: Ewha Women's Univ. Press, 1977), 130.

3. See Song-whan Cho, "Ideological Change and Social Stratification during the Transitional Period from the Koryo to the Yi Dynasty," in *Sohoehak Yongu*.

4. John Duncan, "The Korean Adoption of Neo-Confucianism: The Social Context," in *Confucianism and the Family*, ed. Walter H. Slote and George A. De Vos (Albany: State Univ. of New York Press, 1998), 75.

5. Cho Hae Joang, "Male Dominance and Mother Power: The Two Sides of Confucian Patriarchy in Korea," in Walter H. Slote and George A. De Vos, *Confucianism and the Family*, 189-90.

6. Theresa Kelleher, "Confucianism," in *Women in World Religions*, ed. Arvind Sharma (Albany: State Univ. of New York Press, 1987), 138-39.

7. Lee Kwang Kyu, "Women's Status in the East Asian Patriarchal Family," in *The Structural Analysis of the Korean Family* (Seoul: Ilji-sa, 1975), chap. 10.

8. See Yo Sop Chong, "Women's Social Status during the Yi Dynasty," in *Journal of Asian Women* 12 (Seoul: Sukyong Women's Univ., 1973).

9. Richard W. Guisso, "Thunder over the Lake: The Five Classics and the Perception of Women in Early China," in *Women in China*, ed. Richard W. Guisso and Stanley Johannesen (New York: Philo Press, 1981), 59.

10. Mark Peterson, "Women without Sons: A Measure of Social Change in Yi Dynasty Korea," in *Korean Women*, ed. Laurel Kendall and Mark Peterson (New Haven, CT: East Rock Press, 1983), 37-43.

11. Lee Kwang Kyu, "Confucian Tradition in the Contemporary Korean Family," in Walter H. Slote and George A. De Vos, *Confucianism and the Family*, 253.

12. Ibid., 251-54.

4. The Entry of Christianity

1. Han Sung Hong, *The Stream of Korean Theological Thoughts*, vol. 1 (Seoul: Korean Presbyterian Univ. Press, 1996), 37-53.

2. Kim In Su, *Korean Christian Church History* (Seoul: Korean Presbyterian Press, 1991), 86-129.

3. Kim Kyung Jae, "Korean People's Sprituality and Christianity" in *Religion and Spirituality*, ed. Kang Nam University Committee (Seoul: Kang Nam Univ. Press/Handle Publishing House, 1998), 18.

4. Kim Young Ae, *Han: From Brokenness to Wholeness* (Ph.D. dissertation, School of Theology at Claremont, May 1991), 143.

5. Ibid., 144.

6. Kim Sang Il, "What Is Hanism," in *Hanism as Korean Mind*, ed. Sang Il Kim and Young Chan Ro (Los Angeles: Eastern Academy of Human Sciences, 1984), 10-19.

7. When I define *multi-religion* or *multi-religious*, I do not mean each different religion in its own area; rather, I define *multi-religion* as a complex "melted" layer of different religions within communal as well as individual identity. It includes multidimensional compounds of religious cultural ideologies and experiences in a person or a community. Any religion can be a multi-religion as long as it has multi-religious components. I maintain that Korean Christianity, as it has developed within Korea's multi-religious environment, is a multi-religion. In order to understand Korean Christianity as a multi-religion, other religious influences, the long history of colonial military culture, and the strong patriarchal family system should be critically analyzed along with Western and Eastern Christian history.

Part II: The Social Roles of Women in Korea

1. The names of women with whom I have spoken have been changed to protect their identities.

2. Seoul, the capital city of Korea, is a very urban area and the largest metropolitan area in Korea. Its official name is Seoultuekbyeolsi (Seoul Special District). One quarter of the entire Korean population lives in Seoul. It is the center of finance, politics, education, and culture in South Korea. Its citizens come from different areas and represent different cultures. See

Korean Scholar Committee, ed., *Dong-A's Encyclopedia* (Seoul: Dong-A Press, 1986), 16:608-14.

3. Kyoung Ki Do includes Seoul, and many parts of it became suburbs of Seoul. It is now a megalopolis. See *Dong-A's Encyclopedia*, 2:313-17.

4. The middle part of Korea, Chuwg Chung Do is divided into two sections, Chuwg Chung Nam Do (South Chuwg Chung Do) and Chuwg Chung Buk Do (North Chuwg Chung Do). Most of Chuwg Chung Do is rural, with agriculture the common occupation. In ancient times it had many scholars and educators who were called Chuwg Chung Do Yang Ban (Chuwg Chung Do bureaucrats). See *Dong-A's Encyclopedia*, 26:626-31.

5. Jun La Do is the southwest part of Korea. This province is divided into two sections, Jun La Nam Do and Jun La Buk Do. Most of Jun La Do is rural, with many people involved in agriculture and fishing. For a long time Jun La Do has been neglected in the areas of industrial development and economic support. See *Dong-A's Encyclopedia*, 24:395-413.

6. Kyoung Sang Do is the southeast part of Korea. This province is divided into two sections, Kyoung Sang Nam Do and Kyoung Sang Buk Do. In ancient times this was part of Silla, which united ancient Korea as one state for the first time. In modern times several dictators have come from this province. Agriculture used to be the main occupation in this area, but after the 1960s many cities in this area have been developed as industrial centers. See *Dong-A's Encyclopedia*, 2:380-88.

7. Sometimes women hold part-time jobs; however, while most women have a job before they marry, after they marry they devote themselves to being full-time mothers and wives.

8. Semi-arranged marriages are called *sun* in Korea. While arranged marriages are coordinated solely by both sets of parents with the future bride and groom not meeting, semi-arranged marriages can be arranged by parents, people who know them, or professional matchmakers. Unlike traditional arranged marriages, in the case of semi-arranged marriages, there are several factors to consider, such as province, economic class, and religion. It is common to look for a similar level of education, but it is often acceptable for women to have less education than men. Many people practice *sun;* however, after three or four meetings the couple will decide whether or not to marry. Most women choose to marry, and sometimes quickly, before they reach twenty-seven or twenty-eight, while in the case of men the age varies. Men can often remain unmarried until the age of forty.

5. Women—Always Daughters

1. This woman is forty years old and middle class, with a middle-school education. She was a Buddhist until she was twenty-four and is

now a Presbyterian. She is from Chun La Do and has lived in Seoul for fifteen years.

2. This interviewee is twenty-four years old and is lower-middle class. She is a junior in college and a Presbyterian who lives in Kyoung Sang Do.

3. This mother is thirty years old and is lower-middle class with a high-school education. She married when she was twenty-one. She lives in Seoul.

4. This wife is fifty-five years old and is middle class with a high-school education. She married when she was twenty-four. She is from Chun La Do and has lived in Seoul for thirty-eight years.

5. This woman is thirty-six years old, middle class, and has a graduate degree. She married when she was twenty-five and lives in Seoul.

6. Young Hwa is thirty-one years old, middle class, with a college education. Her parents are from Kyoung Sang Do. Born in Seoul, she lives there today. She married when she was twenty-six years old.

7. Sherry B. Ortner and Harriet Whitehead, "Introduction: Accounting for Sexual Meanings," in *Sexual Meanings—The Cultural Construction of Gender and Sexuality*, ed. Sherry B. Ortner and Harriet Whitehead (Cambridge: Cambridge Univ. Press, 1981), 1-13.

8. Nancy J. Chodorow, "Family Structure and Feminine Personality," in *Feminism and Psychoanalytic Theory* (New Haven, CT: Yale Univ. Press, 1989), 65.

9. Cho Hae Joang, "Male Dominance and Mother Power: The Two Sides of Confucian Patriarchy in Korea," in *Confucianism and the Family*, ed. Walter H. Slote and George A. De Vos (Albany: State Univ. of New York Press, 1998), 189-90.

10. This interviewee is a fourth-year college student from the lower-middle class.

11. This woman is thirty-two years old, from the lower-middle class, with a high-school education.

12. This interviewee is fifty-six years old, middle class, with a middle-school education.

6. Women as Mothers

1. Sun Ja is fifty-eight years old, lower-middle class with a middle-school education. A Presbyterian, she lives in Kyoung Sang Do.

2. Jin-a is forty-nine years old and middle class. She is a Methodist with a high-school education and lives in Kyoung Ki Do. She married when she was eighteen years old.

3. I discuss the relationship between daughters and mothers from the position of daughters in Chapter 5. In this chapter I examine the relationship from the position of mothers.

4. Carol Gilligan, "Exit-Voice Dilemmas in Adolescent Development," in *Mapping the Moral Domain*, ed. Carol Gilligan, Janie Victoria Ward, and Jill McLean Taylor (Cambridge: Harvard Univ. Press, 1988), 141-58.
5. This is from a conversation with a woman who has three daughters. She is fifty-two years old, Presbyterian, and middle class, with a high-school education. She is from Chung Cheong Do and has lived in Seoul for thirty-nine years.
6. See Judith Arcana, *Our Mothers' Daughters* (Berkeley, CA: Shameless Hussy Press, 1979).
7. See Nancy J. Chodorow and Susan Contratto, "The Fantasy of the Perfect Mother," in *Feminism and Psychoanalytic Theory* (New Haven, CT: Yale Univ. Press, 1989), 79-96; Lois Braverman, "Beyond the Myth of Motherhood," in *Women in Families: A Framework for Family Therapy*, ed. Monica McGoldrick, Carol M. Anderson, and Froma Walsh (New York: W. W. Norton, 1989), 230-31.

7. Women as Wives

1. Hee Suk is sixty-five years old, Presbyterian, from the lower class, with a middle-school education. From Chung Cheong Do, she has lived in Seoul for forty years.
2. "The 'good wife and wise mother' ideal was promulgated in Japan in the first decade of the twentieth century as a way to interpolate women into the service of the state during a period of intense industrialization, foreign expansionism, and militarism. It was adopted by Japanese colonial and native Korean political leadership and continues to shape social constructions of gender in contemporary South Korea." See Elaine H. Kim, "Men's Talk," in *Dangerous Women: Gender & Korean Nationalism*, ed. Elaine H. Kim and Choi Chung Moo (New York: Routledge, 1998), 67-118.
3. Ji Eun Hee, "Korean Industrialization and the Research of Korean Women's Work," in *Korean Women and Work*, ed. Korean Women's Organization (Seoul: Korean Women's Studies, 1990), 34.
4. Ibid., 33-37.
5. Cho Hae Joang, "Male Dominance and Mother Power: The Two Sides of Confucian Patriarchy in Korea," in Walter H. Slote and George A. De Vos, *Confucianism and the Family*, 199.
6. Gayle Rubin, "The Traffic in Women: Notes on the Political Economy of Sex," in *Toward an Anthropology of Women*, ed. Rayna R. Reiter (New York: Monthly Review Press, 1975), 183.
7. Cho Hae Joang, "Male Dominance and Mother Power," 197.
8. Hyun Jin is sixty-two years old, Presbyterian, from the lower-middle class, with a middle-school degree. She is from Kyoung Ki Do and has lived in Seoul for forty years.

8. Women and the Nation

1. Carter J. Eckert et al., *Korea Old and New: A History* (Cambridge: Ilchokak Publishers, 1990), 403.

2. Ji Eun Hee, "Korean Industrialization and the Research of Korean Women's Work," in *Korean Women and Work*, ed. Korean Women's Organization (Seoul: Korean Women's Studies, 1990), 33-37.

3. Park Hyun Ok, "Ideals of Liberation," in *Dangerous Women: Gender & Korean Nationalism*, ed. Elaine H. Kim and Choi Chung Moo (New York: Routledge, 1998), 229-48.

4. Carter J. Eckert et al., *Korea Old and New*, 409.

5. Moon Seungsook, "Overcome by Globalization: The Rise of a Women's Policy in South Korea," in *Korea's Globalization*, ed. Samuel S. Kim (New York: Cambridge Univ. Press, 2000), 127.

6. Ibid., 134.

7. Ibid.

8. See Lee Mi-Kyoung, "A Feminist Analysis of the State Policy on Birth," *Yosonghak Nonjip* 6 (1989): 49-76.

9. Family Health International, *Korea: A New Look at the Fertility Transition and Its Impact on Women* (Family Health International, 2005), available at http://www.fhi.org.

10. Moon Seungsook, "Overcome by Globalization," 135.

11. Paulette Thomas, "Success at a Huge Personal Cost," *Wall Street Journal*, July 26, 1995, B1.; Lee Su Kang and Kee Lam Park, "Women and Work," in *The Lectures of Women's Studies* (Seoul: Korean Women's Studies, 1991), 133-60.

12. Park You-me, "Working Women and the Ontology of the Collective Subject," in Elaine H. Kim and Choi Chung Moo, *Dangerous Women*, 203-21.

13. This working woman is thirty-five years old, middle class, with a high-school education. She lives in Kyoung Ki Do.

14. This wife and mother is forty years old, from the lower class with a community-college education. She was married when she was twenty-four years old.

15. See Kathryn Ward, ed., *Women Workers and Global Restructuring* (Ithaca, NY: Cornell Univ. Press, 1990).

16. Ji Eun Hee, "Korean Industrialization and the Research of Korean Women's Work," 33-37.

17. Choi Chungmoo, "Nationalism and Construction of Gender in Korea," in Elaine H. Kim and Choi Chung Moo, *Dangerous Women*, 9-32.

18. Moon Seungsook, "Begetting the Nation," in Elaine H. Kim and Choi Chung Moo, *Dangerous Women*, 46-49.

19. Kim Hyun Sook, "*Yanggongju* as an Allegory of the Nation: Images of Working-Class Women in Popular and Radical Texts," in Elaine H. Kim and Choi Chung Moo, *Dangerous Women*, 175-202.

20. George Hicks, *The Comfort Women: Japan's Brutal Regime of Enforced Prostitution in the Second World War* (New York: W. W. Norton, 1995), 11-12.

21. Testimony by Yi Sun Ok, "The Korean Comfort Women Who Were Coercively Dragged Away for the Military," trans. Keith Howard, in *The True Stories of the Korean Comfort Women*, ed. Keith Howard (New York: Continuum International, 1997), 176; Yang Hyunah, "Re-Membering the Korean Military Comfort Women," in Elaine H. Kim and Choi Chung Moo, *Dangerous Women*, 132.

22. Testimony by Tok-chin Kim, in Keith Howard, *The True Stories of the Korean Comfort Women*, 49; Yang Hyunah, "Re-Membering the Korean Military Comfort Women," 133.

23. Yang Hyunah, "Re-Membering the Korean Military Comfort Women," 131.

24. Testimony by Sunok Yi, "The Korean Comfort Women Who Were Coercively Dragged Away for the Military," 123; Yang Hyunah, "Re-Membering the Korean Military Comfort Women," 132.

25. Testimony by Tok-chin Kim, in Keith Howard, *The True Stories of the Korean Comfort Women*, 49; Yang Hyunah, "Re-Membering the Korean Military Comfort Women," 133.

26. Katharine H. S. Moon, "Prostitute Bodies and Gendered States in U.S.–Korea Relations," in Elaine H. Kim and Choi Chung Moo, *Dangerous Women*, 143-47.

27. See Rita Nakashima Brock and Susan Brooks Thistlethwaite, *Casting Stones: Prostitution and Liberation in Asia and the United States* (Minneapolis, MN: Fortress Press, 1996), 155-204.

28. Katharine H. S. Moon, "Prostitute Bodies and Gendered States in U.S.–Korea Relations," 166-68.

29. I believe that prostitution in any country is not a simple choice of individual freedom. It is also deeply connected to capitalism, militarism, and sociopolitical power in human history.

30. Suk Young is thirty-six years old, Presbyterian, from the middle class, with a middle-school drop-out background. She is from Kyoung Sang Do and has lived in Seoul seven years. She married when she was thirty-one years old. She used to be an atheist, but she converted to Christianity when she was twenty-nine.

Part III: The Transformation of *Han*

9. God as Family

1. Karl Barth, *The Epistle to the Romans*, trans. E. Hoskyns (Oxford: Oxford Press, 1933), 35-41.

2. Korean Protestant churches try to establish identities that clearly differentiate them from the Roman Catholic Church. Because of this tendency, Protestant theologians such as Barth, Moltmann, and Pannenberg have been chosen for study by many Korean theologians. Many seminaries offer courses on these theologians in their curricula.

3. Wolfhart Pannenberg, *An Introduction to Systematic Theology* (Edinburgh: Oxford Univ. Press, 1991), 340; see also Pannenberg, "The Kingdom of God and the Church," in *Theology and the Kingdom of God*, ed. R. J. Neuhaus (Philadelphia: Fortress Press, 1977).

4. Nancy Jay, *Throughout Your Generations Forever: Sacrifice, Religion, and Paternity* (Chicago: Univ. of Chicago Press, 1992), xxiii.

5. Rosemary Radford Ruether, *Sexism and God-Talk: Toward A Feminist Theology* (Boston: Beacon Press, 1983), 61-67.

6. This woman is fifty-nine years old, from the middle class, with a middle-school education. She used to be a Buddhist but is now a pentecostal Presbyterian.

7. This interviewee is fifty-five years old, Presbyterian, and middle class, with a college education.

8. This woman is forty-five years old, Methodist, and middle class, with a high-school education.

9. This interviewee is thirty-two years old, Presbyterian, and middle class, with a graduate degree.

10. Carol Gilligan, "Exit-Voice Dilemmas in Adolescent Development," in *Mapping the Moral Domain*, ed. Carol Gilligan, Janie Victoria Ward, and Jill McLean Taylor (Cambridge: Harvard Univ. Press, 1988), 141-58.

11. Ibid., 84-86.

12. Choi Man Ja, "Feminine Images of God in Korean Traditional Religion," in *Frontiers in Asian Christian Theology: Emerging Trends*, ed. R. S. Sugirtharajah (Maryknoll, NY: Orbis Books, 1994), 84.

13. Ibid., 84-86.

14. Kang Chung Suk, "The Historical Understanding of Korean Women's Experience," in *Korean Women's Experience*, ed. Korean Association of Women Theologians (Seoul: Korean Christianity Press, 1994), 85-112.

15. Lee Young Suk, "The Social Understanding of Korean Women's Experience," in *Korean Women's Experience*, 150-53.

10. God as Liberator in Korea

1. Kwok Pui-Lan, "Discovering the Bible in the Non-Biblical World," *Semeia* 47, ed. Katie Geneva Cannon and Elisabeth Schüssler Fiorenza (Atlanta: Scholars Press, 1989), 27.

2. Kim In Su, *Korean Christian History* (Seoul: Korean Presbyterian Press, 1991), 36-50.

3. Kim Yong-bock, "Korean Christianity as a Messianic Movement," in *Minjung Theology: People as the Subjects of History*, ed. The Commission on Theological Concerns of the Christian Conference of Asia (Maryknoll, NY: Orbis Books, 1981), 107.

4. See Ahn Byung Mu, *Liberator Jesus* (Seoul: Modern Thoughts, 1975).

5. Choi Man Ja, "Feminist Christology," in *Consultation on Asian Women's Theology* (Seoul: Women Theology Press, 1987), 3.

6. Musa W. Dube, "Savior of the World But Not of This World: Postcolonial Reading of Spatial Construction in John," in *The Postcolonial Bible*, ed. R. S. Sugirtharajab (Sheffield: Sheffield Academic Press, 1998), 118-35.

7. Chung Hyun Kyung, *Struggle to Be the Sun Again: Introducing Asian Women's Theology* (Maryknoll, NY: Orbis Books, 1994), 35.

8. Musa W. Dube, "Toward a Postcolonial Feminist Interpretation of the Bible," in *Reading the Bible as Women: Perspectives from Africa, Asia, and Latin America*, ed. Phyllis A. Bird, *Semeia* 78 (Atlanta: Scholars Press, 1997), 11-26.

9. Yang Hyun Hae, "Women and Church in Korean Church History," in *Church and Women's Theology* (Seoul: Korean Christian Press, 1997), 140-41.

10. Ibid.

11. Lee Uoo Jung, *Korean Christian Women: 100 Years' Footsteps* (Seoul: MinJungSa, 1985), 52.

12. Yang Hyun Hae, "Women and Church in Korean Christian History," 163.

13. Kim Yun Ok, "The Feminist Understanding of Korean Women's Experience in the Church," in *Korean Women's Experience*, ed. Korean Association of Women Theologians (Seoul: Korean Christianity Press, 1994), 72-80.

11. God as Friend

1. The Korean language system has two different forms of structure: proper usage is dependent on the nature of a relationship.

2. Martin Buber, *I and Thou*, trans. Ronald Gregor Smith (New York: Charles Scribner's Sons, 1958).

3. Ahn Byung Mu, "Minjung God," in *Christian Thoughts* 54 (Fall 1986): 691.

4. See Song Ki Duk, "Minjung Messiah Theory," in *Christian Thoughts* 96 (Spring 1997): 181-211; Suh Nam Dong, "The Fusion of Two Stories,"

in *Minjung and Korean Theology* (Seoul: Korean Theology Press, 1982), 237-76.

Part IV: New Understandings of God

12. Pastoral Landscapes within Korean Churches

1. Lee Jae Hoon, "A New Vision of Korean Pastoral Counseling," in *Pastoral Counseling for the Korean Church* (Seoul: Korean Christian Press, 1997), 58-61.

2. Carol Gilligan, *In a Different Voice: Psychological Theory and Women's Development* (Cambridge: Harvard Univ. Press, 1993), 23.

3. Oo Sung Chun, "How Do We Apply Pastoral Care to Pastoral Visits?" in Lee Jae Hoon, *Pastoral Counseling for the Korean Church*, 138.

4. Lee Ki Chun, "Korean Church and the Guideline for Pastoral Care," in Lee Jae Hoon, *Pastoral Counseling for the Korean Church*, 91.

5. Park Won Kun, *The Theory and Reality of Pastoral Visit* (Seoul: Korean Christian Press, 1997), 143.

6. Aart M. Van Beek, *Cross-Cultural Counseling* (Minneapolis, MN: Fortress Press, 1996), 14-26.

7. Carol P. MacCormack, "Nature, Culture and Gender: A Critique," in *Nature, Culture and Gender*, ed. Carol MacCormack and Marilyn Strathern (New York: Cambridge Univ. Press, 1980), 1-24.

8. See Suh Nam Dong, "The Formation of Han and Its Theological Thought," in *Minjung and Korean Theology*, ed. NCC Theologian Committee (Seoul: Korean Theological Research, 1982), 319-47.

9. Riet Bons-Storm, *The Incredible Woman: Listening to Women's Silences in Pastoral Care and Counseling* (Nashville, TN: Abingdon Press, 1996), 145.

10. Kim Young Ae, "The Pastoral Context of Women's Experience in Korean Patriarchy," in Lee Jae Hoon, *Pastoral Counseling for the Korean Church*, 169-212.

11. Miriam Greenspan, *A New Approach to Women and Therapy* (Bradenton, FL: Human Services Institute, 1993), 232-315.

12. Mary Ballou and Nancy W. Gabalac, *A Feminist Position on Mental Health* (Springfield, IL: C. C. Thomas, 1987), 10.

13. Ibid., 82-83.

14. Ibid., 89.

15. Ibid., 83-90.

16. Ibid., 90-93.

17. Ibid., 93-97.

13. Reconstructing Women's Understandings of God

1. Rosemary Radford Ruether, *Sexism and God-Talk: Toward A Feminist Theology* (Boston: Beacon Press, 1983), 64-66.
2. Elizabeth A. Johnson, "God," in *Dictionary of Feminist Theologies*, ed. Letty M. Russell and J. Shannon Clarkson (Louisville, KY: Westminster John Knox, 1996), 128.
3. Christie Cozad Neuger, *Counseling Women: A Narrative, Pastoral Approach* (Minneapolis, MN: Fortress Press, 2001), 12.
4. Laurel C. Schneider, *Re-Imaging the Divine: Confronting the Backlash against Feminist Theology* (Cleveland: Pilgrim Press, 1998), 156.
5. Henri Nouwen, *The Wounded Healer: Ministry in Contemporary Society* (New York: Bantam Doubleday Dell, 1979), 88.
6. Ana-Maria Rizzuto, *The Birth of the Living God: A Psychoanalytic Study* (Chicago: Univ. of Chicago Press, 1979), 130-48.
7. Tyron L. Inbody, *The Transforming God: An Interpretation of Suffering and Evil* (Louisville, KY: Westminster John Knox, 1997), 64-67.
8. J. Jeffrey Means, *Trauma & Evil: Healing the Wounded Soul* (Minneapolis, MN: Fortress Press, 2000), 67.
9. Riet Bons-Storm, *The Incredible Woman: Listening to Women's Silences in Pastoral Care and Counseling* (Nashville, TN: Abingdon Press, 1996), 140.

Selected Bibliography

Ahn Byung Mu. *Liberator Jesus*. Seoul: Modern Thoughts, 1975.

Arcana, Judith. *Our Mothers' Daughters*. Berkeley, CA: Shameless Hussy Press, 1979.

Ballou, Mary, and Nancy W. Gabalac. *A Feminist Position on Mental Health*. Springfield, IL: C. C. Thomas, 1987.

Barth, Karl. *The Epistle to the Romans*. Translated by E. Hoskyns. Oxford: Oxford Press, 1933.

Beek, Aart M. *Cross-Cultural Counseling*. Minneapolis, MN: Fortress Press, 1996.

Bons-Storm, Riet. *The Incredible Woman: Listening to Women's Silences in Pastoral Care and Counseling*. Nashville, TN: Abingdon Press, 1996.

Braverman, Lois. "Beyond the Myth of Motherhood." In *Women in Families—A Framework for Family Therapy*, edited by Monica McGoldrick, Carol M. Anderson, and Froma Walsh. New York: W. W. Norton, 1989.

Brock, Rita Nakashima. *Journeys by Heart: A Christology of Erotic Power*. New York: Crossroad Publishing, 1992.

Brock, Rita Nakashima, and Susan Brooks Thistlethwaite. *Casting Stones: Prostitution and Liberation in Asia and the United States*. Minneapolis, MN: Fortress Press, 1996.

Buber, Martin. *I and Thou*. Translated by Ronald Gregor Smith. New York: Charles Scribner's Sons, 1958.

Butler, Lee H., Jr. *A Loving Home: Caring for African American Marriage and Families*. Cleveland: Pilgrim Press, 2000.

Cho Song Whan. "Ideological Change and Social Stratification during the Transitional Period from the Koryo to the Yi Dynasty." *Sahoehak Yongu* [Sociological studies] 1. Seoul: Deyong-sa, 1984.

Chodorow, Nancy J., and Susan Contratto. "The Fantasy of the Perfect Mother." In *Feminism and Psychoanalytic Theory*, edited by Nancy J. Chodorow. New Haven, CT: Yale Univ. Press: 1989.

Choi Man Ja. "Feminist Christology." In *Consultation on Asian Women's Theology*, edited by the Korean Association of Women Theologians. Seoul: Women Theology Press, 1987.

179

Choi So Young. "Female Creator, Grandmother God of Korea, and Their Distorted Story." In *The Feminist Theological Perspective of Female God in Korean Indigenous Religions*. Edited by the Korean Feminist Researchers of Female God. Seoul: Korean Feminist Press, 1992.

Christian Thought Committee, ed. *Pastoral Care and Counseling for the Korean Church*. Seoul: Korean Christian Press, 1997.

Chung Hyun Kyung. "*Han-pu-ri*: Doing Theology from Korean Women's Perspective." In *Frontiers in Asia Christian Theology: Emerging Trends*, edited by R. S. Sugirtharajah. Maryknoll, NY: Orbis Books, 1994.

———. *Struggle to Be the Sun Again: Introducing Asian Women's Theology*. Maryknoll, NY: Orbis Books, 1994.

Clinebell, Howard. *Basic Types of Pastoral Care and Counseling: Resources for the Ministry of Healing and Growth*. Nashville, TN: Abingdon Press, 1984.

Committee of Theological Study. *Minjung and Korean Theology*. Seoul: Korean Theological Study Institute, 1982.

De Vos, George, and Takao Sofue, eds. *Religion and the Family in East Asia*. Berkeley and Los Angeles: Univ. of California Press, 1984.

Dube, Musa W. "Savior of the World But Not of This World: Postcolonial Reading of Spatial Construction in John." In *The Postcolonial Bible*, edited by R. S. Sugirtharajab. Sheffield, England: Sheffield Academic Press, 1998.

———. "Toward a Postcolonial Feminist Interpretation of the Bible," In *Reading the Bible as Women: Perspective from Africa, Asia, and Latin America*, edited by Phyllis A. Bird. *Semeia* 78. Atlanta: Scholars Press, 1997.

Eckert, Carter J., Lee Ki-Baik, Young Ick Lew, Michael Robinson, and Edward W. Wagner. *Korea Old and New: A History*. Cambridge: Ilchokak Publishers, 1990.

Erikson, Erik H. *Identity and the Life Cycle: Selected Papers with a Historical Introduction*. New York: International Universities Press, 1958.

Fanon, Frantz. *The Wretched of the Earth*. New York: Grove Press, 1963.

Friday, Nancy. *My Mother/My Self*. New York: Dell, 1977.

Gilligan, Carol. *In a Different Voice*. Cambridge: Harvard Univ. Press, 1993.

Gilligan, Carol, Janie Victoria Ward, and Jill McLean Taylor. *Mapping the Moral Domain*. Cambridge: Harvard Univ. Press, 1988.

Gorsuch, Nancy J. *Pastoral Visitation*. Minneapolis, MN: Fortress Press, 1999.

Greenspan, Miriam. *A New Approach to Women and Therapy*. Blue Ridge Summit, PA: TAB Books, 1993.

Il Yun. *Samguk Yusa* 5, T. 2039.49.1011c12-22.

Inbody, Tyron L. *The Transforming God: An Interpretation of Suffering and Evil*. Louisville, KY: Westminster John Knox Press, 1997.

Jay, Nancy. *Throughout Your Generations Forever: Sacrifice, Religion, and Paternity.* Chicago: Univ. of Chicago Press, 1992.

Ji Eun Hee. "Korean Industrialization and the Research of Korean Women's Work." In *Korean Women and Work,* edited by Korean Women's Organization. Seoul: Korean Women's Studies, 1990.

Ju Sun Ea. *Presbyterian Women's History.* Seoul: Presbyterian Women's Associations, 1978.

Kim, Elaine H., and Choi Chung Moo, eds. *Dangerous Women: Gender & Korean Nationalism.* New York: Routledge, 1998.

Kim, Harvey Youngsook. "Possession Sickness and Women Shamans in Korea." In *Unspoken Worlds: Women's Religious Lives in Non-Western Cultures,* edited by N. Falk and R. Gross. New York: Harper and Row, 1980.

———. *Six Korean Women: The Socialization of Shamans.* St. Paul, MN: West Publishing Co., 1979.

Kim In Su. *Korean Christian History.* Seoul: Korean Presbyterian Press, 1991.

Kim, Samuel S. *Korea's Globalization.* Cambridge: Cambridge Univ. Press, 2000.

Kim Tae-gon. *The Study on Korean Shamanism.* Seoul: Jipmundang, 1981.

Kim Young Ae. *Han: From Brokenness to Wholeness.* Ph.D. dissertation, School of Theology at Claremont, California, May 1991.

Korean Association of Women Theologians, ed. *Church and Women's Theology.* Seoul: Korean Christian Press, 1998.

———, ed. *Korean Women's Experience.* Seoul: Korean Christian Press, 1994.

Korean History Research Association, ed. *Korean History.* Seoul: Dong-a Press, 1996.

Kwok Pui-lan. *Discovering the Bible in the Non-Biblical World.* Maryknoll, NY: Orbis Books, 1995.

Lancaster, Lewis R., and C. S. Yu. *Introduction of Buddhism to Korea: New Cultural Patterns.* Berkeley, CA: Asian Humanities Press, 1989.

Lee Eun Sun. "Women Theology and Christology." In *Christian Thoughts* 389. Seoul: Korean Christian Press, 1991.

Lee Jae Hoon. *The Exploration of the Inner Wounds–Han.* Atlanta: Scholars Press, 1994.

Lee Ki-Baik. *A New History of Korea.* Translated by Edward. W. Wagner and Edward J. Shultz. Cambridge: Harvard Univ. Press, 1984.

Lee Mi-Kyoung. "A Feminist Analysis of the State Policy on Birth." *Yosonghak Nonjip* [Women's studies] 6 (1989): 49-76.

Lee Su Kang, and Park Kee Lam. "Women and Work." In *The Lectures of Women's Studies.* Seoul: Korean Women's Studies, 1991.

Lee Sun Ai. "Images of God." *In God's Image* (September 1988).

Lee Uoo Jung. *Korean Christian Women: 100 Years' Footsteps*. Seoul: MinJungSa, 1985.

Lee Uoo Jung, and Lee Hyun Suk. *Women's History during Sixty Years*. Seoul: Korean Presbyterian Women's National Assembly Press, 1988.

MacCormack, Carol P. "Nature, Culture, and Gender: A Critique." In *Nature, Culture and Gender*, edited by Carol MacCormack and Marilyn Strathern. New York: Cambridge Univ. Press, 1980.

McFague, Sallie. *Models of God: Theology for an Ecological, Nuclear Age*. Philadelphia: Fortress Press, 1987.

Means, J. Jeffrey. *Trauma & Evil: Healing the Wounded Soul*. Minneapolis, MN: Fortress Press, 2000.

Memmi, Albert. *The Colonizer and the Colonized*. Boston: Beacon Press, 1965.

Miller, Jean Baker. *Toward a New Psychology of Women*. Boston: Beacon Press, 1976.

Moltmann, Jürgen. *The Crucified God: The Cross of Christ as the Foundation and Criticism of Christian Theology*. Minneapolis, MN: Fortress Press, 1993.

———. *The Trinity and the Kingdom of God*. London: Oxford Univ. Press, 1981.

Moon Seungsook. "Economic Development and Gender Politics in South Korea, 1963-1992," Ph.D. dissertation, Brandeis Univ., 1994.

———. "Overcome by Globalization: The Rise of a Women's Policy in South Korea." In *Korea's Globalization*, edited by Samuel S. Kim. New York: Cambridge Univ. Press, 2000.

Neuger, Christie Cozad. *Counseling Women: A Narrative, Pastoral Approach*. Minneapolis, MN: Fortress Press, 2001.

Nouwen, Henri. *The Wounded Healer: Ministry in Contemporary Society*. New York: Bantam Doubleday Dell, 1979.

Ortner, Sherry B., and Harriet Whitehead. *Sexual Meanings: The Cultural Construction of Gender and Sexuality*. Cambridge: Cambridge Univ. Press, 1981.

Pannenberg, Wolfhart. *An Introduction to Systematic Theology*. Edinburgh, Oxford Univ. Press, 1991.

———. "The Kingdom of God and the Church." In *Theology and the Kingdom of God*, edited by R. J. Neuhaus. Philadelphia: Fortress Press, 1977.

Park, Andrew Sung. *The Wounded Heart of God: The Asian Concept of Han and the Christian Doctrine of Sin*. Nashville, TN: Abingdon Press, 1992.

Park Won Kun. *The Theory and Reality of Pastoral Visits*. Seoul: Korean Christian Press, 1997.

Peach, Lucinda Joy. *Women and World Religions*. Upper Saddle River, NJ: Prentice Hall, 2002.

Pedersen, P., J. Draguns, W. Lonner, and J. Trimble, eds. *Counseling Across Cultures*. Honolulu: Univ. of Hawaii Press, 1989.

Peterson, Mark. "Women without Sons: A Measure of Social Change in Yi Dynasty Korea." In *Korean Women: View from the Inner Room*, edited by Laurel Kendall and Mark Peterson. New Haven, CT: Little Rock, 1983.

Rizzuto, Ana-Maria. *The Birth of the Living God: A Psychoanalytic Study*. Chicago: Univ. of Chicago Press, 1979.

Ruether, Rosemary Radford. *Sexism and God-Talk: Toward a Feminist Theology*. Boston: Beacon Press, 1983.

Russell, Letty, Kwok Pui-lan, Ada María Isasi-Díaz, and Katie Geneva Cannon, eds. *Inheriting Our Mothers' Gardens: Feminist Theology in Third World Perspective*. Philadelphia: Westminster Press, 1988.

Schneider, Laurel C. *Re-Imaging the Divine: Confronting the Backlash against Feminist Theology*. Cleveland: Pilgrim Press, 1998.

Schüssler Fiorenza, Elisabeth. *Sharing Her Word: Feminist Biblical Interpretation in Context*. Boston: Beacon Press, 1998.

Sharma, Arvind, ed. *Feminism and World Religions*. Albany: State Univ. of New York Press, 1999.

———. *Women in World Religions*. Albany: State Univ. of New York Press, 1987.

Sugirtharajah, R. S., ed. *Frontiers in Asian Christian Theology: Emerging Trends*. Maryknoll, NY: Orbis Books, 1994.

Terrell, Joanne Marie. *Power in the Blood?: The Cross in the African American Experience*. Maryknoll, NY: Orbis Books, 1998.

Thistlethwaite, Susan Brooks. *Sex, Race, and God: Christian Feminism in Black and White*. New York: Crossroad, 1989.

Ward, Kathryn, ed. *Women Workers and Global Restructuring*. Ithaca, NY: Cornell Univ. Press, 1990.

Williams, Delores S. *Sisters in the Wilderness: The Challenge of Womanist God-Talk*. Maryknoll, NY: Orbis Books, 1999.

Yu Chai-Shin and R. Guisso. *Shamanism: The Spirit World of Korea*. Seoul: Asian Humanities Press, 1988.

Index